THE TOKEN : BOOK ONE

ECHOES

FROM THE

MOON

NATHAN HYSTAD

Cover art: J Caleb Design
Edited by: Christen Hystad
Edited by: Scarlett R Algee
Proofed and Formatted by: BZ Hercules

ISBN: 9798878666503

PROLOGUE

Nothing comforted Peter more than the noises echoing across the lake at dusk. He'd never understood people's fascination with the city. Horns beeping. Sirens ringing out all night. You could go an entire day in Manhattan without an unobstructed view of the sky. The profound significance of that was wasted on everyone there.

Thinking about New York caused Peter to glance at his home. The timber A-frame's top windows reflected the last rays of light as the trees ingested the glowing sun, and a moment later, it was gone. The lake instantly shifted from pleasant and welcoming to ominous and threatening.

The birds chirping in high branches were replaced with the cries of lonely loons. Peter couldn't see the waterfowl, but they'd be in the middle, drifting around like lost spirits.

The Moon was low and fat, the horizon adding to the illusion of its size. Peter stared at it, gritting his teeth. That very hunk of rock had given him fame, and taken his freedom from him. Peter had wasted the rest of his life wondering if he'd rather have declined that mission. He could have done it all differently.

His kids might stay in touch, and Patricia, God rest her soul, would have had a much better life, before the inevitable curse of cancer took her from him.

Peter sighed and used the arms of the wooden chair to help him up. Everything ached, but that was what it was like in your eighties. The hours he'd spent in zero-g and freefall didn't help his case, but he counted himself lucky. He was here, and that had to be enough.

The walk to the house took longer than normal, his body stiffening in the cooling air. His home looked like a beacon on the stationary lake, the illuminated lamps inside drawing the eye in the dark evening. He'd always wanted this quiet existence, as had Patty, but she'd passed a year after the moving trucks dropped their possessions off.

Somewhere down the road, a pair of headlights shone, and a truck slowly crawled by. Probably another tourist searching for the vacation home a half mile to the south. It wouldn't be the first time a frazzled family man from the city came knocking on his door, looking for 21 Beachcomber Way.

Peter went in, grateful for the warmth. It was summer, but he kept the heater on for these particularly chilly nights.

The full Moon lingered in his thoughts as he approached the wall above the mantel, where old photos sat in frames Patty had selected. Peter stared at the nearest, barely recognizing his own face. Twenty-two, graduating from West Point with a degree in engineering. His parents had been so proud, they could hardly contain themselves.

The next shot showed his arrival from overseas, his Air Force tattoo visible on his bicep as he kissed a young Patricia. The third photo caused him to pause. Two men's arms were around Peter's shoulders as he proudly wore his commander's uniform before their infamous Helios 15 mission to the Moon. Had he ever smiled so freely since those eight days in space? He doubted it.

Little did that trio know, nothing would ever be the same after landing on the rock-covered wasteland.

Peter was the last remaining member of the prime crew, his counterparts expiring before him. He'd occasionally thought about what happened to their tokens, but rarely let himself dwell on it. Peter had been in therapy since Patty's death, and with Doctor Joe's help, he realized how often he made up stories to justify his actions.

Let it go. He tried to persuade himself there was no reason to take this trip down memory lane, not after such a peaceful day, and his feet carried him to the kitchen. He put a kettle on the stove, turning it low, and headed into his office. More frames. What was with a human's constant need to reassure themselves of their accomplishments? In the same way an author might display their written words, Peter had his doctorate on exhibition, centered behind his seldom-occupied desk.

He peered toward the window, unable to see past the glass. Guilt overcame him, and he began sweating, without an actual reason to be distressed. He knelt on the floor, worried he might not be able to get up. Peter slid his chair over and lifted the hinged floorboard.

For a moment, his doddering mind almost forgot the passcode. When had he last opened the safe? Two years ago? Four? He remembered that he'd used a combination of his children's birthdays, and though they never called him on his own anniversary around the sun, his attachment to them remained. After entering the four digits, it clicked, and Peter sighed as he retrieved the satchel. This was the diversion should someone manage to break in. It contained exactly two thousand dollars, all small bills, making it feel like plenty more.

He set that aside and pushed his finger into the bottom, revealing a second compartment. Peter nearly returned the bag and slammed the safe shut, but he didn't. They'd been so young, so optimistic, and this contraption was the beginning of their end.

It slid from a wooden case, the shiny metal object no longer than his hand. It was flat, like a ruler, and thinner than a dime. Three identical mementos, one for each of the crew. NASA had no knowledge of the pieces, and rightfully so. Had they divulged these treasures, they would have sent an endless stream of men to the cold surface of the Moon to investigate. Peter and his crew had agreed that what they'd witnessed was better left alone.

They'd each taken one, promising to never again speak of them. And they hadn't, until Colin started losing it and decided to do that interview. But that was a decade ago, and Colin had died shortly after. Peter had spent ten years convincing himself they were safe from what they'd found hidden on the Moon. NASA had grown tired of the pursuit fifty years earlier, marking Peter's Helios mission as the final endeavor, and he was grateful for it.

Peter refused to touch the token with his skin, especially after making that mistake a few times before. He used a handkerchief from his pocket, picked it up, and set the object back. He placed the satchel on top, and he'd started to close the safe when the phone rang.

"Who could that be?" he asked out loud. It wasn't uncommon for him to speak to himself, just for the sake of another voice. Life at the lake was rewarding, but it offered little in the way of socialization, if he didn't count Carol from next door and her yappy dog. She had a habit of showing up most mornings to talk his ear off about the local gossip.

His legs protested, but he made it to the kitchen, grabbing the archaic phone from its cradle on the wall.

"Hello?"

Silence.

"Hello?" he asked louder.

He slowly turned to find a man stalking into his home. Had he not locked the door?

The phone gave off a dial tone, and Peter dropped the handset, facing the intruder. "I've called the police." He tried to make his voice sound authoritative, but it wasn't convincing when it cracked. He pointed at the intruder with his entire arm shaking viciously.

The guy sneered and shook his head. "No, you didn't."

Peter's chest tightened. "What do you want?"

"Where is it?" His accent might have been from Jersey, possibly Staten Island.

"What?" Peter's ears rang, his vision covered with white dots.

"You know what I'm talking about. Where are you hiding it?" The man ransacked the kitchen, opening drawers. He dumped a cutlery tray, the utensils clashing loudly on the floor. "Old man, don't make me ask again."

Peter had spent decades waiting for someone to come for it, so this really didn't surprise him. He couldn't allow it to get into the wrong hands. "Go to hell."

The kettle whistled loudly as the water finished boiling, and the sound was an awful, high-pitched ring. Patty had loved the damned kettle, so he couldn't bear to part with it. Now it would be the last thing he heard.

The gun aimed at him from five feet away, and Peter saw his life in a series of flashes. Some of it was nice, the rest riddled with anxiety and grief. In his final breath, he welcomed his future.

"I'll find it myself." The man shot him, his expression vacant as he pulled the trigger.

Peter collapsed onto the hardwood, the whistle occupying his entire being as he silently drifted into oblivion.

PART ONE
BREAKING NEWS

1

Rory signaled and took the exit, leaving Boston in the rear-view mirror. She'd spent seven years striving to find her place among the intellectuals and artists in her community, but she'd never broken through. That suited her fine, now that she knew them for what they were. Soul-sucking blowhards, with more opinions than talent.

Her hatchback sat crammed full of her worldly possessions. Rory noticed the box of small appliances in the back seat and recalled buying them with Kevin after they'd moved in together. He'd selected all of it. Kevin, who needed everything a certain way. Kevin, who made all their decisions. Kevin, who controlled their finances because he earned more than her.

Rory veered right, slamming the brakes on the freeway shoulder. Enormous trucks sped by; the eighteen wheels squealed over the pavement.

When the coast was clear, Rory climbed out of the car and shouted at the sky. Someone honked, and she screamed in anger, letting out her bottled-up emotions. After a few minutes, she wiped her cheeks and got into her vehicle, firing the engine up with the push of a button.

"Now I can leave," she whispered. No more Kevin. No more pretentious dinner parties that made her uncomfortable. It was time to carve a fresh path. Her own way.

Rory continued on the road, pulling into the first pit stop she spotted. She headed past the gas station to the dumpster behind it, and popped the rear hatch. Rory unloaded her things into the open bin, and one by one, every memento of Boston was ditched. When the car only held her suitcase and a single book, she dusted her palms off and smiled to herself. Gone were the vestiges of her old life.

Rory grabbed her journal from the glove box and scrawled the line down, verbally repeating it. *Vestiges.* Had she heard this quote somewhere, or could she use it in her new book?

Since she was there, Rory headed into the convenience store, moving directly to the carafes of coffee. She walked by the French roast and hazelnut, settling on the third option, and filled a paper cup.

"I remember when they landed. It was such a thrill," an elderly man at the counter said. He leaned on it, like he might fall otherwise. His cane lay hooked around the magazine rack.

"You're that old?" the clerk asked with a grin.

"I was seven when Commander Peter Gunn led them on Helios 15."

Rory's blood pumped faster. "What about it?"

Both men peered in her direction, and she snapped the plastic lid on her cup.

"You haven't seen the news? Commander Gunn died last night. Murdered in his living room. Can you believe it?" the old timer asked. "It's all over every channel."

The clerk, a young kid with longer hair than Rory's, gestured at the dusty TV behind the till.

Rory's voice barely escaped her lips. "Would you mind turning that up?"

"Sure." The volume bar rose, her anxiety increasing with every green line that appeared.

The video showed a beautiful house on a lake, and Rory flinched when she saw the police tape surrounding the yard. A half-dozen squad cars parked out front, their lights flashing.

"Details are slim at this point, but we do know that Peter Gunn lived alone. His neighbor found him this morning at nine o'clock. We're live on scene with Olive." The newscaster's face vanished, and a shaky camera focused on a woman in a trench coat holding an umbrella.

"It's a rainy day on Loon Lake, the home of renowned astronaut Commander Peter Gunn, the last remaining crew member from the final Moon mission. His murder comes as a shock to the community and the entire world. Was it a burglary gone wrong, or was this a targeted event? The police are working tirelessly to find out. We'll report further as specifics are released," Olive said.

Rory recalled the last occasion she'd seen Mr. Gunn. Her grandfather had driven them to the reunion, regaling her with tales of his training for the Helios mission. He'd died a year later, weeks before her high school graduation.

"I have Carol, Commander Gunn's next-door neighbor."

A middle-aged woman with a canary-yellow slicker came into view, her eyes darting between the camera and Olive.

"Can you tell us why you contacted the police?"

"Pete spends every sunrise on his pier with his morning tea. I prefer to get my beauty sleep," Carol said nervously. *"He wasn't there today when I took Bitsy for her morning walk. I stopped in to*

make sure he was all right, and the door was open." Her eye twitched, and she wrung her hands. *"I found him inside. Dead."*

Olive thanked Carol, and the clerk muted the feed.

"It's a shame." The guy grabbed his cane and wandered off.

"Just the coffee," Rory said, reeling from the shock of Mr. Gunn's murder.

"On the house."

"Thanks," she said.

"You're Rory Valentine, aren't you?"

Valentine. Her pen name. It was extremely rare to be recognized, especially by a hippie at a gas station. Rory shook her head, but he didn't let it go. "You totally are. I came to your signing a few years ago. *View from the Heavens* is one of my favorite books."

Rory paused and smiled at him, despite the gnawing sensation in her gut. "Thank you."

"Wait, I think I have a copy." He grabbed a torn cardboard box from under the counter and started rifling through it. She was impressed with the assortment of popular volumes this awkward clerk had collected, and when she saw the familiar lettering of her own novel, she experienced a flash of regret. "There it is."

The corners were damaged, and it had stains on the pages. He'd actually read it—more than once, by the looks of it. "That's my book," she murmured.

He shoved a pen at her. "Can you sign it?"

"No problem." Rory opened the dust jacket and stared at the photo of herself. Credit to Kevin Heffernan. Would she ever be able to escape him? "Who do I make it out to?"

"Bailey."

She scrawled her signature, languidly drawing a heart

over the I in *Valentine*, and slid it back.

"Thanks." He gawked at it. "When's the next coming out?"

Never. I'm washed-up. How do you follow such a success? Rory swept her hair behind her ears and smiled at Bailey. "I'm working on it," she lied, and left. The door chimes rattled as she strolled outside, and Rory exhaled, overwhelmed by the entire experience. Wasn't she leaving Boston to get away from her past? Why did it seem to follow her like a shadow?

She walked by the old man from earlier and glanced at the silhouette of darkness behind him. What was hiding in his past? Did he have regrets?

"Miss?" He scrunched up his face, his bristly white moustache lifting.

"Have a good day," she told him, and hurried to her car. Rory put the coffee in the cup holder and threw the hatchback into gear. Without all her belongings, the vehicle felt lighter, and Rory would have too, if not for the news. Why did that shake her so much? She didn't know Commander Peter Gunn in reality, just from article clippings, or from her connection to her own grandfather. But his murder felt significant.

Rory contemplated this while drinking the gas-station coffee. It tasted like motor oil, and instantly made her miss her first writing haunt, the beanery downstairs from her and Kevin's apartment. Not the fancy brownstone they eventually moved into, but the cramped one-bedroom. The dishwasher and fridge couldn't be opened at the same time, and no matter how hard they tried, you couldn't both get ready for the day without having an argument. But they'd made it work. That was her magic. Tension. The threat of not being able to pay her bills if the book advance didn't come through. She'd been hungry.

Her stomach growled at the thought, and as Rory entered the border for Vermont, she laughed. This was for the best, after all. Was there anything wrong with a thirty-year-old woman heading home for a few months while she figured her life out?

Yes. It's a trap. Her inner monologue always seemed to contradict her conscience, and Rory ignored the warning.

An hour passed, then two, and finally, she saw the sign for her hometown. Rory stopped her car and got out. *Welcome to Woodstock, Vermont.*

The place looked as picturesque as it came. In the spring, flowers bloomed in the community gardens, and she recalled all those fall afternoons with the sun high, her grandfather taking her to the playground, watching Rory as she dove into piles of leaves without a care in the world. This was exactly what she needed.

Rory avoided the city center, knowing she'd encounter someone she knew if she drove straight, and circumvented the town, advancing north to the suburbs. The homes were idyllic, and her own parents' house was no different. As the son of a famous astronaut, her father had done well for himself. First city council, then the mayor. Now he was closing in on retirement, and Rory assumed that would drive her mother crazy.

The hydrangeas were in full bloom, the perfect blend of oranges, red, and pinks. Her mom spent weeks planning the gardens, but didn't do the actual planting herself. They had people for that. The house was a white colonial, the shutters black, six equal dormers lining the roof. Her room was on the right, and she remembered gazing at the Moon through the window for hours, thinking about Gramps flying there. It had seemed impossible then, and Rory still felt that way.

Once she was parked, Rory grabbed her suitcase, then her journal, and marched to the front door.

"Rory!" Her mother was on the veranda, sitting in a blind spot, rocking on the chair. She was pale and had a sweating drink in her grip, mostly empty.

"Mom, are you okay? What happened?"

"You heard?"

"About Commander Gunn?"

"Yes." She downed the last of the beverage, and Rory inhaled the scent of lime with her gin. "What an absolute shame."

"It is." Rory took the seat beside her mom. "But you didn't really know him, right?"

"Not well, but your father is in shambles over it. He spent a lot of summers with them when he was a kid. Your grandfather was his children's godfather, and vice versa."

Rory had no idea. "Peter Gunn was Dad's godfather?"

She nodded slowly. "They had a falling out after that final mission. Rarely spoke, and when they did, it wasn't for long. The reunions dwindled, and he never told us why."

Rory pictured their interactions at the last event, the three older men posing for photos with the press, their smiles not reaching their eyes.

"I suppose there'll be a funeral. We'll have to attend, of course," her mom said.

Rory tried to think about where Peter Gunn even lived, and couldn't remember, despite watching the news feed a few hours earlier. "Okay," she replied, not wanting to tell her mother that she had no desire to travel out of state. She'd been planning on settling in at home, occupying her old bedroom, and finishing this book. To do that, she needed to start it.

Inside, the phone rang, and her mom sighed. "The press has been calling for your father all morning."

Her dad's baritone voice answered, his responses short and clipped. Then it ended.

"Pumpkin, you're home." He smiled from the open door, his phone still gripped.

Rory hugged him, and he took her luggage, carrying it into the house. "Not the best day for our family, but we're thrilled to have you."

Rory and her father hadn't always seen eye to eye, but they were working on it. "Thanks for letting me stay."

"We should have seen the signs earlier. That Kevin…"

"Can we let it go?"

Her dad's frown melted, and his smile lit up the foyer. "Yes, dear."

She walked by the photos on the wall, seeing the crew from Helios 15 centering the collection. They looked so happy. What had happened to them on that mission?

2

Silas threw a rock into the lake, watching it skip once, then drop into the depths. It would stay there forever. Because of his actions, the pebble belonged to the water.

Just like someone had murdered his grandpa. He belonged to the ground.

"Silas?" His father's spotless dress shoes clicked loudly on the wooden pier. "They're done with the house. Come in and see if you'd like anything?"

"Sure, Dad." Silas undid his top button, feeling stuffy in the afternoon heat. He slapped a mosquito, and thought about Grandpa Gunn's obsession with this place.

The police detective met them at the sidewalk, his hands on hips. "We're finished here. Forensics has everything they need, but so far, we're light on the evidence. We'll keep you posted." He shook hands with Silas' father, and finally Silas, who wished to shout at the detective for coming up empty, but that wouldn't help solve the murder.

When the last of the cars left, they were alone, a strand of yellow police tape flapping in the wind.

"What really happened between you guys?" Silas asked.

His dad, the CEO of New York's second-largest furniture company, dipped his chin. "Peter wasn't there for us. He didn't care what we did in school, or who we spent time with. Hell, he was barely around for his own wife."

"He stepped out on Grandma?" Silas reached for the door handle.

"No, it wasn't another woman. It was the Moon," his father said.

"The Moon is a harsh mistress," Silas told him.

"You're a good son, Silas."

His dad had been present for every single occasion in his life, from baseball games to science camp contests. Probably too often. Now it all made sense.

Together, they entered the house, eyeing the damage. Pictures were shattered, glass glinting with sunlight on the hardwood. Every last drawer had been upended.

"The killer wanted something," Silas whispered.

"Or they were hoping to make it look like that. Peter may have had enemies."

Silas tried to imagine a man in his eighties with rivals that would seek to kill him. Couldn't they have just stolen his meds?

His dad pulled a cell phone from his jacket when it rang and wandered over the mess to the windows. "Don't let that shipment go without signing off on it. Yes, Mark has to authorize… This is a big client, Brian. Make sure it's perfect." He hung up. "Where were we?"

"Dad, I'd like to stay for a while," he said.

"Stay? At the lake house?" His dad lifted his arms in disbelief.

"Is that an issue? Do the police need anything?" He shoved his hands into his suit pockets, peering at the place.

"No. We haven't spoken with the lawyer yet, and of course there's the will. He probably gave everything to charity. I wouldn't put it past him."

Something felt wrong, and perhaps a few days cleaning up Grandpa's place would give Silas a connection he'd never made in his youth. "You don't mind if I take some time off?"

"Time off? You're the CFO, son, but you're due bereavement. I'll be in the city. The funeral's in a couple of weeks. Stay until then, if that's what you want." His dad held on to his shoulders, facing him. "I'm sorry you had to witness this."

"He was your father," Silas whispered.

"Peter will be missed by many," he told Silas. "But not me."

He texted his driver, and Silas watched from the front porch as his dad was shuttled away, the tires kicking up gravel.

Silas took off his jacket, righted a kitchen chair, and slung the coat on the top. He rolled up his sleeves and started to clean. He found garbage bags in the pantry, then a broom in the closet, and an hour later, the biggest debris was collected. With the drawers returned to their proper places, and the furniture straightened, it almost looked like a normal home.

His eyes drew to the bloodstain that had to be dealt with. Anger rose in Silas' chest as he pictured an assailant shooting the American hero in the chest and destroying his place in the aftermath.

Silas clenched his jaw and wondered why his grandpa hadn't installed an alarm system. Cameras. Anything.

He saw the phone on the wall and was aware someone had called Peter minutes before his estimated death. The police were working on the lead, but they assumed it was a burner. Another dead end.

The sun began to set, and he made a cup of tea before strolling to the pier, where he was told Peter Gunn liked to watch the changing of the guard.

Silas sat in the chair the former astronaut occupied daily, and immersed himself in the experience. Dusk evaporated, the air grew colder, and Silas closed his eyes, listening to the sounds of nature. His office was on the twentieth story of a midtown high rise in New York. Could he get used to this? A life of stillness?

"Hello?" The voice was kind, and he craned his neck to see a woman approaching.

"Hi." Silas stood, nearly spilling the last of his tea.

"Are you with the police?" she asked, squinting. He noticed a tiny dog with her, its hair tied up with an elastic.

"No. I'm with the family," he said. "That sounded far too formal… I'm Silas, Peter's grandson."

"From New York," she added. "I've seen your picture. But you've grown."

Silas grinned, motioning to the second seat. "Would you like to join me?"

"Yes, that sounds lovely." The woman settled into the chair.

The dog yapped, lunging for his pants hem. "Bitsy! Be nice." Bitsy barked again and did a full three-sixty before lying down at her feet. She sighed and lowered her chin to the wooden pier.

"How well did you know him?" Silas asked.

"Peter? About as well as anyone could, I suppose. We were friendly. I really liked Patty. She was a shining light. Oh, I'm Carol, by the way. And this is Bitsy."

The dog grumbled, but stayed put.

"Nice to meet you."

"Are you planning on taking over the house?"

"I don't think so," Silas said. "I just wanted… to spend awhile here."

"Have you ever visited?" Carol asked. Her questions seemed friendly, not invasive, so Silas didn't mind answering.

"Never. Dad wouldn't allow it."

"That's a shame," she said.

"You didn't see anything that night?"

"Like I told the police, he was absent in the morning when I passed by. I had to check on him. Who would do such a thing?"

"You live next door?"

She pointed down the path, and Silas spotted an orange light through the trees. "Right over there." The shore snaked in beside this property, giving the pier a lot of privacy. Her own dock wasn't visible from his seat.

"Do you have cameras?"

She mimed taking a snapshot. "On my phone."

What was he thinking? That he'd play sleuth and solve the mysterious murder? He was a CFO, and only because of his father's insistence that he stay with the family company. "Can you tell me about him?"

"There's a lot of information on the computers. Dozens of books have been written about Helios 15," Carol said.

"No, not his accomplishments. I want to learn who Peter Gunn was outside of that mission," he told her.

She visibly shrank in the chair. "He was pleasant enough when he noticed me. Peter didn't have much to say, not since Patty died."

"That was the last time I saw him," Silas said.

"But it's been years. Surely…"

"I was in college. Third year. Finance major." He grinned, recalling Grandma's supportive phone calls every few months. When she was gone, he'd lost all connection with his father's side.

"You look like you've done well," she said. "He spoke of you often, Silas."

"He did?"

Carol nodded. "He was proud of his family. Don't you run a big furniture company?"

Silas glanced at the parking lot, remembering he didn't even have a rental car. His dad had taken the only vehicle.

"I guess so. It's all my father's, not mine," Silas whispered, and changed subjects. "Do you think anyone else may have witnessed something?"

Carol wrapped her arms around herself. "The police have already interviewed the neighbors."

Silas stood. "It's getting cold."

Carol smiled at him and stroked Bitsy's back before rising. "That it is. We should chat again before you leave."

"I'd like that."

Silas walked her to the end of the dock, and waited until Carol and her dog left the property before turning his attention on the house. In the dark, it seemed like a menacing place, the lights shining brightly from within the living room. He imagined someone plodding up, finding the door unlocked. His grandpa was near the dining table when he'd been shot. Only once. That showed the perp knew his way around a gun. Or he was scared off, but that didn't seem likely, since he'd had time to properly ransack the home.

Silas ensured the latch was flipped, and he dimmed the lights, flicking one lamp off entirely. He walked through the ranch, stopping at the far side of the hallway. He pushed the door, finding the primary bedroom, which he'd already tidied, shoving the clothes into the drawers rather than folding and organizing them.

Next, he checked the guest room, which had nothing of note. It was as cold as his grandfather's personality. Silas doubted the man had had much company since his wife passed.

Then there was the office. The assortment of pictures from the main living room wall was now stacked on the desk, their frames dented, the protective glass shattered. The murderer had torn the photos out meticulously, to check if something was tucked behind them. The police had dusted everything, but the detective claimed the assailant had been wearing gloves.

Silas had watched footage of the Moon landing, the grainy videos that defied technology. Commander Peter Gunn had looked so poised in them, his voice authoritative, his movements rehearsed and sure.

He flipped through the pictures, and one slid from his grip, drifting to the floor under the desk.

Silas crouched, shoving the rolling leather chair a few inches. "What's this?" A floorboard was slightly agape. He used a fingernail and lifted. A safe sat open underneath, its lock not clasped closed. It appeared to be empty.

Silas recalled the police report, and didn't remember anything relating to a safe. Had they missed this somehow? Whatever had been stashed in this was gone. Silas sat on the floor with his knees up as he wondered about it.

He didn't have many memories of Commander Gunn, but one stood out as he occupied the office. He was ten, and his parents suggested he get his very own desk for doing homework in his bedroom. Grandpa Gunn must have gotten word, and his desk had arrived first. His dad was so upset with Peter. He'd thought the gift to Silas was an insult, a slight against the quality of their family furniture company, and perhaps it had been.

The note that accompanied it was tucked in a drawer, and only Silas knew it was there. It spoke of a hidden compartment, a place where Silas could keep his secrets from his parents and sister.

"You clever old badger," Silas whispered as he stuck his hand into the safe. His fingers prodded the bottom, and he pressed it in all corners, eventually hearing a click. Silas' heart pounded, and he almost closed it. What if Commander Peter Gunn's mysteries were something he didn't want to expose?

But curiosity won the battle, and he relented, tugging a cloth bag from within.

"What is this?" A flurry of random objects flooded Silas' imagination, from old picture negatives to a bag filled with priceless diamonds. But the flat, metallic item he removed was as far from his expectations as anything could have been. He stared at it, the end protected by the covering it came in.

Silas tossed it onto the desk and shook his head. "He'd lost his mind." Alzheimer's didn't run in his family, but that didn't mean that his grandpa was impervious to the disease.

Silas sat on the couch, turned on the flat-screen TV, and watched another news feed dedicated to Commander Peter Gunn's murder.

3

*T*heir countless hours spent on the case led to this moment. Special Agent Waylen Brooks eyed the storage facility from across the street. The streetlights were abnormally dim tonight, the region blanketed by a thick fog emerging from the Pacific.

"Ready, Brooks?" his partner, Special Agent Martina Sanchez, asked.

"Yes. Where are the locals?"

"On the way," she assured him.

Two squad cars appeared, parking at the facility's gate. The lead cop honked, and a man came from the dirty-windowed office. He limped along, stopping to talk with them.

"Let's go," Waylen said, not trusting any of the communication to pass through the police department. He got out and ran, his tie flipping over his shoulder.

The old guy kept asking for a warrant, and Waylen pulled it from his breast pocket, offering the copy to the proprietor. He fumbled for his glasses, which dangled on a string around his neck, and squinted as he mouthed the words. "Fine. I'll show you to the storage unit."

"We could have handled that," the lieutenant said. They'd been abrupt since the moment Waylen and Martina had arrived two days prior. In his experience, the locals were occasionally open to the FBI's involvement, but that was when it included their own issues. This was a federal money-laundering case, and it so happened that they were using this facility to hold certain incriminating evidence.

Waylen had done everything in his power to ensure they arrived before the criminals, and from the look of things, they'd succeeded.

"Stick with us, and make sure no one interferes," Martina told the four officers. The lieutenant nodded, and they escorted the agents behind the shuffling proprietor. He took ages to find the proper unit, endlessly repeating the numbers from the warrant.

Waylen used a pair of bolt cutters, snapping the high-quality lock, and dropped it to the concrete with a thud. "Thank you. We appreciate your cooperation."

If the man realized he'd been dismissed, he didn't act like it. "You can go home," Martina said. She was usually blunter than Waylen.

Waylen rolled the door up and stared at the numerous plastic totes, each meticulously labeled. "Jackpot."

He reached for one of the crates, unsnapped the lid, and checked a file. The transactions were clear as day. "Pack it up, gentlemen. We have what we need."

An hour later, they finished rolling the last of the carts to the utility van, and Waylen was almost ready to leave when he saw the owner waving him down.

"What can I do for you?"

"You FBI?" he asked.

"Yes, sir."

"I had a break-in, but the cops didn't do nothing about it. They told me to file a report. I even have foot-age, but no one cared."

Waylen wasn't responsible for this, but perhaps there was a connection to his own federal case. "Show me."

He sent Martina off with the police and files so they

could start sifting through the information, and went into the man's office. "What's your name?"

"Bart."

"Special Agent Brooks," he said.

The place was dusty: cobwebs in the corners, the glass smudged gray from years of cigarette smoke. An ashtray sat filled near a relic of a computer, and Bart booted it up, finding his security system, which was equally as unimpressive. The tower whirred and choked like the fan was caked with debris.

"This is it." Bart pointed at the screen, and Waylen scribbled down the plates.

"You're certain he robbed the unit?"

"Yes."

"Who does it belong to?"

"The storage unit?"

"Yes," Waylen said.

"Fred Trell."

Waylen grinned. "He must get confused for that other Fred Trell."

"It's the same Fred Trell, and he paid for a decade."

"The astronaut?" Waylen didn't understand.

"Yes. He grew up here. Hell, my older brother went to high school with him. He came about twenty years ago and gave me cash upfront, and a lump sum before he died," Bart said.

He flipped to another grainy image, this of a man moving to one of the smaller units. He wore a baseball cap, but the team name on it was indistinguishable from this far.

"Can you take me to it?" Waylen asked.

"Sure. Now?"

"If you're not too busy."

"My show's being recorded by the machine, so it's no

big deal." Bart headed out, and Martina watched Waylen from the car.

"I thought you were escorting the files," he told her, trying to toe the line of equal partner.

"What are you doing?" she asked.

"Fred Trell had a storage unit here."

"Who?" Martina slid her phone into her pocket.

"Remember? Helios 15… the last mission to the Moon," Waylen said.

"I'm thirty-five. I wasn't even born yet."

"Didn't they teach you this in high school?" Waylen followed Bart, who walked slowly with his limp.

"Probably, but I was too busy being cool to listen." Martina smiled and laughed.

"You think I was the captain of my chess club, don't you?"

"You read nonfiction books. It's the only thing that makes sense."

Bart stopped at the same unit he'd shown Waylen the footage of. "This was it."

"How does it work? Fred died some time ago, and yet you keep his stuff?"

"A lawyer contacted me. Told me to leave it, since he'd covered the cost," Bart said.

Waylen entered the unit after the door was rolled up. It wasn't jammed full like most units, but nothing appeared out of place. "You said he was robbed?"

"No, I told you I had a break-in."

Martina peered into a cardboard box. "What did he take?"

"There was a bag in the guy's hand," Waylen said. "Bart, give me the plates and I'll run them."

Bart seemed pleased someone had showed an interest in his complaint. "Thank you."

Waylen drove off a few minutes later with the out-of-state license plate number.

"Probably stolen," Martina said. She used her laptop to check.

"Any bets?" he asked.

"Drinks on the loser."

"Okay, I say they're legit."

Waylen headed toward the hotel, glad they'd secured the files. He'd been on this case for six months, chasing leads. Financial crimes weren't as riveting as other fields, but Waylen had a mind for numbers, and enjoyed following the money.

"And...?"

Martina grinned from the passenger seat. "Reported stolen a week ago."

"Fine." Waylen parked in front of his room's door, with Martina's next to him. "You need a minute?"

"Don't even think about bailing on drinks," she told him, closing the car door. "We've been working hard, Waylen."

"I'll meet you in five." He used his key and entered the room. The suite was warm, and he undid his tie, draping it on the back of the desk chair. "We did it," he whispered.

After all those hours, they'd hammered the nail in the coffin. The evidence would lead to arrests, and another criminal organization would be one step closer to justice. Waylen sat on the end of the bed and flipped through his notes, seeing the name *Fred Trell* scrawled onto a page.

Someone had killed Peter Gunn in a home invasion a couple of days earlier, and now he was looking into a break-in at Fred Trell's storage unit. "Are they connected?"

He was tired, but Martina was right. She'd put in

more hours than him, her determination unmatched on this case. Waylen used the bathroom, washed his face, and sauntered to the hotel bar. It was the middle of the week, and the place was mostly empty.

Martina sat at the bar, her hand wrapped around a bottle of beer. Another lingered beside it, and she passed it over when he joined her. They clinked their drinks, and Martina let out a heavy sigh. "What's next?"

"We're not done."

Martina finished her beer. "Almost."

"You know we don't choose the next case." The TV was on, showing the end of a basketball game, and he nearly forgot what city they were in. He'd been on the road for so long, he didn't remember what his own bed felt like. These were the times he was grateful to be single. It was no life for someone with a family, though most of his counterparts had them. Special Agent Martina Sanchez was the exception, and he often wondered if that was why they paired them together.

"Can you do me a favor?" he asked.

"What?" Her gaze was fixed on the TV, and she accepted another beer from the young bartender.

"Check something with that plate."

"What's with you and these astronauts?"

"I loved space. You should have seen my bedroom. Shuttles on the walls, stars plastered to the ceiling." He glanced up as if they might be above him.

"Fine." She pulled out her phone. "But this is the last thing related to work I'm doing for the night."

"Run the plate for Cheshire County," he said.

"Where the hell is that?"

"It's where Loon Lake's located."

Martina did as he asked, sending a text to someone in the nearest office. "Gary's not happy to be bothered, but he's doing it." She set the phone on the bar's surface.

Martina cursed when the buzzer rang on the TV and lowered her chin. "I just lost twenty bucks."

"You really shouldn't be gambling on random basketball games," Waylen told her.

"And you should stick to minding your own business." Her words were harsher than the look she gave him. Martina's hand slid onto his thigh, hidden by the bar, and she drank more of her second beer. "Would you like to interrogate me again?"

Waylen had let himself slip a couple of weeks ago after a particularly dismal week in the field, and they'd ended up in bed together for the first time since becoming partners two years earlier. "I think that was…"

"You really are no fun." Martina's text notification beeped, and her eyes widened when she read it.

"Get a hit?"

"You're never going to believe this, but that truck was found parked two miles from Loon Lake."

"I knew it," he said.

"What does this have to do with us?"

He finished the drink and shrugged, waving for another. "Probably nothing, but I want to check it out."

They were his idols growing up. Most kids fantasized about wearing armor and flying through the sky to fight evil villains, and Waylen had dreamed of rocketing to the Moon like these real superheroes.

"But we *are* still going to…" She winked.

Waylen had to admit she was a tremendous partner. "Not tonight."

But a half hour later, he was stumbling into her room, forgetting about the big case, the astronauts, and the stolen truck.

4

*T*he luxury of being back in Woodstock wore thin after a single night with Rory's parents. She'd expected to work without interruption, but apparently, her mother was even needier than she'd remembered.

"I can't go to the farmer's market. I have to write," she complained. The laptop was open, the chapter number the only thing on the entire screen. ONE. The single three-letter word taunted her, the cursor blinking accusingly.

"That's not much of a start." Her mom had the keen ability to belittle, all while acting innocently. She entered the room, leaning on the dresser. "What's it about?"

Rory closed the computer and spun around in the chair. "It's about a woman who's so pathetic, she has to drive home after a terrible breakup and deal with her insufferable parents." She smiled when her mom grimaced.

"Sounds like the main character has some growing to do."

"She does."

"Can your protagonist make time to go to the market with me?"

"Fine!" Rory stood and clapped her hands together. "Another hurdle in a string of many for my heroine."

Despite her misgivings about being in Woodstock, there were parts of it she appreciated. Her childhood room was completely different than it had been as a kid, and Rory was glad her parents weren't the type to cling to their past. Being in it was strange, almost like a dream, with fresh wallpaper and bamboo bedding.

She followed her mom into the living room and smiled at the housecleaner. Kathy Swanson was a lot of things, but a homemaker wasn't one of them.

"What's with you and the market?" Rory asked.

"It's tradition." Kathy flashed her a smile and opened the door, revealing another perfect day. Rory hadn't even peeked outside yet. She'd woken with high hopes of finishing a chapter; instead, she'd stared at the blank screen for two hours. She'd made starts and stops, deleting every passage with reckless abandon the moment her fingers ceased typing whatever gibberish she'd tried passing for a novel.

The car waited in the driveway, a classic convertible from the Sixties. All she needed was a headscarf and a flowery dress to complete the look.

"You drive." Kathy offered the keys, and Rory gaped at them.

"You've never let me touch this car before," she said.

"You were young. Now you're not."

Rory rolled her eyes. "Gee, thanks. I suppose being thirty and single makes me a spinster in Woodstock."

"There are a few eligible—"

"Stop right there. I am *not* here to find love."

Her mother grinned again. "Who said anything about love?"

The car started with a rumble, and Rory noticed how different the exhaust smelled in these old vehicles. It reminded her of Gramps, and she instantly missed him. As she backed down the drive, she wondered what it was like to live in that earlier era, a time during the Cold War, with the space race constantly making headlines.

Kevin always went off on tirades about how the space program was, and continued to be, a waste of money, and that it was a conspiracy to distract the people from the truth about Vietnam and corporate greed. Nixon always played a factor into his rants. She rarely listened to her ex after he began spouting opinions for which he had no real basis. But people at parties seemed to enjoy his debates, and she'd hide in the corner like a meek mouse until they could leave.

Downtown was unlike anything in the big city, a throwback to quaint New England life.

"Park behind the bakery. Mr. Frank saves me a spot on Fridays," Kathy said.

Rory hadn't been there for years, but she remembered the place and turned into the alley, pulling in between two other cars. The aroma of freshly baked bread drifted from a window, and Rory realized she'd skipped breakfast.

Kathy waved and greeted everyone on the sidewalk, most of them chatting with Rory, asking about Boston, and mentioning how much they loved her book. When prodded on the new release, she diverted, changing the subject effortlessly. Rerouting conversations was a real-life skill she'd gained from the woman beside her.

"You really should write it," her mom whispered as they strolled across the street to the outdoor market.

"What do you think I was trying to do?"

Tomorrow, she'd head to the coffee shop for a few hours, and bang out a chapter or two. She'd written *View from the Heavens* in spurts of three thousand words, with her fingers almost moving of their own volition. It had taken two months to write the initial draft, and another year of painfully meticulous rewrites, following notes from her agent and editors. But the end result had earned a few prestigious nominations, and even more pressure to succeed with the next novel.

View told the story of a young girl following in her grandfather's footsteps to become the first woman to walk on the Moon. Her main character let nothing dissuade her from her chosen path, and it was told over the course of twenty years, emphasizing the highs and lows of her youth. Her publisher had denied the idea of a sequel, suggesting that the tale of an ex-astronaut wasn't interesting enough. The comment made Rory understand what Gramps must have experienced for decades after the Helios 15 mission.

"You should write something more contemporary, darling," Kathy said.

"Contemporary?"

"Literary fiction is where the real money's at," she said.

"That's what I wrote."

"No, I'd say it was science fiction."

Rory bit her tongue, not willing to get into an argument over it. She was good at holding back, considering it was how she'd spent the last few years of her life with Kevin. But that was the old Rory Swanson.

"Mom." She grabbed her wrist, stopping them from entering the market. "If we're going to live together, can we cut the veiled attacks? No more passive-aggressive comments about what I do for a living, or the choices I've made. Let's be adults. Friends, even."

"I never meant to hurt you. I'd enjoy that, darling." Kathy hugged her gently, her lavender perfume filling Rory's nostrils. "I'll agree with you, if…"

Here it came, the catch twenty-two. "If what?"

"You stop being so cranky."

"Cranky?"

"You're miserable, Rory. Always finding the negative. You're in Woodstock, and it's the middle of summer. The world is your oyster, and there's limitless potential for someone of your skill set. Write from your heart, and you'll be amazed at what you find."

Rory stared at her mother, dumbfounded by the response. "You believe that?"

Kathy started walking. "Without a shred of a doubt."

That was unexpected, but Rory took it with a grain of salt. "Where to?"

"I was thinking about a dinner party. Tonight."

"Seriously? Such short notice," Rory said.

"Not really. The invitations were sent a week ago." Kathy stopped at a nearby booth to chat with a middle-aged woman selling microgreens. She bought a couple of packs and paid with cash.

"You weren't going to tell me?"

"You're the special guest of honor," Kathy told her. "Rory Valentine, local best-selling author, returns home to where it all began."

"Who's invited?"

"Just ten or twelve of our closest friends," Kathy said.

Her mother hadn't mentioned it, because Rory would have talked her out of hosting the event. "Fine. But I'm not doing a speech or anything."

Kathy smiled widely, delighted in the lack of protest. "Wonderful. Help me with the ingredients. I'm thinking lobster."

They strolled with purpose, Rory at peace with the idea of a Friday night dinner party. These people were a far cry from her usual crowd in Boston, and she thought they might spark an idea for her new book. Without experiences, a writer was nothing.

The market was busy in the morning heat, and they

waited in line a few times, chatting with the vendors, picking the best produce and seafood they could find. Rory actually found herself enjoying the event. Kathy Swanson was the consummate New England delight, complimenting everyone on their outfits, offering to donate to some fundraiser or another.

When they were finished, they carried their bounty in large reusable bags, exiting the market. "You must be exhausted," Rory told her.

"Why?"

"Being so social. I'd probably die."

"I've had a lot of practice, darling. Your father spends his days trying to make Woodstock a better place to live, and I do my part to help. You don't become this... *entity* without decades of work, Rory."

Rory had never thought of her mother in this light, and guessed it wasn't easy putting her own career behind her to support her husband. She'd been a schoolteacher early on, and according to Rory's dad, a hell of a good one.

She stopped before crossing the street and noticed a man watching them. "Who's that?" she asked, as a large semi-trailer crept down the road.

"I'm not sure where you're looking."

When the truck passed by, the man was gone. "Nothing. Let's get home."

"We've only just begun." Kathy motioned to Rory's outfit. "We'll have to do something about this before the party."

Rory started the car, glancing in the mirror to check if she was still being watched, but there was no one behind them.

5

Silas opened the fridge, finding nothing remotely edible. His grandfather had a few cans of unopened sardines in the pantry, along with some generic soup and crackers. This appliance was even sadder, with expired cream and a jar of pickles with exactly one gherkin remaining in the green brine.

He'd searched for evidence of just who Peter Gunn was until late into the night, but had learned little. There wasn't a personalized memoir outlining his historic career with NASA or the subsequent years afterward.

It was like being given free rein in an unfamiliar house. Silas had hoped to grow closer to the idea of his paternal grandfather, but the visit left him even emptier than before.

He sighed, closed the fridge, and threw on his shoes. He'd seen a town a mile or two from Loon Lake on the way in, and the walk would do him good. Silas enjoyed doing that back home when he was stuck on a work problem. Stretching his legs always helped line up the dots, and more often than not, he returned with a smile.

As he strode down the pathway to the looping road that circled the lake, he realized how different this was from the city. There were no traffic noises, and the birds sang loudly for anyone who listened.

The sun was high, and with no clouds to disarm the

heat, Silas began to sweat within minutes of his hike. Every time he passed someone's property, he peered toward the home. Some were visible; others were tucked behind a dense woodland area for privacy. The last one on the right had the owner's name carved into a cracked placard, and it swung with the breeze, the metal rings squeaking slightly.

The sound of tires behind him caused Silas to step aside, and the driver slowed, rolling down the passenger window. "You lost?"

"No. Just out for a walk."

The middle-aged guy pointed at him. "Doesn't look like walking clothes."

Silas had wingtips and a pair of three-hundred-dollar pants on. His dress shirt was unbuttoned at the top, and he'd ditched the tie. "I'm visiting on short notice."

The man's eyes widened. "Wait, you must be related to Peter."

He lifted a hand. "Silas."

"Gabriel." The guy tilted the beak of his baseball cap. "Need a lift? I'm heading into town."

Silas wasn't used to this kind of open trust, not where he came from, and his parents had been very strict on rules about getting into vehicles with strangers, but he wasn't in middle school. "Sure."

Gabriel looked harmless, and obviously, he'd met Peter Gunn. The truck smelled faintly like the Earth: damp soil and vegetation. With a quick peek at Gabriel's nails, he noticed they were coated in dirt. "You knew my grandfather?"

"Not really. Mean SOB, that one. But we've talked. I helped his late wife with the garden. I run a landscaping company," Gabriel said, picking up a business card. He passed it to Silas. *Mr. Greenthumb.* He started for town, and Silas left the window down. "How long you sticking around for?"

"I might leave tomorrow," he said, defeated. There was nothing for him at Grandpa Gunn's house.

"That's a shame. He was an important figure, your grandpappy. Once, ages ago. I don't think he ever got used to being grounded. He always seemed to be thinking about something else, like he'd never left the Moon," Gabriel said. "But my experiences with him were few and far between."

They came up to the town's borders a few minutes later, and Gabriel slowed. Silas read the sign labeling the place as *Gull Creek*. He sensed a theme. "Where you want to go?"

"I need some groceries."

"Coming right up." Gabriel signaled and turned onto what had to be their Main Street. Silas spied a diner, a bank, a bodega, and a lawyer's office on one side of the road. Gabriel parked out front, then gestured at the store. "I can drive you back."

"I'll get something to eat at the diner first, then hike it. Thanks for the ride." Silas exited the truck and patted the top. "Appreciate the kindness."

"Think nothing of it. Sorry about your loss, Silas." Gabriel threw it in reverse and drove toward the lake.

The grocery store had flowers in the windows, and when he entered, the brass chimes sounded his arrival. An old woman stood behind the register, face stuck into a newspaper. She peered at him without a word and continued reading.

Silas toured the store, carrying a shopping basket, filling it with a few fresh ingredients. He tried to think whether he should stay or go, because that would determine how much food he required.

"Can I help you with anything?"

Silas looked up and saw an attractive woman standing with a hand on her hip. She wore a red smock, covering a rock and roll band t-shirt. She had half a dozen piercings in each ear and a hoop in her nostril. "I…"

She narrowed her eyes, tapping her foot. "You're not from around here, are you?"

He lifted both eyebrows. "I could say the same about you."

That made her laugh. "Okay, you got me. I'm here for the summer, working with my mom." She glanced at the lady with the newspaper. "Dad had a heart attack, and she can't run this place on her own. Surprise, surprise, a town this size doesn't have many decent employees."

"That was nice of you." Silas set the basket aside, and she peered into it.

"Lots of produce."

"Is that a problem?" he asked.

"Nope. Just don't see many men coming in for anything but frozen dinners."

He glanced at her nametag, trying to be casual. "Well… Leigh, I'm not most men." Was he flirting? It sounded like a stranger speaking through his lips.

She frowned, watching him intently. "What's your name?"

"Silas."

"Now you have my interest piqued. What did you do to get a name like that?"

"My mom has Greek in her blood, and it was an ancestor of ours."

"I think it's badass."

The chimes rang, and mother and son entered, the boy running straight to the candy section.

Silas guessed Leigh was a couple of years younger

than him, and since they were both visitors, he swallowed and blurted it out: "When do you get off?"

Leigh smiled at the comment. "It's not that busy. What are you thinking?"

"Is the diner any good?"

"No, but there aren't many options." She walked to the register and whispered to her mom. The white-haired woman lowered the paper, stared daggers at Silas, then muttered a response. "I have an hour."

Silas paid for the food, and Leigh stuffed the groceries in a paper bag before leading him outside. "You have a car?"

He shook his head.

She gestured to an old Gremlin. "Toss them in mine for now."

"Haven't seen one of these in person."

"Drives like crap, and breaks down every other week, but I still love it," she said.

"You look too young to be her daughter," Silas told her.

"I was adopted. They couldn't have kids. Once they hit their forties, they were lonely, and I was up for the taking. I'm glad for them. Kind of boring around these parts, but it's a safe place to grow up."

"I'm from New York."

"Upstate?"

"Manhattan," he said.

"I should have known by the shoes," she said. "Why are you in Gull Creek?"

Silas strolled ahead, holding the diner door for Leigh. "Do you know who Peter Gunn is?"

She nodded and shrugged, combining the gestures. "I didn't until a couple of nights ago. He was killed. Everyone was talking about it. That stuff doesn't happen in these parts."

"He was my grandfather. I'm staying at the house."

"I'm sorry, Silas. I wouldn't have given you a hard time—"

"It's fine. We weren't close or anything. I thought it might be good for closure, but now I'm just kind of depressed. He's gone, and I never got to know him." Silas stopped while they waited for the server to come over. "Sorry, I won't bore you with the details."

The server was in her fifties, and she smiled at the sight of Leigh. "Back so soon?"

"Carrie, this my friend Silas. Can we have your finest table, please?"

"Right this way." Carrie brought them to a booth that looked identical to the rest. There were only five other customers, but it was also the middle of the afternoon. The witching hour in the restaurant world came between lunch and dinner, not that Silas assumed the joint was ever packed full.

When Carrie left, Leigh laid a finger on his menu, lowering it. "Get the burger and fries. Trust me." He noticed a tattoo on her arm, a thorny rose that shed a few petals.

"Okay," he said, taking her suggestion. She didn't order, and he quickly learned she'd been there two hours ago on her lunch break.

"Peter Gunn was your grandfather. What was that like? Having a hero carving a turkey at Christmas?"

"That never happened. He and my dad didn't…"

"Say no more. What about you? You enjoy being in the big city?"

"I guess so."

"I'm in Denver. Or was, until I came back."

"Is your dad doing better since the heart attack?"

"No. Mom's fooling herself, but I don't think he has more than a year or two," she said indifferently.

They sipped coffees and discussed their lives, skimming over the many details of their past that had brought them to this very point. Silas enjoyed her company more than he did most people's. She was far more refreshing than the usual women he dated in Manhattan. Leigh had a confidence that didn't require designer clothes or fancy shoes, and he appreciated her candor.

When the food came, he ate, painfully aware that she watched him while he chewed the messy burger. It was good. Better than good.

Carrie returned with the coffeepot, and he asked a question. "Did Peter Gunn ever come into the diner?"

She spilled while pouring, and apologized, dabbing up a handful of drops. "Mr. Gunn wasn't a regular, but he did like the burger." She nodded at his plate. "Ordered it the same as you, without onion and double pickles."

That threw Silas for a loop, and it made him grin. That alone was the only connection he had to the old man, but it was enough to make his decision. He'd stay for a while longer, trying to learn more about what made Peter Gunn tick.

He paid the bill after the food was cleared, the last of their coffees drunk.

"What are you doing tonight?" Leigh asked when they were outside.

"Probably staring at the lake again."

"Want some company?"

"Sure," he said.

"I can bring the groceries with me if you like."

"You sure?"

"No sense in walking home with your hands full." She grinned and asked for his phone. He handed it over, watching her quickly add herself to his contacts. "In case you need to cancel."

"I won't," he assured her.

Leigh waved as she entered the grocery store, and Silas stood on the sidewalk, feeling lighter than he had in months.

6

"*T*hey'll never let us go to the boondocks without a good reason," Special Agent Martina Sanchez said.

"There is a reason," Waylen claimed.

"Not for a financial crimes agent!" Sanchez was grinding his gears.

"It's fine. Head to the field office and tell them I had to leave. I'll be back in a couple of days. A week, tops."

"Seriously?"

"We closed on the biggest case of our careers. They're being indicted as we speak. I deserve personal time," Waylen told her.

"But you're not taking personal time. You're going to Loon Lake with your badge," she said.

Waylen got out of the car and helped Martina with her suitcase, which made her even angrier. "I can do this myself."

"Just trying to be a gentleman," he muttered.

She rolled it to the sidewalk and glared at the airport terminal. Finally, her expression softened. "You did good. On the case, I mean. Don't get excited about your performance last night or anything."

Waylen put a hand on his chest. "I would never…"

"I'm not sure why you want to be involved with this astronaut business, but be careful, okay?"

"Why?" He stepped aside while a family strolled

through, the four children following their mother like ducklings, each dragging a tiny piece of colorful luggage behind them.

"Because things like this tend to get blown out of proportion. The moment the FBI is involved, it's more than a break and enter gone wrong. It's a conspiracy. You know the press these guys from that Helios 15 flight had, right? The last trip to the Moon. Then the interview from Swanson a decade ago… that man sounded off his rocker."

Waylen recalled the interview, but would have to watch it again as a refresher. "Someone broke into Fred Trell's storage unit, and Commander Gunn was killed the same week. The truck we caught in the footage was found ditched near Loon Lake. There's something bigger than a break and enter, and you know it."

"Possibly." Martina walked over and set her palm on his cheek. She lifted onto her toes, glancing around first, then kissed him gently. "If you need backup, call me. And keep me posted. Assistant Director Ben is going to be pissed."

"Then it's a good thing you like wearing Kevlar," he told her, returning the kiss. He watched her leave, knowing they shouldn't be engaging in a relationship, and definitely not displaying open affection. It was one thing to share a bed after winning a big case and drinking a couple pints of beer, but the rest of it… that was different.

When Martina was in the airport, a taxi honked from the road, and Waylen lifted both hands. "Okay, I'm leaving."

Waylen headed to the car rental kiosk, wishing the Bureau would approve something flashier for once. They were instructed to go for the sedan with the clunkiest doors, the baldest tires, and broken windshield wipers.

His own car was in the garage two thousand miles away, in his home outside Atlanta, Georgia. Some days, he wondered why he even owned a house, considering he visited it less than these remote field offices.

After ten minutes of navigating complicated airport traffic, he was on the freeway, moving south. He could have flown to Wyoming, but preferred the road. It would give him a chance to unwind after months of tireless efforts on the last case.

Growing up, he'd always wanted to be a police officer, and unlike most kids, it stuck with him after high school, girls, sports, and any other distractions. When he graduated college, he got into the field with the Atlanta Police Department for five years, working the beat for the first couple, until his finance degree led him into financial crimes. He'd helped the FBI on a counterfeiting case, and Assistant Director Ben, a lowly Special Agent at the time, had recruited him. The FBI! Who could decline that kind of opportunity?

Now his old friends from the precinct were rising up the ladder, sitting behind desks, going home to their precious families, and taking vacations at the beach.

Waylen considered this as he drove, wondering if he'd trade this life for another, a more stable and comfortable one, and decided there was absolutely no way. This was his freedom.

He turned on the radio, listening to a local rock station play hits from the late 80s until he crossed the border into Idaho a couple of hours later. Waylen had been in every single state, most of them a dozen times, and it never grew old. He slowed at the sign and parked on the shoulder, clenching his teeth as a large truck sped by, shoving wind in his direction. Waylen snapped a photo of the *Welcome to Idaho* sign, blurring out the backdrop, and examined it. One of his friends had suggested he should eventually publish a book showcasing these 'Welcome to States' signs, but Waylen took them for himself as a reminder of their country and his purpose.

When he got into the car, he received a text notification and saw it was from Martina.

Landed. Wish me luck.

He smiled and typed back. *You just solved the fourth largest fraud case in Bureau history. Don't worry about the fallout from me.*

Three dots appeared, and he started the engine, waiting for the response, but it didn't come. The dots vanished, and he tossed the phone to the passenger seat, returning to the highway.

Waylen continued, then stopped to refill the tank and to empty his, while grabbing a cup of coffee in the middle of Idaho. His eyes were growing tired, and when he checked his distance from Loon Lake, he found it was still three and a half hours away.

Instead of pressing on, he stopped an hour later in Idaho Falls. He'd been there a few years earlier, tracking a fugitive, but hardly remembered the place. The sun was barely up when he entered downtown, and he found a hotel chain that had a corporate rate. It sat by the river that wound through the entire city.

Waylen changed out of his dress shirt, put on a pair of sneakers, and decided to stretch his legs before hitting the bed.

He looked at his phone, expecting a message from Martina, but he only had a spattering of work emails he was cc'd on. It was no wonder most people never got anything done. They were constantly being bombarded with unnecessary minutiae that had nothing to do with their job. He ignored them all and walked to the water, admiring the falls. He strolled by a statue of a moose, where a young couple stood taking selfies, and eventually arrived at a brick building with live music drifting through the propped-open door.

Waylen was tired, but the idea of a beer and something to eat won out. He breezed past a bouncer, who gave him no attention, and took a seat at the bar. A couple of women were nearby, discussing an issue at the office, and Waylen did his best to filter out the noise. He listened to the music and peered at the tight makeshift stage, where a man strummed an acoustic guitar, singing a folk version of a classic Zeppelin tune.

"What'll ya have?" The guy could have been born a bartender, with a stocky torso, a mistrusting gaze, and a bar towel draped on his left shoulder.

"Beer. Something light. Is there a menu?" Waylen asked.

The man poured the pint, slid it over before the foam dissipated, and tossed a small, laminated menu into a damp spot on the wooden bar before moving on.

Waylen sipped his beverage, reading the minimal food offerings, and peered around to check if anyone else was eating. He noticed more sandwiches than anything else, and ordered a club with fries, knowing that one day it would catch up with him. But he thanked his mother for a good metabolism and waited for his late dinner to arrive.

Waylen watched the artist on stage, and as time ticked by, people started leaving. By nine thirty, only ten remained, and the guy packed his guitar into its case, gathered his tips, and left without a word to any of the employees.

"Here's your club," the bartender said.

Waylen saw the coworkers were gone, and caught

sight of the TV. Country music played in the bar's background, and he motioned for the man behind the bar. "Can you turn that up?"

He shook his head.

"Subtitles?"

The bartender grabbed the remote and offered it. "You figure it out."

Waylen used it easily enough, and soon words scrolled in white letters on a black bar across the bottom of the screen.

"The Air and Space Museum had an incident this afternoon. Let's go to the Udvar-Hazy Center for more on this story. Bill, can you explain what transpired?" the news anchor asked, and the camera switched to the largest of the hangars at the Virginia museum. Being a fan of the space program, Waylen had visited the location a few times, and could still hear his own footsteps echoing through the massive room as he toured it privately at an event years earlier.

"Jennifer, the representatives for the center are uncertain what was taken. As you know, the hangars hold complete shuttles, landers, and modules from past space missions. They have the very module from the final mission to the Moon, Helios 15."

Waylen sat upright, leaning closer even though the sound was off. *"While security has often dealt with people eager to touch or even take pieces of the memorabilia, they've never had someone raid their warehouse. Inside the hangars are dozens of historical jets, planes, helicopters, and shuttles, but often the artifacts deemed less interesting to the general public are held in another room."*

"Define less interesting," Jennifer said.

Bill had the decency to smile. *"A toilet seat, for example. Peter Gunn's toothbrush."*

The mention of the recently murdered astronaut grabbed Waylen's attention even more.

"Speaking of Commander Gunn, we at APN News are still shocked by the tragic accident. Bill, what was stolen?" Jennifer asked from inside the studio, and the split screen displayed Bill shrugging while holding his microphone.

"It's unclear. There were dozens of labeled crates containing various items." Bill nodded at the camera. *"The museum is requesting the public to come forward if they have any information."*

Waylen stared at the TV while it showed an unmarked white van backing up to the docking bay. A man hopped out, wearing a black jacket and matching black hat. His sunglasses concealed the top half of his face. The feed switched to a view from in the warehouse, and he carried a clipboard, walking into the facility like he owned the joint.

A few minutes later, he reappeared, rolling a cart with a few crates on it and loading them into the van. He then pressed the bay door closed and drove away. They zoomed on the license plate, and Waylen marked it down into his phone.

"And now, something more uplifting from Arkansas… a little girl had a wish to…"

Waylen gave the remote back and tried to piece it all together. What happened on that Helios 15 mission that triggered a murder fifty years later? The incidents were too far apart to be the actions of an individual, unless they had a boatload of frequent flyer miles.

His phone vibrated, and he scowled when he saw the name. Waylen answered, prepared for a reaming out, but Assistant Director Ben surprised him. *"Waylen, good work on the case. We're proud of you and Sanchez."*

"Thank you, sir."

"Sanchez filled me in on your current distraction."

Here it was.

"Keep at it. I just had a call from above regarding the Center's

theft today, and we're being asked to place feet on the street. I have Special Agent Charles on it in DC. You two can link up. Check out Commander Gunn's situation and see how it correlates with Trell's storage unit. Can you do that?"

"Yes, sir," Waylen said.

"Good man. I know this falls under the Science and Technology Branch, but maybe it's time for a change? What do you say?"

"You're moving me from Financial Crimes?"

"It's not permanent unless you choose otherwise. But for the sake of saving face, I think it's for the best. Understood?"

"Yes, sir. What about Special Agent Sanchez?"

"She's sticking around."

"Okay," Waylen said.

"Are you in Wyoming?"

"Close. I'll arrive in the morning," he said.

"Good. I don't know what the hell these guys are doing, but NASA wants answers, and so do I. Commander Gunn was a real-life hero of mine, and I need you to find the people responsible. Do I make myself clear?"

"Yes, sir. Crystal." Waylen smiled as he ended the call. His food sat uneaten, and he picked at the fries, dipping them in ketchup.

"Another beer?"

The place was almost empty, and Waylen shook his head, paying the tab.

Now that he had approval from the bureau, Special Agent Waylen Brooks was officially on the case.

7

Rory dreaded the sound of the doorbell. When she was a kid, she'd run from upstairs, racing down the banister-lined steps to the front door, trying to beat her parents to see who visited.

Tonight, each press announced the arrival of another guest, some stuffy Vermont elitists with plans to drink her father's rare wine and Scotch, and bore her with tales of their own literary attempts over their lives.

"Rory, what are you doing up here?" Her dad's tie was askew, and she walked up to him, straightening it like she'd seen her mother do a thousand times. He didn't thank her, but a smile creased his eyes.

"I was…"

"Go downstairs before your mother has a fit."

Rory's hair was bouncier than she preferred after the trip to the salon, and her dress was far too colorful. It was bright and form-fitting, unlike her usual roomy black attire in Boston. "How do I look?"

"Like a million bucks." Her father led them down the stairs, and she paused when she saw the man being greeted by her mother.

"I'm thrilled to have been invited to dinner," he said.

"Sorry there wasn't more notice. Rory only got into town yesterday," Kathy said.

"Not a problem. I was supposed to be heading to a

pharmaceutical conference in the city, but it was postponed." He glanced at Rory, and she tried to ignore his gaze.

"Rory." Her mom stopped her from passing by. "I'd like you to meet Greg." She grinned casually. "*Doctor* Greg Palmer."

Rory fumed at the gall, but put on a strong front. She offered her hand, making sure not to shake with too much vigor. Men hated that, or so her mom had taught her. "Charmed."

"Rory, I'm a big fan. I have a copy of *Tears of the Heavens* in my waiting room," he said.

"It's *View from the Heavens*," she corrected him, and her mother bristled.

"I'm certain you two will have a lot to discuss. I've seated you beside one another." Kathy Swanson left the entryway, waving down a member of the serving staff.

A dinner party at the mayor's house was quite the spectacle. The surprising thing was, Kathy had done most of the cooking, despite hiring caterers for dessert and appetizers. She loved control of the main courses, and with her, that meant a lot of seafood and butter, which the people of Woodstock treasured. It was a trait Rory could appreciate, but if it were up to her, Rory would be at the fireplace with a mystery book, or on the back deck sipping a sweet tea and listening to the frogs sing.

More guests arrived while Rory stayed at the entrance, fighting her instincts to leave and lock her bedroom door. These were her parents' friends, and she knew many of them. She noticed Greg had lingered in the sitting room, and Rory headed there when she thought all the guests were present.

"You didn't grow up here, did you?" Rory appraised him, guessing he was a few years older, but Woodstock wasn't large. She'd have heard about him from someone.

"No. I came with my… we broke up."

"Sorry about that." Red flags ran up Rory's mental flagpole, and she pictured a baggage cart behind Greg, being dragged around by a chain on his ankle. She had a tendency for what she called imagination drama.

"Water under the proverbial bridge." Greg stared at her with a smile. "Look, Rory. I really did read your book."

"Yeah?"

"Yes," he declared.

"What was your favorite part?" She smirked and saw the wheels in motion as he searched for a lifeline.

"Madeline was under this immense shadow."

"Go on," Rory said, her curiosity spiked. He knew the main character's name. Rory wondered if he'd spent the previous five minutes web searching the title.

"Her grandfather was this icon, the last person to set foot on the Moon. Then the funding was cut, and you could tell from Madeline's internal monologues how important his career had been. He treated Madeline with such care and attention, it was difficult to see that inside, all he thought about was the Moon. Those near weightless strides, the view of Earth from another surface. Madeline had no choice but to follow in his footsteps, and the scene where she actually did … Forty-nine years after he walked the crater, she did too, and on the anniversary of his death." He paused, his gaze out the window. "She was so connected to him… her boot in the print, the edges blurred and slightly larger than hers. The shadow was gone after that. She'd done it."

Rory stood still, her heart pounding in her chest. "You did read it."

"That's what I said."

"No one's ever mentioned it so eloquently, Greg. Not even my editor."

He flashed a grin, the moment of vulnerability vanished. "I could relate. My grandfather was a doctor, then my dad. I realize it's not identical, but the feelings resonated. A paternal shadow is much the same, no matter what the occupation."

She nodded and gazed to the dining room, where her mom was waving for them to join. "Thank you." Rory touched his arm and kissed his cheek.

"For what?"

She felt rejuvenated. Creativity suddenly coursed through her bones again. That was what it was all about: connecting to people, giving them something to hope for while offering a story they might be able to relate to in some form. She didn't answer his question, and entered the dining room, leaving him behind.

Greg moved faster, sliding her chair out before she arrived at the table, while waiting to push it in after she'd sat. Her mother was watching their interactions, and Rory blew at a strand of hair falling into her eyes.

Kathy Swanson stood at the end of the table with Rory's father, the mayor placed at the far side. Rory's mom tapped her palms together. "I'd like to thank you all for coming tonight to celebrate my lovely daughter's return to the nest. Oscar and I couldn't be happier to have her for the summer."

Rory silently expressed gratitude that her mom made it sound like there was a limited timeline, because truthfully, she had no plans to leave, and no destination in mind.

"Rory's working on her second novel, and a dinner party is just the event to spur on her imagination, isn't it, dear?"

Rory nodded. "I'll do my best not to air any of your dirty laundry."

The various couples stared at her until Mr. Farrow rapped a fist to the table while laughing. "You know us too well, Rory. It's great to see you again."

She'd always liked Mr. Farrow, and his wife sat there with a vacant, medicated look in her eyes, hands folded on her lap.

"I'm glad you could make it."

"What happened to Boston?" Brian Weaver asked. He was the local lawyer, and a regular in her father's Thursday afternoon golf foursome for the last decade.

Rory half-expected her mom to come through with the deflection, and so she didn't answer while Kathy sat. "Rory gets bored with things easily. Apartments, cities, men…"

This got a big laugh, and the party was on.

Rory ate little, as was her usual custom at these events. The food arrived slowly, giving everyone a chance to experience the several courses, and by the time the lobster made an appearance, she noticed some guests sitting back, their stomachs already full.

Greg didn't seem bothered by the endless options, and he chose a lobster tail, offering it to Rory before taking one for himself. He was thin, athletic even, which made her wonder where it all disappeared to. He used the melted garlic butter, dipping a chunky piece in before eating it, and making a small noise of enjoyment.

Rory left hers on the plate, and a server refilled her wineglass. She'd been nursing the first one, not wanting to make a fool of herself in any form, but didn't stop the woman from pouring. Rory took a sip, listening to bits of five different conversations. One centered around her father's choice to not rerun for mayor in the upcoming election. That evolved to discussing retirement; then, of course, golf with Brian. Her mother chatted with Mrs. Farrow, who did more listening than responding.

She and Greg seemed the only pair not interacting, and when she looked in his direction, he'd finished the course.

Once the plates were cleared, Duncan Brown, a retired professor from Rory's own alma mater, leaned his elbows on the table, and a hush fell over the room. "Shame about Commander Peter Gunn."

Everyone murmured their agreement, and Rory nodded.

"Oscar, it made me think about your father."

"Likewise," her dad said.

"Did you know Commander Gunn was Oscar's godfather?" Kathy Swanson asked, her eyebrow raised.

Duncan looked surprised, as did the rest. "I did not. Then I'm doubly sorry. When and where is the funeral?"

"The details aren't firm yet, but I've been contacted by his son, Arthur Gunn. He'd intended on having a ceremony in New York, but they found a will. Peter wanted to be buried with his wife at Loon Lake, or whatever the nearest town is. I presume it'll happen out there," Rory's dad said.

"His lander is at the Smithsonian. Shouldn't there be a pomp ceremony for the press? A lot of good Americans would like to say goodbye," Mr. Farrow added.

"Speaking of the Smithsonian, did you read about the robbery at the Center?" Brian Weaver asked with a mischievous expression. His cheeks were red, and he downed another glass of her father's imported Burgundy.

Rory sat up at that. "What happened?"

"Some guy backed up, gave them a list on a clipboard, and drove away with crates of memorabilia," Brian said.

"When?"

Brian waved at the server, lifting his glass. "Today!"

"I bet that stuff shows up online… or the dark web," Duncan said. "You guys hear of that dark web? Bad bad bad."

Rory let the news wash over her. Peter Gunn had been murdered and his place ransacked. Then someone had the nerve to steal items from the Helios 15 mission? It couldn't be a coincidence. "Dad, where are Gramps' things?"

He stared for a moment; then his face lit up. "We stored some of it in the guest house."

"What do you have of his?" Greg asked.

"Not much. His books, binoculars… he loved watching birds at the lake… and that telescope. Thing cost more than a car, but he wouldn't part with it, even when he moved to the retirement home."

Rory pictured her grandfather in the backyard when he'd visit, setting up the telescope to gaze at the Moon. Always the Moon. The memory filled her with sadness, but also made her grateful that she'd been able to spend so many years of her life with him, at a formative time where his genuine influence had helped make her the woman she'd become.

Rory talked with the guests, finally answering questions about her next book, but keeping them vague. When the clock struck eleven, they began funneling out, everyone kissing her on the cheek or shaking her hand as they left through the front door. Most of them shouldn't be driving, but no one seemed to care.

Soon, only Greg remained, and her mother linked arms with her husband, whispered something, and they entered the den.

"Thanks for being such a great dinner partner," Greg

said.

"Was I? I just kind of sat there most of the night."

He laughed, but didn't deny her claim. "If you're going to be around this summer, why don't we…"

"Greg, you seem like a nice guy, and you're a doctor, tall, and quite…" Rory stopped. "But I really need to focus on my book. That's what I came here for, and it takes priority."

His disappointment was palpable, and he seemed ready to respond, but must have thought better of it. "If you change your mind, your mother has my office's number." He left her alone.

The serving staff exited through the garage when she crossed to the kitchen, and she poured herself a glass of water. Her parents talked in the other room, but she didn't want to join them, so she headed upstairs and walked to the hallway window that overlooked the sweeping backyard. Thick trees hung heavy with foliage, and she could almost smell the sweet fragrant flowers, even from here.

The guest house sat at the rear of the yard, a beautiful structure that Rory used to sleep in when her friends came over. They'd stay up late, talking about boys and watching movies with subject matter no preteen should be privy to. As much as she wanted to investigate what her astronaut Gramps had stored in there, she was too tired tonight, and her book wouldn't write itself.

Rory went to bed, picturing the scene from *Views*, and instead of Maddy's foot in the spacesuit stepping on the light gray regolith, it was her own.

8

Silas slapped a mosquito and checked his phone again. Nothing from Leigh. He should have carried the groceries himself, rather than trusting them to a stranger. He'd thought they'd hit it off at lunch, but clearly Leigh didn't feel the same way. His stomach grumbled, and he opened the pantry cabinet, knowing the contents wouldn't have changed.

The lake was quiet, the Moon sheltered by a thin layer of clouds. Silas smelled the familiar odor of ozone that came with a storm, right before a single raindrop fell, splatting on his forehead, then another. Soon the heavens unleashed their fury, and Silas sped onto the dock, his bare feet slapping on the wooden slats.

Headlights shone on the driveway, drifting sideways, then straightening on the bending gravel road. The old Gremlin car parked, and the lights flashed off before Leigh climbed out, grabbing the groceries as she was soaked.

"Let me help you!" Silas called over the booming thunder. Their hands touched, and Leigh smiled at him under the storm when he took the paper bag.

"Sorry I'm late. My mom decided it was a great time to start an argument about my future, and then my dad had an episode, and when they all settled down, I tried to text you, but the service in this area is a nightmare." She was rambling, and must have realized it.

"Don't worry about it. I was just sitting in the rain," he said.

"How melancholic of you." Leigh darted ahead, rushing to the shield of the front porch. The house was bright compared to the darkness surrounding the lake, and Silas was grateful for the warmth as he entered, his clothing dripping on the hardwood.

Leigh laughed as she closed the door.

"I'll find us something to dry off with." Silas did his best not to slip on the floors, and returned a moment later with two bath towels. Leigh bent at the hips, rubbing her hair before draping it on her shoulders. Her eye makeup was slightly smudged, but Silas would be lying if he didn't find the entire situation slightly appealing. "Come in."

He set the bag on the counter and began filling the cabinets and fridge while Leigh walked into the living room, staring through the tall panes of glass. "This is a nice place."

"Grandpa Gunn would sit out there on the pier for hours a day. He loved watching the sun rise and set."

"He wasn't looking at the sun," Leigh whispered.

"What do you mean?"

She'd moved to the wall where Silas had replaced the photos. Some frames had been broken, but he'd salvaged what he could. She pointed at the image of the three-man crew from Helios 15. "What if he was really observing the Moon?"

"I guess so."

Leigh had a backpack with her, and she unslung it, pulling a bottle from inside. "My dad was a tequila guy, but he can't drink anymore with the medication. So I borrowed this from his cabinet."

Silas didn't have a taste for the stuff. "Is it good?"

"Let's find out." Leigh took it to the kitchen and removed a couple of limes from the bag, making herself at home by grabbing a knife and a cutting board.

"I'm going to change," he said, plucking at his soaked t-shirt. Leigh was damp, but nowhere near as bad as him.

"I'll be here." She poured two glasses.

Silas wasn't confident where tonight was headed, but a beautiful woman was in his grandfather's house after ten at night. He wondered if Grandpa Gunn would be proud or disgusted with the fact. That showed Silas how little he knew about the man.

Silas had borrowed that shirt from the closet, and found another, this one slightly too large, with some charity run from the city on the front. Grandma Gunn had been into supporting various causes, and this was for a children's hospital. He smiled while looking in the mirror. The woman must have been a saint putting up with Peter.

The sounds of music drifted into the hall, and Silas recognized the jazz album he'd been listening to last night before bed.

"He has a nice collection." Leigh thumbed through the plethora of records. Silas had done his best to return the albums to their proper sleeves after the break-in.

"That he did." Silas sat on the couch and used the remote to activate the gas fireplace. The flames took a moment, but the pilot caught the hissing gas and erupted behind the glass, adding to the cozy ambiance. Leigh glanced at the fire, then at the carpet.

"He died here, didn't he?" She hadn't sat yet, and offered him a drink.

Silas had cleaned everything with bleach and covered the area with the throw rug, but the restoration company couldn't come for another two days. "Yeah."

She hugged herself and sat across from him. "Do you believe in ghosts?"

"No," he blurted. "Do you?"

"Kind of. I believe they might exist."

"Why?"

"There's so much we don't know, Silas; millions of things science can't explain. What if there's another realm on this very Earth that we can't see? What if heaven is really here, but through a veil of some sort?" Leigh downed the contents of her glass and followed it up with a lime slice. Silas shrugged and did the same, wincing at the sharp taste.

"So you believe in ghosts *and* heaven?"

"You're making fun of me," she said.

"I don't mean to. I guess my family is just more pragmatic. My mom grew up Catholic, but my dad wouldn't go to church, so none of us did."

"Not even your grandfather?"

"No." Silas recalled the photos in the album of Peter Gunn as a child. He'd been baptized, and there was a black-and-white photo with the date written on the back to prove it. "He used to, but not later in life."

"Being on the Moon probably changed his view on things," Leigh suggested. She had the bottle, and refilled their glasses. "Can you imagine what it would feel like to be up there?"

"I can't," he admitted.

"I think it would be cool."

"I guess," Silas agreed.

"What do you do… for work?"

Silas leaned back on the couch, watching the rain drip down the windows. A bolt of lightning flashed across the lake, briefly illuminating the region. "I'm the CFO of my father's furniture company."

"Nepotism. Gotta love it."

"That's what I told him," Silas said. "It's a family affair. My sister Clare runs manufacturing, and I oversee the financial side."

"Do you like it?"

Silas doubted anyone had ever asked him that before. They usually heard his job title, assumed he made good money, and moved on. "I ... don't hate it."

"That's not the same thing."

"I haven't given that much thought either," he said.

"Seems like you need to do more thinking." Leigh grinned, and he couldn't help but smile back, despite the playful insult.

"What about you? Came from the city to work out here at your parents' store? Running from something?"

"Myself, mainly," she said.

"I can understand that."

"My dad's heart attack was a wake-up call, but now that I'm here..." She sighed heavily. "I just want to leave."

"You don't like Gull Creek... or Loon Lake... Also, what's up with these names?"

"There's a lot of lakes and creeks, I guess."

"And birds."

"They wake me up every morning," she said.

Leigh was on her feet, and she strolled to Grandpa Gunn's office. Silas followed her, and stopped at the desk. He had all sorts of paperwork strewn out, seeking anything personal he could on Peter.

"What's this?" Leigh touched the cloth satchel and slid the object from the case.

Silas recalled finding it below the safe, tucked under the hidden compartment. So far, he hadn't a clue what it was, and told her so.

Leigh picked the metallic object up, her eyes going wide. It fell from her grip, clanging to the desk, and toppled to the floor. "What the hell was that?"

Silas frowned, wondering what frightened her. "What?"

She shuddered and did her second shot of tequila, stepping away from the flat piece of metal. "I…"

"Leigh, tell me."

Leigh glanced at the exit, and Silas noticed a pair of headlights shining from the end of the drive. Thunder boomed, and another flash of lightning sparked from above as the rain continued to pelt on the roof.

"What spooked you?" he demanded, probably louder than was necessary.

She stared at the object. "Have you touched it?"

He thought back to when he'd discovered the satchel. "I don't think so."

She backed up another step and leaned on the office door frame. "Try."

Silas hesitated, but bent to pick it up. The moment he skimmed the surface, the sensations rushed into his mind.

A triangle. No air. His lungs pressurized. Eyes threatening to bulge. Dust below his feet. Blackness. A hole.

He fell to his seat and pried his finger from the object. It slid to the hardwood, landing lightly. Silas scrambled to the wall and stared at the cold, narrow piece of metal. "We shouldn't have done that." His chest ached, and everything was momentarily blurred. Leigh was a shadowy shape with floating black specks rising from her head.

Neither of them spoke for a minute. Finally, he left it on the floor, and they returned to the living room. The moment he was free of the office, his heart slowed, his breath evening out. Leigh looked lost, and he hugged her, feeling the warmth of her body. It grounded him.

"Did you…"

She nodded. "It was like being in space without…"

"How did he get this?" Silas plopped on the couch, with Leigh beside him. The headlights were gone, the driver probably just turning around.

"There's nothing here that mentions it?" Leigh asked.

Silas struggled with his balance, but his eyesight had returned to normal. "Not a single note. He didn't keep a journal or any voice recordings that I could find."

"He was the last of the astronauts, right?"

"From the Moon missions, yes," Silas said. He stared at the fireplace and remembered something from a decade earlier. He'd gone to Colin Swanson's funeral. His own father had made them, even though they didn't sit with Grandma or Grandpa Gunn. It had been a solemn affair, after a long battle with dementia.

Silas grabbed his phone from his pocket and opened a browser.

"What are you doing?"

"Checking something." He quickly found the video and saw it had over 10 million views. He hit play, and they both watched intently as Colin Swanson, seated on a comfortable chair across from the host, sipped a coffee.

When they spoke, Silas could barely hear it with the raging storm, so he turned the volume up.

"You were on the last trip to the Moon, correct?" John, the host, said.

"Yes. It was a remarkable time," Colin answered.

"Do you have any idea why NASA didn't send more missions afterwards? Is it true that the Moon holds no value to us on Earth, besides the obvious?"

Colin set the coffee aside, his face stern. *"There's a lot NASA doesn't know about that mission."*

John looked amused. *"Is that so? Pray tell."*

"I'm getting old, John. We all are, and it's time to come clean," Colin said.

"We're listening."

"We found something and promised to take it to the grave. Me, Fred, and Peter."

John scooted forward and glanced at the camera, as if he was making sure they were catching the interview.

"We should have told them, but we were worried about what might happen." Colin's lip quivered, and his fist balled up.

John, the host, sat still, allowing the dreaded dead air to choke out the set.

"They're out there. Waiting for us."

"Who?" John whispered. *"Who's waiting?"*

Colin shook his head, as if he'd thought better of it, and removed the mic clipped to his lapel. He stood and walked away, with John calling after him. The video ended, and Silas began scrolling through the comments.

"Does that have anything to do with... what just happened in his office?" Leigh asked.

"I have no idea."

Leigh offered the faintest smile. "I should go."

"Already?" He felt like they were delving into a mystery together, and didn't want to part ways. "You could stay the night...if you wanted."

Leigh shook her head and peered at the office, then the carpet in the living room. "I can't be here." She took off without another word, leaving the front door wide. The Gremlin's engine fired on, and she sped around, shooting gravel from under her tires. Soon he was alone with the rain, and a peculiar object.

They're out there. Waiting for us. Silas thought about the comments, and remembered the first time they'd watched the interview, after his father told him that Colin, his godfather, was ill. He died two years later.

Silas locked the door, turned off the fireplace, and carefully placed the metal strip into the bag without touching it. He dropped it into the secret compartment beneath the desk, and found the bed, staring at the ceiling as rain battered the house. He didn't think he'd ever sleep again.

9

Gull Creek looked like any other rural lakeside community in the region. Waylen drove through the main drag and checked the time, finding it was just before eight in the morning. He'd forgotten what day of the week it was, and realized it was Saturday. Nothing around here would be open yet, with the exception of a diner—if he was lucky.

He passed a store with colorful signs, and a young man moved out scooters and dragged rental canoes on trailers to display them. Waylen slowed and rolled his window down, the kid leaning closer.

"Need a boat? We're closed for another hour, but I'd take cash," the worker said, with a hint of hope in his voice.

"You guys busy?" Waylen asked.

"Not bad. Weather's been good. My dad—he owns the place— he thought with the news of the murdered old guy that Loon Lake wouldn't be tourist friendly this year, but he was wrong."

"Peter Gunn?" Waylen knew that was the only murder in the area.

"Yeah, that dude."

"You ever see him?"

"In the paper after he was shot. Kinda freaky that some guy would break in and kill an astronaut or whatever," the kid said.

Waylen doubted he'd get any more information. "Thanks. Have a nice day." He pressed the window up and headed for the sheriff's office. The nearest detective lived twenty miles away, but Waylen heard they'd been on the site because of the nature of the crime, and that it had made national headlines. When he pulled up to the depressing building, he cringed. There was a single squad car, the paint chipped, the door dented.

The sheriff's office wasn't in any better condition. Its roof was in disrepair, the gutters growing a green moss, and he spotted a bird's nest in the eaves. The front door was unlocked, and he entered, finding a woman in uniform, bent over a newspaper and eating a donut. She didn't seem to notice she had company, and upon closer inspection, music leaked from earbuds. He waved a hand to gather her attention.

"Oh, good morning," she said. The woman removed the earbuds and brushed donut crumbs from her lips. "Can I help you?"

"Yes. Are you the sheriff?" Waylen doubted it, but it was a tactic he often employed when first meeting an officer like this. It gave them a sense of purpose, a notion that yes, they could be in charge if the man in a suit thought they were.

"No, sir. I'm Deputy Hunt." She dusted her hands off and extended her arm. "And you are?"

Instead of shaking, he reached for his credentials, flipping the wallet open to display the picture. It wasn't his best. His hair was shorter in it, done last minute at a barbershop he'd never been at before. "Special Agent Waylen Brooks, FBI."

"FBI?" She coughed. "What are you doing here?"

"I'd like to speak with you about Peter Gunn."

"Most of the details will be with Detective Frank Desjardins, out of Campbelltown."

"But you did visit the scene?" he asked.

She nodded. "Yes, sir."

"And you saw Peter?"

"Yes. He'd been shot and left to bleed out."

"I assume it was your first body?"

"No, sir. We see a fair bit of death. Traffic accidents. A young girl drowned out in Loon Lake a couple of years earlier. But nothing like this… not murder."

Waylen saw a toughness in her expression that hadn't been there a moment earlier. "Are you the only one on shift?"

"The sheriff is having breakfast at the diner like he does every Saturday morning."

"Then he comes in?"

"That's right," Hunt said.

"You found the stolen truck outside of town, correct? Can we see it?"

"Sure, it's in the yard. From what I've seen, the insurance company is waiting for news on damages."

They walked through the building, and Waylen noted the coffee pot was on. He almost stopped for a cup, until he detected the rat droppings on the floor by the trash can. "What's with this place?"

Hunt genuinely looked confused. "Sir?"

"Do you have no funding?"

She shook her head. "It's a small community, and we're lucky to have any support at all. Plus, the pay sucks, and we're dealing with a meth epidemic in the county. Most of the state is, truthfully."

Waylen held the rear door for her, and Hunt stepped into the yard. "What about you? Why do you stay?"

"It's a job, and… I've always wanted to help."

Waylen had seen the type a few times, and appreciated her more for it. She'd probably grown up poor in the area, wishing to improve her town. Unfortunately, he gave her three years before she realized it was fruitless and she pulled the plug, seeking a transfer to a larger city with opportunities of advancement.

The yard was fenced with chain-link, but the gate was wide open, the lock hanging loose. Eleven vehicles were parked within it, all of them in rough shape, most rusted and tireless—except the one truck linked to the crime.

He pulled a pair of gloves from his pocket and slipped into them, snapping the vinyl on his wrists. Hunt looked surprised to see him using the protective barrier, and that didn't give him much hope for the continuity of their crime scene investigation. Waylen opened the passenger door and checked the glove box. An old map, a user manual, and a multi-screwdriver. Not much to go by there. He searched under the seats, finding nothing of note. Whoever had stolen this truck had cleaned it as they dumped it.

"Can you show me where they ditched it?" he asked.

"Sure. Hop in." Deputy Hunt led him to her car, and he narrowed his gaze, pointing at his rental.

"Do you mind if I drive?"

"No. Just let me lock up." She went to the doors and mumbled into the radio on her shoulder. The conversation was quiet, but Waylen could tell the man on the other side of the discussion wasn't expecting to hear that an FBI agent had arrived this early on a weekend morning. "The sheriff would like to meet with you after."

"I'd like that as well," he said. Truthfully, he wanted to get to Peter Gunn's house and check out the scene. He had to tour this region and paint a picture of what happened last week.

Waylen signaled despite being the only guy on the road out here, and noticed the grass was in desperate need of being cut. "How's the town office?"

"Gull Creek is reliant on tourism, and since the bigger lakes have built a resort on the other side of Campbelltown, we've struggled a bit. Our campsites get busy enough, but that doesn't bring in a lot of income for the local businesses."

"The kid at the boat rental store seemed to think they were doing all right."

"Chet? He's stoned half the time. And he's always trying to get cash for the units, since his dad is letting him take the reins."

"He mentioned it," Waylen said.

He continued through the town, nearing a humble market where a young woman placed fresh flowers on an outdoor display. "Who's that?" he asked. The diner was next to it, with the sheriff's car out front, the paint faded from the sun.

"Her name's Leigh. We went to high school together. Never really got along, but it wasn't my fault. She stuck to herself, mostly."

Leigh's gaze tracked their car as Waylen slowly rolled down the main street.

"Her dad almost died. Hell, it would have been better if he had."

"Why do you say that?"

"His wife, Mrs. Kettle, is a real cow. She runs the store. Leigh was adopted when they were in their forties, and it's no wonder she ran away at seventeen before graduating."

Waylen let the deputy talk, not really interested in the sordid details of the locals, but he wanted Hunt to feel comfortable with him, so he listened. "Hunt's not your first name, I assume."

"Dear lord, I hope not. It's Gail."

"Where do I go from here?" He followed her directions, and they exited Gull Creek, heading on a narrow road toward the lake. The ground was elevated in this area, and as he crested a hill, Waylen spied the water through the tree cover. It glimmered with the sunlight, and the street dropped again, the view becoming spoiled by dense spruces. Waylen opened the window, inhaling the scent of nature.

"You like it out here?"

"I'm usually working in an office, poring over financial reports and filling out paperwork, so yeah, this is nice."

Deputy Hunt shrugged her shoulders. "Summer is my least favorite season. Bugs are bigger than bats, and everything seems sticky all the time. People get drunker, more violent. Tourists make litter, fires erupt from cigarettes when it gets too dry. I prefer the winter myself. Warmth of the hearth, stockings on the mantel."

"I can appreciate that," he said, and meant it. Waylen usually spent his Christmases alone in Atlanta, but had once been on a case in Montana during the holiday season, and he'd witnessed snow for the first time on the day of. He'd never forget it.

"Sorry, I'm not usually so chatty. We can turn here." She pointed to the right, and he slowed, pulling into a service access road. "It was there."

"In the open?"

She nodded.

Waylen parked and got out. "Which direction was it facing?"

Deputy Hunt paused and tapped her chin with a plain fingernail. He noticed the ends were chewed. "That way."

Forward, toward the access gate.

"And no one has reported a stolen vehicle since?"

"Nope."

Waylen pictured the murderer ditching the truck after shooting Commander Gunn. Why here? He stared at the land in the distance, and at the road leading to Gull Creek. Loon Lake lay a few miles to the east in the other direction. "He wouldn't have walked away in the dark."

"I suppose not."

"Then he had a ride. Someone picked him up," Waylen whispered.

"No one's thought about that," she said. "At least, not that I've heard."

Waylen knew it had to be more than one person from the beginning. There was too much ground to cover. Were there just this pair? Could they have reached DC in the span of two days to steal crates from the NASA collection at the hangar?

Waylen texted Martina, hoping she'd offer some support in the case, or put it on someone who could make the time. He needed to know if tickets were bought from the nearest airport, with DC as the destination.

The pieces of the puzzle were slowly shifting into place, and Waylen thought he might get somewhere in rural Wyoming after all. "Can you show me the house?"

The radio beeped, and Deputy Hunt lifted a finger. She stepped toward the field and consulted her boss in private before returning. "Detective Desjardins will be at the diner in ten. The sheriff asked to speak with you both."

Waylen nodded. The visit to Gunn's house would have to wait.

10

For the first time since her breakup, Lauren feels the weight of her existence vanish with the morning mist. She's meant for so much more than fetching coffees at the office and cleaning up after her slob of a husband. Lauren smiles, entering the greenhouse, inhaling the scent of damp soil and herbs.

Rory paused, looking at the computer screen, and her chest filled with relief. She finally had something. It was just an idea, an inkling of the bigger picture, but the premise was there. Madeline had been a version of herself in *View from the Heavens*, and Lauren was born from her trauma with Kevin in Boston. She could let it out on paper for the world to experience, and hopefully grow as a result.

The clock on the bottom left corner of the laptop told Rory that it was almost lunch, meaning another extravagant dining experience with her parents. Seven pages. That was better than her usual, even at the peak of her last novel, and with a quick word count check, Rory read that she'd done over two thousand words.

Her mother's knock came as no surprise, and Kathy Swanson entered with a smile. "I heard you clicking away. That's good news, I hope?"

"You're seriously out in the hallway listening to me type? Can't you be like those other WASPs and drink rosé and discuss summer beach reads at the park?" Rory closed the laptop and had a rush of satisfaction. She was an author, no longer a mere budding writer.

Even after the success of her debut novel, Rory never felt worthy of the literary circles. Maybe with the follow-up, she could banish the self-doubt once and for all. This story was more grounded. Her agent swore that *View from the Heavens* deserved a film or TV option, but the budget would be too high, considering the space modules and scenes on the Moon. This new project might fit the broader readership she needed to reach the next level.

"Your father and I thought we could go out for lunch today."

Rory should have known that by the fancy outfit her mother wore. Her dad was at the front doors, his suit jacket draped over his arm, and he held the exit wide for the ladies to go through first.

"Do we have to leave the house?" Rory asked. "I'm on a roll and wouldn't mind continuing this afternoon."

"Pumpkin, you don't want to burn out," her dad said.

"I've been writing for three hours." And eighty hours staring at the screen in the past month, randomly hitting keys until she deemed the prose bad enough to delete. "I don't have to worry about that."

"It'll be good for you," Kathy told her, holding the convertible's door open for her to climb in. Rory glanced at her own attire, realizing she wasn't as smartly dressed as her parents.

The moment the car started and her father drove off the property, Rory had a sinking feeling. "You're not setting a trap here, are you? Bring unsuspecting Rory to the club to be surprised by Greg the doctor or something?"

"Nonsense, dear. I wouldn't have let you leave looking like that," her mother said offhandedly.

Rory grew even more self-conscious as the wind blew

through her hair, ruffling it. They pulled up to the private club, which catered to Woodstock and the surrounding areas. It was a couple of miles from town, down a stretch of estate properties larger than their own.

Rory inhaled and smelled old money. She reached into her purse and grabbed her cell phone, marking that sensation down for her book.

"What are you doing?" her mom asked.

"Making a note."

"Your head is always elsewhere, isn't it?" Her father tossed the keys to a young valet, who smiled as Rory climbed from the backseat.

They strolled the cobblestone pathway to the restaurant. Rory heard someone swearing, and glanced at the tennis courts, finding two middle-aged women with a pair of tennis instructors, working on their backhands.

Rory almost got clipped by a golf cart, and the guy muttered an apology through a cloud of cigar smoke. They didn't slow or check on her.

Her parents stalked ahead, everyone waving to them like they were royalty. Rory trailed behind like an invisible servant, wondering why she'd never grown used to the lifestyle. She'd ventured off from college with the aspiration of doing life on her own merits. Her roommate had come from nothing, and was the most eloquent, intelligent woman Rory had ever met. Karli had inspired Rory to forgo the condo her father offered to purchase in Boston for her and Kevin. Because of that, she'd struggled with two jobs while finishing the manuscript.

Now, walking through this idyllic setting, she wondered if it wouldn't have just been easier to accept their wealth and use it to her advantage. How much farther ahead could she be if she'd stayed at home in those early years, writing rather than serving as a barista at a coffee shop, and a cashier at the local bookstore?

That hadn't lasted long, because Kevin Heffernan couldn't dare tell people at parties that his girlfriend was scraping the bottom of the societal employment pool. Kevin wasn't much better, but he wouldn't admit it. No, Rory had to be this fledging authorial star, with multiple publishers interested in her manuscript. That was the story, but maybe there was something to Kevin's assurance that it would happen. Because she'd finished the book, found an agent, and had sold the manuscript for a hundred thousand dollars.

Life-changing money.

Which was all gone, because of Kevin.

She glanced at the tall trees, limbs hanging low with plush green leaves. Flowers were everywhere; bright azaleas sat in pots beside orange and red daylilies. Rory took a deep breath, desperately not wanting to think about Kevin. He could rot in hell.

"After you," her dad said, waving her into the clubhouse restaurant. It was Saturday, meaning the place was packed, but her father, as usual, had a standing reservation, and they were ushered to the window seat overlooking the eighteenth green. Older couples stood in the shade outside, sipping drinks and laughing about something as they compared score cards.

"Mom, why don't you pick up golf?"

"It's not for me," Kathy answered, slinging her purse over her chair. "Ask your father."

"She came once and refused to take lessons. We played eight holes, and I almost got hit twice, even though I stood behind her." He laughed.

Rory tried to imagine her mother being bad at anything, but couldn't.

They ordered drinks: her mom white wine, her dad a

bourbon, and Rory requested a cup of coffee, which got a glare from her parents, like it was a sin to not have booze on a Saturday lunch at the club. People would talk. Newspapers would be notified.

Rory requested the fish, and after the server left, her father removed his glasses and set them on the table. She knew that look. "Oh God, are you two getting a divorce?" she groaned.

Kathy and Oscar locked gazes and broke out in matching smiles. "Divorced? Never!"

"Then what's this all about?" she asked.

"We've been talking…" Kathy started.

"Great."

"Maybe it's time you put that degree to good use," she said.

Rory froze.

"You went to an Ivy League school, darling. What if this book stuff isn't meant to happen? You already lost the advance from the first one, and you have nothing to your name, do you?" Kathy tried to give her a supportive nod, but all Rory heard was the condemnation behind the words.

Rory bridled in her seat, but before she could offer a rebuttal, the drinks arrived. She poured cream into the cup, slowly stirring it into a caramel color. When they were alone again, she leaned closer. "Kevin spent my money. He wasted it all on poor investments. He treated me horribly and stole from our accounts. I'm a talented author. I've won awards and have a contract on another—"

"But you're not writing it," Kathy interjected.

"Because I'm here at the *stupid club* when I should be *working*. You won't stop dragging me around town like I'm your little doll." Rory raised her voice, but settled down when a few tables watched their interaction. "I can do this. I just need to focus."

"That's fine, we'll leave you—"

"I'm going to take the guest house," Rory said, shocking herself. The idea came from nowhere.

"It's filled with… stuff." Oscar sipped his bourbon, a large spherical ice cube clinking on the crystal glassware.

"I'll move it to the second guest room," she said.

"Okay." Oscar clapped his hands gently. "If that's all it takes, but promise us one thing."

"Sure," she relented.

"If this fails, you'll get a job. You can stay with us for as long as you like while you get on your feet, and the offer to buy that condo in the city still stands. But it doesn't have to be Boston. What about Montpelier? You'll be much closer. It's only an hour's drive."

Rory tried to defuse her anger, because they meant well, but this conversation proved they didn't fully believe in her abilities. "That's very kind of you." She didn't verbally commit, but her parents seemed to take it as some version of an agreement.

The rest of the lunch was spent discussing a planned renovation on the library in their house, and what Oscar would do when he retired. Rory listened with one ear, her other hearing tidbits of exchanges from around the club. She spied older men with younger wives, flaunting smooth foreheads and pouty lips. Everywhere she looked, there were diamond tennis bracelets, Rolex watches, designer bags, and expensive champagne being trickled into stemmed glasses. She suddenly felt very out of her element.

Her father signed off on the tab, and they walked through the gardens on the way to the car. Oscar wandered off, chatting to some friends, and her mom came closer. "Honey, we didn't mean to ambush you."

"It's okay."

"I do have confidence you'll continue being success-ful," she said.

Rory didn't respond, waiting for an elaboration.

"Your father just wants you to have a safe and stable life. You're almost thirty, and he believes you should have something to fall back on if this book thing doesn't take off." Her mother smiled and took her hands. "He loves you and only desires the best for his princess."

"I appreciate it," she said. Truth was, Rory couldn't really complain. They'd received her return home with open arms, and the offer to buy her a condo when she was ready.

When they made it home, Rory had the desire to keep writing, but she opted to investigate the guest house. Oscar gave her the key, and she went alone while her parents took a leisurely stroll before cocktail hour at their swimming pool. They were creatures of habit.

It was three o'clock when she stood at the small home's front door, the shutters closed. She glanced up at the pair of dormers from the second floor and tested the handle, which was locked. Rory dangled the key, smiling as she slid it in. The door clicked, and Rory stepped into her new temporary home.

11

"Pick up, pick up," he muttered. She didn't.

Silas paced the living room, his gaze eventually falling on the spot where Grandpa Gunn had been murdered. He couldn't stick around any longer. Leigh had gone dark, not responding to him.

Silas hadn't slept for more than two hours, and those had been riddled with dreams of another place. He tossed and turned on the bed, his lungs aching, his vision blurring. When he woke, he was fine. Twice, he almost touched the slender piece of metal again, but the memories were so fresh that they held him at bay.

The time on his phone showed 1:12 PM, so it was after three on the East Coast. He dialed his father's number, and it rang once before the familiar gruff voice answered.

"*Silas, good to hear from you,*" he said.

Silas was quickly comforted by the sound of his father. "Dad, you doing okay?"

"*Me? I'm fine. We're finishing up the arrangements for the funeral. It's next Friday at Campbelltown.*" He spoke with little emotion. "*Apparently, the old man already had most of it set up, and he'd paid for the plot beside Grandma Gunn.*"

Next Friday. Could Silas stay here another week alone? With that… thing in the other room? "Dad, did Grandpa ever mention…"

"Mention what?"

"An object?"

"Son, what are you talking about?"

Silas thought better. "Never mind. When are you coming?"

"Thursday. Your mother and sister will be joining me. Clare's bringing the kids. You need anything? A suit?"

"Sure, please."

There was a brief pause. *"Silas, did you find what you were hoping for?"*

Silas didn't know how to respond. "Not really."

"That's because the man was a vacant shell. You're staying until the funeral?"

This was it: his opportunity to leave. His dad would get his assistant to book him a flight out today if he wanted, and he could be at his apartment by dark. The phone buzzed, and he checked to see Leigh's number. "Dad, I gotta run. I'll be here. Love you."

"Love you too." It ended, and Silas answered the second call.

"Leigh!"

"Hey, Silas." She sounded scared.

"You haven't answered…"

"I've been working all day," she said. *"And… I didn't sleep well."*

"Can we get together?" He looked outside, desperate for some fresh air, then exited the front door. Silas went to the porch, feeling a hint of the sun breaking through the canopy of trees above the property. Silas kept on to the pier, the heat rising with each step.

"Sure. Hey, there's a guy in town wearing a suit. Looks like a G-man."

"G-man?" Silas asked.

"Government agent. CIA, FBI…"

"Gotcha."

"*I think we should talk to him. He met with the sheriff earlier. I asked Carrie about it, and she said they were discussing your grandfather's case after breakfast. They stayed for a couple of hours and left around eleven. He might come to see you,*" Leigh said.

"What do we tell him? About the… thing."

Silas grew protective, knowing that his grandfather had gone to lengths to keep it hidden. Was that why he'd been killed? For a stick of metal that makes you sick? "Let's meet up first. Discuss the options."

"*Okay,*" she conceded. "*I'm off at two. Should I come over?*"

"I'll make the hike. I have to get out of the lake house," he said.

"Meet me at the bar. I don't need my mom seeing you again. I already heard about it last night when I got home."

Silas wanted to tell her she was twenty-five and could make her own decisions, but refrained. He didn't know enough about their family dynamic to form an opinion. "Be there in forty minutes." He clicked END and wandered to the edge of the pier, glancing at his grandfather's chair. "What were you doing with that thing? And where did you find it?" he whispered, receiving an answer from a pair of ducks floating by. His grandfather had always been the same: calm on the surface, but moving a mile a minute below the water.

Silas examined his reflection back at the house and straightened his hair. He wore another of the old man's shirts, this one a short-sleeved button up that, no matter how many times he washed it, still smelled like a stranger. He checked the safe, ensuring the item was in its hiding place, and locked the doors.

The area was serene, the breeze barely offering any

reprieve, and he listened to the leaves rattling a song you rarely heard in the city. The longer Silas stayed at the lake house, the more he understood why Peter Gunn and his wife had chosen to escape the hustle and bustle of a metropolis. They were retired and could spend their days together in peace.

Silas took his time, deciding to use almost all of the forty minutes to walk the two miles. He paused as the road peaked and took in the view from this perch. People were out in droves, some waterskiing behind expensive boats; others basked in party pontoons, drinking in the sunlight. Silas hadn't had fun like that in ages, not since he'd taken on the responsibility of CFO at his father's company. The sounds of summer echoed over the lake, and he inhaled the scent of a bonfire. Country music carried from a speaker nearby, and a girl screamed loudly before diving off a pier by the beach.

Silas closed his eyes and saw only darkness. A hole. His chest burned, his temples feeling pressure. When he opened them, the sensation had passed, and the scene in front of him focused into clarity.

He shook it off and strode into town twenty minutes later, the strange moment a distant memory. Silas didn't know where the bar was, but Gull Creek wasn't a large place. He spied it a little after two, the wooden building painted brown. It was peeling from the sun, and the sign labeled it as Dawn's Lakeside Bar and Grill, though there was no lake in sight. The Gremlin was in the parking lot, one of three cars occupying the large gravel space.

He pressed through the doors, and someone glanced up from the bar, his eyes narrowing at the sudden infusion of natural light. When the entrance closed, he turned back, hands wrapped around his beer.

"Over here!" Leigh called, and he found her in a corner booth.

The joint smelled like every hole-in-the-wall dive Silas had ever set foot in, right down to the musty scent of beer on the creaky wooden plank floor. He glanced at the seat and brushed aside a few crumbs before sitting across from her.

Leigh was half covered by shadows in the dim room, her eyes black. "No issues finding the place?"

Silas shook his head and peered at the plate of untouched fries.

"Want some?" she asked.

Silas realized he hadn't eaten today, and took one. "We should talk …"

"Where did you find it?" she interjected.

He finished the fry and told her about the safe, along with the secret compartment on the bottom.

Light poured in, and two men entered. Their gazes drifted across the floor, casually observing the handful of patrons, and they took a seat at a booth on the far edge. Silas returned his attention to Leigh. "We can't tell anyone."

"Why not?" she asked.

"I think that's what got my grandfather killed," he said. "If whoever broke in was searching for it…"

"Let's say it was a targeted attack—and that might be pushing it—then wouldn't they be gone? They killed Peter Gunn and left empty-handed. You said the entire place was ransacked. They'd probably think he didn't have it. And what kind of killer hangs out in town after murdering someone?" Leigh asked.

"I don't know," he admitted. "What do you think it was?"

"Your guess is as good as mine." She finally tried the food.

"It has to be poisonous. Like radioactive or whatever. Why else would we have seen things?"

"I didn't just see them. I felt it."

"Same here," he whispered. "Maybe it has lead in it. Or uranium. I didn't do well in chemistry."

"Me neither," she admitted. "I still say we talk to the FBI agent."

"I'm not sure that's a great idea." Silas ordered a water, to the chagrin of the haggard server, but she brought it without complaint. "The funeral is next Friday."

She watched him. "You're staying?"

"Yeah."

This brought a smile to her face. "Good." Silas warmed at the reaction. "I figured you'd be on the first train outta here."

"What about you? The way you escaped last night, leaving me to the wolves," he joked, but her grin faltered.

"I was scared."

"Me too," he said.

"What if they discovered it on the Moon?"

Silas let the remark sink in, recalling Colin Swanson's comment from the interview. *We found something and promised to take it to the grave. Me, Fred, and Pete.* "If they all knew about it, why did my grandfather keep it?"

"He was the commander in charge of the mission. He pulled rank," Leigh suggested.

"Could be. Or…"

"You don't think there are more, do you?"

"I saw a shape when I touched it."

"So did I."

"A triangle. It might have been made of three tokens like the one in his safe," Silas said.

"Someone broke into the museum in DC and stole containers from the Helios 15 mission." Leigh dropped her French fry. "That has to be related."

"There was Fred Trell too. But we haven't heard anything about him." Silas brought his phone out and did a quick search of the man. "He never married. Lived in Oregon. Died there eight years ago."

They hadn't paid their respects at that funeral, with Silas' father claiming not even Peter Gunn talked to Trell any longer. Colin had been Silas' dad's godfather, but Fred Trell never fit the mold, and Silas had only seen him at the reunion years earlier when he was a kid.

"If he had one of those...where would it be?" Leigh asked. "What about the guy from the interview?"

"I know the family," Silas said. "They have a girl close to my age. She's an author." Silas owned a copy of Rory Valentine's hit release, but he hadn't read it. He'd heard enough about the space program over the course of his life, and didn't need to read a fictional account of it.

"You should contact them and subtly ask if they know anything."

The guy at the bar slid a bill to the bartender and left. The pair sitting in the other booth were gone, and Silas hadn't seen them slip out. They weren't familiar, but he was new to town, and had really only met Leigh and Gabriel, the landscaper that had given him a lift yesterday. And Carol, the neighbor.

Silas checked the various social media apps on his phone and found Rory's name listed on an older one. He noticed a page for her pen name, but skipped that, and sent Rory Swanson a friend request.

"Now we wait."

"Want to go to the beach instead?" Leigh seemed lighter, her dark mood subsiding as they made an effort at solving their riddle.

"I'd love to." Silas paid, and they went to the car,

Leigh revving the engine before speeding down the road toward the public beach access.

Leigh smiled at him as they parked in a busy lot. Silas kicked off his shoes and socks, like Leigh did, putting them in the trunk, and they strolled to the sandy cove, his mind on something other than the mystery his grandfather left behind.

12

"I appreciate all the details, Detective Desjardins, but I'd like to see the house now," Waylen said for the second time.

"Sure, sure." Desjardins seemed competent, but he'd obviously never worked with anyone from the FBI before. It was as though he was seeking to impress Waylen, when that wasn't necessary.

The sheriff had left the room an hour ago, and Waylen thought he heard snores emanating from the office down the hall. Desjardins rolled his eyes and closed the file folder. "Most of these small towns are the same thing. I worked in Kentucky for a spell, and it was no different there. Old timers with no ambition, hoping nothing happens on their watch."

Waylen couldn't fully disagree, but he'd seen enough capable sheriffs and police chiefs throughout the country to shake his head. "They aren't all like this."

The detective blinked and pointed at the exit. "Shall we?"

Martina hadn't responded yet, and Waylen quickly sent another text.

They'd gone in after lunch, and it was getting later than he'd wanted. All he knew was the man who'd killed Peter Gunn had an accomplice, but there was no lead on either of them.

"No one saw anything suspicious in town?" he asked in the parking lot.

"Where?"

"Gull Creek," Waylen said.

"We didn't canvass the town, just Loon Lake," he said.

Waylen stared at him. "They're like two miles apart. Where do you believe the killer stayed? At the campsite?"

Desjardins swallowed and wiped his forehead, even though they'd just stepped into the heat. "I'll ask around."

"Don't bother. If anyone saw something suspicious, they'd have come forward," Waylen said, unsure how true that statement was. "Let's go. Is the house still taped off?"

"No," Desjardins said.

"Why not? It's a crime scene."

"We took all the samples, ran forensics. Fingerprints. Blood analysis. So we gave the keys to the family."

"They were here?" he asked. Waylen hadn't read that part in the paperwork.

"Yeah, Arthur Gunn and his son Silas. From New York."

Waylen was upset the house hadn't been kept off-limits. "Bring me there. Did the family stay?"

He shrugged. "I gave them my card, but no one's called. I assumed they took off right after I did."

Waylen stewed over the incompetence as they headed to the lake. He followed Desjardins in his rental. They passed the location where the truck had been ditched, and continued to Loon Lake, until he came upon 18 Beachcomber Way. The lot was large, made private by mature trees.

Since he saw no car parked in the gravel driveway, he guessed it was vacant. By law, Waylen couldn't enter it now, not without the family's permission, but he could tour the property.

"This is where Commander Gunn spent his retirement." Waylen took it in, appreciating the man's choice. Loon Lake was a decent size, but from this spot, they were a distance from the boat paths. The cove kept the pier private, and Waylen went there first, ignoring the comments by the detective.

Waves gently lapped against the shore, the weeds meticulously trimmed to make the water clear. He suspected Gunn had done the work himself, probably to keep busy. He was a widower, and a brilliant man by all accounts. Waylen figured a guy like Peter Gunn needed stimuli to get him through a day.

"No forced entry?" he asked when they reached the porch.

"No. Tea kettle must have been on, because it made a mess in the kitchen."

Waylen peered through the windows, seeing a record in the player and a cup of coffee on the counter. "You said the place was a mess when you left it?"

"Yep. Ransacked."

"They've cleaned it." Waylen guessed the coffee cup meant someone was still there, or they'd have washed it too. He glanced at the detective and offered his hand. "Thanks for the help today. I think you can head home. Enjoy the weekend."

Detective Desjardins hesitated before shaking it. "If you're sure. What are you going to do?"

He plopped onto the front steps, loosening his tie. "Wait for the family to return."

"We can put you up in Campbelltown. There's a nice chain hotel by the river."

"Thanks, I'd appreciate it."

Desjardins seemed to hesitate, probably seeing if Waylen might change his mind, then walked to the car. He started the engine and backed up.

The Assistant Director wanted answers, and Waylen was certain there was a connection. It had to be tied with Fred Trell's storage unit, and the burglary in DC. Someone was making a move. But why now, fifty-plus years since the last Moon landing? Had information been released?

Waylen used his phone, searching news about NASA, and discovered they'd updated the details of the Helios 15 mission to the public, along with countless years of never-before-seen data on their progress with the ISS, but there was nothing Waylen could find pertinent to Gunn's murder.

After an hour, he finally received a message from Martina, and instead of responding, he called her.

"Hey. Enjoying your vacation?"

"Sipping a Mai Tai as we speak. What about you? What kind of crazy case does Ben have you on?"

"Nothing exciting. A hedge fund operator has been flagged by the SEC, and they want someone to run an analysis on the transactions," she said.

That was usually his job. "I'm sure you'll find anything fishy."

"You know I prefer steak."

"How could I forget, after you stuck me with that last check at the expensive place in Boise." He laughed, picturing her enjoying the comment. "So there was no one leaving for DC."

"Not on a direct flight, and not on any connectors. Whoever did the job is either still there, or they drove away. I ran a check at the five nearest international airports, and no dice."

Waylen heard an engine and stood, tossing his jacket

to the porch before returning to the pier. He ambled down the wooden planks, watching the boat. For a second, he thought the man driving it was staring at him; then he saw the woman appear from the water, clutching a wake board. She climbed onto the boat, and they sped off.

"You there, Brooks?"

She always used his last name on official calls. "Yeah. I'm here. Thanks for the help."

"Have you found anything?"

"Not enough."

"Where to next?"

"DC, I guess," he said, thinking about the other astronaut, Colin Swanson. If the first two had been hit, why not the third? He was dead, but perhaps it would be wise to notify his next of kin in case someone was on the way. No one else was aware of the Fred Trell storage unit incident, which could give him a leg up. If the media caught wind, it would be a different story. "Actually, I might not get to DC yet. I'll have to make another stop."

"You keep in touch, and let me know if you need anything else. I better run. These financial reports won't analyze themselves," Martina said.

"You're ready for this," he told her. "Remember to seek the patterns. If there's something to be discovered, it will always stand out."

"Spoken like a true nerd," she joked.

"A nerd you occasionally have..." He stopped, remembering they were talking on company property. "Lunch with."

"When you're back, maybe we can... have lunch again. I'm in the mood for a... bowl of soup," she said.

"Soup? Is that what I... Have a good night." He ended it and shook his head, laughing at their banter. He'd screwed up by sleeping with her. It complicated things, and Waylen preferred his life to be straightforward.

Waylen sat on the wooden chair facing the lake and settled in, eager for one of Peter Gunn's relatives to come home. It was after dinner time when he fell asleep.

When he woke, the sky was dark, the last hint of dusk vanishing from the lakeside. He'd overdone it on the coast, with weeks of no sleep, and rushed to Loon Lake for this case without realizing how burnt out he was. He touched his brow and realized he was also sunburnt. How fitting.

The house was still empty, the lights off. It looked menacing in the moonlight. The large A-framed windows reflected the stars onto the deck.

Waylen was about ready to give up for the night and come back in the morning when he heard glass shatter, followed by a woman's scream. He didn't hesitate to gather his gun from the locked car and chase the direction of the noise. It came from the neighbor's place, and he cut through the dense forest separating the properties.

According to the files he'd been reading today, her name was Carol, and she lived alone. He barreled into twigs, spiderwebs clinging to his cheeks, and he scratched at them, emerging from the trees on the other side. A truck was in the drive, blocking a van in. The taillights were aimed at the porch, backed in for a quick exit. Waylen noticed a guy in the driver's seat, and a second large, shadowed figure beyond the blinds of the home's living room.

When another muffled cry escaped the front door, Waylen had to make a choice. He ensured the driver didn't see him and circled to the house, pressing against the wall. The window was open, and he peered into it, finding an old woman clutching a yipping dog.

"Where is it?" the man demanded.

"I don't know what you're talking about!" the woman claimed.

"I hear you and Peter Gunn were friends. Do you want to end up like him?" The man's voice was even, as if he was just having a conversation with his local butcher about the cut of beef he needed.

"Y... You murdered him?" She backed up, and the guy raised his gun.

Waylen's issued 9MM Glock 17 filled his right hand, ready to burst in and defend this woman. It wasn't often he'd pulled it while on duty, being in the Financial Crimes division, but he kept up with his required training, and found the act of firing it at the range soothing after a trying week on the job.

"I'll kill you too, if you don't tell me where it is."

"What are you looking for? Peter never gave me anything, I swear!"

"You have one more chance."

The dog scrambled from her arms and ran at the guy, biting his pant leg. He shoved the dog off and fired a shot at the animal.

"Bitsy!" the woman shouted.

That was enough. Waylen rushed to the door while the driver got out of the truck, clearly noticing his sidekick might need help. Waylen aimed his Glock from the shadows. "Don't come any closer!"

The guy was skinny, wearing a black baseball cap, and had a light blond mustache. Waylen expected him to shoot, but he surprised Waylen by running.

Carol screamed again, and the barking stopped. Waylen entered, ignoring the escaping culprit, and saw Bitsy lifeless by the fireplace. Carol was a mess, sobbing on the floor, and Waylen took aim, ducking when the gun fired.

He dove behind the couch, and instead of moving forward with the momentum like the shooter would expect, he circled back and rolled to the right, using the handgun as he'd been trained. The bullet struck the stranger in the chest, and Waylen tapped the trigger again when the man didn't let go of his weapon. Waylen hadn't tried to make a kill shot, but he'd just reacted, trying to save Carol and himself.

The truck tore down the driveway, gravel flying into the porch, and Waylen climbed to his feet, still focusing his 9MM on the perp. He stood over the body while Carol continued to cry, but it was quieter now. She muttered about not knowing what he was after, that she barely knew Peter. Carol clutched the dog to her chest, rocking back and forth.

Waylen crouched, finding a pulse, then used his phone to call the local dispatch.

Deputy Gail Hunt answered, and sounded shocked when he called for backup, describing the truck. "*We're on the way!*"

"Carol," Waylen whispered, reaching for her hand.

Bitsy bounced her head up, shaking her neck, and her tongue stuck out. "You're alive!"

Waylen guessed the dog had been knocked unconscious, and he breathed a sigh of relief. He'd saved a woman, but for the first time in his long career, he'd pulled the trigger at something other than a paper target.

"I've called the cops!" a voice shouted from outside. "Carol, are you okay?"

Waylen stepped through the door and saw a man arrive, with a woman at his side. They looked half cut, their hair messy, the female in pink flip-flops.

"Are you staying at Peter Gunn's house?" Waylen asked them.

The man raised his arm. "Yes. I'm his grandson, Si-las."

13

Rory transferred the last of the boxes and appraised her work. Why did her parents cling on to all this junk? She recalled ditching her belongings on the trip from Boston to Woodstock, and relished in the feeling it gave her afterward. All Rory desired was her laptop and some privacy.

The guest house was the perfect space for her, and she wondered why she hadn't thought of it earlier. It had its own kitchenette, and a spacious bathroom with a soaking tub. When they'd built it, her father had the notion that either his parents or Kathy's would retire and move in to stay closer to their family, but it hadn't happened. They'd offered it to visitors, but soon it became a graveyard for discarded clothing, photo albums, and apparently, Rory's old school assignments.

She'd hefted out three fake Christmas trees, along with a handful of containers filled to the brim with kitschy Halloween decorations. Rory almost asked if she could call one of those junk companies to get rid of it, but that would end up being a fight she didn't want, so she shoved the bins into the second bedroom, stacking them floor to ceiling, and covered the queen-sized bed.

The cuckoo clock chimed, and the bird darted from the small wooden doors, announcing the hour change. That might be annoying during the night, but the sound was comforting. It had been her grandfather's, and he'd given it to Oscar, his son, years ago. Her mom didn't like it, so it had ended up in the guest house the moment Colin had died. Rory couldn't believe it was already midnight.

She remembered the ticking of the clock in Grandma and Grandpa Swanson's house and pictured their beautiful dwelling on the shores outside of Portsmouth, New Hampshire. Rory distinctly thought of a time she'd gone to their house for a couple of weeks in the summer, probably when she was eight years old.

Grandma was a saintly old woman to her then, but now, Rory knew she'd only have been around sixty. She was vibrant, her hair always dyed bright red, her dresses full of patterns most people would have avoided. On her, they were marvelous. Rory spent her days in coloring books, listening to Grandpa talk about his time in the military, or his adventures training for the Helios mission. Sometimes he'd stop mid-sentence, his eyes glazing over, and Grandma would have to poke him, bringing him home with a simple touch.

Rory realized those had been the first hints of dementia, the disease that eventually killed him.

Her phone rang, and she didn't recognize the number. She clicked 'ignore' and waited, but no voicemail came. When it started again, she answered, "Hello. You know it's after midnight, right?"

The voice on the other end sent shivers down her spine. "*Rory…*"

One word, and it all flooded back. "Why are you pestering me, Kevin?"

"*Is that any way to talk to your husband?*"

"We're not married, you jerk."

"*Look who got a backbone. We're not married yet.*"

She lowered the phone from her ear and moved to hang up with a shaky finger. When she heard his voice continuing, she sighed and decided to finish this once and for all. "Why did you call me?"

A slight hesitation. "*I miss you.*"

Rory actually laughed. "Miss me? You're a loser, and I will never— *ever*— set foot in the same room as you, let alone the same city."

"*It's too late for that,*" he said, and she noticed a light near the street. Rory turned the lamp off and crept to the window, flicking the blinds an inch. Someone was on the sidewalk, beside a black sedan.

"Is that a threat? Are you in Woodstock?"

"*Maybe.*"

She looked at the number and realized it was the local area code.

"*Just meet me. Tomorrow. In the daylight, for breakfast at whatever passes for a diner in this podunk town,*" he said.

Woodstock was about as far from insignificant as Rory had seen, but she kept her opinions to herself. "No." She gathered her courage and hung up. She wouldn't deal with his crap any longer. She was a new woman, distanced from a cruel relationship. He'd spent her money and played every possible mind game to make her feel worthless. He'd even gone as far as hitting her. Once. The final straw.

Rory kicked on her sneakers and hurried from the guest house, racing across the yard. "Get out of here! Leave me alone!"

The man near the car held a camera, and he lowered it, his jaw dropping. "I…"

"Who are you?" She peered around, trying to see if Kevin was in the area.

"The name's Jack." He offered his hand, but she just

scowled.

"Why are you at my parents' house in the middle of the night"—she pointed at the camera—"with that?"

"I…" Jack stuttered, but finally found his voice. "I'm doing an article on the Helios 15 mission."

Rory's hackles were raised. The light on the back porch flashed on, and her father came out with a baseball bat. "What about it? Why are you here? You didn't answer my question."

"Rory, who's this?" Oscar asked, the bat still up.

"Sir, I apologize for any missteps. I work for a digital media company, and we're running an article about the crew from Helios 15 in time for the last member of the crew's funeral next week. I knew that you were his godson, sir, and we decided to take some photos of the house Colin Swanson stayed in when he visited. He was the lunar module pilot, after all."

"I know what my father did on the Moon, junior." Oscar checked his watch and shook his head. "Go home."

"Sir, would you be willing to discuss—"

"No."

Jack looked dejected, and Rory couldn't help but sympathize with the guy. He was kind of cute, the polar opposite of Kevin in almost every way. Shorter, with a thin build and blond hair.

"I could come back… tomorrow?"

"No."

Rory smiled at her father's insistent tone, and Jack flipped a business card from his pocket, handing it to her. "If you change your mind?" He said it like a question and got into the car, driving away.

"I should have called the cops," her dad muttered. "Come on, Pumpkin. How about a nightcap?"

"Sure." Rory didn't want to, but she also didn't want to be alone, not after the ominous call from Kevin. She thought about telling her father, but he was already worked up. If she mentioned it, he'd drive to the hotel, or the bed-and-breakfast, and do something stupid. She hadn't told her parents just how bad Kevin had been, but she suspected they were reading between the lines.

She glanced at the guest house and ran back to it, locking the doors before rejoining her dad.

"Was that necessary?"

"Can't be too safe," Rory said.

"We're in Woodstock, Vermont. This is as safe as it comes. Short of nosey wannabe journalists with bad timing," he joked, and held the door for her.

"Where's Mom?"

"She fell asleep reading. I left her up there." Her father cut an imposing figure and managed to look mayoral in his sweatpants and white t-shirt. He headed to the bar. "Wine?"

"Okay." Rory accepted the glass of red and saw the French label. He had a basement filled with rare vintages, and she'd always gone down there as a young girl, running a finger over the dust-covered bottles, pretending they held secret messages from across the seas.

"Do you miss him?" Oscar sat in the leather chair, and she took the one facing it.

"Kevin?"

Oscar nodded.

"Not at all. Why…"

"I ran into him at the market," Oscar said.

"What? Why didn't you tell me?" She'd only been apart from her parents for a few hours while working in the guest house.

"He seems remorseful."

Rory took a sip and felt the walls shrinking. Her vision grew fuzzy, and a piercing noise reached her ears. She set the glass down and rubbed her temples.

"Pumpkin, are you okay?"

"This can't be happening."

Her dad came over, grabbing her hand. "What is it?"

"Kevin's a dangerous man." She was supposed to be safe at her parents' house. They were hundreds of miles from Boston. Rory had only wanted to escape the relationship and visit for the summer to write a novel in peace. She'd hoped to be surrounded by flowers and sunshine, but the darkness had crept back into her life.

"Then I'll tell him to pack his things and get right back to Boston," he said adamantly.

The noises subsided, her eyesight improving, and she breathed, trying to calm herself from the impending panic attack. "Thanks, Dad."

He walked to the edge of the room, turning the speaker on. He linked his phone, and jazz played softly. "I wish you would have come home sooner."

"I know."

"And I'm sorry we've been hard on your... career choice."

"I have to do it," she said.

"I understand." He plunked into the chair, taking another drink. "I'm going to drive everyone nuts when I retire."

"You should do something on the side," she suggested. "You're too young to be finished working."

"That's what your mother says."

Rory looked at him. He was the same age as her grandparents had been in her memory, but he didn't seem it. A full head of hair, a glint in his eyes. "What ever happened to their house?"

"Whose?"

The topic was changing on a dime, which wasn't unusual in their conversations. They were both used to it. "Grandma and Grandpa Swanson's."

"It's still there."

"Yeah, of course it is. But who bought it?"

"No one."

"What are you saying?" Rory drank a mouthful of the wine and melted into her seat. The adrenaline from the phone call and the stranger on the street had faded, and she was plain tired.

"I kept the house," he told her.

"You have their house in Portsmouth?"

"Technically, it's in Rye, New Hampshire. But yes, I haven't sold it. I pay a company to cut the yard and spray for weeds. Another guy checks the property every week for insurance purposes. Otherwise, it sits empty."

"Why? It's probably worth a fortune."

Her father sighed, and she finally saw his age creep through the visage. "I can't bear to sell it. I loved my parents, and they were nothing but great to all of us. Without them, I wouldn't have this." He gestured at the luxurious room. "Your mother couldn't have stayed home to raise you, and you couldn't have gone to an Ivy League school. The house is just a house, but I grew up in Rye, and it's special to me."

"Does anyone else know it's yours still?"

"Maybe. The deed is under a corporate name, but," he shrugged, "it's not a secret."

Rory took it in. "Can I visit it this summer? Maybe spend a while to write?"

"It's a two-hour drive, and you remember how touristy it gets in the summer," he said.

"I need to focus, and clearly I won't be able to do that

while I'm being stalked by exes and journalists."

"Okay." He picked up his phone. "There's a lockbox on the door. I've texted you the code. But promise me you'll come to the funeral beforehand."

"Deal." Rory had no desire to head inland to a stuffy funeral for a man she'd barely known. But her parents were being super generous, and she wanted to support them, like they'd done for her. She stood, leaving an ounce of wine at the bottom of the glass, and peered out the window.

"I'll walk you back," he said without needing to be prompted. It was the first time in her entire life that she didn't feel protected on her own property.

When she closed the guest house doors, she flipped the bolt, then saw the text message from her father. A notification appeared, and it was from Kevin. She'd already blocked his cell number, so now he was resorting to social media. She rarely used it, to the chagrin of her publisher and agent, but there were more important things in life than pumping your followers. Rory opened the app, typed the password, and quickly deleted the message from Kevin without reading it.

With the press of a button, he was removed from her friends list, and eternally denied to the application. She smiled and was about to close it when she noticed the friend request.

Silas Gunn wants to be friends! Confirm/Ignore/Deny.

Rory pictured the brooding young man at Grandpa Swanson's funeral and clicked *Confirm*.

PART TWO
THE SECRET

1

The clock blinked over from 4:59 to 5:00 A.M. The sun rose in the east, marking a new day, but Silas had yet to sleep. The crime scene next door was still active, but they'd left an hour earlier after the police excused them.

Special Agent Waylen Brooks had asked Silas to stick around the house, saying he wanted to speak to them privately when he finished filling out the paperwork. Brooks had killed a man. Silas couldn't imagine what that must feel like. The FBI agent seemed to take it in stride, but Silas doubted it was ever that easy.

He'd saved Carol's life, making him a hero. The older woman was clearly shaken up, and she held on to Bitsy like the dog might disappear at any moment. Once the body had been removed, the sheriff and the detective he'd met earlier in the week had allowed Silas to return to his grandfather's lake house. Leigh had reluctantly stayed with him, and she dozed on the couch while Silas made a pot of coffee.

Silas walked through the house in socks, his steps nearly silent, and wondered if there was anything he'd missed. Was the dead man the same guy that had killed his grandfather? Special Agent Brooks claimed he had a partner that escaped, and so far, no trucks matched the description. He'd warned Silas to lock the doors, which he'd done, but Silas doubted a motivated killer would have a difficult time breaking in, not with half of the exterior walls being glass.

He peered through the bedroom window, seeing a flashing police light near Carol's house. Two dead bodies in a week, and both were right beside each other. He was grateful the FBI agent had shown up, because Silas would have probably been killed too, rushing into danger like that.

A knock on the door startled him, and Silas clutched a chef's knife from the kitchen.

"Who is it?" he called, rousing Leigh from her slumber. She sat up, wiping a string of drool from her lips.

"It's Waylen!"

He relaxed and let the agent in. "Thanks for waiting," Brooks said.

"No prob," Silas said, locking it once he was inside.

"Nice house." Waylen's gaze drifted to the floor where the carpet sat, then to the office and kitchen. Silas almost heard his thoughts as he ran over the police reports and compared them with the actual crime scene.

"It's not mine. We haven't found out who's getting it," Silas said. "In the will, I mean." He felt terrible for even talking about himself after what this man had just gone through. "Have a seat."

Waylen didn't oblige, but stayed on his feet, exploring the house as if watching the scene unfold. Silas peered at the entrance and pictured the perp's footsteps approaching his grandfather. Waylen's gaze drifted to the photos Silas had restored to their positions on the wall, though they may have ended up out of order.

Leigh stretched her arms overhead, yawning widely. "How are you doing?"

"I've had better nights."

"They let you keep the gun?" she asked. "I thought you needed to relinquish it or something?"

"It was self-defense, and besides, he didn't die," Waylen said.

"He didn't? He looked dead to me." Silas had stayed out of the way when the paramedics arrived, while being grilled by Deputy Hunt.

"Truthfully, he probably won't live to see the morning." Waylen stared at the picture of the crew before the Helios 15 mission. "Did you know Peter Gunn well?"

"Not really. My dad didn't get along with him."

"I've heard rumors that Gunn was a tough nut," Waylen said softly.

"That's the understatement of the year."

Leigh stood at Silas' side, her hand slipping into his. It was the first time they'd had any contact, and he wasn't sure how to react. "Did that man kill Silas' grandpa?"

Waylen stopped what he was doing and finally took the chair he'd been offered earlier. "I believe so. If not him, the other guy in the truck."

"Why did they do this?" Silas urged. The coffee pot beeped, so he went to the kitchen, asking if anyone wanted a cup. They both agreed, and he returned with a serving plate holding cream and sugar cubes, along with a few cookies. They'd been in the cupboard, and Silas felt foolish, like an imposter, as he set the tray down. Waylen plucked a cookie and bit into it before answering his previous question.

"He was looking for something," Waylen said. "He had an accent. Staten Island, probably."

Silas was familiar with the accent, since their primary warehouse on Long Island had a hundred or so commuters from Staten. "What kind of *something*?"

"He just said *it*, as in *where is it*?" Waylen peered past Silas to the office. "What were they searching for, Silas? You've been here a few days. I assumed whoever killed Commander Gunn had walked away with their treasure, but clearly, that's not the case."

Silas's hand grew clammy, and he released Leigh's grip, and wiped his palm on his pants. "I don't..."

"Seriously?" Leigh shoved him on the arm. "You have to tell him."

Waylen grew more attentive when he finished his cookie. "Tell me what?" His voice was low, and his posture stayed upright, like he was about to pounce.

"It's better if I show you." Silas glared at Leigh, wishing they'd leave the strange object in its resting spot. He'd considered tying it to a rock and throwing it into the middle of Loon Lake, but couldn't bring himself to part with the metal piece. His grandfather had deemed it important enough to hide in the safe's secret compartment.

Or dangerous enough.

Silas strode into the office, rolled the desk chair off the carpet, and pulled the satchel out. He returned to set it on the coffee table. "Don't touch it."

"Why not?" Waylen gazed at the cloth bag, the ties cinched tight.

"No." Leigh grasped it, loosening the strings. The slight metal sheet slid out to rest on the table. "He should. So he knows we're not messing around here."

"What is that? A bookmark?" Waylen reached for it, but Silas cleared his throat, stopping the FBI agent from making contact.

"Wait!"

Waylen watched him expectantly.

"If these people are searching for anything, this is it."
Silas seized the coffee cup and spilled a few drops. "Leigh
touched it, then I did…"

"And?"

"We can't explain. Special Agent Brooks, I have to
know we can really trust you," Leigh said.

"Yes. I'm on your side. If this can connect the case—
"

"Connect what? There's more?"

Waylen blinked twice and nodded. "No one knows,
but Fred Trell's storage unit was broken into," he said.
He grabbed his phone and tapped on a video. A man with
a baseball cap closed a unit's door, walking off with a
satchel. He paused it and zoomed on the bag. "They look
the same to me, don't you think?"

"I can't tell."

"Even if they found these on the Moon, why would
they have the same bags?" Leigh asked.

"The Moon?" Waylen interjected. "You guys are suggesting this"—he gestured to the flat metal object—
"came from outer space?"

"It's possible. We checked out the interview Swanson
did years ago, and he admitted there was an incident during the landing. He said, and I quote, *'They're out there.
Waiting for us.'*"

"Say you're remotely right. The astronauts fly to the
Moon on Helios 15. Colin Swanson piloted the lander,
nicknamed *Pelican*, and Fred Trell remained in orbit, cir-
cling above as they conducted their business. Commander
Gunn and Swanson did a moonwalk," Waylen said.

"They didn't go to the Sea of Tranquility. And they
were out there longer than any others, spending eighteen
hours on the surface. The pair used the rover and loaded

almost eighty kilograms of material. NASA planned on it being the last mission, or at least the second last, unless they found something worthwhile. Grandpa believed they were already planning to cut the program, and the next mission was canceled. We've never returned." Silas had read countless books and watched documentaries on the subject when he was younger, striving for a connection to his estranged grandfather.

"And you're suggesting they found that on the Moon?" Waylen reached for it again, but his fingers only hovered, not landing.

Leigh flipped over the sack to reveal an embroidered label on the bottom. "It's an old whiskey container. They used to sell bottles in these limited-edition bags to make them seem classier. My dad has a couple in his liquor cabinet. He says they'll be worth money."

"She's right," Waylen agreed. "I've seen them too."

"Okay, what does that tell us?"

"That the murderers have one of those metal bookmarks," Waylen said.

Silas brought up the interview to replay it.

Colin Swanson's eyes were round, his mouth twisted like he'd swallowed a lemon. *"We found something and promised to take it to the grave. Me, Fred, and Peter."*

Silas stopped it. "He mentions all three of them. Do you think there are three of… these?" He nearly grabbed it to wave it around, but recoiled when he remembered the sensation.

"Possibly." Waylen let the bag go and sipped his coffee, making Silas do the same. It had gone cold.

"That leaves the Swansons." Silas spotted the social media site notification from a few hours ago. He'd been too distracted at Carol's to check. "And I've contacted Rory Swanson."

"She's related to Colin?"

"Granddaughter."

Leigh peered at his phone. "She's cute. Were you two ever…"

"No. We've barely spoken."

"She accepted your request."

"She'll know who I am, and my grandpa just died. I expect they'll be at the funeral. It's kind of tradition among the old crew's extended families."

"We have to talk to her about this. She can fill us in if there's anything like that sitting in Colin's old belongings. Rory should also be warned they might be in danger," Waylen said.

"Do you want me to—"

"No. I'll call the house. Do you know where she is?"

There were no posts from the last year. Her profile picture showed her with a man, and the bio said she was with a Kevin Heffernan, but when Silas clicked the name, he noticed Rory and Kevin had no mutual friends, which suggested Rory had blocked him. "It doesn't say."

Waylen checked his phone and scrolled, smiling a moment later. "I have the son's number in Woodstock, Vermont. I'll try it"—he looked at the time—"later. It's Sunday morning, and only seven thirty on the East Coast."

"This might be life or death," Leigh whispered.

"I doubt these guys are that big of an organization," he said. "Since they were just here, she should be in the clear for the time being."

Silas wasn't so certain, but he conceded to the agent in charge of the case.

"Okay, now that I've listened to your theory, which I must admit is out there, let's see what has you two so rattled. Then I'd better get on to Campbelltown to visit my friend in the hospital."

Waylen grabbed the metal token, and his eyes shot wide.

2

*T*he triangle burned brightly, imprinting in his mind. When Waylen saw a hole, a dark mist rising from it, the vision threatened to take the breath from his lungs. He glanced up at Earth, a perfectly unspoiled marble in the black canvas of space. The sun was behind him, a giant mass of hot gases. Instead of being yellow, like at home, it appeared white, and Waylen recalled reading about the phenomenon before, which had to do with scattering and atmospheres.

Waylen peered at the strip in his palm. He heard voices, but struggled to make out the words. The hole called to him.

The mass floated on the surface, the inside dark and menacing. No color dared enter the void, the misty tendrils rising and vanishing in the Moon's tenuous environment.

He felt a grip on his shoulder and turned, seeing no one.

Waylen took another step, his body lighter than should have been possible. He bent at the hole to reach for it.

"Waylen!" Silas and the girl were over him, their faces etched with concern.

He was on the floor, his palm bleeding where he'd gripped the object, and he let it fall to the hardwood.

Air didn't come. Waylen closed his eyes, picturing the Moon again. He was there, on the surface, with a view of their planet. Everything ached, and his chest burned like it was in a vise.

Finally, he opened his mouth and inhaled before coughing ferociously. Leigh thrust a glass of water at him, and he drank greedily until it was empty and he no longer had the urge. Instead, he turned his chin and threw up on the carpet. When he tried to stand, he couldn't get to his feet.

"Are you okay?" Silas asked, and Waylen lay back, not even coherent enough to be ashamed.

"I traveled there," he croaked out.

"Where?"

"The Moon," he said. Each breath came slightly easier, and he finally climbed to the chair, sinking into the cushion. "Did you both do it?"

"Not like that. We touched it for a moment. You wouldn't let us pry it away from you," Leigh told him.

"A warning would have been nice," he muttered. "Okay, I'm a believer. What the hell is it?"

"All I know is that my grandfather didn't want anyone to find it," Silas said.

Waylen's mind felt cluttered, and he pictured cobwebs on his brain. He needed to focus, to make rational assumptions. "My body never left, right?"

They shook their heads as one.

"So it's not real. Maybe it's holding a memory. I read something in a science journal about an alloy that can retain information for several hours. It might be similar."

"Like an echo," Silas whispered.

"Yeah, an echo of an event."

"We're guessing it's radioactive," Leigh said.

Waylen checked his palm and fingers, but they appeared unaffected. "I doubt it. Wait until the lab analyses this."

"Hold up," Silas said. "It's not yours."

Waylen composed himself, and Leigh refilled his empty glass, which he drank within seconds of receiving. His throat burned like he'd swallowed fire. "This is a federal case, and that has just become evidence."

"There's a reason Grandpa Gunn never told anyone, and I should honor that," Silas said.

"You don't want to learn what it is?" Waylen asked, understanding the younger man's motivation.

"Sure I do, but let's figure that out before we go announcing it to the world. And you have to find the other two. If Trell had one, then these... *guys* are walking around with the first token." Silas paced the living room, his steps long and well-timed.

"It's too dangerous for you to hold on to. Especially here."

"I'll go home. To the city."

Leigh looked disappointed, and Waylen wondered if they'd only recently met, or if they were old flames. He guessed the former. "They may have seen Leigh. She'll be in danger if the other perp is sticking around Gull Creek or Loon Lake."

"She can come with me," Silas said before Leigh could comment.

"Me... to New York? What about my job?"

"There has to be someone else your mom can hire. Aren't you curious?" Silas asked, like they were on an innocent adventure.

"Silas, I shot a man tonight, and he might have killed your grandfather. This isn't a game," Waylen said.

"Clearly." His gaze displayed his determination.

"This can't be happening." Waylen stared at the metal

object while Leigh carefully slipped it into the cover.

"You saw a triangle, didn't you?" Silas whispered.

The shape of light burned into his eyes. "Yes."

"That means there are three." Silas took the bag, and it was apparent he wasn't about to offer it to Waylen.

"I'd better get to the hospital to see if I can make the guy talk. Are you leaving?"

Silas glanced at Leigh, who gave the smallest of nods. "Yeah. We'll head to my place. I'll keep it with me."

"That's too obvious. If there's really a larger organization involved, they'll be watching it. Do you have anywhere else you can bring it?"

"We have a house in Cape Cod," he said.

"Good. That'll work."

"Cape Cod?" Leigh asked. "Who are you guys?"

"The furniture business has been good to my family," Silas responded.

Waylen used his phone. "What's the address? And your phone numbers?"

He marked them all down and looked at the mess he'd made on the carpet.

There was a knock on the door, and Waylen's gun was out in a flash. He lifted a finger and stepped cautiously for the exit. He peered through the blinds, seeing two women in coveralls, a cleaning company brand logo patched onto the shoulders.

"Can I help you?" he asked through the glass.

"We're with Cover Up, the cleaning service. Silas called…"

"I wasn't expecting them until tomorrow," Silas admitted, stalking to the door to open it.

The women stared at Waylen, and he realized the Glock remained in his hand. He shoved it into its holster and smiled at them. "Good morning, ladies. Sorry about the mess, but I have to be going."

Waylen walked to his car rental, his head pounding, as the women brought in carts filled with supplies. He sat in the driver's seat, watching a darkness spill onto the road, the hole spreading as tendrils of mist rose from the black void. He blinked, and it was gone.

"You're losing it," he muttered, pulling out of the driveway.

Waylen tried not to think about the past few hours as he left Loon Lake, driving through Gull Creek and toward Campbelltown. He called the hospital, and discovered that their John Doe had survived and was currently in serious, but stable, condition.

Instead of going straight there, Waylen drove to the hotel, learning that the detective had booked him a room. He carried his bag with a change of clothes, and took the stairs to the third floor. His limbs were dead, his brain fuzzy.

Waylen was at the door, holding the keycard, and saw a housekeeping cart exiting an elevator. He realized he'd been standing there with his eyes closed. With a tap of the card, he quickly entered the suite and tossed the bag onto the nearest double bed.

He'd started this case by happenstance, but how quickly the 'right place at the right time' had turned into bad luck. Waylen wished he'd ignored the storage unit proprietor. Then he'd never have held that damned piece of metal, and…

He was near the mirror, staring at himself, but didn't remember walking there. The Moon's surface appeared in the reflection. Darkness surrounded the horizon, making it seem like he might fall off and float into oblivion. The only real option was the hole, waiting for Waylen to climb in.

Waylen spun to gaze at the rocky landscape, but there was a tub and shower, the curtains drawn. He opened them, half expecting the misty blackness to be behind the covering, but it was a chipped porcelain tub.

"You need to sleep." He'd shot someone, and narrowly avoided being killed himself. This was trauma, nothing more. The metal bookmark had probably just played off that. His otherworldly vision was based on the near-death experience.

John Doe could wait.

Waylen showered, lingering in the hot water for thirty minutes. Time didn't feel relevant any longer.

He laid out his change of clothing on the second bed, and almost didn't recognize the articles. Were they his?

Waylen lifted the blankets and slipped underneath, pulling them over his head for comfort. The pillow was too soft, the bed lumpy, but he drifted into a sleep he desperately needed.

The first thing he saw in the dream was a triangle of light.

3

"*H*ow are we out of coffee?" Rory's mother asked. "Seriously, what do we have Rosalita for if she's always letting us run out of staples?"

"Calm down, Kathy," Oscar said. "She's off this weekend. Remember her kids have that band thing?"

"Right," Kathy said. "Sorry, Rory. I know you had a late night."

Sunday was the perfect day for living in Woodstock, except for the fact that nothing really opened until ten. "I'll go to the store."

"It's closed until…"

"Yeah, ten. I'll hit the market."

"Pumpkin, would you like to take the car?"

"Nah, I'll walk." Rory had a lot of pent-up energy after last night's conversation with Kevin, and the scare from the journalist. She often wondered why her parents didn't have a dog. She'd grown up with one, a fat Labrador that gained weight no matter how many miles he walked, or how little they fed him. Rory remembered crying when he'd died. She'd been nine, just a year younger than Bach. Her father was in a morose piano mood when they'd adopted the puppy, and weeks later, they'd discovered they were pregnant with Rory. She figured neither of them had gotten over the loss, so they never tried to replace him.

Rory decided to avoid writing for the morning, given the lack of valuable rest, and hoped to return to the desk in the afternoon before dinner. Sunday dinners were a constant at the Swanson home. Rory realized that nearly every trivial occasion was a 'thing' at home, but that was the comforting part of being there. Routines were important to her mother and father, and she'd been without them for so many years. Kevin didn't believe in routine. He said it made people sloppy and uninspired.

Well, Kevin could go straight to hell, handbasket included or not. She didn't care.

Rory slipped into her white tennis shoes and peered through the window, seeing another picturesque summer day. No need for an umbrella or jacket. "See you guys in a few."

"Take your time," her dad said.

"But not too much. I get jittery without my coffee!" her mom called.

Rory hoped Kevin was already on the road home after his failed attempt at a reunion.

She strolled down the sidewalk, passing the neighbors' houses. They were each as equally impressive as the next, and she experienced a surge of pride at her parents. Oscar had grown up under a heavy shadow, but he'd escaped it and thrived in a career—not because of his family name, but because of his hard work and perseverance. Their town had never been in a better state.

Rory grabbed her cell and checked her social media, but found no message from Silas yet. He'd friended her, and she was curious to see what he wanted. His grandfather had recently died, and she figured it was up to her to reach out to offer her condolences.

The walk wasn't too far, and Rory slid the phone into her belt bag, enjoying the morning sun. It was obviously going to be a hot one, and she thought she might go to the club's pool in the afternoon, instead of writing. She'd learned early on that writers required down time to recharge, but she'd been in a perpetual state of inactivity. Those words wouldn't write themselves.

Rory strode by the doctor's office and saw Greg's name on the window, under two other partners' names. They were old school, practicing since Rory was a kid, and she recalled her visits to the family doctor, always with a lollipop upon leaving. The office was closed, and she peered in, seeing he hadn't lied about that either. Her book sat on the waiting room table, atop a mound of tattered magazines.

Rory spied the town's fanciest bed and breakfast and cringed, suddenly worried that her ex might not have left town. His car was nowhere in sight, but there were two vehicles in the driveway, one with a rental company sticker on the bumper. She kept her chin down, walking faster, until she was a block clear, and finally slowed her dramatic pace.

"He's gone. He got the message," she said.

Downtown was beautiful, with a long street of brick buildings, many with American flags jutting from window casings. Lots of the businesses were new since she'd left town, and she smiled while exploring. Ice cream shops. The old bookstore she'd visited nearly once a week as a kid. She froze at a display with a picture of Rory Valentine, claiming her as 'Woodstock's own.' It made her wonder why she'd never offered to do a book signing there. But then again, she hadn't been able to return home in ages.

Rory noticed a woman inside, and knocked.

"Hello?" It was Mrs. Habbishire. She squinted through the glass and quickly unlocked it, raising her arms to embrace Rory. "As I live and breathe. Rory Valentine."

"Swanson," she said.

"Of course. We have your book. Isn't this a treat?" Mrs. Habbishire was looking good, and Rory put her at about sixty-five. She removed a pair of reading glasses and let the chain dangle them around her neck. She smelled of vintage perfume, and Rory liked the scent. It was the same stuff she'd worn all those years ago when Rory would listen to her recite stories for kiddie hour.

"I'm sorry I haven't stopped by before."

"You're a busy lady, up in the city."

Rory shrugged. "I'm here now."

"In Woodstock?"

"For the summer. I'm trying to finish my new novel." *More like start it.*

Mrs. Habbishire clapped her hands. "That's good news. I can't wait. Is it anything like *View from the Heavens?*"

"No, but I'm hoping it delivers an equal sentiment to the reader," Rory said with confidence.

"How wonderful."

"Mrs. Habbishire, would you like me to sign any of these?" Rory gestured to the end cap with two dozen copies of her novel in hardcover.

"Please, call me Wanda."

Rory hadn't known her first name. Even her parents called her Mrs. Habbishire.

Wanda looked at the books. "An in-person signing would be much better. For the townsfolk."

"Sure." Rory suddenly wished she hadn't offered, but it was already out there. She'd done fifty readings at the request of her publisher in the early days, but that had been two years ago, and she was rusty.

"What about tonight? The book club meets here at

seven, but we'll stay open late and do an entire event."

"That's short notice. For you."

"Nonsense. I'll get coffee in from the beanery, and Florence will order the pastries." Wanda's eyes welled up with tears. "My little Rory, all grown up and so successful."

"I wouldn't say…"

Wanda hugged her again. "I'm so proud of you."

"I mentioned you in the acknowledgments," Rory said.

"I saw that." Wanda jogged to the display, and she opened a copy, running a finger down the page. She returned her reading glasses and cleared her throat. "…*and I can't forget the woman that inspired all the children of Woodstock to dream big, Mrs. Habbishire.*" She closed the cover with a thud and held it to her chest. "I showed anyone and everyone."

There was no backing out now. "Do I need to bring anything?"

"We'll have it all ready. Do you mind coming at six thirty? And tell your friends," Wanda said.

"Will do." Rory didn't really have many friends, not on her own, and didn't know anyone in town. She retreated to the sidewalk, with Wanda muttering excitedly as she planned.

Rory continued past a boutique clothing store, then a place that sold candles and kitchen accessories, and saw her destination. The corner store was quaint, with a wooden sign always neatly painted at the start of each spring. She gazed up at the billboard, seeing layers of old paint beneath it. Still the same store, just adding coats. Rory felt like she had a few coats of paint on herself, and wondered if she'd be able to find the old version once more while in Woodstock.

A few cars were parked on the street in front, and Rory pressed the large, worn golden handle, entering another era. The chimes were probably the ones from her childhood, and the floorboards creaked as they always had. It smelled like candy, and flour, and bread, all intertwined into a musty fragrance that should be bottled and sold as nostalgia. The town had a chain grocery store now, but in the earlier years, this had been the primary source for locals to shop without driving to the bigger neighboring towns and cities.

Rory walked the aisles, memories flooding into her mind. She pictured a twelve-year-old Rory gathering items to make her parents an Italian meal after she'd binged a season of *Primo Chef*. She was dead wrong, but it hadn't stopped her from trying. That night, her father choked down the food with a smile, but her mother had been unable to hide her disdain. Rory had run to her room, slamming the door closed, and told herself she'd never cook again.

"Rory."

One simple word, and her blood turned to ice. She twisted slowly, and there he was. Kevin Heffernan in the pasty flesh. Rory didn't respond. She walked on, accelerating her steps.

He appeared at the end of the next aisle, grabbing for her. "I just want to talk."

"No." She headed in the other direction and sprinted. Rory reached for her phone, and it fell to the floor. Kevin beat her to it and clutched it with a sadistic grin.

"I assume a fool like you hasn't changed her password." He typed it in and laughed when it worked.

Why hadn't she done that? It hadn't even crossed her mind. "Give it back!" She lunged, but he held it higher, like a bully in the schoolyard, playing keep-away.

"Hold on, Rory. We can be civilized, right?" He started to lower it, and Rory clenched her teeth, searching for someone—anyone—a witness, but the store seemed empty.

She'd had enough being a victim. Rory balled her hand into a fist, and he glanced down, still smiling.

Rory hit him square in the nose. He hadn't been expecting it, and the bones crunched from the impact. Her phone dropped, and she grabbed it protectively. "Leave me alone, or I'm going to the police for a restraining order."

The chimes rang, and a man walked in. "Everything okay?"

Kevin was howling in pain, blood dripping from his broken nose. "No, this woman assaulted me. I'll sue!"

"I don't think so." The newcomer hauled on Kevin, tossing him out the door. He fell to the sidewalk, and Rory finally recognized the man as Jack, the journalist from last night. He stood over Kevin as her ex scrambled to his feet.

"Screw you!" Kevin cocked a fist, but Jack moved right before it struck. The momentum brought Kevin off balance, and he lashed out again, missing for the second time.

"Go home—"

"Kevin," Rory finished.

"Beat it, Kevin. Rory doesn't want to see you," Jack said calmly.

Rory recognized the moment Kevin lost his courage, and his shoulders slumped as he staggered down the street, cursing them and shouting about lawyers.

"Who is that guy?"

"My ex," she said.

"Really? That loser?" Jack's expression evened out,

and he just looked sympathetic. "I didn't mean—"

"No, you're right. We met when I was young, and I had trouble getting out of it." Rory stopped. "Why am I telling you this?"

"Because I'm a good listener," he said. "It's kind of my job."

"Aren't journalists writers?" she asked.

"Well, that too, of course," he answered. Jack smiled and swept his blond hair to the side.

"Thanks for the help." Rory was still shaking, and her hand ached from the impact.

"Let's get some ice." He opened the door for her, and they entered the store. Rory grabbed coffee as she'd promised her parents, and Jack paid for it, and a bag of frozen peas. "We should stop for something to eat so I can make sure you're okay."

Rory shook her head in disbelief, but didn't decline. They wandered through town, finding a quaint coffee shop. After a few minutes with a cold compress on her hand, it already felt better. She should have hit Kevin harder.

The place was half-filled with younger hipster types Rory rarely saw in their town. Its energy was vibrant, and she decided this might be a decent spot to park her laptop and do some writing in the coming weeks. They ordered breakfast sandwiches and lattes, sitting at the window.

"Are you going to the funeral?"

Rory unwrapped the food, appraising the man next to her. "Already? Really?"

"What?"

"Always looking for that interview." She took a bite.

"Can you blame me? You do owe me." He gnawed at the egg jutting from the bun.

"Okay. I'll talk. But I should get home soon. I have a

thing at the bookstore later."

He lifted both eyebrows. "A thing?"

"I agreed to do a signing tonight."

"Can anyone come?"

"Yes, it's open to the public, so you could make an appearance."

"We can talk after that." Jack chewed, looking contemplative. "I'd rather this breakfast be two new friends getting to know each other."

Rory wasn't sure how to take that, but Jack was charming, and he had a very peaceful demeanor. "Sounds good."

Her phone chimed, but she ignored it. Instead she stayed for a while, talking with Jack about growing up in what he called a movie set.

4

"I sent the message. We'll see if Rory responds," Silas said. He couldn't wait around for Special Agent Brooks to contact the family, not after recent events.

"My mom's going to be pissed," Leigh muttered. "She's already so hard on me, and with Dad…"

"You don't have to come." Silas judged her posture, and it was obvious she wasn't joining him. There was no point in arguing with her. They were strangers, this odd scenario thrusting them together.

Leigh stood at the doorway while Silas threw his jacket on. He didn't really have any belongings, since he'd only been planning to be there for a few hours. Instead, it had turned into a handful of days.

"That agent scared the other guy off, and one of them is in the hospital or the morgue by now. I'll be safe." She glanced at the ground. "Sorry, Silas."

"Don't be." He hugged her. She backed away, and he realized she'd felt the bag in his chest pocket.

"I don't like that."

"Neither do I. Do me a favor and keep in touch, okay?"

"I'll drive you to the airport."

He nodded, glad to have the company; not to mention, there was nothing close to a taxi service in the region. Leigh started her car, and Silas took his time, making sure Grandpa Gunn's house was secured. The cleaners had done their best on the blood, though Silas was sure they'd eventually need to replace the wood before they sold the house. He shuddered at the thought of putting it on the market. He'd grown attached to it, despite the atrocity that had occurred here last week.

"Goodbye, Grandpa," he whispered, and jogged down the front porch, climbing into the Gremlin.

The airport was an hour away in Jackson, and it passed slowly, with little conversation. When she pulled to the terminal, she stared at him with misty eyes. "I wish… we'd met under different circumstances."

"Me too," Silas agreed. He leaned over the center console, aiming to kiss her cheek, and she averted her gaze to the road. He left the car, and the moment the door closed, the tires squealed as she drove off, leaving him at the airport. Leigh had come and gone so quickly, he wondered if she'd even remember what he looked like after a week.

It was a few miles from the town, centered in the Jackson Hole Valley, and the views were incredible. The mountains of the Teton Range overlooked the entire tarmac, as if standing guard.

He strolled to the proper airline desk and eventually found a circuitous path home that would only require one layover. Silas recalled that he wasn't going to New York, and changed the plan before paying, choosing Boston instead. He'd get a rental, then head to Cape Cod. After arriving, he'd let his parents know where he was, and that he was safe. He couldn't imagine telling his father about the object in his pocket.

At security, he'd kept the bag within reach, not wanting to take his eyes off it. Silas expected someone to flag it as the tray rolled through the scanners, but no one did.

He returned it into the jacket and found a place selling coffee. His flight to Cleveland left in thirty minutes, and he was the third passenger on.

Three and a half hours later, he was boarding the second flight, and Silas slept for the last segment, his exhaustion beating out the adrenaline rush he'd been surviving on. Would they try to track him? Or had Special Agent Brooks done his job, breaking up the duo behind the thefts?

It was two in the afternoon when he left the airport, heading south on the Pilgrims Highway toward Cape Cod, and the sense of unease had finally subsided, making Silas wonder if he'd overreacted. There was no way to be certain the killers were searching for this specific object. No one had straight out said, "Give me the flat, shiny artifact from the Moon."

The more miles he put behind him, the calmer Silas became. When he spied the 'Welcome to Cape Cod' sign, he was confident there wasn't even a reason to be hiding at their family's vacation home. He thought he should go home and return to his normal life.

But he drove to the hideout. Silas hadn't been out there since Thanksgiving the previous year. His sister had come with her two kids, and they'd made a lot of noise, breaking a window with a baseball. He remembered his mother stressing out the entire time. She'd been an exceptional mother, but being a grandmother didn't suit her. Usually, it worked in the opposite manner. But that didn't stop her from pressuring Silas to meet the right woman and start a family, because that's what successful people were supposed to do. What else was being wealthy good for if you couldn't spoil your children rotten?

Silas drove to the north end of the peninsula and slowed as he approached their home. It was a classic Cape

Cod with cedar shingles and siding, the white trim a stark contrast to the wooden coloring. There were shutters, and a sign with their family name on it. It suddenly bothered him that Peter Gunn hadn't once visited the estate. Had his father ever called him and invited him, or was it a two-way street?

He pulled into the driveway and struggled to recall the code for the garage opener, so he sat there for a moment with the engine off as it started to rain.

I'm at the house. You good? He sent it to Leigh and scrolled on their earlier conversation. She'd been in a better mood, and said she was taking a shift for her mom so her parents could spend the afternoon together.

When she didn't respond, he got out of the rental and dashed to the front door. Rain came harder, and he ran through puddles, splashing his way beneath the awning. He checked under the clay pot, but the key wasn't there. The numbered panel faced him, and Silas came up blank.

"Damn it," he muttered, grabbing his phone. His father answered on the second ring.

"Silas, what's up?"

It was Sunday, meaning his dad had the day off. One day a week to rest and reset, he called it. "I'm at the Cape Cod place and need the code."

Thunder boomed, making him flinch. *"Cape Cod? I thought you were at Loon Lake."*

"Dad, there's been another shooting." The rain blew sideways, hitting him even under the porch's awning.

"Shooting?"

"What's the code? I can barely hear out in this storm!"

He listened and entered it, making the deadbolt retreat. The noises quieted as he closed the door, and Silas kicked his shoes off. He opened the closet, finding a couple of pairs of his own shoes. He left things here so he could pack light. They all did. It was musty, and he slid a window wide, letting the fresh air waft in on the breeze.

"What were you talking about?"

Silas informed his dad of the incident at the neighbor's house at Loon Lake, and his introduction to the FBI agent on the case.

"The FBI? For what?"

"They think there's a connection between Grandpa and the break-in at the Smithsonian's hangar. Apparently, Fred Trell has a storage unit, and someone broke in last week. It's what spurred the investigation on."

"I don't know what your grandfather might have had that would elicit this type of behavior," Silas' father said.

"I do," he muttered.

"What aren't you telling me?"

Silas removed the satchel, slipping the mysterious piece onto the table. How could something that appeared so trivial be the cause of two shootings? "You won't believe me anyway."

There was a pause. *"Silas, did you find it?"*

Silas took a seat, noticing the hint of panic in the other voice. "You knew?"

"Not really. I remember the metal strip. I went in his office when I was five years old. He'd fallen asleep in his chair, which wasn't that uncommon, since I don't think he slept at night. I'd hear his footsteps at three AM, pacing the hallway. Mom told me it was sleepwalking, but I've always wondered if there wasn't something more on his mind."

"Dad, the metal ..."

"The token sat on the desk with an old whiskey bag undone next to it. I reached for the strip and set a finger on it."

Silas pictured a little boy touching the odd piece.

"Just for a second, because my father woke and snatched my

wrist, slapping my hand away. But I saw something… I still do, every few months."

"A hole?"

"I thought of it as a pit. A dark and dangerous one."

A tingle crept down Silas' spine at the words. "I have the token."

"And you think that's what these guys were after? Did he get killed for that?"

"Yes."

"And Special Agent…"

"Waylen. Waylen Brooks."

"He knows too?"

"He held on for a few minutes. Waylen made it sound like he was actually on the Moon, and he saw the pit as well."

Another pause. *"I'm coming."*

"No. Stay put. If they're watching us—"

"Who are they?"

"Waylen's going to interview the guy at the hospital when he comes to, but I have a feeling he won't be very forthcoming to the man that just shot him."

"I really should come."

"Stay there. The funeral's soon. I've reached out to Rory Swanson."

"Rory… I have Oscar and Kathy's number." His father mumbled something, and a text came through. *"I sent their information in case you can't connect. You're suggesting there were more of those… strips?"*

"Three total."

"The triangle," his dad said.

That his dad recalled so many details from fifty years ago revealed the power of the token. "I'll be in touch."

"Be careful. I asked your grandfather about it only twice, and both times he warned me to never bring it up again. I don't know

what it is, but he was protective."

They said their goodbyes, and Silas stared at the shard, his hand hovering directly above it. What had Waylen seen? Could he step on the Moon too? Silas returned it to the bag without making contact, and realized there was no food in the place. He checked the phone, not seeing a response from Rory or Leigh, and nothing from the special agent yet either.

He took a long shower, washing off the day of travel, and after refreshing some of his clothes from the closet, he headed to the store for supplies. Silas was certain someone would respond soon.

5

*T*he hospital looked newer than the rest of Campbelltown. Not that the city didn't have a lot to offer. It was charming, an upgrade from the smaller surrounding hamlets, and the police headquarters from where Detective Desjardins operated was state-of-the-art. Waylen wished some of that funding would be thrown to the older departments like the one Deputy Hunt was stationed at in Gull Creek.

"I'm here to see the John Doe," Waylen told the receptionist. She smiled at him and picked up a phone, turning and speaking quietly before hanging up.

Desjardins chatted to a nurse at the elevator, and they both laughed. Waylen wasn't in a joking mood. He'd slept away five hours of the day, which was unlike him, but his body needed it. Even with the rest, he was still groggy, his eyes scratchy and his chest tight.

"You can go in. ICU on the third floor, section 3-A," the woman told him.

"I can show you," Desjardins said, waving at the nurse.

"Friend of yours?" Waylen glanced at the detective's hand, seeing a wedding band. He bet the guy's phone had family pictures with his wife and a couple of kids too.

Desjardins lost his grin and pressed the elevator button. "I'm a cop. We come to the hospital often enough, okay?"

Waylen let it drop as they rose, the doors chiming and springing open on the third floor. He followed the detective through the corridors, doing his best not to think about the death and illness around him. He'd always hated hospitals. The chemical scent, the patients sitting alone with machines attached by tubes. Waylen had watched his own father wither away until there was nothing left, and he'd vowed never to return. Being in the financial division of the Bureau had kept him from places like this, but Waylen knew his luck would eventually run out.

"You okay?" Desjardins asked as they approached the intensive care unit.

"Sure, why?"

"Kind of pale."

"I'm about to grill a guy I almost killed," he said.

"Right." Desjardins took charge, talking to the nursing staff, and Waylen waited to be shown to John Doe's room. A weary security guard was at the door, and he seemed thankful to see the pair of them arrive, like he had to use the washroom. Desjardins nodded at him, and the guy sauntered off for a break.

When they got there, Waylen put a hand on the detective's shoulder. "I'll do this alone."

"But…"

"If I need you, I'll call," Waylen said.

Desjardins plopped into a seat and fished his cell phone out of his pocket. "It's Sunday. I should be at the lake with my family."

Waylen ignored the complaint and entered the room. Most of the patients were in curtained-off sections, their life-preserving apparatuses beeping and pumping air. John Doe's room was no different. His gunshot wounds were bandaged up, and he sat propped at a forty-five-degree angle. His eyes were closed, but Waylen noticed a twitch of the hand when he entered, suggesting he was awake.

When the door clicked shut, he stepped closer, noting the handcuff securing the patient to the bed. "Hello."

The perp's eyelids remained tight.

"I'm Special Agent Waylen Brooks. What's your name?"

No response.

"What were you doing at 19 Beachcomber Way last night?" Waylen paused. "Besides trying to scare an old woman to death?"

Finally, he reacted. "Screw you."

"It lives," Waylen muttered. "The name?" he asked again.

"Why do you care?"

"I want to know what to write on your toe tag," Waylen said softly. He touched the bandage on the man's shoulder and grabbed it, pushing his thumb into the wound. Fresh blood welled at the injury. The guy didn't scream, but he tried to shove Waylen with his free arm, which made him wince even more.

"Okay, it's Bobby," he gasped.

Waylen glanced at the door, where Desjardins' head appeared. "We're good, aren't we… Bobby?" Waylen released him, and the perp nodded. Sweat beaded on his brow.

The detective grinned, indicating he wasn't below a little aggravated assault to get answers either. Waylen wasn't the type, but he believed the only way to this bastard's truth was to out-bully him. Sometimes you had to fight fire with fire. "Tell me what you were doing last night."

"Go to…" Bobby stopped when Waylen reached for

his holster. "You may as well end me."

"Why?"

"I'm screwed. They told me if I was caught, I'd be cut off. That's the best-case scenario." He shifted on the bed, grimacing when he peered at the bloodied bandage.

Waylen needed to keep it going. "I'm with the FBI, Bobby. We can help you in a situation like this." He was technically lying, because he had no authority in judicial matters, but he could heave it up the flagpole to the Assistant Director and see if there wasn't a plea to be had. "But we're talking about murder here."

"It wasn't me!" he proclaimed.

"Is that so?"

"Shane offed the old guy. I met him afterwards," he said.

"When Shane ditched the stolen truck from Oregon, right?" Waylen crossed the room, hands on his hips.

Bobby's expression gave him away. "How did you…"

"Because I'm paid to know, Bobby. We've been keeping tabs on you for a while. And your boss," he added.

"Then you're aware there's nothing you can do to stop him," Bobby said.

"Why?"

No response.

"Where is Shane?" Waylen asked, still not sure if Bobby was telling the truth.

"Probably already on the East…" He stopped again.

"East Coast? Woodstock, perhaps?" He added a bit of bait, since Bobby wasn't going anywhere and they'd ensure he had no visitors, or access to a telephone.

"If you know that much, why haven't you arrested him?"

"Who?"

"The boss? What if I can survive this after all?" Bobby grunted.

Waylen needed more information. "How do I reach him?"

"You don't."

"How did you stay in touch?"

"He called me."

Waylen strode to the far side of the room, where Bobby's personal effects were stashed in a clear bag. He removed the phone and turned it on. The facial recognition didn't work. "Look up," Waylen said, and the guy closed his eyes.

"You shouldn't do that."

"Why?"

Bobby sighed and relented, letting his face unlock the device. Waylen instantly went to the texting app, and saw most of them were wiped. One remained, and it said *SA* as the label. "SA is Shane?"

He nodded.

"Shane what?"

"Adams," Bobby admitted, and Waylen made a note on his own phone.

There was only a scattering of messages between the pair, mainly two words, with a time or a place. "How do I ask where he is?"

"He knows I'm caught. He won't respond."

"How?"

Bobby peered at the door, then at the large round clock on the wall as it passed four in the afternoon. "He won't stop until he has them all."

"You did find it in Trell's unit, then?"

Bobby nodded in agreement.

"But Peter Gunn had nothing?"

"Shane believes he gave it to someone. He upended that place and it wasn't around," Bobby said.

Waylen leaned closer and shoved the phone at Bobby. "How do I ask?"

"Type this: The weather is clearing up. Same for you?"

Waylen did, but hesitated before sending it. Would that alert him and the invisible boss? "You better not be screwing me."

"If I was, I'd buy you dinner first. Hospital food, though." Bobby making a joke was a good sign, or so he thought. Waylen hit send.

The response came a moment later. *Rain.* "What's it mean?"

"He's moved on to the third target."

"How did you two get to DC and back so quickly?" Waylen asked.

Bobby began to laugh, then coughed, making his brow furrow in pain. "If you have my boss in your crosshairs, are you really shocked?"

That got Waylen thinking. There were more than Bobby and Shane working to steal these... artifacts from dead astronauts. Did he mean someone at the CIA? A political figure?

Bobby's face slackened. "Damn it, you don't know."

Waylen smiled. "You could tell me."

"He's going to have me killed."

"We'll protect you," Waylen promised, but Bobby shook his head.

"You can't."

Desjardins poked back into the room, his expression grim. "Special Agent Brooks, we have to leave. There's been an incident."

Waylen peered at Bobby. "Was it Shane?" he asked the perp.

"Probably." Bobby's chin dropped to his chest. "Failure isn't an option."

Waylen rushed down the corridors of the ICU, trailing after the detective, and they quickly made it outside. "What's the call?"

"Gull Creek. A fire."

Waylen kept his mouth shut as Desjardins sped out of Campbelltown and to the small town twenty miles away. Fire trucks were on the scene, along with the sheriff and Deputy Gail Hunt. She met Waylen's gaze as the hoses sprayed the town's only grocery market. The Gremlin sat on the street, the glass shattered, the paint melted. He'd expected Leigh to leave with Silas, but clearly she'd stayed. He wondered if Gunn's grandson had left, or if they'd find both of them inside.

Waylen found his voice. "Anyone in there?"

"We don't know yet," Hunt said.

The fire was out, and smoke billowed from the damaged strip of buildings. The diner's occupants were on the street, watching in terror as their town experienced another tragic event. Waylen followed a pair of firefighters into the smoldering building and shielded his mouth and nose with the crook of his elbow.

There was one body, and he suspected the autopsy would show a fatal gunshot wound occurred before any smoke inhalation. It was Leigh. He recognized the tattoo on her arm.

A text came through, and Waylen staggered back to the sidewalk, seeing it was from Silas.

Any updates?

Waylen sighed and thought about his response. Instead, he dialed the number, walking away from the scene.

"*Hello?*"

"Silas, it's Waylen."

"*Yeah, I know. What's going on? Did you learn anything?*"

Waylen paced as the emergency crews carried Leigh out on a gurney, her body covered by a white sheet. An older woman wailed at the sight, and Waylen guessed it was her adoptive mother.

"*What's that sound? Where are you?*" Silas demanded.

"There's been an accident."

"*Accident?*"

"Silas, she's dead. Leigh is dead."

6

Rory straightened her collar and flattened her shirt at the sides before exiting the bookstore office. She heard another chime and saw a third message from Silas Gunn. Rory would respond later, after the book reading. Whatever he wanted couldn't be that important, considering they hadn't spoken in a decade, and even that conversation had been nothing more than simple pleasantries.

Rory expected twenty people to fill the small section of the store, but the sight nearly took her breath away. She slowed her approach, guessing there were over two hundred in attendance. Her lectern faced the chairs, which were filled with recognizable people. Rory's own parents were in the front row, her mother giving her a nod of approval.

She'd done readings for larger crowds, but her hand still shook slightly as she set the book on the stand, adjusting the mic to lower it.

Wanda Habbishire, the owner, watched her with pride, and strode down the middle aisle, taking over the podium for introductions. "Welcome to Woodstock Books. I'm Wanda, and I'm thrilled to host tonight's event with local author Rory"—she caught herself at the last moment—"Valentine. She'll be reading from her hit release *View from the Heavens.*"

Rory was surprised when Wanda gave her a light hug,

then fluttered back to her spot next to Florence, the bakery owner. The gathered people clapped, and she scanned the crowd for Kevin, but he was nowhere in sight. She noticed her father doing the same, since she'd put him on alert. Oscar had called the police department earlier and talked to his buddy, the chief, making sure Kevin Heffernan was gone from their town. It appeared that their altercation earlier had scared him off, and he'd checked out of the B&B only an hour later. But Rory wouldn't put it past the creep to stick around and seek vengeance for the bloodied nose.

She cleared her throat as the room grew silent, and took a moment to appreciate the support of her hometown. When she was younger, she couldn't wait to escape Woodstock and venture to the big cities. She'd pictured herself sipping cocktails with the wealthy at nightclubs, and be asked to dinner by rich men who drove convertibles and showered her with gifts and affection. Coming back had made her realize just how nice of an environment it was here.

One of her old friends, Caroline, waved from the second row, and lifted her copy of the book. Rory smiled, wondering how long it had been since they'd spoken. Five years? Before she'd started writing the novel, that was for certain.

"Good evening, everyone," Rory started with a scratchy voice. She sipped the water and flipped open her book. "I wrote *View from the Heavens* six years after my grandfather, Colin Swanson, passed away from his battle with dementia. It was an honor to place a version of him into the story, though the main character, Madeline, had a very different relationship with her astronaut grandfather than I did. Grandpa Swanson was a sweet man who constantly made time for his family, no matter what stage of life he was in. The town Madeline grew up in wasn't listed as Woodstock, Vermont, but if you've read the book, you'll see countless similarities. This bookstore inspired the one in which Madeline first started reading about space travel and NASA."

Rory waited while a few people whispered to themselves, a couple standing in the back, nodding like they'd known this detail.

"Without all of you influencing my life, I wouldn't be where I am today, with a book in its fourth printing, so I want to thank you. Woodstock, while my temporary home for the moment, will always be *home* to me."

The crowd cheered at the comment, and it made Rory flush with joy. When they quieted, she flipped the novel to a section she'd pre-marked and tapped the mic, then gulped a mouthful of water.

"I've chosen to recite two excerpts. One from young Maddy's point of view, then one from closer to the end. If you haven't read the book, I apologize for any spoilers, but I don't think either will affect the overall experience." Rory set a finger on the page and took a deep breath. "*Madeline strolled through the park, but something had changed. The sky was darker, the Moon brighter, the stars flickering with clarity. Her grandfather's revelation at dinner stunned her, but now she was more determined than ever to set foot on the distant hunk of rock. If these men from fifty years ago did it, why couldn't she? She had the grades to enroll in the ideal school, which would set her on course for a position with NASA. Madeline Baker would be the first woman to do a moonwalk.*"

Rory paused, peering up when the door chimes rang. For a second, she thought it was Kevin coming to ruin her evening, but instead Jack, the journalist from earlier, entered, crossing his arms as he grinned and leaned near the exit.

She continued the reading, pausing at the proper moments, getting into the story herself. When had she last reread her own work? From start to finish, not since the day before shipping the final manuscript to her agent. Rory stopped, closing the book, and glanced up at the quiet crowd. They applauded politely, a few going so far as to cheer her boisterously.

"Any questions?"

"Would *you* fly to the Moon?" The question came from Greg, the doctor, whom she hadn't noticed in the crowd. People laughed while Rory composed herself.

Her mother raised an eyebrow, waiting.

"*View* is a fictitious account of Madeline's life. There's a common misunderstanding about authors. We do put elements of ourselves into our stories, but she's a lot braver than I am. I don't think I'd cut it as an astronaut. Sorry to disappoint you," Rory answered, receiving a few claps.

"Being the granddaughter of a famous astronaut must have been interesting," someone else said. Rory didn't recognize the man. "In your book, it made Madeline even more determined when he claimed NASA would never send a woman to the Moon. Did that happen?"

Rory shook her head and thought about a similar discussion she'd had as a child with Grandpa Swanson. "No. He told me I could be anything I wanted. President. Air Force aviator. Nobel-winning laureate. With him, there were no barriers, because he saw stuff differently than regular people. He once told me that his entire life changed the moment he stepped onto the Moon. Witnessing Earth from another vantage point made him realize how petty humanity was. He tried to support real changes in the Seventies, while his fame propelled him to the top of the headlines, and it worked for a while, before the space program grew nearly defunct. The Eighties brought a different mindset, and people stopped caring what he had to say." Rory lifted her hands. "His words, not mine."

The same guy, she noted, had a recorder in his hand. "What are your thoughts about Peter Gunn's murder?"

"This is a book reading, not a press conference." Wanda Habbishire strode through the aisle, pointing at the man. "You either sit down or leave." She frowned at him, and added, "Please."

He flipped the device off and took his seat.

"While Peter Gunn has nothing to do with my book, I want to express my deepest condolences to the Gunn family," she said.

When no one interrupted her, she went to the last section and read for another ten minutes. At the end, the crowd applauded again, and her mother was already on her feet, hitting the refreshment table, pouring a coffee. Rory waved at a couple other familiar faces from around town and took a seat behind the table Wanda had set up, complete with her author profile picture enlarged until she couldn't stand the sight of herself. She averted her gaze and grabbed the pen, testing it on a blank sheet to ensure the ink was distributing properly.

The line formed, but not with any real urgency. Even if all two hundred guests wanted a signature, Rory would wait until they were all satisfied. The first up was an older lady in a wheelchair, and a younger man pushed her.

"Hello," Rory said.

"You won't remember me, but I was an acquaintance of your grandfather's. He was a good man, and I can only imagine how proud he would be of his little Rory hitting it big," the woman said.

"What's your name?"

She looked up at the man behind her, as if seeking help. "It's Bernadette," he answered.

"I knew that. I was just checking if you did," she snapped. "My son. He's always worrying about me."

Rory signed the book, making it out to Bernadette. "How did you meet Colin Swanson?"

"I used to own a pub in town. The Twisted Tie," she said. "Do you remember it?"

"Mom, she's not old enough," the son grumbled.

"What if she heard about it? How should I know?"

Rory imagined their conversations were all equally loud. The line was getting larger, and she had only signed one copy. "I wasn't aware my grandpa visited the pub in town."

"Yes. He used to carry something with him. A whiskey bag," Bernadette said, her eyes growing hazy as she stared at the sign with Rory's picture on it.

"A whiskey bag?" Rory didn't recall that, but from the sounds of it, Bernadette knew him before she was born.

The man ushered his mother away while she scolded him about talking over her.

Rory signed the next few and accepted a copy of the book, not looking up. "Who can I make it out to?"

"Your biggest fan," he said. She glanced at the figure, finding Jack there. Greg was two behind him in line, and he made eye contact. Rory almost laughed that there were two men vying for her attention on the same day her crazy ex had stalked her in town. Her own life could have been in a book. Maybe she'd end up on the Moon like her character Madeline.

"Hello, Jack," she drawled. "Or do you prefer something else?" Rory pointed at the open page. "I think it's almost worth face value with my signature on it."

"Why are authors always so self-deprecating?" He

laughed.

"It's a defense mechanism. Otherwise, our reviews would kill us."

"Jack is good."

"Glad you could make it," she told him.

"Wouldn't miss it." Jack accepted the copy and slid it under his arm. "Mind if I stick around?"

Rory gestured at the line. "It'll be a while."

"I have nothing else to do."

Rory continued with the signings, Greg asking her about dinner this week, and she kindly rejected him, claiming to be swamped with work. He exited a few minutes later, and Rory caught a glare from her mother. In another hour, her wrist ached, and a headache began to spread in her temples, but she was done.

"That went splendidly," Mrs. Habbishire claimed. "Good thing I had all those copies, though half of the people in town already owned it. You did well up there."

"Thanks." Rory stretched after standing, and slung her purse over her shoulder. "I appreciate the support."

Wanda and a couple of younger men began folding and stacking the chairs, and when Rory attempted to assist them, the proprietor waved her away. "Go home. It's getting late."

Rory's parents waited outside, and someone honked from ahead. "You want a ride?" Jack asked.

She glanced at Kathy and Oscar, and her dad finally relented, giving her a nod. Her mother kissed her cheek. "Congrats on tonight. I foresee more of these events in your future."

It was about the nicest thing her mom had ever said, and she watched them walk to their convertible. The top was up, and Rory felt a raindrop falling from the sky.

Jack leaned over the front seat and opened her door.

"Come on in."

Rory did as the rain came harder. "I could have gone with my parents."

"But then you'd miss out on inviting me back to your guest house," he said, pulling a wine bottle from a brown bag as she climbed in. "Your big night deserves a celebration."

Rory recognized the label, aware it was an excellent vintage. It was after ten, and she really wanted to be writing first thing in the morning, but Jack smelled wonderful, and after Kevin's presence that morning, she might feel better to have someone around for a while. "Okay."

They drove to her family's estate as the storm blew in.

7

Silas, she's dead. Leigh is dead.

The words from Special Agent Waylen replayed in his mind, and Silas circled the room, his steps causing the oak hardwood to creak. He remembered his mom remodeling the place about a decade earlier, and couldn't recall what it had looked like before.

This wasn't happening.

Silas kept peering at the bag, holding the flat metal token, wishing he had somewhere to ditch it. Whatever it was, someone was willing to kill for it. Leigh. They'd barely talked, but it was obvious she'd been running from something in the city. Now he'd never learn the truth, because she was murdered. All as a result of getting involved with *him*.

Wind blew against the shutters, rattling them, and Silas walked to the drapery, shoving it aside. Tiny motes of dust fell, and he spied the trees bending with the growing storm. His phone made an alert, and for a second, he thought it might be Waylen checking in, but it was his weather app. The area was on a hurricane watch, with the massive cyclone coming from the southeast. It would strike off the coast of Florida, but the region would experience high volumes of rain and damaging winds. An evacuation notice was issued, but not implemented.

A text appeared from his father. *Silas, I saw the weather*

report. I think you should come home.

He stared at it for a minute, unsure of what to do. He should have handed the object off to the FBI, then walked away unscathed. At first, he'd just been angry at Leigh's death, but the more he thought about it, the worse his stomach tightened. Keeping this put his entire family in danger. The bastards had already killed his grandfather, and now Leigh. Who was next?

The phone rang, and he recognized Waylen's area code. "Hello."

"Silas, you okay?"

"Sure. Not really," he added.

"Bobby is gone," Waylen said.

"Gone as in… dead?"

"No. Gone as in, the hospital let him escape. I guess there was a bomb threat called in, and Bobby vanished during the commotion."

A noise sounded at the window, and Silas wished he had a gun. Then he recalled the safe in his parents' bedroom. They did have one. It was only a branch tapping the glass, but Silas' overactive imagination had him picturing the two men stalking up the driveway, soaking wet from the storm, ready to demand he give up the satchel. Silas would, if it came to that.

"Silas, are you there?"

"Yes. Are they coming here?"

"Bobby mentioned going to the third target. I think that's the Swansons."

"Damn it," he whispered. "I've sent Rory a few messages, but she's not responding."

"The house line didn't get me anywhere, but I left a message," Waylen said. *"I'm at the airport in Jackson Hole, waiting for a flight to Vermont, but the storm is delaying all the trips. I'll go to Albany and drive the rest of the way. That option's leaving in thirty*

minutes."

The fact that the FBI agent was on the move, about to visit the Swansons, made Silas slightly less stressed. "Good plan."

"These two can't travel any faster than that, not with the weather, so my suggestion is to batten down the hatches and wait to hear from me. Keep pestering the daughter, and make sure she understands the danger."

"Will do," Silas agreed.

"Have you… touched it again?"

"No."

"Good. Don't." There was a brief pause while a voice carried through a speaker in the airport. *"That's me. I'll make contact when I land."*

The call ended abruptly, and Silas noticed a second message from his dad.

Silas dialed him, but it failed. He lowered the cell, finding no service. The lamp flickered and cut out. He barely had enough light through the window, so he checked the kitchen, finding a flashlight. The branch continued to tap the pane of glass, casting lengthy shadows on the hardwood. When he was a kid, he always thought of them as witch's fingers.

Silas turned the flashlight on and strode down the hall to his parents' primary suite. He rarely went in there, but it looked completely normal, the bed made after the housekeeping company had cleaned up since their last visit. Silas pushed past the sundresses and sports coats to the rear wall of the closet and slid the painting off, wondering if it was connected to the main power grid. When he touched the digital keypad, it glowed, telling him it wasn't. What was the passcode?

He tried the house's code, and it blinked green, the bolt receding. Leave it to his father to get lazy when it came to passwords. He used the same one for everything at the office, so why would his vacation property be any different? Silas reached in, seeing a stack of cash and the handgun case. He pulled the 9MM free and clipped a magazine into it. With murderers stalking anyone involved with the Helios 15 mission, he wasn't going to stay unprotected.

He sealed the safe up and returned to the living room. Silas wanted to warn Rory, like Waylen suggested, but the network was down. He held the phone, willing it to work.

Rory woke up.

The spot in the bed next to her was messy, a glass of water half empty on the stand. The night had been a blur, starting with the wine. She'd had the vintage a few times with her father, and this one had tasted off.

Rory pictured Jack pouring a refill, smiling and asking her questions about her grandfather. She'd gone to bed, but there was no way they'd slept together. Right? She was still fully clothed, so that answered her question. The clock told her it was three in the morning, and she swallowed with a dry throat. Her mouth was pasty, her lips sticking shut. When she got out of bed, her legs wobbled, and her feet hardly lifted as she tried to walk. Something was wrong.

"Jack?" she called, but the noise barely escaped. Rory held the door frame and stepped through it. He was there. The lights were on in the second bedroom, where she'd placed all of Grandpa Swanson's possessions.

Rory grabbed her phone, seeing it was off. She returned to the bedroom, pressing it on. The startup seemed to take forever, and when she looked, the battery was nearly dead. Rory lumbered to the nightstand and plugged it in, frantically trying to text her dad.

Rory had read about things like this, women being drugged, and was confident that was what had happened. But why was Jack still there, and sifting through their belongings? Did he drug her for the story on Helios 15?

She noticed the messages from Silas Gunn and realized she'd never even read them. It had been a busy night, and then Jack came over to distract her. Rory clicked the first unopened note.

Hey Rory, not sure if you remember me, but I'm Peter Gunn's grandson. We've met a couple of times.

The next grew more erratic. *They might come for you. Peter was murdered for … something in his possession, and we think your family might have one too. It looks like a metal bookmark.*

An hour later. *Oh, and if you find it, don't touch it.*

"What are you doing up?" The voice startled her, and Rory dropped the phone.

She had to play it cool. "I heard a noise." She tried to sound confident, but doubted it came off that way.

Jack filled the frame, his eyes covered in dark shadows. "Where is it?" he seethed.

"What are you looking for?"

"You're not fooling me, Rory. I read the book. You know everything about Colin Swanson," he said. "They lied to their government, and I'm going to find them."

"Who are you?"

Jack smiled, the expression unsettling. "I'm your worst nightmare. I see the drugs wore off. No problem. Now we can have a nice chat."

Rory peered at the floor where her phone sat. She hoped he hadn't seen it there, but the screen brightened as another message appeared from Silas.

He lunged, beating her to it, and snatched the cell, shoving her to the bed. "Stay there!"

Jack brushed the hair from his face and tapped the incoming note. *"Power just came back on. They killed another person. A girl in Gull Creek. Rory, get out of there."* While he read the previous few, his grin grew larger. Jack pocketed the device. "You've been in touch with the Gunn family."

"I didn't talk to him at all. I just saw the messages," she said truthfully.

"I already have a piece, and you'll help me secure the other two, since this Silas character clearly has the one from Loon Lake," Jack said.

"What are you even looking for?" she demanded.

"The triangle," he said.

"What is it?"

"It's going to change everything." Jack pulled a bag from his back pocket and dangled it near her face. "Have you seen its counterpart?"

She recalled the old woman, Bernadette, mentioning her grandfather hanging out in the bar, holding one like it. "No."

"I don't believe you," Jack said. "Stand up."

She did.

"You sorted all of his things?" Jack asked, dragging her roughly by the arm into the living room.

"Yes."

"Then where is it?"

"I have no clue what you're talking about!" she yelled, hoping her parents might overhear her. Jack struck her on the cheek. She saw stars and clutched the aching spot with her palm.

"Rory, we can make this simple. Hand it over, and I won't kill your family. Deal?"

Rory had had enough of people like Jack and Kevin.

"Screw you," she hissed.

The gun appeared, the hammer cocking back as he touched the trigger. "Don't make this harder than it has to be." The barrel pressed to her head, and Rory saw her life flitter before her eyes. It wasn't nearly as satisfying as she'd hoped by this age. She wasn't done living.

"You need me," she said.

The gun moved a few inches. "Is that so?"

"I know where it is."

"Then show me," Jack said.

"It's not here." She moved across the living room and entered the bedroom. The boxes were all open, and it was a disaster. Despite the mess, Rory found a photo album, and she flipped through the pages, trying to remember where she'd seen that bag before. Finally, after five minutes of Jack rushing her, Rory stopped on the proper one. She yanked it from the album and shoved it at him. "There."

Jack clutched it, his gun aimed at her. "Where was this taken?"

"At his house."

"I thought all his things were donated or brought here," Jack said.

"My dad wouldn't sell it. It's on the coast, and I have the passcode to get in."

Jack stared at her, but the gun remained in place. "Are you trying to trick me into leaving so your parents don't die?"

"You also need me to contact Silas."

"I could just use your phone and pretend to be you."

"That'll only work for so long," she said. Rory needed to survive the night and figure out the rest along the way. She'd spent years placating a psychopath. What was another couple of days?

"Get moving. We're off."

Rory watched the photo drop to the floor, hoping someone would see it and follow her.

8

Normally, a drive from Albany to Woodstock, Vermont would have taken him two hours and forty minutes, according to his GPS. Waylen made the trek with thirty to spare, since he didn't stop at the state border to take a picture of the sign. The sun rose early this time of year, and it blinded him as he entered town.

Waylen had visited countless areas over the course of his career with the Bureau, but rarely did he find a hidden gem. Everything was flawless, as if the town was wearing a veneer. He expected there was a seedier side, like all places, but from the exterior, it was perfection.

He slowed while dialing the Swansons again, and finally, after five rings, someone picked up.

"It's five in the morning," the man said, presumably Oscar Swanson.

"Sorry about that. This is Special Agent Waylen Brooks of the FBI, and—"

"FBI? Is this about the bank deal with the town? Because it's totally legitimate. Judge Sando signed off..."

Waylen signaled as he headed for their street. "No. We believe someone might be after an object your father had in his possession. You've heard about Peter Gunn?"

"Yes, he was my godfather," Oscar said grimly.

"The same people are coming for your house."

"Where are you?" Any sign of sleepiness had vanished

from Oscar's voice.

"A block away," Waylen said.

"*I'll be outside.*"

Waylen expected a barrage of questions, but the man was clearly composed. He pulled the rental along the street, eyeing their home. No, this was an estate. The place was palatial, the landscaping immaculate in the morning sunlight. Dewy drops clung to the green grass, the flowers stretched toward the sky, petals bright and vibrant. He exited the car, peering in both directions. From what he could tell, no one was casing the house.

Oscar Swanson looked to be about sixty, his hair gray, his shoulders wide. He was fit, with a deep bushy scowl on his brow. "What's this about Peter Gunn?"

Waylen checked the front door. "Is your wife home?"

"Yes, but she's in bed."

"Does anyone else live here?"

"Rory's in the guest house."

Waylen followed his gaze to the structure at the rear of the property. A light was on, the dim glow carrying through open blinds. "Is she usually up at five?"

"She's writing a book," he said, as if that explained everything.

Waylen usually let his gut guide him in situations like this, and with Bobby escaping the hospital, and his partner Shane evading capture, he had a bad feeling. He started down the stone pathway toward the guest house.

"Where are you going?"

"Your daughter might be in danger," he answered, his gun quickly retrieved from its holster.

Oscar chased after him, wearing his bathrobe and slippers. He lost one of them halfway, but didn't stop to pick it up. "She's fine. Had a book reading last night at the local—"

Waylen lifted a hand, silencing him as they neared the structure. The door was closed, but the welcome mat sat slightly askew, like someone might have been forced out. He glanced at the street, then to Oscar. "Do you have security cameras?"

"Of course." He gestured to the side of the porch.

Waylen knocked, rapping his knuckles on the glass pane.

"She wears those headphones." Oscar mimed putting on a pair. "Noise cancelling."

Waylen took gloves from his pocket and depressed the door handle.

"What do you need those for?"

Waylen ignored the comment and stepped in. Oscar pushed past him and rushed to the bedroom.

"Don't touch anything," Waylen warned.

"Rory?" Oscar walked through the small place and stopped at a bedroom door. "The room is trashed. Rory spent an entire day moving my father's things into there."

Waylen observed the mess, the open boxes, the spilled contents of numerous packages.

"Call your daughter," he whispered.

Oscar did, and quickly hung up. "It says the number is out of service."

"He probably removed the SIM card." Waylen sent Special Agent Martina Sanchez a message asking for her to track the phone's movement, but he doubted they'd get far. "Those cameras. I have to watch the footage."

Waylen examined the place and saw the open wine bottle, the two dirty glasses. "Someone was here with her."

Oscar shook his head. "That journalist... he drove her home."

"What journalist?"

"The guy was here the night before, and scared Rory half to death. I guess they hit it off, and he helped her get rid of her ex earlier in the day. Kevin was quite the nuisance. If I ever see him again…"

Waylen relaxed slightly, but still worried for the daughter. "Her ex-boyfriend was in town?"

"Yes. But she was sure he left."

Waylen eyed the glasses and gazed at the bedroom, seeing the disheveled sheets. Could this be something different? A reunion with her old fling? "Let's check the cameras."

"It's on my laptop in the house." Oscar blinked three times and sighed. "Is Rory going to be all right?"

"I don't know."

Waylen stopped in the living room and noticed a photo on the floor. He crouched to pick it up, and the hair on his arms rose. The picture showed a young Colin Swanson holding a bag, like the one Silas had in his possession. "What is this?"

"It's an old picture of my dad," Oscar said.

"Where was it taken?"

"His house."

Probably a dead end.

"Rory was asking about it the other day. She wanted it for a couple of weeks to write her book."

"You still have the house?" Waylen asked.

"It's a beautiful place, and I have such fond memories of it…"

"That's where he's taking her," Waylen muttered.

"Who?"

"We're about to find out."

Five minutes later, they were in Oscar's office, with his wife Kathy hovering behind them as he powered the computer on.

"Rory probably took a walk. You know how she is," Kathy said. "Restless."

Waylen had seen enough people in denial over the years to keep quiet and let her ramble on. She left and returned with two cups of black coffee, sliding them to the pair of men at the desk. Waylen gave his thanks and stared at the screen while the program activated.

In it, Rory arrived with the potential perp, his car parking directly under the streetlight. Waylen thought there was something familiar about his gait as they approached the guest house. Their voices were muffled, but the conversation sounded light and happy.

"Any other angles?" he asked.

"No."

Waylen drummed his fingers on the mahogany desk, thinking this through. They viewed the next motion, and the timestamp told them Rory had been abducted at 3:27 A.M.

"That's only two hours ago," Kathy said. "She's really gone?"

He tried to understand why this man would have kept her alive. If he had the location, what was stopping him from going alone and breaking in? It wasn't Bobby or Shane, which suggested the operation was much larger than that duo, as Bobby had outright proclaimed in the hospital.

The guy had a gun, and he glanced up at the camera, darkness shrouding his face. Waylen reached over Oscar and paused it. He dove into his pocket, grabbing his cell, and checked the ancillary surveillance footage Sanchez had sent him from the hangar in DC. When he got to the right frame, he paused his screen. Upon comparison of the two images, he was sure it was the same man. Whoever'd broken into the Smithsonian-owned warehouse had taken Rory Swanson hostage.

Before he put the phone away, Silas texted him, asking for an update.

"Excuse me," he said, stepping from the office. He dialed Silas, who answered after the first ring.

"Are they okay?"

"Rory's with him," Waylen whispered.

"With him?"

"She was taken two hours ago."

"Damn it. Wait, I just got a message from her," Silas said.

"You did? What's it say?"

"Hey, Silas. Long time no talk. I'm heading to the coast. Any chance you want to meet up in the next couple days? I can come to the city, if that works?"

Waylen cringed. "It's him. The guy running this operation. He has the one from Trell's storage unit, and now he's heading to get Swanson's. Then all he'll need is yours."

"For what? What's their purpose?"

Waylen closed his eyes, seeing the eternal blackness of the hole. The Moon's surface was cold and lifeless, the pit beckoning him. "I don't have a clue, but it can't be good. There was a reason these three didn't tell a soul about what they discovered, and why they tried to keep them separated."

"I'll meet you there," Silas said.

"That's not a great idea."

"Too bad. Where are they?"

Waylen hesitated. "Outside Portsmouth, New Hampshire."

"Send me the address."

"Bring the bag, Silas. I should be the one to hang on to it."

After a moment's hesitation, he finally responded.

"Okay."

Waylen suddenly regretted offering to carry it, since he'd be tempted to touch the foreign object again, to learn if it offered any other secrets of the Moon. "Be careful. I'm on my way."

"Have you checked the weather? It's getting worse," Silas said.

It was growing cloudy in Woodstock, but dry for the time being. "I'll call you in a while."

Waylen heard a door close, followed by an engine starting. Wind whistled in the distance, and the rain came down so hard, it could have been hail. *"We can't let anything happen to Rory."*

"We won't," Waylen promised, more for himself than Silas. He'd allowed Leigh to be caught in the crossfire, and he wouldn't stop until this baffling treasure hunt was over.

He looked into the office, but the Swansons weren't there. The image remained on the man and Rory, and Oscar's voice shouted on the phone. "...No, he's here! The FBI agent!"

"Who's he talking to?" Waylen asked.

Kathy looked up, her eyes red and swollen. "The police."

"Oscar, give me the phone."

He paced the kitchen. "Rory's gone. Send someone, Bill. He already murdered Peter Gunn... now he has my daughter..."

Waylen grabbed the cell and thrust it to his own ear. "Bill? Special Agent Waylen Brooks, FBI. We need a team to come to the Swanson residence with a full dusting kit. The perp was in the guest house, and I believe you can ID him with a print. Wine bottle. Glasses. Door handles. He wasn't being overly cautious." He ended the call and tossed the phone back to Oscar. "I have to leave. I'll be in touch."

Waylen exited as they began to protest, but he didn't have the luxury of hanging around to explain anything. The clock was ticking, and he suspected Rory would be dead in a matter of hours, whether they found the hidden prize or not.

9

Gusting wind threw the car around. Even with the wipers on full power, Rory couldn't see the road. She continuously gripped the handhold above her door, clenching her jaw as Jack drove on.

"We have to stop!" she urged, but he didn't relent.

"No, you need to shut up," he said. The gun was in his lap, and Rory was surprised he hadn't tied her up or tossed her in the trunk. Instead, she rode in the passenger seat, the two of them looking like a normal couple speeding into a hurricane.

Rory squinted as they passed a sign indicating they were twenty miles from Portsmouth. Her grandparents' house was about ten minutes farther, right on the coastline, where the storm would be even worse. It shocked her that her father had kept the property without ever mentioning it.

"Why are you doing this?" she asked.

"Which part?"

"Any of it. You killed Peter Gunn, didn't you?"

"Not me. I prefer to let others handle that side of the business," he said. "These days."

She didn't believe that, considering the threats he'd made with no compunction. "Then who did?"

"Rory, there are things you can't fathom."

"That's not an answer," she said.

"What if I told you the members of the Helios 15 mission found something on the Moon? That Commander Gunn and Swanson stumbled upon a secret, and never shared it with anyone, including NASA?"

"I'd say you're lying."

"That's what everyone thought, but there was a hole in their plan," Jack muttered. "Your grandfather exposed them on national television."

Rory observed him, and found Jack seemingly normal. He was clearly worked up about getting this... whatever was hiding in the whiskey bag, but otherwise, he didn't come across as delusional. "You're obviously not a journalist."

"No, Rory, I am not."

"What's so important about these? Why kill for them?"

"They might change the world," he said.

"How?"

"Do you believe there's life on other planets?"

Rory shrugged. "Sure, I do."

"What if we could travel to them?"

Rory pictured the footage of Peter Gunn's shuttle leaving the cape in the early Seventies. The flames propelling them upward, toward the Moon. "We can't even get to Mars."

Jack grinned, but it didn't meet his eyes. "That's irrelevant. Mars is dead. A lifeless husk. No, I'm talking about actual planets with lush landscapes, vibrant beaches, colorful oceans."

"You've lost me," she said.

"Never mind."

The wipers sloshed water around, the blades speeding back and forth. Wind blew at the trees, and Rory watched a billboard flip onto its side. A plastic garbage can bounced across the road, and Jack slowed to avoid it. There were no other cars out, no one for Rory to flag down, even if she freed herself from the confines of the vehicle.

"Don't even think about it," he cautioned her.

"Think about what?" she asked innocently.

Jack set a palm on the handgun. "Just don't."

The GPS directed him past Portsmouth and toward the water. The street was flooded near the house, and Jack splashed into it before slowing. Rory guessed it was up to the door, but they moved on, eventually rising as the road inclined up a hill. Colin Swanson's house was perched on the top, with a million-dollar view of the squalls in the distance.

They reached the end of the way, the Swanson residence on their left. It was a beautiful colonial, with a giant American flag flapping with the wind. For a moment, she remembered the famous image of the flag being planted on the Moon.

Even in the storm, Rory recognized the care the landscapers continued to put into the property. Her father was still paying for the upkeep. How much were the taxes alone? Colin Swanson had left everything to the family, but this seemed excessive.

Jack parked and snapped his fingers, drawing her attention. "We're going in."

It had taken them two hours to drive from Woodstock, and Rory wondered if her parents were even up yet. Likely they were, her dad probably reading the paper while sipping a coffee. Her mom would be laying out her clothing, excited for lunch at the club. How long would it be before anyone noticed she was missing? Another two, three hours? Rory needed to stay alive. Jack seemed distracted, which meant she might find a way to escape, or at least contact someone. Local police? Her parents? Hell, she'd give Kevin a call if it was possible.

The rain poured onto the driveway, gushing from a clogged gutter near the entrance. It flowed like a waterfall, and Jack sidestepped to avoid being soaked. Rory trailed after him, her socks wet by the time she found cover at the door.

"Hit the code." Jack glanced down the street nervously. The gun remained in his hand, and he shifted on his feet.

Rory typed the four digits, and it unlocked, the light flashing red, signaling the battery was at the end of its life. There was no alarm, which surprised her. But the town of Rye was safe, and the neighbors probably watched out for one another. It was seven thirty, and some of them might be awake. If she could notify …

Jack shoved her in, and she almost tripped on the carpet.

"Easy," she called. "You don't have to be a jerk. I'm here, aren't I?"

"Where's his stuff?" Jack moved deeper into the place, his shoes leaving wet marks.

"How do I know?" She glanced at the door and thought about running. But despite the threat to her life, Rory was extremely intrigued by what Jack had mentioned on the way in. She didn't have much to go on, and Jack wasn't going to openly discuss more than he'd already done, so she tried to connect the dots herself.

He'd suggested that the Helios 15 team had discovered something on the Moon, and that there were three sections, each astronaut taking one, with the vow to never speak of it again. But Grandpa Swanson had cracked, and that was how Jack, or whoever he was working for, learned of the mystery.

Rory imagined her own grandpa, the kindly old man, but he hadn't always been elderly. He'd been extremely intelligent, fit and confident in a way most weren't these days. He'd exuded a calm energy, and people normally reacted well in his company.

Rory realized she was still at the door, the water beginning to pool. She closed it with a sigh when Jack returned, holding his pistol up. "This will all be over soon."

"If you find it, will you let me leave?"

His eyes crinkled at the corners as he squinted. "Yes."

Rory wasn't an expert, but the one word was undoubtedly a lie. He planned on killing her. She resigned herself to being her own savior, a hero like a character from a book, not a woman who'd been pushed around her entire life. Madeline wouldn't have allowed anyone to stop her in *View from the Heavens*, and neither would Rory. "Take what you want, and I'll pretend we never met. There's no need to notify the police. I'll go home to Woodstock, and you can have the bag."

He studied her for a moment and pressed his lips tight before turning around. "If you try anything, I will shoot."

"But I should be there for Silas…"

"The Gunn kid won't know what hit him." He stowed the pistol into his jacket pocket.

Rory searched for something to strike him with, but the living room was mostly empty. The fireplace tools at the hearth were gone, and a single couch was centered on the polished cherry hardwood floors. The kitchen was off to the right, but she'd never reach it without him noticing. Besides, the cutlery was probably packed in boxes like the rest.

Rory followed Jack to the stairwell, and he motioned for her to go ahead. She obeyed while considering how to stall him. If she found the object he sought, she'd need a distraction.

"Where would he hide it?"

"He had dementia."

"So?"

"If he recalled how important it was, it would remain somewhere secured, but at the end, he didn't know his own name. If he stumbled on this... part of the triangle, he could have done anything with it."

Jack paused at the top of the steps and gestured down the hall. "Did he have an office?"

Rory nodded and led the way. It was surreal being in the home. The place was in desperate need of a makeover, but she found the faded wallpaper comforting. It was almost like her grandparents' ghosts remained, and she stared at the bathroom as she passed, recalling getting her hair braided at the sink when she was ten.

The office door was closed, and Jack tried to open it. "Locked."

Rory started for the next room, but Jack lifted his leg and kicked under the handle. The frame splintered, and the slab banged, hitting the wall hard enough for the knob to stick in the plaster.

She recoiled from the sudden noise, and flinched when he reached for her arm, dragging her into the space. Photos sat on the white wall, each meticulously framed and staggered to make a circular pattern from a distance. Her grandpa was so proud of his training, and his mission to the Moon. It was all he could talk about in the later years, when his knees gave out and his hip flared after dinner.

Jack set to his search with a level of intensity usually reserved for emergency surgery. He looked focused, his fingers quickly sorting through the paperwork on the desk. Grandpa Swanson had no computer, just a phone and a Rolodex with real business cards. She stared at the telephone, wondering if her dad continued to pay for the utilities on the property. Rory pressed the light switch, and the fixture snapped on, startling Jack.

"Figured we could use some light." Rory went to the closet and began the search. It was filled with medals and certificates of various accomplishments. He always ended up being an honorary something or other. Libraries and museums would invite him for the pittance of press an old astronaut might draw in, then offer him a piece of paper to display. He'd told her privately that it was all BS, but he couldn't imagine disappointing the event coordinators. From what Rory understood, Peter Gunn had no issues in denying public appearances, and preferred to live his later years by secluding himself at the lake.

"Where would he put it?" Jack rifled through the drawers, upending them one at a time until the entire desk had revealed nothing of note.

The closet wasn't large, and after checking the handful of technical educational volumes on physics and propulsion from the Fifties, Jack stood at the door, fists clenched. "I was certain we'd find it here."

"Let's keep checking," she said, not wanting Jack to give up. If he did, he wouldn't need her any longer.

Her captor peered at his watch, and she wondered what had him on a tight timeline. His phone beeped, and he groaned, then dialed someone. "Where are you?"

Rory didn't have any idea who he was talking to, but his tone suggested it was an underling. If he brought reinforcements, she was doomed. Rory walked toward the bedroom as he spoke on the phone.

"Yeah, near Portsmouth. I'm leaving soon. Do I have it? That's none of your business, Shane!" He was obviously growing agitated, which decreased her odds of survival.

Grandma had outlived her husband, but only by three years. Her heartache had never left, and she'd passed in her sleep at the age of eighty-one at home, in this very bed. The sheets were tucked pristinely, and the bedding was familiar. Rory went to it, wishing she could talk to them just one more time.

The reality of her situation returned when Jack stomped down the hall, cursing into his phone.

Rory pulled open the nightstand on Grandpa's side and found it empty. No, there was a book in it.

"Get to DC. We'll have all three by tonight." Jack entered. "It better be here."

Rory read the title and laughed. He'd loved old Western books. Movies, too. He thought there was something romantic about finding a property and staking claim to it.

Jack stormed through the room, knocking a lamp over. It shattered loudly, and he stepped past the fragments, entering the closet. He tossed boxes, complaining about doing the task himself. He made quick work of the stuff, grumbling about their useless junk. Jack griped, then exited, leaving her alone.

Rory dropped the worn paperback, and something fell out.

The metal was shiny, drawing her eye.

Rory reached for it, stopping an inch above as Jack glanced back into the bedroom. "You going to help me?"

"Sure. Be right there." The clock on the wall was out of batteries, and stuck at 11:11, which Rory took to be a fortuitous sign.

She grabbed the flat rectangular object, and the ground gave out from under her.

10

Silas rarely drove, let alone in the middle of a storm this bad. Being from Manhattan, he'd take rideshares, taxis, or the Metro. His confidence had been low at the beginning of his trek up the coast, heading north toward New Hampshire, but after an hour, he felt comfortable enough to ease his grip on the steering wheel. His hands ached, and his wrists burned.

But as he neared his destination, the rain that had been pouring for the entire trip turned to hail. It walloped the car, and he was glad he'd bought the extra insurance.

"It won't matter if you get shot," he reminded himself. His voice was scratchy after not speaking to anyone since his call with Special Agent Waylen. He'd promised to offload the secret object to the FBI, and Silas still believed that was the best idea. But he also worried they might be stepping into a trap that would see this… organization, or whatever they were, secure the second and third pieces of the triangle in one fell swoop.

The ocean swelled and bashed against the rocky coast, and it carried over the stone wall separating the street from the shore. Water gushed onto the road, and Silas steered into the wrong lane, avoiding it. Traffic was non-existent, because they were all smarter than him. Silas wished he'd gone home. He could have hidden the object in a bank's safe deposit box until the FBI showed up and took it from him.

Silas dialed the special agent, and Waylen answered. "*Where... driving... stuck.*" He sounded like he was underwater.

"What's that? I'm almost there. You said we should meet up first."

"*Is that better?*"

"Yes."

"*I stopped under an overpass. This storm is getting worse, and the highway's washed out. I have to go around.*"

"How long?"

"*Give me another forty,*" Waylen said. "*Where are you?*"

"According to my GPS, I'll be there in ten."

"*Park down the block and stay hidden. It'll be obvious if he sees someone. They'd have to be stupid to be out in this.*"

"Like us?"

"*Yeah, like us.*"

"If he's hurt Rory..."

"*No heroics, Silas. Just wait for me. We'll stop him and save your friend, okay?*"

'Friend' was pushing it, but they shared an important connection. "Deal."

Waylen said something that was too garbled to make out, and the call died. Silas pulled onto the road, and when he arrived on the proper block, he slowed and parked under an enormous oak tree. Silas peered at the giant branch swaying in the wind.

"Please don't break," he whispered.

Silas gathered his bearings, locating the Swanson-owned residence. A car was in the driveway, suggesting they'd arrived. He sifted through his texts with Waylen to retrieve a photo of the abductor. He'd been driving earlier, so he hadn't viewed the face up close.

Silas zoomed, pinching his fingers on the screen, and

realized he'd seen the man before. But where? Those eyes…

"Damn," he said, and tried to dial Waylen. His phone showed no service again. He pictured the event in New York last autumn and remembered bumping into the guy near the bar when he'd ordered a gin and tonic for his date. The stranger had stared at Silas, then quickly apologized and asked about the charity event. After that, Silas discussed the cause a bit.

Silas usually left social obligations to his father or sister, but both had been tied up, so he'd gone in their stead. The only reason he recalled any of the details now was that the man had asked about Commander Gunn. At the time, he'd found it off-putting. Silas didn't even know if he'd said his last name. Later, he asked an acquaintance about the man in the tuxedo, and they just shrugged, saying he worked for some rich investor.

He returned his attention to the house and saw a shadow walk by the windows on the second story. The hail clicked on the hood, but probably not hard enough to cause much damage. The massive tree limb swayed languidly, and he worried it would damage the car. But it also offered the best cover from the storm, and a view of the place across the street and down a hundred yards.

The same silhouette advanced to the next window, then the next, and the head bobbed down the stairs. If Rory was with this man, she might be alone on the second floor. Silas reached under the seat for the gun and shoved it into his pocket. He confirmed the safety was on and left it in place.

With a deep inhale, Silas checked the time, judging Waylen a good ten or fifteen minutes away, and that was if the roads hadn't been washed out to the north. Rory might not have that long. Silas had never claimed to be brave, but he'd truthfully rarely been tested. If Commander Gunn could fly to the Moon in a tin can, he could save Rory from her abductor. Whoever the man worked for, his people had killed Silas's grandfather, and Leigh. Neither deserved their fate, but this guy did.

Silas scanned both ways and exited the car, staying low to cross the street. The property had two oaks centering on either side of the yard, and he rushed to the nearest, pressing against the gnarled bark. Water dripped from above, but the branches, thick with large leaves, blocked most of the incoming rain. Bits of hail clipped the sidewalk, quickly melting in the warm air.

For a minute, the inclement weather seemed to subside, and Silas glimpsed clear skies to the east. The winds died off, making the entire area silent. The leaves no longer splattered and slapped one another, the puddles growing calmer as the rain ceased falling.

A woman opened the door across the road, peering out. "Harry, I think we might be in the clear!" She closed it again, and Silas breathed a sigh of relief when she didn't spot him standing in the middle of an abandoned house's yard.

His phone vibrated in his jeans pocket, and he grabbed it. He had reception again. Before he could dial Waylen, a second message came from Rory's social media login.

The weather's crazy, but I'd love to meet up.

Silas glanced to the house, finding the man's shape bent over a cell phone. He winced and hovered a finger near the screen's keyboard. *Can't do it. Went to Oklahoma for a last-minute work emergency.*

The guy stood taller, and Silas heard the swear through the glass, then saw three dots appear on his cell.

Where you staying? I'm near the airport. I can come meet you.

Silas thought about the traveling conditions and was surprised anyone would believe he'd gotten on a plane in the middle of a hurricane warning. *It's downtown. I'll check the name.*

Where was Rory? He hadn't seen any sign of her since arriving, and it had him worried.

Listen… I read what you said earlier, about someone coming for me. I think he's close. I have the object. Let's get together.

Silas read it twice, and noticed the guy turn his head toward the stairs, like something had alerted him. The momentary relief from the storm was at an end, and the wind blasted in with more ferocity than before. He tried to send a message, but the network failed again. Hail came in sideways, battering his jacket, and Silas rotated around the trunk, staying out of sight.

"Hurry up, Waylen," he pleaded.

He watched as the guy returned to the stairs and ascended to the second floor. When the figure could no longer be seen, Silas walked to the front door and tested the handle. The lever depressed, and he entered as quietly as possible. He carefully avoided the slippery pools of rain as he sneaked into the home, securing the door behind him. With a quick peek outside to make sure Waylen hadn't arrived, he grabbed hold of the stair banister while removing the gun from its hiding place. Silas flicked the safety off and shuddered a breath, his nerves getting the best of him. This wasn't a game. It was life or death. For what? A piece of metal? He wanted to throw the thing at the abductor, and trade for their lives.

With a new plan in mind, he tip-toed up the steps.

"Great, what the hell's happened in here?" a voice asked from one of the rooms.

Silas crept closer, emulating the protagonists from movies he'd seen in similar situations, but he'd never noticed their hands shaking like this. He had to keep his finger farther from the trigger to prevent himself from accidentally firing it.

"Rory, quit messing around!"

Silas arrived at the right room, seeing shadows on the carpet. He risked a glance, and found a woman sprawled on the floor. The man lingered over her, snapping a finger inches from her face. Was she already dead? Had he been too late? But the captor seemed as surprised by her position as anyone.

"I know you're faking it."

With a better view, Silas spotted the familiar metal object in Rory's grip. Without thinking, he dashed into the room. "Get that out of her hand!"

11

Rory knew precisely where she'd been transported to, and it immeasurably terrified her. There were a few foot-prints on the gray sand, which she knew from her extensive research was called lunar regolith. She briefly wondered if she'd been shot by Jack, and was possibly bleeding out in the very room her grandmother had left the world behind in. If so, Rory could accept her fate. This truly was a view from the heavens. She smiled to herself, feeling a slight burning in her chest. Her eyes were dry, and she lifted her hand, finding her fingers to be paler than a phantom's.

She gazed up, staring at the Earth. It was the most spectacular sight of her life. Of course she'd seen photos taken by lunar landers, but nothing could prepare you for the real thing. When she was a kid, her parents took her to the Grand Canyon, and she'd spent a week reading about the geological wonder. But when she arrived, the sheer scope of the canyon had shocked her to tears.

Rory had heard of the Overview Effect, and finally understood why people experienced it when seeing Earth from afar. She tried walking forward, but her feet were planted on the ground.

Rory…

The voice was distant, from inside her head.

Then she noticed it.

The blackness was darker than anything she'd ever witnessed. It hovered a foot over the ground, and she crouched, peering below it. Grainy bits of dust lifted from the Moon's surface into the opening. Above it, inky blotches rose into a thin atmosphere before vanishing.

"It's a hole," she said, but her voice didn't extend past her own mind.

Rory, come back…

She didn't recognize the voice, and it felt like a trap. Rory struggled to recall why she was here. Her fingers reached for the hole, her arm an apparition.

Rory looked at her hand, finding the metal piece she'd discovered in her grandpa's paperback Western. Blood welled around her palm, and she jolted upright, letting it go.

She was in a bedroom, the blood real, the bookmark on the floor with red splattered around it. Rory's breaths were labored, like there wasn't enough air in the world to fill them. Her legs gave out, and she fell to the carpet, landing in a heap.

"Don't touch it!" someone shouted.

"Why? I don't get it," the other said. Rory recognized the voice as Jack's. She tilted her chin and dry heaved, coughing and hacking until her eyes filled with white light.

"I have to find a glass of water," the first one said.

"Move and I'll shoot you," Jack told him.

Rory managed to control the coughs, and she wiped her lips with her forearm, sitting against the nightstand. Her gaze flicked to the second man, who also held a gun. "Silas?"

Jack laughed, the sound uncomfortable. "You brought it here? Saved me traveling around to search for it. Nice try, Oklahoma. How did you know I had her here, of all places?"

Rory wondered if this was all a dream, and her experience on the Moon was reality. Silas had come to rescue her?

The object lay on the floor, and Jack's gaze lingered on it. "Pass it over."

Rory shook her head, moving farther from the thing. Her hand stung where the edges of the metal had dug into her flesh. "No."

A switch flipped in Jack, and he kicked a plastic garbage can, sending it flying across the room. "Give it to me!" He fired the gun at the ceiling, blasting a hole into the plaster. White flecks drifted down to land on his shoulders.

"I'll do it." Silas walked to it, not letting his gaze leave Jack. He turned toward Rory. "We'll be okay," he whispered. "You can have both. Just let us leave."

Jack grinned and nodded. "Sure. Whatever."

Silas picked up the stained bookmark by using the whiskey bag in his hand, and Rory noticed how carefully he avoided touching it. Instead of offering them to Jack, he tossed both onto the bed and helped Rory to her feet. His grip was firm, but didn't hurt. Silas propped her up, taking half of her weight, given the weakness lingering in her knees. Her breaths came in ragged gasps, as if her lungs had been damaged.

"Downstairs!" Jack yelled.

"We're leaving," Silas told him.

Jack smirked and shot Silas.

Rory tumbled to the floor again, this time landing with a semblance of grace. Silas's shoulder recoiled, and the gun fell. Jack was on it, snatching the weapon, and he booted Silas in the wound. Blood welled through Silas's sleeve where the bullet had struck, and he grunted in ago-ny. Rory peered behind him, finding spatter on the wall. She thought that meant there was an exit wound, which gave him a better shot at recovery. If they could get out alive.

"You okay?" she asked him.

Silas' face was pale, and he cradled his injured arm with the other hand. "I will be."

"I said, downstairs." Jack hauled Rory up while Silas climbed to his feet, glaring at his attacker.

Rory and Silas went ahead, plodding down the steps with Jack muttering to himself as he clutched the bag.

"You said we could go," Silas said.

"The boss will be happy," Jack mumbled. "On the couch."

Silas waited for Rory to sit; then he took the spot right next to her. She already had her belt off, and wrapped it around his shoulder, cinching it tight. "Is that bearable?"

"Think so." Silas groaned, but she thought the flow was already improving.

Outside was dark, despite there being most of the day left. The overhead clouds were enraged, the wind blasting the home. Shutters clattered against the window frames, and Rory watched as the oaks danced back and forth. A large limb sat broken and drooped to the grass in the yard.

Jack set the bag on the coffee table, out of reach, and slid his cell from a pocket. He peered at them as he dialed a number. A muffled voice spoke from the speaker, but Rory couldn't decipher the words. "Hey, I got the artifacts."

Jack's eyes grew wider, and he blinked, looking at the floor. Rory peered at the gun in his pants that he'd taken from Silas, then at the front door.

"Okay. I'll report back."

A pause.

"Two."

Rory's throat ached as she swallowed.

"Understood." Jack met her gaze, and she realized he'd been instructed to kill them.

"We can help," she said with tears in her eyes. They began to fall, and Silas, despite his gunshot wound, held her hand while they awaited their fate.

Jack slipped the two flat metal pieces out and dug into his jacket, removing another matching whiskey bag. Rory could only assume this came from Fred Trell. He had all three side by side, and she noticed he hadn't touched any of them with his skin.

Jack appraised the tokens, and from this angle, all three appeared to be identical. "He told me to kill you."

"Who is he?" Silas asked.

"That's none of your business."

"He's an investor or something."

Jack looked at Silas for a moment. "We've met, haven't we?"

"At the gala."

"Right."

Rory had no idea what they were talking about.

"You asked about Commander Gunn. I should have realized something was off," Silas said.

"Those were the early stages." Jack grabbed the metal bookmark on the right edge, the one he'd already been carrying.

Rory gasped, expecting him to have an out-of-body experience like she had. But nothing happened.

"Why can't you touch them?" Jack flipped it around, showing them how harmless it was.

Silas squeezed her hand once, comforting her.

"They only affect the family members," Rory quickly said.

Jack's brow furrowed. "How would that even work?"

"They must be linked to our grandparents' DNA."

Jack paced while holding his prize. "That complicates things, if you're telling the truth. Are you, Rory?"

She nodded as sincerely as possible. "Why would I lie now that you've found it? Grandpa Swanson used to regale me with tales of his Moon landing, and how they stumbled upon the hole."

"The hole?"

"It's how you access other worlds," Rory said. It was a theory, but the evidence made it seem plausible. Jack had spoken about visiting worlds with the triangle earlier, and then she'd encountered the mysterious darkness mere minutes ago.

"I need to test it," Jack said.

"Let us help," Silas told him. "We're as invested in this as you are."

Jack eyed Silas with suspicion, but clearly he was curious. "My boss warned me not to connect them."

Rory observed with nervous energy as Jack stretched his finger toward the second metal strip. This was it. He stopped an inch short and shuffled to the fireplace. The lights flashed off as the storm grew in intensity. She'd seen Jack agitated earlier, but now he looked ready to explode.

"I don't trust either of you," he said.

"We're being honest. Put them together, and we'll show you how to use the triangle," she lied. "Imagine how impressed your boss will be when you can demonstrate its power."

Jack's cheek twitched, but he returned to the coffee table. "Fine."

The shutters bashed into the frames, and Rory flinched as another oak branch snapped off, falling to the sidewalk outside. Jack didn't even pay attention. He took the second metal bit, making Rory tense.

The moment he had hold of it, his eyes rolled into his head, and he fell sideways, hitting his temple on the coffee table's ledge. Rory was out of the seat, speeding to the kitchen. She searched the drawers and eventually found a roll of duct tape in the pantry. Her grandfather had used it for everything, and she silently thanked him for leaving this behind.

Silas had Jack flipped onto his stomach, and Rory tugged on the tape, wrapping it around his wrists to secure them. She was careful not to brush the object in his palm. When they felt confident he couldn't escape, Silas hauled him up with a grunt, and pushed him into the couch.

"Now what?" Rory asked, glancing at Silas.

"We wait for the FBI."

"What's this really about?"

Silas checked his arm, and Rory helped keep him steady. "I don't know, but we're going to find out."

12

Special Agent Waylen Brooks parked out front, beyond a broken tree branch. When he dialed Silas' number, the man answered in a flash. "Have you seen anything?"

"*Come inside*," Silas responded.

It had taken Waylen an extra fifteen minutes, and he had a sinking feeling that Rory was already dead and the abductor gone. The hurricane had hit the southern coast, and the weather had pummeled his current location. He fought the deluge and jogged up the steps, gun in hand. Waylen didn't knock as he bolted into the home.

He was shocked to find Rory and Silas standing over a man in the dim room. "What happened?"

"Who are you?" the woman asked. Her eyes looked red and puffy, and he'd appeared much the same after his lunar experience. He wondered if she'd had a similar vision.

"Special Agent Waylen Brooks, but you can call me Waylen. You're Rory Swanson," he said, and she nodded. "And who is that?" It was the guy from the camera footage he'd watched mere hours ago.

"He went by Jack, but I doubt it's really his name," Rory told him.

The man's head bled from a scalp wound, and his arms were tied behind his back. Waylen noticed his straining breaths. "Is he…"

"Yeah, we tricked him into touching the real token," Silas said.

Waylen finally noticed that his younger friend had been shot. "You okay?"

Silas shrugged and grumbled from the motion. "Maybe we can visit a hospital."

"We should take it back." Waylen pushed Jack forward and slipped on a pair of nitrile gloves from his pocket. Jack threw up the moment Waylen removed the object in his grip. The man that had abducted Rory from her guest house and broken into the hangar to steal NASA property stared blankly into space.

Waylen gazed at the piece, and then at the other two on the table. "We have them all?"

"I don't think so." Rory walked to the pair on the wooden surface and shakily reached for one. She snatched it, but there were no ill effects. "I believe Fred Trell had a fake."

"I'll be damned," Waylen whispered, and processed the information. They had footage of the guys they'd met in Loon Lake stealing the whiskey bag from Trell's storage unit, but nothing else had been sorted through, which suggested Fred had left the duplicate in plain sight. Waylen gathered them all, slipping them into one bag, and pocketed the treasures. Two people had already been killed because of these, possibly more in the earlier stages of their hunt. He needed to be extra cautious with them.

"You don't know who you're messing with," Jack spat, finally coming to.

"Then enlighten me," Waylen said.

Jack's phone beeped, and Waylen patted the guy's jacket, finding its hiding spot. The text was from someone labeled as: B. "Is this Bobby?"

Jack's surprised expression told Waylen he was right.

When Waylen had interrogated Bobby in the hospital, he mentioned traveling to the East Coast. "We're about to get some company." He rushed to the windows and flipped open the blinds.

"Who? Those goons that killed my grandpa and Leigh?" Silas asked.

"Yes."

Silas had a gun in his non-dominant hand, and he aimed it at the front door. "Good." It was fairly obvious to Waylen that his aim was off, but he didn't comment.

Waylen tried to think, but all he could do was concentrate on the meaning behind the trio of objects presumably brought to Earth from the Moon. They only had two, if Trell's was a fake. That left the last a mystery. Waylen didn't know what their purpose was, but he had a very strong and validated suspicion it was important.

"We can't stay here," Rory said. "Let's get the hell out."

Rain splattered hard against the windowpanes, filling the room with white noise. "I can't do that. I'll call it in and have the local PD pick him up. Then we'll bring Silas to a hospital."

Another text appeared, and Waylen read it.

Is the storm passing?

"What will convince them to leave and not come back?" Waylen asked Jack.

"Like I'd tell you." Jack struggled to free his wrists, but Rory had used half the roll on him.

Waylen took a chance. *All clear. No need for umbrellas.* He hesitated and hit send. No message came in response, and Waylen hoped that was a good enough signal that Jack didn't require his henchmen's help.

Rory waited at the living room window, peering at the street as the weather battered the area. "Someone's here."

Waylen grabbed his own phone and dialed 9-1-1. "Yes, we need assistance at…" He gave the address, and quickly explained to the dispatcher that there were already gunshot wounds on site. Waylen mentioned he was an FBI agent, reciting his credentials. He hung up before she could respond and ran to the edge of the room, watching as the thugs he'd encountered halfway across the country strode up the sidewalk.

"What do we do?" Rory asked.

Jack had dropped the third gun, and Waylen passed it to the woman. "Go hide in the kitchen. I'll come for you when it's over. You too, Silas."

"No way," Silas muttered. "They killed my grandfather. I won't let them hurt anyone else."

Waylen cringed, knowing he shouldn't be agreeing with this condition.

"They're inside! Kill them all!" Jack shouted so loudly, it hurt Waylen's ears. He clipped the guy in the head with the butt of his gun, silencing him as he slipped from the couch to the hardwood floors.

"Do you have any more of that tape?" he asked, and Rory quickly obliged, slapping a length over Jack's mouth.

Bobby and Shane obviously heard him, because they ran faster. Waylen lunged to the entrance, flipping the bolt before they arrived, and stood there while they tested the handle, banging ferociously. He didn't react until a gun was fired, and he worried the bullet would penetrate the thick door. Waylen jumped to the side, staying below the window, and watched as Rory slipped into the kitchen. Silas was in the hallway, peering around with wild eyes.

Waylen hadn't needed to shoot anyone during his tenure on the police force or with the Bureau until a day ago. Or was it two? He couldn't even recall. The duo no longer made any noise, and Waylen risked a peek through the blinds, finding the front steps devoid of the figures.

"Where are the other exits?" he asked Silas, but he shrugged.

"I came in there." Silas pointed at the door. "Then I went upstairs."

"Stay put." Waylen rushed into the kitchen, and didn't see Rory. The pantry was closed, and he silently thanked her for obeying his command. The rear entry had glass panes covering the top half, with curtains tied at the middles, giving a full view inside the home. Bobby arrived with a sneer.

Waylen listened for sounds of sirens, but couldn't hear any beyond the noise of the storm surrounding the house. They were close to the ocean, and the waves battered loudly against the cliff side. From the back, all he saw were black twisting clouds, their fury about to be unleashed on the coastline. They didn't have long.

Bobby's arm was in a sling after his visit to the hospital, but he shattered the glass with his gun, reaching in to turn the lever and unlock the door. Waylen hesitated for a moment, waiting for his attacker to step into plain sight, and the man saw him at the last second.

Waylen's bullet went wide, striking the cabinets. Bobby barreled into Waylen's chest. They tumbled to the ground, his back hammering into the wall. A serving bowl fell and shattered on the tiles.

"This is going to be fun," Bobby said, standing and cracking his knuckles. Waylen's pistol had fallen in the altercation, and he lunged for it. Bobby moved faster, and it skidded across the room, hitting the kitchen island.

"We can work something out," Waylen said.

"No. We can't."

Bobby aimed, but didn't have a chance to pull the

trigger. Rory stalked in, firing three times, each punching the broad assailant. Two blasted his chest; the third hit him directly in the neck. He wobbled on his feet for a gurgling exhale and dropped hard.

"I told you to hide in the pantry," Waylen scolded. He tapped Bobby with his shoe, making sure he was really dead, and retrieved his gun.

"You could say thank you," Rory told him. She didn't seem shaken by her actions, but the shock would eventually come after the adrenaline disappeared.

Silas arrived, gawking at the sight. "He's…"

"Yeah, Bobby's gone."

More glass shattered, this time from another wing on the main floor. "What's over there, Rory?"

"Garage," she said.

When they returned, Jack was missing. "Silas, you should have stayed with him!"

"Sorry, I heard the gunshots—"

"Get upstairs. I'll handle this." Waylen removed the bag and gave it to Rory. "If anything happens to me, keep these safe. Understood?"

Rory took them hesitantly. The duo turned and hightailed it up to the second level as Waylen paused, trying to detect Shane's location.

The storm worsened by the minute, making him worry they might be swept into the ocean before the hour was through. The police were likely dealing with a million issues, and with half the streets overflowing, it could be hours before help came.

Jack's arms were secured, and his mouth covered with tape, but if he met up with Shane, that would change. Waylen wished his partner, Martina Sanchez, was there. He'd grown used to her constant presence during a case.

The hall was long, with a few rooms connecting onto

it. He passed what resembled an indoor greenhouse. Dried-up plant husks remained in earth-scented pots, the musty smell lingering after sitting empty for years.

He slowed at the next with the sound of whispering. "That's right. Shane says he's with the FBI. Yes, *the* Bureau. Don't worry, they won't know you're involved, sir. It'll look like the storm took them to sea. Yes, sir. I believe we're missing Trell's. Yeah, it's a fake. We'll take care of Sanderson after this."

Waylen absorbed the one-sided details of the conversation, and it became obvious they were done on the phone. Jack had been speaking to his boss. Even if Waylen got Jack's cell, he assumed the boss wasn't dialing from his personal number.

The footsteps clipped behind him before he noticed the shadow on the floor, and something struck the back of his neck. Waylen gasped and staggered to the open doorway, where Jack faced him, holding a gun. Shane was behind, a metal barrel pressed into Waylen's spine.

"My boss wants to know why the FBI is involved in this case, and who's in charge of your operation," Jack said.

Waylen knew this was about to become a hostage situation with the police on the way...he hoped. "Go to hell."

Jack punched him in the gut, and the air rushed from his lungs.

"I saw the Moon when I touched it. Have you experienced that? It's real, and it works," Jack said. "Drop your weapon, Special Agent."

Waylen slowly rose, considered his odds, then did as ordered. He caught a reflection in a framed picture on the wall coming from the front yard.

13

Silas glanced outside, smiling as Rory bolted from the property, heading to his car rental. The lights flashed on as she fired the engine to life, and he continued watching until she was farther down the street.

With the mysterious items extracted from the scene, Silas almost considered bolting too. But Waylen had done his best for them, and he wouldn't abandon him in his moment of need.

Silas's shoulder hurt, but the tourniquet had stopped the blood flow. He couldn't feel much in his right arm as he tested the mobility, finding he could lift it high enough to aim a gun. He knew there was a better chance of defending himself with his dominant grip. The pistol was heavy on his sore side, but he left it there anyway, and started to creep from the second floor. He used both hands, helping burden the weight.

"Toss them over," someone said.

Silas stayed crouched by the banister, and spied two figures, then the third. Waylen was on his knees near the fireplace, his fingers intertwined behind his head. They'd kill him the moment they discovered the bag was missing. Jack and his sidekick had their backs facing Silas, but he doubted he'd get a clean shot off, not from twenty feet away. He'd need to be closer. Shooting and missing would get Waylen and himself killed.

"Sure, give me..." Waylen reached into his pocket slowly, probably trying to buy time. Despite the phone call to the police a few minutes earlier, there was no audible sound that help was coming.

Silas kept low and slipped from his shoes, deciding that socked feet would be far less disruptive. He left the shoes on the steps and slunk behind the couch. His knees ached as he waited, but he'd cut his distance to the men in half. He could make that shot. At least one of them would be injured, letting Waylen stand a fighting chance.

"I've misplaced them. They must be in the kitchen... with Bobby."

"Jack, this guy's messing with us."

"Shane, stay with him. I'm checking."

The big man oversaw Waylen, who remained in position on the floor. Silas circled behind the end of the sofa, keeping out of sight as Jack went by.

"Son of a bitch!" Jack kicked something in the other room, and the cookware clattered onto the tile. "You killed Bobby."

"I failed at Loon Lake, so I had to finish the job," Waylen said with an unforgiving level of callousness.

Jack stormed back, and Silas noticed Waylen peering at his position. Silas met his gaze, and Waylen blinked three times.

Silas raised three fingers. *On the count of three?* he mouthed, then Waylen nodded.

"Tell me where they are." Jack shoved a gun at Waylen's cheek, nearly knocking the agent over.

One.

"I hear something." Shane cupped a hand to his ear. His accent placed him from Staten Island.

Two.

"Police are on the way," Waylen said.

Three.

Silas rose, supporting the weight of the pistol, and shot at Shane. He figured Jack was in worse shape, and he was far smaller than the lumbering man with a beard. It didn't hurt that Shane was the one who'd ended Silas' grandfather's life.

The bullet hit him in the stomach, and the moment the sound rang out, Waylen was on his feet, tackling Jack. Another shot blasted into the ceiling, sending more plaster to the floor, and Waylen shoved a knee on Jack's chest, decking the man in the cheek. Even with the remnants of duct tape on his wrists, Jack punched at Waylen, but the FBI agent had the upper hand, and the training to subdue his opponent.

Silas arrived, ready to put a bullet into either of the men, but it wasn't necessary. Shane bled as he thrashed, and Silas snatched his weapon.

Jack gave up, resigned to his fate. "He'll never stop. It's too important."

Sirens grew closer, and spinning lights finally shone through the glass as they parked across the street. One squad car didn't stop there. He drove into the yard, a pair of armed officers quickly sprinting the distance to the house.

They were followed by a guy with a battering ram, and both stepped aside as he bashed it near the handle. The door flew open, and they entered, weapons raised.

"I'm Special Agent Waylen Brooks!" Waylen shouted before they could act. "This is my friend. And these two men need to be in custody."

"Are there any more?" An older officer asked, his face covered with deep wrinkles.

"In the kitchen," Waylen said. "We have another victim on the second floor. She was the one abducted from

Woodstock."

"Rory's gone," Silas said. "She took my rental."

"What's your name?"

"Silas."

"I'm Police Chief Wolanski. What kind of rental, son?" the gruff officer asked. "So we can put an APB out."

Silas described it, giving the make, color, and rental company he'd borrowed it from, then observed as they secured the duo, Shane bleeding from his gut wound.

Waylen chatted with the officer in charge and returned to Silas' side. "Let's get you examined. The EMT's here."

Silas had lost a decent amount of blood, and now that the threat was finished, he stumbled down the steps. Waylen caught him, and Silas noticed the aging cop on his cell phone, not the radio.

"…Rory Swanson. Yes. Bring her in…" The words were muffled in the fury of the storm, but Silas was sure he'd heard something about a bag.

Silas gaped at Wolanski as he ended the call, acting completely innocent. "Waylen," he whispered as a young female EMT unbuttoned his shirt to examine his wound.

"You're in expert hands," she told him.

"Waylen!" Silas snapped, getting the agent's attention.

"What?" Waylen's eyes were dark slits.

Silas glanced around, making sure no one was listening. The EMT continued her assessment, and he grimaced when she pressed the bullet wound with a gloved finger.

"They know about the bag. I overheard Wolanski mentioning it," Silas said.

Waylen squinted at the chief, who happened to be directing the pair in custody into a second ambulance. Silas finally realized the storm had slowed, moving farther north, but the road was still covered in a foot of water, the drains doing their best to redirect the flooding.

"Damn it," Waylen muttered.

"What should we do?" Silas asked.

"Stop them." Waylen pulled a set of keys from his pocket, and as much as Silas wished to go with the FBI agent, he stayed, gritting his teeth while the EMT patched him up.

Rain battered into the windshield, and the wipers couldn't move fast enough. Rory looked for her phone, but realized it must have fallen out at some point. The storm wreaked havoc on the area, and not only were the streets filled with water, but many trees had also fallen, dropping across sidewalks, crushing cars, and blocking her path.

Rory didn't slow, opting to crash through the debris. Her lights barely seemed to be on, even with the glimmer of the sloshing water, and everything was too dark. She continued to check behind her, worried the goons might have escaped the house to track her.

It seemed like she was in the clear.

"Where do I go?" Rory hadn't thought that far ahead when Silas handed her the rental's keys and the satchel filled with the metallic pieces. Water seeped through the crack at the bottom of her door and began pooling near the pedals. If it became any deeper, she would come to a halt.

There was no one else stupid enough to be on the roads, not in the aftermath of the storm. While it was improving, it remained treacherous out, though it was much better than twenty minutes ago. Rory wondered if the worst was over, or if this moment of reprieve was a fleeting thing.

A pair of headlights shone from ahead, a large SUV facing her. It flashed the brights, and Rory slowed, trying to see past the windshield. They blinked again, the white glare blinding her. Now she was angry. Rory hit the gas, seeking to drive around the SUV, and it hurried to attempt a block. Were they well-wishers, warning her of some hazard, or had Jack's boss sent someone to retrieve the bag? She'd rather risk flooding the car than dying at their hands.

Rory sped up, which wasn't easy in the deep overflow, but she managed to skim the bumper of the opposing vehicle. It clipped her rear end, but she stayed straight, moving past them.

The SUV turned and followed. Rory cursed under her breath and kept going. The other vehicle was faster, more equipped for the poor weather conditions.

Rory stared forward, avoiding tree limbs, parked cars, and anything else floating in the water. She concentrated so hard on not crashing, she didn't notice the SUV right on her tail. It bumped into her, and the car slid sideways. Rory gave the pedal everything she could and pulled away. The SUV quickly caught up.

Her breathing picked up speed as adrenaline coursed through her. This was it. She'd never write that new novel, or prove to herself that she even had it in her. Rory Swanson wouldn't get her second chance after wasting a decade in an abusive relationship. This summer was supposed to be the start of her transformation into a new woman, a better author, daughter, and friend. Instead, these men would kill her, take the artifacts from the

Moon, and leave her corpse behind.

The SUV hammered her bumper, and she tried to steer out of the skid. It didn't work, and the last thing she saw was the fire hydrant poking from the flooded street. Her hood smashed with the impact, deploying the airbags. Rory's face struck the fabric, and she saw white.

The horn sounded, and the lights flickered. Rory heard a car door opening and the muted noise of two men speaking in low tones.

They were coming.

14

"Where are you?" Waylen grumbled. The rain had started again with a bang, and the clouds were dark and perilous above the ocean. He'd witnessed a few big storms over the course of his life, being from Atlanta, but none quite this extreme.

This was no longer about the tokens. It was about saving a life. Rory Swanson hadn't done anything to deserve this kind of attention, and there she was, torn from her own home in Woodstock because of some artifact her grandfather had discovered on the Moon fifty years earlier. As incredulous as it sounded, Waylen believed it, because he'd touched the damned thing.

Each secondary route looked worse than the main drag running parallel to the coast, meaning Rory had likely stayed on this path. Waylen ignored the steps that it had taken to get to this point, and focused on nothing but the road and finding her.

Those men were killers. Waylen couldn't wait to retrieve Rory, then return to his office to discuss the case with Sanchez and Assistant Director Ben. They'd have insight, and he needed a team to fish out the head of this organization. Maybe the President would get involved. NASA. It would be huge.

Waylen gripped the wheel tightly and urged the car forward. Water slowed his passage, but he eventually found something. An SUV parked at a harsh angle ahead, the brights aimed at a crashed car. Had it been a Good Samaritan? His gut told him no.

Waylen killed his own headlights and pulled to the side, keeping a half a block down. It didn't appear like anyone had spotted him, or if they had, they didn't show it. With his gun in his grip, Waylen exited the car, quickly shutting the door to keep the water out. It was up to his knees, but he did his best to disregard the fact his shoes and socks were soaked.

Just when he thought he'd arrived too late, he glimpsed the first figure. The man was in a dark suit, and he held a woman. The other man was halfway in the crashed vehicle. Water shot from the damaged hydrant, making it hard to hear anything but the wind and gushing liquid.

"It's not in there!" Rory shouted when he was closer, back pressed to their SUV.

Waylen risked a glance and saw the second man shrugging at the car and grabbing a cell phone.

"We don't have it," he said into the cell.

"Where is the bag?" The bigger guy hauled Rory to the sidewalk, a meaty hand on her throat. She coughed and gripped his arm.

She tried to shake her head, but clearly couldn't move.

Waylen took a deep breath and considered giving them a chance. Instead, he rose like a shadow and slowly walked toward the rental.

"We'll tear it out of her. Yes, sir. We won't fail you."

Waylen waited until the man had ended the call, not wanting to alert whomever these hired guns answered to. Then he fired.

The bullet struck the guy between the shoulders, and Waylen shot again as he spun around in shock. The man's gun dropped from his grip, splashing into the water, and he slid down the door, bubbling below the surface.

"Let her go!" Waylen shouted.

The big man continued to hold Rory at the neck, and rotated her like a shield. He had the audacity to smile, exposing a missing tooth where the canine should have been. "The FBI agent, I presume," he said in a deep voice. He didn't give a moment of concern for his dead partner.

"Sorry, I'm at a loss. Who are you?" Waylen asked. The grip on Rory appeared to have loosened slightly.

"Do you have the bag?"

"What bag?"

"Don't play coy. We all know what we're after. Give them over, and I'll let your friend live."

Waylen glanced at Rory, then focused on the oaf holding her. "Tell you what. You let Rory go now, and you can leave."

While the man contemplated his response, Waylen lifted the gun a few inches and fired.

Rory screamed into the wind, and she fell when he released her, his hand flying to block the seeping blood from his throat. Rory scrambled away, jumping behind Waylen. He staggered, using the hydrant to hold him upright for a second, before falling face first into the water-logged road.

Rory sobbed as she hugged Waylen. When they separated, he noticed her neck was red, and he urged her to his car.

"Hold on," she said. Rory ran past the crash site, and she crouched in someone's yard, fumbling through a foot of water.

"What is it?"

She held the bag in victory, clutching it to her chest.

"I threw it out before they got here." Rory had tied the end of the satchel to an empty water bottle to keep it from sinking.

"Good plan." Waylen hesitated when she tried offering the metal shards to him. "We can't go back. The chief gave these men the order to find you."

"How deep does this go?" she asked.

"I won't know until I can follow the trail. Come on, let's get somewhere to camp for the night."

"What about Silas?"

"We'll fill him in soon."

Waylen left the two dead bodies and threw his car in reverse. As he sped for the coastline, the rain let up, and the clouds began to lighten.

Silas knew something was wrong when they packed him into the ambulance and drove him from the scene. While the paramedic bandaged his arm, he'd misplaced his cell phone, and no matter how many times he asked the woman riding with him where it was, she denied having seen it.

"I'm fine," Silas told her.

"Not my call. We've been asked to escort you," she said.

"To the hospital?"

She pursed her lips and looked toward the front of the ambulance. Silas shifted on the bed, sitting up, and winced when the bullet wound twisted. He'd thought his night was over when the cavalry arrived. Rory had escaped, and they'd managed to survive a gun battle with a gang of murderers.

Unfortunately, Silas still had a sinking feeling in his gut when they stopped a few minutes later. The rain continued to batter the ambulance's roof, but the wind had slowed.

"This is us." The woman opened the doors and helped him out.

"Silas Gunn?" an officer asked.

"Yeah."

The man's hand never wavered off his holstered pistol. The buckle was open, giving him quick access should he require it. Silas lifted his good arm and shook his head. "What's this about? Where's Special Agent Brooks?"

The officer acted confused. The paramedic shut the doors, and the vehicle sped off, the sirens coming on a moment later as they ran a red light, splashing through the waterlogged streets. "Come with me."

Silas backed up a step. "No way."

His gun lifted an inch. "Son, don't make me say it again."

"Am I under arrest?" Silas asked.

The cop flinched. "No, but Police Chief Wolanski wants a word with you."

"I've been shot, and nearly killed today. I just want to talk to my friends."

"It's okay, Barnes, I'll take it from here." Wolanski emerged from the entrance, his stride cautious.

"Sir…"

"I'm sure there are two hundred calls we're behind on, thanks to the storm." Wolanski strolled up to Silas, narrowing his gaze. Officer Barnes obeyed the command, leaving the pair of them on the sidewalk alone. "Silas Gunn. I was a big fan of your grandfather."

Wolanski wasn't young, and Silas guessed he was probably around ten when Peter Gunn made the trek to the Moon. "Me too. That man you have in custody, Shane, killed him in Loon Lake."

This seemed to surprise Wolanski. "Is that so?"

"We have to call Special Agent…"

The police chief grabbed Silas' arm, right under his bullet wound, and dragged him close enough for Silas to smell the coffee on his breath. "Listen here, you little shit. Where are they?"

"Who?"

"Not who… what. The metal triangle things. I was told they'd be here, and I need the payout."

"Who's paying you?" Silas yelled when the man's thumb pressed into his injury.

"Do you have them?" The police chief started patting him down, and Silas shoved the older man.

"Get off me."

Wolanski grinned. "Assaulting an officer. Thanks… that's all…"

Sounds of a helicopter distracted them both, and he watched the vehicle descending from the sky. The clouds had shifted from black to a dark gray, and the tops of the trees barely swayed with the wind. The leaves fluttered as the copter continued to descend, and it landed in the middle of the quiet street.

"What in the …" Wolanski reached for his holstered piece.

A woman exited the copter, and she was followed by two men in matching black suits. "Silas Gunn?" she called over the noise.

He didn't move, wondering if this was another deception to get him into the enemy's custody.

She stopped a few yards away and eyed the chief. "I've heard of corrupt cops before, but seriously? Getting paid off to release murderers? Where are they?"

"I don't know what you're talking about!" Wolanski claimed.

"I'll be taking the two into custody." She flashed her ID, and Silas relaxed slightly when he saw she was with the FBI. "I'm Special Agent Sanchez, and they're involved in a federal treason plot. They're coming to DC with me."

Wolanski visibly shrank. Likely he'd been contacted during the storm, with promises of a fat stack of cash for the simple task of recovering the metal shards, should the investor's hired goons fail to do their job. "We're investigating—"

"Let me put this to you so you understand," Sanchez said. "Bring the suspects now, and I won't run you up the flagpole in your underwear, *capiche?*"

Wolanski blanched, and Silas couldn't help but grin at the incredible woman before him.

"And give me my phone back!" Silas added.

The chief glanced at him, frowning. Sanchez backed Silas up. "You heard the man!"

Wolanski muttered something and fished it from a pocket, passing it to Silas. Then he vanished, leaving Silas in the FBI's custody. "Thanks," he said.

"No sweat." She checked her watch. "He should be here any…"

The black car slid around the corner, water shooting from the tires, and came to park right beside them. Waylen came out first, followed by Rory Swanson, and she beamed when she saw Silas.

"You're okay!" She hugged him, and it hurt his arm to return the gesture, but he did it without complaint.

"Did you…" Silas glanced at their hands.

Waylen patted his jacket pocket. "If the chief sniffs them out, he'll probably do anything to keep them. We're leaving. Sanchez, I appreciate the support."

"Do you have any idea how much trouble I'm going to be in? The pilot almost refused to leave in that storm. Ben's already been calling me every five minutes." Her phone rang again, and she grinned, flipping it to show Waylen the number. "Do me a favor, you talk to him." She tossed her cell, and Waylen caught it, hitting 'answer.'

"Assistant Director," he said. "Sorry about everything. Yeah, I asked Sanchez…" He stopped, and Silas could hear the tirade of the voice on the other end. Waylen kept the phone a foot from his ear and waited for the guy to calm before speaking. "Yes, sir. I'll be there. Tomorrow. Yes. They're coming with Peter's killer and his boss. No, sir, I don't have the top of the food chain yet, but we're working on it." He grimaced and passed it to Sanchez. "That went well."

"You still have a job?" she asked.

"Time will tell. If you don't mind, can you personally escort them to Virginia?"

Another two officers exited the police station, each hauling a perp with them. Silas had to use all his restraint when he came face to face with Shane and Jack. Shane had his stomach wrapped, and didn't look in any position to be traveling. His boss must have ordered Wolanski to keep him there.

"We'll be free within a day," Jack spat.

"Unlikely." Waylen shoved him toward the FBI agents. "Make sure they're not too comfortable." He whispered something to Sanchez. Silas wasn't certain about Bureau protocol, but the action seemed out of place. She smiled and winked at Waylen before ordering the duo into the helicopter. They watched it take off.

"Now what?" Rory asked when they climbed into the FBI agent's rental.

"I don't know about you, but I'm starving. Burgers?" Waylen turned the engine and drove inland. He retrieved the bag from his jacket and set it in a cup holder. "Just what have we gotten ourselves into?"

Silas recalled the sensation of touching the objects and realized there was still one missing to complete the triangle. "As much as I want to return to my normal life, I doubt that's possible."

"Me either," Rory said from the back seat.

Waylen glanced at Silas, then into the rear-view mirror. "The bad guys are in custody. I assume we'll encounter more, but that means we need to work faster."

Silas nodded and took a deep breath. He was alive. His phone beeped, and Silas saw a message from his dad.

You okay? Hell of a storm. With everything, we thought it best to move the funeral. It'll be in the city. This Friday.

"We'll have to find out who had Fred Trell's artifact," Silas said. "I heard them mention someone named Sanderson."

Waylen looked at him from the driver's seat. "I know where we might find some answers."

PART THREE
THE FUNERAL

1

*T*he birds chirped, drawing Rory's gaze. The sun's rays clung to the perfectly manicured hedges at the far end of the yard, and she noticed how damp the grass was. Somewhere in the distance, the sounds of underground sprinklers caught her ear, and she considered shutting the window.

Instead, she tried to ignore it, and closed her eyes. She pictured the man grappling with Waylen, and felt the trigger depress as she shot him. Rory couldn't remember how many times she'd fired, but in her memory, the chamber clicked empty as he lay on the kitchen floor bleeding. The image froze, and Waylen paused in motion. The analog clock on the wall no longer ticked, and a drop from the faucet hung in the air, pausing before it splashed into the empty sink.

Waylen? she asked, and the lapse faded while the agent rushed to the back door, stepping over the broken shards of glass. Rory followed him, and they were suddenly transported to the Moon. Her feet kicked up gray dust, and she halted when Waylen did. From nowhere, Silas appeared, staring at the hole before them. Inky black mist clung to the outer edges, and Rory glanced past her own shoulder, expecting to find her grandparents' house. Instead, the lunar module filled her view. She gazed at the Helios 15 spacecraft's blinking light from fifty miles away.

Silas reached for the hole, but Rory snapped out of it when someone knocked.

"Come in." She rubbed her bleary eyes and spun in her chair to see her father carrying a tray with coffee and a croissant.

"It's chocolate drizzle, your favorite," Oscar said, and set the tray onto the desk.

"Thanks, Dad." Rory exited her manuscript, which she'd been unable to add a single word to since returning home late yesterday afternoon.

Without comment, he sat on the bed, hands resting on his lap. "You've been through a lot."

Rory took a bite of the breakfast pastry and spilled a few crumbs onto her jeans.

"I'm sorry about Kevin, Pumpkin. And then this Jack character… I didn't know anything about whatever your grandfather was hiding. I remember that whiskey bag, but he used to tell me it held his secrets, and he'd say it so casually, I never questioned him. He was like that. Grandpa Swanson had the power to disarm anyone with a kind phrase or a simple expression. I should have sold the house, and that damned…metal bookmark would be gone."

"Then it would have ended up in someone else's possession. I'd rather the FBI keep it."

"Rory," Oscar whispered, and the mattress squeaked as he leaned forward. "I've set up a meeting with a therapist."

"Dad, I'll be okay."

"You shot someone, Rory!"

She shakily placed the croissant on the plate. "You don't think I'm aware of that? Dad, it's been a day. Can you let me process things so I can move on?"

He crossed his arms defiantly. "We shouldn't go to the funeral."

"Dad, he was your godfather."

"I don't care. They brought something back that almost got my daughter killed. None of them deserve our respect," he said.

"Or they were trying to protect us."

"Protect us? From what?"

Rory considered what Jack had told her. "He said they might change the world."

"How, Rory?"

"Jack asked if I believed in alien planets. He thought these artifacts were connected, and that they held the power to transfer us between worlds."

Oscar sat still, his brow furrowed in a deep frown. "He was clearly mad."

"Certifiable," she said. "But I touched it, Dad. I saw the Moon."

"Your mother and I are worried, and if you'd give Justine a shot, you'd feel better."

Rory had considered therapy before, but she had too much to unpack. "I really should be writing."

Oscar smoothed out the corner of the bedding and walked to the door. "I'm selling the house."

"Grandpa's?"

"Yes."

"Okay," she said, understanding she'd never set foot in it again.

"I've also called my lawyer, in case the cops decide to press you on this," Oscar said.

They'd brought Rory in for questioning, with Waylen refusing to leave her side, since their chief was obviously on the take. Wolanski had been stripped of his badge and weapon while waiting for an arraignment.

Waylen had told her that was the end of it, but she loved that her dad was prepared. "Thank you."

"The appointment is this afternoon at two. Her office is a block from Main, in the old Elmwood house."

Rory smiled, more to get rid of him than to accept. He left the door slightly ajar, like he had when she was younger.

She reopened her file and stared at the screen. It had been going well, but after the hurricane and her kidnapping, Rory was a different person: stronger, yet more depleted. She highlighted the entire ten thousand words and, without hesitating, hit delete.

There was another story to tell, one buried deep within her.

By the time she stopped typing, the sun was almost above the house, and her wrists ached. Rory checked the count, finding she'd bashed out five thousand and eleven words of a conscious stream of thought. Of course, she'd have to change the names later, but Rory had something here, a book worth writing.

She chugged the half-cup of cold coffee, and gathered the plates, bringing them to the kitchen after a brief stop at the hall bathroom. The house seemed empty, and for a moment, that frightened her. What if someone broke in? What if they held a gun to her head and…?

"There you are," her mom said, peering in from the sunroom.

"Where's Dad?"

"At the club."

"You didn't go for lunch?"

"I wasn't hungry."

Her mother never missed lunch on Tuesdays. It was her church.

"Rosalita made sandwiches. There's egg salad." Kathy stood and removed her reading glasses. Rory spied the copy of *View from the Heavens* on the coffee table.

"You're reading my book," she said.

"Yes. It's been a couple of years, and I figured I should relive Madeline's adventure."

Rory should have been honored, but she felt nothing. She methodically grabbed two of the quartered sandwich pieces and refilled her coffee cup, joining her mom in the sunroom. The windows were cracked, and a soft breeze blew in, sending the scent of fresh-cut grass through the air.

Woodstock, Vermont was so idyllic, it almost sickened her. The world was a harsh place, but Rory had grown up in the cover of all of this—the house, the wealth, the town... No wonder she'd been so weak when she finally emerged from college with her degree. She'd expected big things, but then she'd met Kevin and wasted an entire decade.

"Rory," Kathy murmured.

Rory wept into her hands, the plate of food falling to the area rug. Ten years! She sobbed, unable to hold her emotions at bay. Somewhere in there, her mother's arms wrapped around her, comforting her with gentle noises and pats on her back, but Rory wasn't in the sunroom. She was in the small bedroom in Boston, hearing Kevin shout through the paper-thin walls, breaking glasses in the kitchen and telling her how worthless she was. The tears didn't stop until she'd expunged all her pent-up frustrations and she sat with her chin drooping, the energy sapped from her body.

Her mom hadn't moved, and she kissed Rory's forehead. Rory didn't know whether to run or embrace Kathy. When she pictured the dead man's eyes staring at the ceiling, sticky blood pooling beneath him, it was Kevin's face she saw.

They remained silent for a full minute, then Rory used a napkin to dab her cheeks. "Mom, I'll go see Justine after all."

"You get cleaned up. I'll walk you there." Kathy left without another word, and Rory moved through the house like a ghost, floating up the steps to her old room from a different time in her life. She'd returned to this bedroom, not willing to spend another night in the guest house after Jack had defiled it.

Ten minutes later, they strolled down the sidewalk in silence. Kathy looked impeccable, her walking shoes matching her outfit. Rory wore scuffed black runners, jeans, and a white blouse that seemed a little too formal for her first therapy session.

They passed the bookstore, and Miss Habbishire waved, but from the look she gave Rory, she'd heard about the abduction. That meant the entire town knew. Rory recognized similar attention as they continued, and she cut into the alley, not wanting to be seen.

Her mom didn't remark, and she took Rory's hands when they reached the house. Justine's home was beautiful and one of the oldest in town, making it smaller than the massive estates, but it was pristine and well-manicured. Rory was overtaken by the scent of blooming flowers, and for a second, the scene seemed fake.

"I'll be at the coffee shop. Join me there in an hour." Kathy wandered off.

The front door opened, and a girl poked her head out. "Rory?"

"That's me. I'm here to see…" *Your mom? Your employer?* Rory couldn't tell, so she just walked up to the porch.

"I'm Justine." Rory shook hands with her. The woman had to be five years younger than her, and from Rory's experience, twenty-five-year-olds were in no position to be offering life advice.

She turned. "This was a mistake."

"I'm good at my job. Try it once and see what happens."

Rory paused and sighed, glancing at the fragrant lilacs. "You hire a landscaper?"

"Me?" Justine pointed to her own chest. "No. I'm starting out, and I do all the work by myself."

"Are you married?"

"No."

Rory squinted and gave the woman a smile. "Sorry, I've had a rough few days."

"Why don't you come in and tell me about it?" Justine asked.

Rory did, and Justine locked the door behind her. "You must be new to Woodstock."

"I've always locked the house," she said.

"I suppose with kidnappers on the loose, it's a good idea." Rory meant it as a joke to break the ice, but Justine looked alarmed.

Her office was off the living room, which notably was missing a television. Rory gazed at the built-in bookshelves, filled to the brim with countless novels, true crime volumes, and nonfiction books.

"In here." Justine motioned to the office, and Rory was glad there wasn't an actual couch for her to lie down on. They sat on opposite ends of the compact room, and Justine picked up a leatherbound journal, along with an expensive fountain pen.

Rory nodded at the pen. "A gift?"

Justine grinned and removed the cap. "Good eye."

"My parents gave me one too. When I signed my deal."

"Graduation," Justine said.

Rory glanced at her accreditation, framed in mahogany on the wall, and was impressed with the school. Justine was young, but she'd worked to get here, and had her own house and practice in an expensive town. She was already miles ahead of Rory.

"How do we begin?" Rory flexed her fingers, still aching a bit from the heavy workload that morning.

"We talk." Justine's pen touched the paper, and she glanced at Rory expectantly.

"If I start talking, you might require a refill on the ink."

"Don't worry about that," Justine said.

Rory shifted on the chair, which was actually more comfortable than it appeared. "Well, I grew up here, I left home, and now I'm back."

"Why don't we delve into the moments between those monumental occasions?"

"Anything we discuss is between us, right?"

Justine tapped the pen on the book. "Yes."

"If I told you I've been to the Moon, would you call someone to drag me out in a white jacket?"

"I've read *View from the Heavens*. Are you comparing yourself to Madeline?"

Rory considered her answer, and shook her head. "No, because Madeline had a spine. Maddy didn't let a man tell her what she could or couldn't do. She buckled down and showed the world what it meant to be a strong woman."

"And you? What is it you dream of?"

Rory laughed and covered her mouth.

"What did you find funny?" Justine asked.

"No one's ever asked me that before."

"They haven't?"

"No. My dad told me to get a proper job last week, in case my writing career doesn't take off. Does he think that's my dream? Working in a library, or teaching at a community college?"

"What do you want from life?"

"That's a loaded question," Rory said.

"That's what we're here for."

"I used to think signing a book contract was the goal. Get married. Have a kid or two."

"And now?"

"My illusions have been shattered. There's more than this Earth, this body, this life…"

Justine scribbled notes. "How do you mean?"

Rory bit her tongue and changed topics. If she spoke the truth, she might not even believe it herself. "Why don't I tell you how I met the devil?"

"Go on," Justine prompted.

"Kevin Heffernan hung out at the bookstore coffee shop near Harvard Square. Since he didn't attend, I'm now assuming he did this to find potential prey." Something odd happened. A tension in Rory's chest lifted as she spoke about Kevin to this young woman. "We're only scheduled for an hour, but this might take a while."

2

Special Agent Waylen Brooks hated waiting, and doubly so in the Atlanta field office. Even though he lived in a suburb only twenty minutes away, he rarely utilized this building. Waylen figured he spent ninety percent of his year on the road, meaning he was usually operating out of some local PD's office or a hotel room.

Compared with their headquarters in DC, this was abysmal. The water cooler was empty, the left lever broken. The fridge hummed loudly anytime someone opened the door, and the coffee always tasted gritty, like the filters were bought in bulk in the Eighties.

While he anxiously sat in the cramped boardroom, Waylen combed over his emails. There was information on the case they'd cracked before he learned that Fred Trell's storage unit had been robbed. Waylen wished he'd never talked to that proprietor, because he wouldn't be carrying around the bizarre metal tokens in his suit jacket.

Special Agent Martina Sanchez was on her own financial case, working out of DC. Waylen had wanted to visit the capital, but Assistant Director Ben had demanded he go home after the events in Rye, New Hampshire.

Waylen closed his laptop and checked the time. Twenty minutes late.

The door finally opened, and in strode Ben, his bald head beaded with sweat. He removed his wire-framed glasses, sliding them onto the table. "Waylen, you came."

"You didn't expect me?"

"I did. Sorry, I had a hell of a time getting in this morning."

"We should have talked on the phone. Or on the computer…they have this feature where you can meet with anyone around the world…"

"Cut the funny guy routine." Ben sat, and the receptionist entered with a paper coffee cup. She offered it to Ben, then slipped out without a sound.

"What's so important you flew to Atlanta?" Waylen asked.

"I gave you the go-ahead on this astronaut business because there was something happening."

"Right."

"Now we've got five bodies and two in custody. Thanks to your stunt, we've taken them from the local department and pointed fingers at their chief, claiming he was working for an unnamed clandestine organization. You also let Rory Swanson leave the state. Did I miss anything?"

"Let me break this down for you. I assume you read the report?"

"I skimmed it."

Waylen struggled to keep his composure, but did his best. "I have evidence of a guy breaking into Fred Trell's storage unit on the West Coast last week. Days later, the same truck was spotted at Loon Lake, the place where Fred's crewmate, Peter Gunn, was killed and his home ransacked. The *killers*, plural, returned and attempted to rob Gunn's neighbor, figuring she knew the location where some mysterious treasure was hidden. I shot the man, who I now know to be James Denton from Staten Island. Shane Adams is in custody, as is Francis Jack

Barker. They work for an operation in DC, and from what James told me when I interrogated him in the Campbelltown hospital, he's a man of note and plentiful resources."

Ben listened, and didn't interrupt the tightened report.

"Francis used the name Jack, and he broke into the museum, pilfering items from the Helios 15 mission. Only someone with credentials could have advised him how to pull that kind of stunt off."

"What are they after?" Ben asked.

Waylen removed the bag from his pocket and dumped the contents. Three of the tokens fell to the table. He shoved one at Ben. "This is the fake. Trell left it in the whiskey bag as a distraction."

"And those?" Ben gestured to the pair Waylen kept on his side.

"They're real."

"Real what?"

"That's what I intend to find out."

Ben sighed. "I've been asked that you stop this investigation."

"By whom?"

"You won't believe it if I tell you."

"Sir, we're onto something here. People were killed. Leigh in Gull Creek...an innocent local caught up in—"

"I said it's over. Special Agent Charles in DC is already off the case—not that he'd made any gains."

Waylen gathered the objects and returned them to the interior of his jacket. "No."

"You sent a helicopter against protocol, and you're lucky I haven't suspended Sanchez for that one. Do you have any idea how many strings I needed to pull after the hurricane? We're already under scrutiny, Waylen. The FBI isn't here on your personal whims."

"Sir, there's a person of power in DC behind this, and they're trying to find three artifacts from the Moon. We're talking about a monumental cover-up at NASA. Gunn and Swanson were on the surface, and I'm convinced they found these." He patted his chest. "Jack told Rory the combination of three might transport him to another planet."

"Do you hear yourself?" Ben laughed and sipped his coffee, scowling after he swallowed. "Give me those. I'm putting you back on Financial Crimes, but you're to take the rest of the week off."

"Sir, with all due respect—"

"Now, Special Agent Brooks. Unless you want to hand over your badge instead? I heard the retired guys make a decent living working security at the arena."

Waylen bristled and removed the bag. "Touch it."

"What?" Ben stood, but Waylen reached and grabbed his wrist.

"I'll drop the case if you hold one of these and still want me to stop," Waylen said.

"Have you lost your mind?" Ben whispered. "It might be best…"

Waylen slid the metal piece from the Swanson house out of the satchel and carefully shifted it beside Ben's coffee cup. "What's the worst that can happen?"

Assistant Director Ben exhaled loudly and lifted a finger. "All I have to do is…" He set his fingertip on it, and his eyes flew open. It was only a few seconds before he hopped to his feet, his seat clattering to the wall behind him. "What in the holy hell?"

Waylen retrieved the rectangle without making contact. "*That* is why you can't take me off the case."

Ben shook, his breathing coming in ragged gasps. "I saw the goddamn Moon."

"I'm aware."

Ben righted the chair and sat, but on the edge, as if he might bolt through the exit at any instant. "Okay, I have to tell you something."

Waylen waited, nervously kicking his leg beneath the table.

"The Department of Defense asked me to move you," Ben said.

"What? How do they have my name?"

"I assumed it was the big case you and Sanchez solved. That made headlines, or have you been too busy to notice?"

"I guess so."

"Secretary of Defense Plemmons called me himself," Ben said.

"And you didn't find that odd?"

"Not at first." Ben gazed at the bag. "But I do now."

"Ben, we've been colleagues for a long time, haven't we?"

"Sure."

"Then you can admit I've never steered you wrong."

"What about the Barbosa job?"

"Once. Sue me." Waylen smiled, but Ben wasn't there yet. He rubbed his fingertip and glowered. "I have to find the last token, Ben. There's someone in power trying to gather them, perhaps an agency."

"You're not suggesting the CIA has anything to do with this, are you?" Ben inquired.

"No. Well, probably not, but I won't rule it out. The guys he used weren't overly professional. Silas said he'd met Jack before at an event in New York, which means—"

"That's an issue too. You already got that Leigh girl killed in Gull Creek. No more consorting with civilians, do you understand?" Ben's commanding voice had returned, and he'd regained some of his color.

"Does that mean I'm still on the case?"

"I'll delay your transfer and respond to Plemmons in a few days. Whatever you have to do, get it done by this weekend," Ben said. "Because by next Monday, you'll be so deep in financial paperwork, you won't know which way's up."

Waylen doubted it would be sufficient, but at least he'd be able to follow a few leads and attend Peter Gunn's funeral. "Thank you, sir. You won't regret it."

"Oh, I already do, Waylen." Ben gestured at the middle of the table. "What are they?"

"My assumption is they were found on the Moon, sir. The trio each took a token, which implies they're meant to connect. Whatever they accomplish, Peter Gunn, Colin Swanson, and Fred Trell went to great lengths to assure no one obtained them."

"Ideas?"

"This is beyond my wheelhouse," Waylen said.

"I have a guy in Boston. He's done a few jobs with us, strictly on a contract basis. He's a bit…out there, but this might be something he could help you with. I'll send you his details."

"What kind of *guy?*" Waylen asked.

"He specialized in…alien topics."

Waylen wanted to object, but that had to be what these things were. Clearly they hadn't been designed by humans, because how would they have reached that region of Moon before the Helios 15 mission? "I'll check into it."

"Keep this discreet, Brooks. If word leaks that one of my top agents is chasing aliens, we're both in a world of trouble." Ben rose and offered his hand. "Be careful.

While I don't really understand what you've fallen into, it's obvious there are people willing to kill for…those." His gaze fell on the tokens covered in their velvety satchels.

"They already have, sir."

"What about you? Do you need to speak to someone about what happened?"

Waylen shook his head. "Not yet. Possibly when the dust settles, sir."

"Don't forget." Ben stopped at the exit, fingers resting on the lever. "And leave the civilians alone. I don't care how eager they are to help. I can't have any more deaths, got it?"

"Yes, sir." Waylen stayed seated, and a few moments later, the contact information appeared in his inbox. Assistant Director Ben moved quickly.

Waylen clicked it, and a website popped up. "UFO and UAP specialist Darren Jones."

He had to search the web to determine what the second acronym meant and read it was short for "unidentified aerial phenomena." "You learn something new every day," he told himself.

Waylen grabbed the suitcase he'd been hauling around the country and saw his reflection in the lobby mirror. He looked exhausted, with bags under his eyes and a few days' worth of stubble. His hair stuck straight up, and he realized how insane he must have looked while discussing the case. No wonder Ben wanted to pull the plug. But Waylen had the ace up his sleeve, and there was no disputing the significance of the metal tokens once they gave you a vision of the Moon.

He'd already ditched the clunky rental, and used an app to catch a rideshare home. He barely remembered waiting, but he was certain he'd fallen asleep on the way there. The driver called to him when they arrived, and Waylen offered a good tip after exiting the car.

Waylen stared at his house and tried to recall the last time he'd been home. Three weeks? A month? The grass was getting long, but the neighbor kid usually took care of that. He always made sure the house looked occupied, so he had no flyers or newspapers cluttering his front steps. It wasn't as big as most of the homes on the block, but that suited him fine. The cheapest house in a pleasant suburb was a smart buy. Eventually, he was sure, he'd move from the Atlanta area, and when he did, he'd turn a nice profit on the sale.

He used his key to unlock the deadbolt and stepped in.

Something was wrong.

Waylen separated his sidearm from its holster, flicked the safety off, and strode into the living room with caution. He toured the main floor, checking the bedrooms and closets, then stopped at the bathroom. Nothing seemed out of place.

Once he inspected the basement, he saw the unlocked window, and lifted on his toes to press the latch. Someone had been in his house, but they hadn't upended anything. Waylen sighed and guessed what had happened.

He grabbed his cell phone, calling the field office. "Hey, Reggie, it's Waylen. Can you send a team over? I need a sweep for cameras or bugs." He spoke softly, and with his mouth covered.

Reggie said they'd be over in an hour, and Waylen threw his clothing in the laundry, attempting to pretend everything was normal while he waited. These were professionals he was dealing with; that much was clear.

3

Silas shoved his hands into his pockets and walked from his suite to the elevator. The lights blinked lower as it descended, then stopped on the fourth floor, letting a woman on. She smiled politely at Silas and turned to face the metal doors.

They both got off at the lobby, and Silas waited while she left the building. He felt eyes on him everywhere he went. The doorman nodded at him, then continued reading a newspaper. Did people still do that?

"Where's Roger?" he asked the guy.

"Roger?"

"The usual doorman."

"Sure, Roger. He's sick. They called me in yesterday."

Silas glanced at his nametag. "Carl?"

"That's me."

"Have a good day."

"You too." Carl returned to the sports section.

Silas was probably being too cautious, but he couldn't get the fiasco out of his mind. He lifted his arm, noticing a slight pucker where he'd been shot a couple of days earlier. It didn't hurt all that much, but the fact they had actually hit him with a bullet was a constant reminder. He was in over his head.

He stood at the sidewalk with his cell phone as he clicked on Rory's name. *Hey, just wanted to check in.* He reread it, then deleted the text. Silas noticed he'd sent the last two messages. He almost called for a ride, but walked instead. He decided to catch the train, to prove to himself he was able. New York was a big city, and he doubted anyone was searching for him.

It was chilly for the middle of summer, and the skies held dark, angry clouds. The moment he reached Canal Street, it rained. Silas ducked into the metro station as it pounded the pavement and slid his card through the turnstile. He hopped on the local heading north, and the car halted at every station until he exited on 59th. Silas circled back, running the few blocks south, and caught the metro to Queens after being thoroughly soaked.

Where are you? The text came in from his father, and Silas waited a moment before responding.

On the train. Be there in 30.

The train? I would have sent a car.

Silas shoved the phone away and gazed outside as they bypassed the East River, then trundled on to Long Island. The car was nearly full at the start, being Tuesday at four in the afternoon, but the number of passengers quickly depleted at every stop. Soon it was only Silas and a man wearing a black trench. He wore earbuds, and the sounds of an audiobook or podcast leaked into the aisle.

Silas watched him from behind, then rose, as if he planned to leave at the next station. The guy did the same, and when the doors opened, Silas stepped out. Trench coat also left, but Silas waited and dropped into the train as the car beeped. The other man didn't so much as glance back.

"You're being paranoid," he told himself.

He walked out and was grateful the rain seemed to be isolated over Manhattan. Silas strode with purpose, taking the route he'd followed as a teenager when coming home from school. Retracing those steps was comforting, and he wondered when he'd last used public transportation to Queens.

His parents were well-off, but they lived in an upper middle-class home. The neighborhood was safe, and everyone minded their business and maintained their yards, so Silas' parents claimed there was no reason to upgrade. Plus, they had the place in Cape Cod to weekend at when they wanted to get away. To Silas, this was an escape from the city.

His sister's huge SUV was out front, and he noticed her husband's stick figure denoting their family on the rear window had been hacked off. Pieces of the sticker remained on Clare's left, then her two kids, with Buffy, her Pomeranian, next to them.

Silas had never cared for Ike, and apparently, Clare had clued in on what a jerk he was after seven miserable years. He felt for the kids, but figured they were better off with one caring parent than two distracted and miserable ones.

Before he got to the front door, it swung wide, and his mom was there with outstretched arms. "Oh my God, Silas."

"Mom, I'm fine."

She hugged him regardless, then held his hands while giving him a once over. "Does it hurt?"

"It's fine."

"Silas, they *shot* you."

"Close the door, you're letting a draft in!" Clare called from the kitchen. Buffy yipped and scratched her way across the hardwood, barking incessantly until Silas crouched and stroked her back.

The place was warm, with a fire in the hearth, and a calming classical piece drifted from the record player. Silas' mood instantly improved. "Is it okay if I crash here until the funeral?" he blurted.

"Of course, Silas." His mom ushered him in. She flipped the lock, which might have been a new thing, but he didn't recall.

"You didn't bring any clothes." His dad entered, wearing his work outfit: jeans, a dress shirt, and a black tie.

"I hadn't really thought it through," he said.

Arthur lifted his empty tumbler. "Drink?"

"I'd take a beer."

Silas ambled into the kitchen, finding Clare at the table with her two kids: Eva, six, and Branson, three. They were both in fancy outfits, Eva's locks loosely braided. Branson had a hundred-dollar cut, and a sweater that would have gained him entry into the yacht club. "Hey, gang." He moved to ruffle Branson's hair, but the boy put a protective hand up. "Right…"

"Hi, Uncle Silas." Eva smiled, showing off her missing tooth.

"What are you guys doing?"

"Drawing." Branson showed his page, which was pretty good for a kid barely out of diapers.

"Dinosaur?" Silas asked.

"Brontosnorus."

"It's a brontosaurus, honey," Clare said.

Branson frowned. "That's what I said."

Silas excused himself and got a beer from the fridge. He loved the kids, but they were well on their way to being pretentious private school brats—not that he had been much better at that age. He peered at them, and decided he wasn't nearly that bad.

The kitchen was filled with the scent of a roast, and he glanced at the stovetop, where a large pot of potatoes boiled. "Thanks for having us," he told his dad.

"We figured we should all get together before the funeral, and… I don't know. Remember your grandfather." His father took a drink, and Silas assumed it was the good stuff he kept for special occasions.

"You've never really spoken about him," Silas said, scooting a stool at the island out. Arthur sat on the one beside him, hands folded around his glass.

"Yeah, Dad. I wish we hadn't been estranged," Clare said from the table.

Arthur sipped his whiskey. "Peter Gunn grew up in difficult times. He was born after the Depression, right when things were improving, but only for those with any money or influence. His parents, my grandparents, were live-off-the-land people, and Peter was put to work as soon as he could walk." Arthur glanced at Branson, as if picturing his own grandson tilling a field, and he grinned.

"But he became an astronaut," Clare said.

"No one told that man what he should do—or, more specifically, what he shouldn't."

Silas had read the books about Peter Gunn, but they always glazed over his early years. "Did you visit their farm much?"

"Rural Kentucky. It was about everything you'd expect. Flat, unforgiving in the summer, and cold as sin in the winter, though not a lot of snow. Why they settled there is beyond me," he said.

"Dad, it's cold here in the winters," Clare said.

"But it's different. The city keeps us warm, doesn't it, honey?" Arthur asked his wife, who was in the kitchen stirring a pot. "Alice?"

Silas' mom looked up from the stove. "Sorry, I wasn't listening."

"Never mind." Arthur got up and gave himself a refill. "My grandfather was a hard man. From what I gather, he'd hit Peter, slap him with a leather belt… There were days I wished my father would do the same to me, just so I knew he saw me."

"Clare and I are grateful for you."

Arthur's smile crinkled his eyes, and he squeezed Silas' shoulder. "You were good kids and deserved your parents' attention. My mother was a different story, a real gem. I miss her."

"Mom, do you need help?" Clare asked.

"Can you check the roast? The thermometer is beside the oven."

Heat filled the room as the oven sprang wide. Silas hadn't had a home-cooked meal in far too long. While he dabbled in the kitchen, he was more prone to eating out, or having food delivered to the office. Most nights, he'd stay until seven or eight, with no real purpose other than to go home to an empty unit. Maybe his mom was right about finding someone and settling down.

He surprised himself with that train of thought, considering he'd been shot over the weekend. These people also might still come for him. Silas finished the beer, and let the effects soothe his busy mind. He wanted to relax for the night, and this was the safest option. Staying here for the week was exactly what he needed. Without him asking, Arthur grabbed him another beer and popped the cap off with an old bottle opener. It said *World's Greatest Dad* on it, and Silas remembered buying it for him when he was around ten.

Silas pointed at the opener. "It's still true."

"You're only saying that because I'm the boss," Arthur joked.

"I work there too, but I'm above sucking up," Clare said while removing the roast tray from the oven.

"Let it rest for a few, and I'll slice it." Arthur unwrapped his chef's knives and polished a blemish on the carver.

"Did Grandpa like roast?" Clare asked.

"He ate anything Mom prepared. Raised as he was, I'm sure he preferred meat and potatoes." Arthur kissed his wife on the forehead and plucked a steamed bean from the colander. "I never saw him eating sushi, if that's what you're asking."

"He liked Chinese food," Alice quipped.

"That he did… Remember that one Christmas where they came into the city and we burned the bird?" Arthur sat and smiled at the memory.

Alice removed her apron, folding it. "We took them to that dive a few blocks away. What was it called?"

"Hank's."

"Yes, Hank's. We thought we'd ruined Christmas, but Peter seemed happier to be out and eating pineapple chicken rice."

"They never came back," Arthur said.

"When was this?" Silas asked.

"Clare was two." Alice gestured to the table. "Kids, clear up your drawings. Everyone grab a plate and utensils. Dinner's ready."

That was how it was in their house. Each person set their own place. It was an odd tradition to other guests, but among their family, it was normal. Silas brought his dinnerware and occupied his usual spot, to the right of his dad at the head. Or the foot, if you asked the woman of the house. Alice always stayed the closest to the kitchen, claiming it was easier to monitor dessert.

They dug in, with Silas grateful no one discussed his recent adventure in Loon Lake, then on the East Coast. He ate, devouring the delicious roast, and poured extra gravy on the mashed potatoes. They talked about Eva's school project, and how Branson was at the top of his pre-pre-something-school.

His phone vibrated, but he ignored it, following that very important rule at the Gunn household. No devices at dinner.

"Let me clear them," Silas said, gathering the plates when they were all stuffed to the gills. Eva surprised him by offering to help, and he gladly accepted, making quick work of the task. They filled the dishwasher, and the scent of apple pie lingered in the air.

He stared at the dessert, and instead of seeing lines of steam rising from the perfectly browned crust, black misty tendrils spread above it.

"Son, are you okay?" Arthur's voice grounded him, and he blinked the echo away.

"I'm fine," he lied. "Excuse me for a second." He hurried up the stairs and jogged through the hall, into his old room. His parents hadn't waited to remodel it, and now it was a study for his father and a guest room. Reprints of Monet were on the walls in place of his old baseball posters.

Silas fished his phone from his pocket and checked the messages.

Silas, give me a call when you get this.

It was from Waylen. Silas considered responding, wishing he could just put all this mess behind him.

He scrolled to the next message and saw it was from Rory. *It's been a day. How are you doing?*

Silas sat on the corner of the twin bed and dialed.

4

Rory hung up the phone and tossed it onto her pillow. It was seven, and she hadn't smelled dinner yet. Talking with Silas had been just what the therapist ordered. Literally. Justine had suggested that connecting with the other person involved in her traumatic incident might help her cope with the situation.

He'd told her about staying with his parents for the week, and it eased her anxiety that another grown human was doing the same as her. It was embarrassing to be thirty at home, but after Jack's actions, Rory couldn't imagine being on her own.

She ventured to the main floor and checked the kitchen. Empty.

"Mom?" Rory walked into the living room. "Dad?"

The front door burst open, and Rory's heart lunged in her chest.

"Rory, where have you been?" Oscar demanded. He had a suit jacket on, and his leathery cologne wafted closer.

"In my room, writing."

"We're going to the club for dinner. I tried calling you, but…"

"I was on the phone."

"You said you were writing."

"Dad, what's gotten into you?"

"Get ready and we'll head out." Oscar smiled, but he was obviously nervous.

"Dad, what's the matter?"

"What's the matter?" he repeated. "Someone came onto our property and took you away, Rory."

She hugged herself, suddenly growing cold. "I was there."

"We should move," he said.

"Move? You can't be serious."

"Then what? These people have our address."

"Waylen…"

"Rory, would you listen to yourself? He's just one man, and from what I gathered, he works in Financial Crimes."

"He does?"

"Yes, I made a couple of phone calls. He wasn't even on this case with a partner. He randomly fell into it."

"Does that change anything?" Rory knew her father well enough to see his mind was made up on the subject. Kevin had a similar trait, and listening to Oscar was irritating her.

Her dad sighed and set his hands on her shoulders. "Pumpkin, you're everything to me. To *us*. We have to keep you from danger."

"By moving," she stated.

"Okay, that might have been impulsive. We'll go to the city for a while. Check into the Plaza under an alias."

"For the funeral?"

"I'm second-guessing whether we go or not."

"You're kidding me." Rory grabbed her shoes, slipping the flats on. "He's your godfather. Colin would be rolling over—"

"I know that!" Oscar shouted, and flopped onto the couch. "Why did my father have this *thing*? What happened on the Moon?"

Rory blinked, an idea coming to her. "Oh my God." She fumbled for her phone, dropping it. The screen was already cracked from the grocery store when she'd encountered Kevin the other morning. She found Waylen's number and dialed it, pacing the living room while Oscar stared at her blankly.

Kathy came from outside, and it was obviously raining. "What's the holdup?"

She lifted a finger while the phone rang. "Pick up, pick up."

"*Brooks,*" the voice said.

"Waylen, it's Rory."

"*Good to hear your voice. Everything okay?*"

"NASA."

"*What about them?*"

Rory stopped her long strides and viewed a photo of Grandpa Swanson with his other crew members from the Helios mission. "They have audio of the entire landing. Most of it's public, or at least available by requisition or something. I heard about it on a podcast."

"*I'll contact them in the morning,*" Waylen said. "*If anything strange occurred, we should be able to determine when it was. But I have a feeling there might be segments missing.*"

"Can they do that?" she asked.

"*Perhaps, but if they really found alien artifacts on the surface, NASA wouldn't have pulled the plug on the program. They'd have spent billions to explore the entire Moon.*"

"Grandpa Swanson must have been scared enough to want them to stay away."

"*That's what I'm thinking too. Good idea.*"

"You were already on this same trail, weren't you?"

"*Yes. But I've had a lot of time today while my place was being scanned for bugs.*"

"Termites?" Rory asked.

"No, the other kind. They did a sweep and found surveillance in three of my rooms."

Rory instinctively glanced at the ceiling. "That's horrible. Do we have anything to worry about?"

"I've been gone from home for weeks. I bet they did it while I flew into Albany," Waylen said.

"You're far calmer than I would be."

"I'm just glad I noticed something was off."

Rory lowered her voice, cupping the base of the phone in her palm. "We're heading to the city tomorrow. Will you be there?"

"Soon. By Friday, at the latest. I have a couple of leads to follow up on," he said.

"Sanderson?" she whispered.

"You got it."

Jack had mentioned a man by that name giving him the location of the fake token, but the storage unit was all the way across the country in Oregon.

"Rory…"

"Yeah?"

"How are you doing?"

She pictured his face, brow scrunched up with worry. "I shot someone that wanted to kill us. I'm fine." Rory glanced at her parents, who were trying their best not to stare while she spoke to the FBI. "I saw a therapist today."

"That's a huge step."

"I had a lot to unload; the shooting's not even halfway up the list." She laughed nervously.

"Don't we all? Keep in touch, and I'll see you at the funeral."

"Have a good night."

"You too." There was a brief pause. *"Rory?"*

"Yes?"

"Do you see it?"

"The Moon?"

"I still sense the echoes," he said.

"So do I."

"We'll figure this out."

The call ended, and she shoved the phone into her pocket.

"What was that all about?" Kathy demanded.

"I had inspiration and wanted to share it with Waylen."

"You're giving the FBI advice now?" her mother asked.

"I guess so."

"We should order in," Oscar said.

"No, let's go out." Suddenly, the house felt like a trap, and it seemed to shrink around her. Rory snatched her purse from the coat hook and walked outside, inhaling the scent of the rainstorm. The drops pitter-pattered on the cedar shingles and careened through the gutters, draining into the yard.

I still sense the echoes.

Rory closed her eyes, picturing the hole floating above the gray regolith. When she opened them, the sensation was gone.

The club was quiet, even though Tuesday was their themed night. Those kinds of places always tried to lure patrons in during the week with half-priced wine or sushi events. Tonight was an Indian buffet, and Rory peered at the offering, smiling as she recalled her favorite place in Boston, which she frequented for butter chicken and biryani. Kevin couldn't stomach the stuff, which had suited her fine. She'd go with friends, or sometimes alone, claiming she needed to do research at the library for her new book. She doubted Kevin believed her, considering she always came home with curry on her breath.

Stop thinking about him, she chided herself as they sat at their reserved table.

It was half-full, with a group of men a few tables over deep into their second bottle of red wine. Doctor Greg was with them. He waved as she took the menu off the table, and she smiled at him politely.

The restaurant grew silent when the guests recognized them. "Looks like word spreads fast around Woodstock," Rory muttered.

"They're only worried, my dear," Kathy said. "And rightfully so. If we don't watch out for each other, who will?"

Rory ignored the stares and ordered a cocktail, which she rarely did. She had a feeling it might be the only way to fall asleep. It came, and she downed half before grabbing a plate for the buffet.

The moment she got to the salad bar, Greg was behind her, refilling his dish. "I heard."

She turned to face him. "Yeah, messed up."

"Do you want to talk?"

She laughed lightly, shaking her head. "Anything but." Her parents kept going, and she caught Kathy nudging her husband with an elbow, as if to say, "Our daughter is actually talking to the doctor."

"Then how about those Red Sox?"

"I didn't put you as a baseball fan," she said.

"Why?"

"Do doctors even have time for sports?"

"Not really, but I watch the highlights," Greg said.

"I'm living in the highlights," she replied.

"What does that mean?"

Rory put a few veggies on the plate and headed to her favorites, steaming under the heat lamps. "In the last ten years, I have five moments worthy of recalling."

Greg nodded. "I guess that makes sense. I spent a decade in school, and barely remember any of it. Graduating, getting my residency, then moving to Woodstock. There were other flashes, like my sister's wedding, and the birth of their firstborn."

Rory realized that her kidnapping and the fact she'd murdered someone might rank at the top of her memories from her thirties, and that didn't sit well. "I'm leaving town."

"For good?"

"For Peter Gunn's funeral." Rory eyed her meal, watching the various portions melt into one another, blurring their edges. Kevin hated it when his salad got soggy. She dropped more butter chicken sauce on her veggies, just to spite him.

"You said you didn't want to discuss what happened, but…" Greg reached for her arm, and it took all her restraint not to flinch. It wasn't anything against the doctor, just the timing of it. He must have noticed, because he stopped and let his arm dangle. "When you're home again, I'd love to take you for coffee, dinner, a walk, whatever you want."

Rory forced a smile and glanced past him, finding her mother staring at their private conversation from across the buffet. "I'll think about it."

Greg nodded and backed away.

"Everything will be okay," Kathy said, startling her.

Rory didn't respond and followed her to their table, where her father had already begun eating dinner. He had an embroidered napkin tucked into his dress shirt above his tie, and for some reason, the sight made her laugh.

Oscar glanced behind him. "What's so funny?"

"Nothing." Rory dug in. She found herself ravenous

after a day of anxiously sitting in her bedroom.

Her gaze kept lifting to the exit, almost expecting Jack to barge through the doors, seeking vengeance, but he was locked up somewhere. Waylen had seen to it. Then she thought about his house being tapped, or bugged, with possible hidden surveillance.

The food was actually better than she expected from a WASP-y club in Vermont, and Rory drank another cocktail while finishing the last of her plate. Oscar, who often overindulged when stressed, returned with a second heaping dish, and her mom refrained from commenting, even though she looked pained to do so.

By the time the table was cleared, Kathy was on her fourth gin and tonic, and Rory declined when the server asked about a refill.

"That was nice," Oscar said decidedly, despite them having little to no conversation for the past forty minutes.

Rory recognized the cogs spinning in both of her parents' minds. Oscar was thinking about selling and getting a beach house in Florida, while Kathy was regretting ever allowing Rory to come home. At least, that was how it played in her head.

"We'll go tomorrow afternoon. I've already booked the hotel," her dad said as the valet brought their car up.

"Are we flying?" Rory asked.

"A drive would be more cathartic, don't you think?"

Rory shrugged, but dreaded the idea of sitting in the backseat for five hours with them. "Why not?"

They headed to her temporary home, and Rory checked her phone, hoping for an update from Silas or Waylen. The unlikely trio was linked to something beyond them, a mystery from fifty years ago involving her own grandfather and a flight to the Moon. Rory cleaned up in her bathroom, wiping off the spattering of makeup she'd put on, then brushed and flopped onto her bed.

She was grateful when sleep came without the misty phenomenon on the surface of the Moon grazing her periphery.

5

*W*aylen dialed the number before pulling away in his car rental.

"*Baker, Schwartz, and Klein,*" a friendly woman's voice said.

"I'm trying to reach Mr. Klein. Is he available?"

"*May I ask who's calling?*"

"Special Agent Waylen Brooks," he told her.

That always got a pause on the other end. "*And what is it pertaining—*"

"Is he in?"

"*Please hold.*" The line filled with elevator jazz, and Waylen connected to the rental, letting the Bluetooth echo the music through the car speakers.

"*Daniel Klein.*" The man sounded older, like he'd smoked a thousand cigars and washed each of them down with five cups of coffee.

"Mr. Klein, I'm Special Agent Waylen Brooks with the FBI, and I'm investigating the Peter Gunn murder."

"*A shame, what happened to him.*"

"Did you know Mr. Gunn?"

"*No, but Fred spoke highly of his commander.*"

"So you're Fred Trell's lawyer."

"*Well, I was,*" he corrected. "*Fred's estate is handled, but there are a few loose ends.*"

"Like his ongoing payments for the storage unit,"

Waylen said.

"*Yes. Among other things.*"

"It was broken into last week by the same people that killed Peter Gunn," Waylen said, knowing he was divulging too much information. In his experience, estate lawyers were mostly trustworthy, especially ones with high-profile clients.

"*I hadn't heard that. What was taken?*"

Waylen hesitated. "A trinket. Mr. Klein, who inherited Fred's estate?"

"*That's private, Mr. Brooks.*"

"It's important. We're talking about life and death."

"*I see. It's about the Delta, isn't it?*"

Waylen's arms covered in goosebumps. "Delta?"

"*The triangle,*" Daniel said.

"You've heard about it?"

"*Fred was a conservative man with a modest life. He wasn't married, had no children, but he had friends. I was grateful to be among them. It was obvious from the moment we met there was something…off with Fred, but I couldn't put a label on it.*"

"When was this?" Waylen asked.

"*In the late Eighties. We played tennis together. I was a decade younger than him, and he still walloped me on the court, nearly every match.*" Daniel gave a light laugh. "*We'd meet for dinner, joined a wine club. My wife would come on occasion and try to set Fred up with women from her charity, but he was always standoffish. It wasn't until the mid-Nineties when I realized how messed up he was from his trip to the Moon. Fred didn't go to the surface, and I think that bothered him.*"

Waylen stayed in the parking lot, rolling his window open. The sounds of an airplane taking off filled the skies.

"*One day, he invited me over for drinks. It was fall, and the sun set early on the Pacific. He had a beautiful home, a charming log cabin with views for days. I remember it like it was yesterday.*"

The fire crackled in the hearth, and he gave me expensive Scotch, the kind you only drank if you closed a big deal or were celebrating something of note. After awkwardly sitting on his leather chairs staring at the fire, he pulled a whiskey bag out."

Waylen closed his eyes, picturing the scene Daniel had set.

"It wasn't what I expected. Fred slid the metal object onto the coffee table. He told me it couldn't be melted, cut, or damaged. He'd tried everything."

Waylen touched his pocket, where the other two sat.

"I asked him what it was, and he broke down. I'd never seen him tear up before, and there he was, almost sixty, trembling with a stiff drink in his hand. I wanted to suggest he talk to someone, but kept watching the fire glint off the metal."

"What did he say next?"

"That they found it on the Moon. He wouldn't go into detail. They'd made a pact—Swanson, Trell, and Gunn—never to tell a soul what they'd discovered."

"And what did they see?" Waylen asked.

"I don't know. Fred must have realized I didn't believe him, or that I thought he was off his rocker, because he asked me to place a finger on the section of the Delta. That's what he called it."

"Did you?"

"Special Agent Brooks, have you found them?"

"Yes."

"Have you experienced what it's like?"

"I was on the Moon," Waylen said.

"Interesting."

"Interesting how?"

"Look, I shouldn't be talking about this. Fred was a private man, and they didn't want it getting out."

"It's a little late for that, Mr. Klein."

"Call me Daniel."

"Okay, Daniel, the bodies are piling up. Whoever is

after the Delta won't stop until they possess all three. I'm carrying two of them, and I need to learn where Fred's is. He had a phony in the storage unit, did you know that?"

"*Yes. I put it there after he died. It was spelled out in a letter,*" Daniel said.

"Where's the third?"

"*I couldn't tell you.*"

"Who's Sanderson?"

"*I should have seen this coming.*"

Waylen stayed silent.

"*Sanderson's a nut. He collects memorabilia. Spacesuits, back-up flags from Moon missions, bags of regolith.*"

"He lives in Oregon?"

"*California. San Diego. He befriended Fred in his final years and made off with a lot of his personal items. I always thought it was a bizarre friendship, but Fred was coherent until the end, and he could make his own decisions.*"

Waylen knew, without a doubt, that was who had the last piece of the Delta. Jack had mentioned Sanderson, and it seemed apparent that he was the one who'd pointed Shane, Bobby, and Jack at Trell's storage unit. He was probably throwing them off his own scent. It was what Waylen would have done.

"Do you have his number? Email? Address?" Waylen opened a blank note on his phone, ready to copy it down.

"*Nothing. I didn't stay in touch with him.*"

"First name?"

"*Cody.*"

"Is there anything else you can think of that might help? They murdered Peter Gunn, Daniel. I have to put a lid on this entire case," he said.

"*Be careful. Fred didn't give me the details, but whatever the Delta can do, it's dangerous. In the wrong hands, at least.*"

"Can you explain—"

"I'm sorry, Mr. Brooks, but I'm late for a meeting. Good luck."

Waylen glanced at the phone as the speakers crackled. He hung up.

"The Delta." Waylen searched the name, learning it referenced the triangle shape in Greek. It symbolized a door, according to the ancient Phoenicians. The shape was the uppercase for the fourth letter in the Greek alphabet. "A door." But where did it lead?

The Moon. Interesting. Waylen thought about those three simple words and the heavy connotations they carried. It implied that Daniel Klein had touched the metal piece, but was transported elsewhere, not to the Moon like Rory, Silas, and Waylen had witnessed. Daniel had also said it was dangerous.

One of the rental workers set a hand on the top of the car and frowned. "Everything okay, sir?"

"Just reading the manual," he lied. "Have a good day." Waylen clicked his seatbelt on and pulled away, setting his GPS for the Archives. He'd spent a lot of time in DC, but never entered the National Archives before. NASA had backups of their files all over the country at various government facilities, but this was the logical location for Waylen to stop on short notice. He'd called the headquarters, but was told the wing was conveniently being fumigated. He wondered if that was even true. Unfortunately, he didn't have the time to drive around and investigate.

His stomach grumbled as he drove. He'd gotten home yesterday, and with the crew coming to sweep the house, he hadn't been able to grab groceries. The morning's coffee and bagel were a thing of the past, and he decided to have lunch before meeting with his contact at the Archives. Against all odds, his flight had been on time, and he pulled into the underground parking lot at precisely noon.

It was hot, the kind of humid summer day everyone on the East Coast consistently dealt with. Waylen was used to it, but as he walked up the ramp, he could already feel his temperature rising. He adjusted his tie, looked both ways, and jogged across the street, remembering visiting this very diner four years earlier.

Charlotte had worked in the White House as an aide, and their relationship had lasted for a year before it sputtered out. He almost expected to find her at the table smiling up at him, but they hadn't spoken since she'd broken it off over text three summers ago.

Waylen gazed at the Archives, seeing he had an hour before his scheduled appointment, and sat at a two-person table near the window. The place was quite full, with people from all walks eating sandwiches and sipping sodas. It was simple to spot the tourists, because they were in shorts and red or blue shirts, often wearing flip-flops, while the locals had on dress shirts, or skirts and heels.

Waylen ordered a burger with a side salad, along with a coffee, even though the diner's air conditioning seemed to be on the fritz.

His phone rang, and he turned the volume down, finding Martina's face on the caller ID.

"This is a surprise," he said.

"*I heard you're still on the case,*" she told him.

"For now, but Ben has me on a short leash. How's your thing going?"

"*It's okay. Boring.*"

"Boring is better than what I'm dealing with."

"*Anything I can do for you?*"

"Is that a genuine offer?"

"Sure, I have some downtime. This guy I'm partnered with is a snoozer. I miss you, Brooks."

"Same here," he said truthfully. "Can you track down a man named Cody Sanderson? He lives in San Diego."

"What do you want, specifically?"

"Get me the rundown. And if possible, find out where he is now." Waylen smiled as the server slid a plate of food near him.

"The rundown, hey? This is going to cost you."

"Send me the bill."

Martina laughed, but it stopped a moment later. *"You were almost killed, Brooks. You shouldn't have gone without me."*

"It wasn't like we had a choice."

"Still…"

"Just find Sanderson. It's important."

"Will do."

An uncomfortable silence filled the airwaves, and Waylen cleared his throat. "I better go."

"Later, Brooks."

The food barely passed muster, but he scarfed it down just the same. He remembered the diner being much nicer when he met Charlotte, but that might have been the company. Waylen contemplated looking her up, but considering what he carried in his jacket pocket, he decided against it. A woman in DC with her smarts and social skills was likely married by now.

Waylen finished his coffee, and people-watched while he waited for the check. He slipped out enough to cover it with a decent tip and left. The National Archive had a tour bus parked out front, and a load of visitors paraded from the vehicle.

Waylen hoped his luck was about to change for the better.

6

Silas munched on his hot dog and wiped the spurt of ketchup that fell onto his forearm. He struggled to recall when he'd last gone to a baseball game. He guessed he'd been in college. Back then, his circle of friends had been into the Mets, and they tried to attend a game every couple of weeks. Since they'd all graduated and moved to various states, they'd drifted apart.

"Come on, you schlub! He's always going low and fast!" the guy beside Silas shouted, cupping his hands over his mouth. He turned to Silas, nudging him. "Can you believe it? Any more strikeouts, we might as well leave before the seventh."

Silas nodded and scooted farther to the left of the aisle seat. The place was only a quarter full for the Wednesday afternoon, so he meandered from his spot, picking a more isolated location. He doubted anyone would check his ticket. He waved down the woman carrying a tray of beer, and exchanged twelve bucks for a plastic cup filled with a flat lager.

He adjusted his baseball cap and sank into the chair while the teams traded positions on the field. The Mets were losing to the Pirates by three, but Silas didn't care about the score. He just wanted to be alone, but not too alone. His dad had asked to meet at the office in the morning, but he couldn't imagine sitting there combing over the financial reports for a furniture company any longer.

He hadn't said that to his father, not yet. Maybe he'd decide about his future after the funeral, but Silas currently felt incapacitated. He'd experienced something traumatic, and Leigh had paid the price. He'd barely gotten to know her, but her loss ate at him. It was all his fault.

The shortstop for the Pirates smashed a two-run homer past the fence, and the crowd murmured their discontent. Silas peered up, finding the guy next to his old seat throwing his hat into the stands before walking off.

Silas drank the beer, and when it was time for the seventh-inning stretch, he headed to the can. He preferred afternoon games, where the lines for the restrooms were nonexistent.

He emerged a minute later and caught someone watching him. The man averted his gaze, pretending to scroll on his cell phone, but Silas was certain of what he'd seen. He started away, and Silas followed him from a distance.

He looked to be about forty, wearing a blue Mets hat and a black t-shirt with some band on the front, and the concert tour listings on the back. Silas almost lost him in the crowd as everyone began finding their seats again, given the volume of matching caps, but picked him up as the stadium concession area emptied.

The man locked gazes with Silas, and his eyes went wide.

Silas found his voice and strode toward the guy. "What do you want?"

"You're Silas Gunn."

"Who wants to know?" Silas clenched his right fist, and the bullet wound on his arm flared.

"Do you have them?"

"I'm going to call security," Silas said.

"Wait, I'm on your side. My name's Cody."

"I don't have a side," Silas proclaimed.

The man anxiously peered around the concourse and removed something from his back pocket. It wasn't in a whiskey bag. Instead, it was a brown sack, the kind you'd throw a sandwich in as a kid. "Does this look familiar?"

Silas backed up. "Get that away from me."

He didn't lower it. "Silas, do you have the others?"

"Don't come any closer," he warned.

Cody didn't seem menacing. He actually appeared frantic. His cheek twitched, and his cap sat too high on his head.

"Is there a problem?" a security guard asked. He set down a huge soda and frowned, touching a walkie-talkie at his hip.

Cody gave Silas a pleading expression.

"No. We were arguing about where to go for beers after the game," Silas said.

The guy shrugged, grabbed his drink, and sauntered off, whistling the song about Cracker Jacks.

"Thanks," Cody muttered.

Silas wondered how he could have explained their situation anyway.

"About that beer…"

"I wasn't serious."

"Please give me ten minutes."

Silas glanced at the token in Cody's grip and knew Waylen would want it. Plus, he had to learn what they did when placed together. He was far too invested, even with every bone in his body shouting for him to stop. They'd have the funeral, and Silas would return to his life, or quit and move. Maybe California. He'd always loved the redwoods of the northern region. Napa Valley. Lush farmland.

"Ten minutes." Silas gestured at the bag. "And put that away."

Cody obliged, and they took the stairs, jogging through the empty concourse. Silas idly checked the score on a TV before exiting the building, and the Mets were being blown out of the water. Hundreds of disappointed fans were already marching outside, heading to the train or the parking lot.

"You have a car?" Silas asked.

"Rental." It took a moment for them to find it, and Cody had to use the fob lock to make the lights flash before he remembered which was his. "Only got in last night."

Silas paused at the edge of the passenger door. Getting into a car with a stranger was stupid, especially after what he'd recently endured. "This is a bad idea."

Cody tossed his hat into the back seat and tried to straighten his thinning brown hair. "I'm not dangerous. I'll tell you my story when we're"—he pointed at the steering wheel—"not out in the open."

Silas took a photo of the license plate and sent it to Waylen with a message. *Sanderson found me. Going for a ride. Thought you should know.*

"Who did you send that to?" Cody asked when Silas climbed in.

"Just a friend."

"Where to?" Cody backed up, nearly being creamed by a minivan. The driver swerved and honked at him, then ripped from the lot, various Mets stickers covering half the rear window.

Silas considered bringing him to the bar a few blocks from his parents' house, but he might run into someone the family knew, and he didn't want to explain himself to anyone. So he directed Cody farther east.

It was three forty-five in the afternoon, and only a few vehicles were near the sports lounge. They went in, and Silas instantly heard the cracking of pool balls. Eighties rock played quietly while a bartender watched the TV, a white cloth draped on his shoulder. He nodded at them, then Silas chose a booth in the rear corner, out of sight. He took the seat that allowed him to view the entire place. Silas hadn't needed to think about things like that before, and hoped his paranoia was temporary.

Cody set his hands on the table in a peaceful gesture. "Where are they?"

"What'll it be?" A woman came over, one hand on her hip. She chewed gum and was about to offer them menus when Silas lifted two fingers.

"Two lagers on tap."

She didn't respond, and walked to the bar.

"I prefer an IPA," Cody mumbled.

"Talk."

"I heard about the incident in New Hampshire."

"Incident." Silas stretched his arm. "I was shot, and my friends were nearly killed. I also overheard them mention you."

Sanderson visibly shrank into his seat. "That's bad."

"When Jack discovered his was a fake, he wasn't pleased. I'm guessing his boss has your name too."

Cody's knee bounced up and down nervously. "Damn it."

"You planted the fake?"

"Not me, but I knew it was there. It was Fred's idea, but when the right people came knocking, I admitted that I may have seen something like it in his storage unit."

"Fred gave you the—"

"Piece of the Delta," he said.

"Delta, as in the Greek letter?"

Cody drew a triangle in the air. "Yeah, that's the one."

The server returned with their beers, foam spilling over the edges. She smiled dully and headed to the pool tables.

"Tell me everything," Silas urged.

Cody wrapped his hands around the thinnest part of the glass, like he was strangling it. "I'm a collector. I was that kid in school who wore NASA t-shirts, went to Space Camp, and dreamt of flying to the ISS. Fred and I met during an event at the college, before I graduated," he said.

"What do you do?"

"IT. Nothing too exciting."

"I have some friends in IT."

"It comes naturally to me." He let go with one hand and took a sip, making a face. "Fred was nice to me, and he agreed to meet up for dinner so I could pick his brain about the Helios mission. He was a little odd, but so am I. We hit it off, and after a few chats, he invited me to his house on the coast to see his own collection."

"When was this?" Silas asked.

"Ten years ago. Not long before he died, really. I really liked Fred. He asked me about my life. By then I'd realized I'd never meet the physical requirements of being an astronaut, but I could work on the back end. It takes more than a pilot to fly to the Moon." He smiled at his own comment. "Fred confided in me." He took another drag from the beer and glanced at the entrance when a couple walked in.

Silas waited, holding his breath.

"Gunn and Swanson went to the surface, and found something."

"The Delta," Silas whispered.

"It was sitting there like a miracle, all the pieces fully intact. An artifact on the Moon. At first, they assumed it was the remnants of a damaged satellite, or a piece that had fallen off one of the previous Moon landers, but they knew those vehicles inside and out. It wasn't until Gunn picked it up that they realized something was seriously wrong."

Silas leaned forward. "What happened?"

"Fred didn't tell me. They were gone, Silas. For two hours. Fred was freaking out, but he figured they only lost communication."

"But NASA must—"

"They swept it under the rug. Fred's erratic contact attempts were relayed, but Commander Gunn swore afterward that they were just gathering regolith and stone samples as required when the comms went wonky."

"Don't you have to touch the…Delta components with your flesh to make them work?" Silas said.

"Not when they're assembled into the triangle. Then you can use them."

"Use them?" Silas asked. "For what?"

"You still don't know." Cody sipped his beer. "They're a gateway to other worlds."

"I thought it took you to the Moon. In a vision."

"That's how the sections work by themselves. Together they—"

A group of men plopped into the booth beside them, talking loudly. "…my route was a disaster," one said. "Leave it to the Queens municipal board to tear up those lanes in the middle of summer. They're clueless."

"I got a flat behind the bank on Linden. Took me an hour to change it." Another guy sniffed his shirt. "Sorry about the smell." This brought a raucous round of laughter.

"Where are you staying?" Silas asked Cody Sanderson.

"In the city. East Village."

"Special Agent Waylen Brooks will be here tomorrow. Can you keep that safe and meet us?"

Cody nodded.

"Be careful. Whoever's searching for these will kill you for it, understood?"

"I won't let it out of my sight."

Silas exchanged numbers with the collector and asked Cody to verify it with a text.

"You didn't hear the rest of the story," Cody said when they'd cleared the tab.

"Save it for Waylen. Let's talk tomorrow."

"You want a lift?"

"Nah, I'll take the fresh air."

Silas didn't want to have Cody know where his parents lived, even though he didn't deem Cody himself a threat. Someone was on the search for Sanderson, and likely for him as well. It was no secret where his family lived, and Silas' gut sank when Cody drove by, waving as he passed.

"So much for a relaxing afternoon," he told himself, and began the trek toward his temporary home.

7

Rory tossed her suitcase onto the bed and unzipped it. She methodically went through the process of unpacking the handful of outfits she'd brought for the funeral and the few days surrounding it. New York differed greatly from Boston, but she was glad to be out of Woodstock for the time being. There, her parents' home was a giant bullseye, a target for this clandestine group trying to find the three mysterious tokens. Here, they could be out of sight, hidden among the crowds.

She checked her reflection in the mirror and reapplied some makeup. Rory primped her hair with her fingers, but it fell flat the moment she let it go. It was four o'clock, and the trip with her parents had been as tense as she'd expected. At least they'd gotten Rory her own room. The idea of sharing with them would have driven her mad.

She heard a knock, and realized it came from the adjoining door connecting their rooms. Rory sighed and opened it, finding her mother.

Kathy looked perfect, her clothing well-tailored and expensive, her pearls marking her as one of the wealthy people that could afford a hotel room like this. "Are you ready?"

"For what?"

"I thought you and I could walk down Fifth, take in

the sights. Maybe do some shopping." Kathy's smile seemed genuine.

Rory glanced at her room, wishing she could work on her book, but with everything that had transpired, Rory wasn't able to concentrate. Maybe once the funeral was over and Waylen figured out who to arrest, she could return to her original plan.

"That sounds nice, Mom. What about Dad?"

"He's going to meet Barkley at the Met, remember?"

"Right." Rory briefly recalled them discussing it in the car on the way down, but she'd been too busy watching the green tree-lined roads. She grabbed her purse, strapping it across her body.

They left, taking the elevator to the main lobby. The front desk concierge waved emphatically at Kathy. "Excuse me, Mrs. Rippen. We don't seem to have your husband's ID on file. Can you see he drops by with it before too long?"

"Absolutely. I'll make sure he does that tonight," her mom said.

They exited, and Rory watched Kathy. "Mrs. Rippen?"

"Your father borrowed his friend's credit card. We couldn't very well check in under our own names, not after what's happened. It's safer this way. Don't worry, we'll keep forgetting until it's time to check out," Kathy said.

Rory smiled as they strolled south on Fifth Avenue. Her parents were trying to be covert, and she loved it.

They gazed at a luxury department store right around the corner, and Kathy slid her arm into Rory's. "Shopping really is the best medicine."

Rory always detested these places, with shirts that cost more than her entire wardrobe and handbags worth more than her hatchback. But it made her mom happy, so she entered the alien world of high fashion, already eager to leave.

She followed Kathy through the store like a loyal child, trying not to frown at the pretentious staff. In the end, they bought nothing, but her mother seemed to be in a great mood.

After a trip to a world-famous jewelry store, they meandered farther south, her mother with a little blue box stuffed into her shopping bag. Rory peered into the window of a bookstore, feeling like a failure. She'd worked so hard on *View from the Heavens* and had secured a very lucrative advance. How could she have allowed Kevin to burn through it?

"It's all right, honey," her mom said softly. "Come on."

Rory hesitated when Kathy held the door, but she finally went in and found three copies of her debut novel in a staff-recommended position near the entrance. Rory lifted a copy and flipped it open, reading her acknowledgments page.

"You'll do it again. And again. I believe in you," Kathy told her.

"You mean that?"

"Yes. When this mess is dealt with, take all the time you need. And your father will buy you that condo when you're ready. I'm sorry we weren't more supportive before. If I had any inkling of what that fraud was doing to you, I would have dragged you home years ago."

Rory sniffled and gave her mom a hug. "Thank you."

"Can I help you?" a woman asked. She was young, with thick black glasses and a name tag labeling her as Elinor. Either she was a Jane Austen fan, or her parents were.

"This is Rory, and she wrote that book," Kathy said proudly.

"*You're* Rory Valentine?" Elinor asked.

"Guilty as charged."

"Do you mind if I get a picture for the store's social?" Elinor's phone was already out, and she angled it crookedly for a selfie with her. Kathy stayed in the shot, putting a hand on Rory's waist. She took two, Rory trying to smile, but it probably came off as a sneer. "Appreciate it." She thrust a black marker at Rory and stared at the books. "Sign them?"

"Sure." Rory did, leaving them open for a moment to let the signature dry. The girl tapped on her phone and shoved it into her pants pocket.

"Do you have any books on Helios 15?" Rory chanced.

"The Moon thingy?" Elinor glanced at the front desk, where five people waited in line. "Think we sold out. That old guy was shot or whatever, and his funeral is this week. Sorry. Duty calls." She strolled away with no urgency, leaving them alone.

"Moon thingy?" Kathy muttered. "Kids these days. You were never like that, were you, Rory?"

She shook her head. "No, Mother, because I am a people pleaser…"

"What did you say?"

"Nothing. Can we leave?"

Kathy led her outside. "Where should we go next?"

"How about the hotel bar?" Rory said.

"Darling, we're in the greatest city in the world. Your father said he could get us tickets to a show. Would you like that?"

Rory contemplated seeing a Broadway musical with her mother, and actually thought it would be fun. She'd tried doing things with Kevin, but he thought Broadway was just another way to remind the lower classes they couldn't afford the finer things in life. He called them price gougers, and a string of other economically-related expletives she forgot because she'd zoned out. It was a common reaction to Kevin's tirades.

Kathy's cell came out, and she wandered down Fifth, talking to Oscar while Rory waited. "Since it's last minute, our options are limited."

Rory chose a long-standing musical, and it was settled. Maybe this trip wouldn't be so bad after all.

———————

"Special Agent Brooks, I'm afraid we're closing up in ten minutes," Donald said.

Waylen had gone through everything he could find on the Helios mission, but the two-hour gap was a giant hole in the lunar landing event. A hole. The thought brought images of the misty black void he'd seen in his vision.

"Did you hear me?" Donald's arms were crossed in the private room's entrance.

"Yes. Don, you've been doing this a long time, haven't you?"

Donald checked his watch and sat across from Waylen. "For twenty-one years."

Stacks of paperwork, along with countless file folders, were strewn about. An image from the moonwalk was paused on Waylen's laptop, showing a grainy picture of Gunn and Swanson gathering samples. These were Rory and Silas' grandfathers. His own grandpa had worked in a lumber mill until he died from lung cancer at sixty-seven, a year after he finally retired.

"Why is there a two-hour window of missing data on the Helios 15 landing?"

"Look, Mr. Brooks, we're the Archives. I don't specialize in NASA documents. If you want answers to that, I suggest you go to the source. We only store certain federal programs' information as a precautionary measure."

Waylen had already contacted NASA again and heard the same runaround on the subject. He was waiting for a return call from someone in their own archives, but he doubted it would happen while he was in town. He wished that Assistant Director Ben hadn't given him such a brief window on the case. "Is there anything like this reported from the previous lunar missions?"

"Not that I'm aware."

"One hundred eighteen minutes of dead air. That seems odd," Waylen said.

"It was the 1970s. They were on the Moon. Count your blessings." Donald motioned to the stacks. "Please clean them up and ensure everything is in the proper order. The interns will just put it back how you leave it, and I don't want to double check in the morning."

"Thanks for letting me come on short notice," Waylen said, shaking Donald's hand.

"You're welcome. Doing anything entertaining while you're in town?"

"I'm off to New York when I'm done here."

"Safe travels." Donald let the door close, and Waylen sank into the chair, staring at the picture. He scrolled to the next still shot and continued through all of them.

He froze on one and zoomed. "I'll be damned."

Commander Peter Gunn's helmet faceplate had a reflection in it. Waylen checked the time stamp, finding this the first captured picture after the lapse. Waylen zoomed until it was nothing but pixels blown up too large on his screen, but the reflection was exactly what he'd feared. The black mass covered half of Gunn's face.

"It really happened," Waylen whispered. He took a screenshot and shut the laptop. After quickly organizing the materials, he hurried from the Archives as a tour bus took off. It shot a stream of thick exhaust into the warm air, nearly choking him, but he kept running, entering the parking lot where his rental sat.

He hadn't found exactly what he'd been searching for, but he did get confirmation that Gunn and Swanson had seen the same strange anomaly he'd observed in the echo after touching the token.

Waylen pulled from the lot, programmed his destination into the GPS, and sighed when it showed four hours until arrival. "I should have flown."

Before merging onto the interstate, he dialed Martina.

"Twice in one day? You must miss me—or our…meetings together."

"Saw right through me," he said. "Anything on Sanderson?"

"Who is this guy? Seems smart."

"Number and address?"

"Just sent to you."

Martina sounded off, and Waylen pictured her working in the office, with boxes threatening to topple over on her. He'd be doing the same come Monday, meaning he needed to move fast. "You're the best."

"Can you fill me in on the case?" she asked.

"Ben's already pissed. It's best to stay clear of this one," he said.

"I literally stuck my neck out when I took that helicopter for you. You owe me."

"I'll make it up when I'm done with this."

That seemed to settle things, and Martina spoke on

the other end, talking to another agent. *"I have to go. More evidence coming in."*

"Don't forget to sleep," he told her.

"Right, sleep. Later, Brooks."

"Bye, Sanchez." Waylen selected a classic rock station and rolled his windows down a crack on both sides while he soared toward Baltimore. Traffic was already slowing as he approached the bypass highway, and he let out a deep breath, knowing it would be dark by the time he neared his hotel.

He patted the two pieces of the Delta in his suit jacket and glanced at the water as he drove over the Patapsco River in Baltimore. Could it be so simple? The flow came to a halt, and he noticed the closure and blinking arrow directing everyone into a single lane.

Waylen removed the bags and rolled the window fully open. He could throw them into the water. No one would ever find them. He could return to his usual job…

He dropped them into his pocket and knew that whoever was trying to gather the Delta wouldn't stop. These people would hunt him down—and Rory and Silas too. They'd already gone through enough, and it was up to Waylen and the FBI to protect the pair. He emerged from the backlog, and as his car exited the city limits, the interstate grew far emptier.

Waylen stepped on the gas pedal.

8

"*T*hat was really something," Rory said, exiting into a different Manhattan. When they'd gone into the theatre, it was muggy and bright. Leaving, the air had a chill, and it was well after sunset.

"Your father missed out. He would have loved that show," Kathy said. She staggered slightly after indulging in a couple of martinis during the intermission. Rory had joined her, drinking a glass of white wine, but her mind was clear and focused as she searched for a taxi.

"We can walk, dear."

"I'd rather…"

Kathy was already strolling north. "It's only twelve blocks, and these are short city blocks."

They were on Seventh Avenue, heading for the hotel. They passed a series of enormous billboards, and a lot of the restaurants were brightly glowing, their signs attempting to draw in the post-Broadway crowds. It felt good to be alive, to walk through the vibrant city.

"I had a great day with you, Mom."

Kathy smiled and stepped around a pile of garbage bags on the sidewalk. "Maybe we should do this more often."

"I'd like that." She'd never had a fun day out on vacation, not in Rory's recollection. Even as a kid, they'd usually travel somewhere warm, and Kathy would ignore her while she swam in the pools alone.

They passed Carnegie Hall, and she could see the first hint of Central Park in the distance. "Maybe we can tour the park tomorrow. Have a drink by the rowboats?"

"We'll drag your father with us," Kathy said.

Foot traffic was lighter the farther they got from Times Square, and Rory slowed, glancing behind them. The sidewalks were empty, except for one man across Seventh. His head was down, and he had a black cap on. He seemed like a local, with hands shoved deep into his light jacket pockets. She'd noticed the same thing in Boston. No one who lived in the big cities ever looked up. They did everything possible to avoid eye contact, drifting with purpose and determination, the opposite of a tourist. Rory's mother was constantly observing every little detail of the cityscape.

When she checked for the man, he was further up, turning onto 56th Street. Rory sighed and kept walking, staying closer to Kathy.

An ambulance siren rang out, and she grabbed her mom before crossing on the Walk signal. The emergency vehicle sped by, and both of their gazes followed it as two police cruisers trailed, their lights flashing brightly.

Rory heard the footsteps before she saw the figure approaching, but it was too late. He shoved Kathy, knocking her to the curb. Rory made a fist and backed up a step as his gloved hand smacked her in the cheek. A white light filled her vision, and she was on the ground, clutching her stomach after a second attack. Her purse had been wrapped around her body, but it came free. Rory noticed the glint of the large blade when he sliced right through the strap. He snatched Kathy's bag and ran without hesitation.

"Mom, are you okay?" Rory clawed her way to her

mom's side, and spied blood on the sidewalk beside her. "Mom!" She reached for her phone, but it had been tucked into her purse.

Another police car flew toward them, and Rory stumbled into the street, waving her arms. He kept going, but she flagged another thirty seconds later.

"Is there a problem?" the officer asked, and his gaze lingered on her, then on her mother sprawled out in the bike lane. "What happened?" He and his partner left the lights on, and Rory shielded her eyes from the flashing.

"A man…he robbed us. There was a knife…"

The female police officer turned her head, using the radio attached to her shoulder. Rory's ears rang, and she crouched by her unconscious mom, holding her hand.

An hour later, Rory glanced up as Oscar entered the waiting room. "Where is she?"

"I don't know. They took her into the emergency room and no one will talk to me." Rory couldn't keep the tremor from her voice. Oscar looked torn between comforting his daughter and getting answers about his wife. "Go find out what's happening."

He strode off with determination and used his best authoritative tone when he spoke to the nurse behind the glass barrier.

Oddly enough, Rory wanted to call Silas or Waylen. She'd just met them, but after their excitement during the storm, she was bonded to them. But her phone was gone, along with their contact information. Rory realized she was friends with Silas on that social media site, which meant she could reach out through her laptop.

Oscar whistled, gathering her attention, and waved for her to follow. They entered a chaotic space with nurses and doctors everywhere, prepping and assessing various figures in beds and gurneys. A hospital in the heart of

Manhattan was a constant stream of incoming and outgoing patients.

Rory felt the tears when she saw Kathy, her head bandaged with white gauze. Her eyes were squinty, but she was awake, and she reached for her husband.

"How are you doing?"

"I've been better," Kathy said. "Rory, you were right."

"About what?"

"We should have taken a taxi."

She'd already told the police everything she could about the incident, but they'd been distracted when the ambulance arrived, finally assuring her they'd do everything they could to find the perpetrator. Rory wondered how often that happened in this city.

The doctor came twenty minutes later, letting them know Kathy had briefly been knocked unconscious and that she had a mild concussion, but the scans didn't show any internal bleeding or serious complications. It was obvious they wanted Kathy to leave, to free up the space, but Oscar demanded they keep her overnight for observation.

"I can stay," Rory told them.

"No, you go," Oscar said. "I'll stick around."

"And, dear." Kathy clutched her wrist.

"Yes, Mom?"

"Don't walk back."

Rory waited until an attendant rolled her mother from the ER and went outside, ready to call a rideshare, which she couldn't without a cell phone. She flagged a Yellow cab, paid with cash her father had given her, and returned to the hotel. After getting to their proper floor, she realized she didn't have the room key, so she wandered to the front desk.

"Can we help you?" The woman glanced at her outfit, then at her head.

Rory self-consciously patted her hair. "I'm in 412, but I lost my key."

"Name?"

"Rory…" She paused, remembering the alias they were under. "Rippen."

"Here we go. Okay, Miss Rippen." The employee kept a finger on the card, eyeing her. "Are you in trouble?"

"I was mugged. My mother… Mrs. Rippen is in the hospital at the moment. He took our purses," she said.

"Oh, my." The clerk put a hand to her mouth in shock. "Where?"

"Three blocks south. We were walking back after a show."

"That's just horrible. Please, order anything from room service on the house. And I'll have a bottle of champagne sent to the room…"

Rory was about to argue, but nodded instead. "I appreciate it." She snatched the key and hurried to the elevator.

Had the robber noticed two women alone on the street and taken advantage, or had they been targeted? Did someone think she had the tokens with her? Rory bolted the door when she entered and flipped her laptop open.

"How did they know I was in the city?" Rory thought through her afternoon and paused at the memory of the bookstore. "…You have to be kidding me."

She brought the boutique shop's social media link up and found a picture of herself with Elinor and her mother. *View from the Heavens author Rory Valentine stopped by her favorite NY bookstore. Three copies signed. Come by today!*

@rory_valentine

She'd been tagged. Anyone with half a brain could have an alert sent to them if this happened, and clearly that was the case. Rory almost shut the laptop, then brought up Silas' profile.

You around? I lost my phone.

His message appeared a second later. *Video chat?*

She glanced at her own reflection on the screen. *Gimme five.*

Rory washed her face, brushed her hair, and changed into a t-shirt. Every ounce of strength in her body had been depleted, and before calling Silas, she ordered a cheeseburger and fries. The champagne arrived as she sat, and Rory confirmed it was a staff member through the peephole before allowing them in. The man rolled the cart in and stood there awkwardly.

"Sorry, we were mugged tonight. I have no cash."

He exited without a word, leaving her with the champagne chilling in a bucket and two flutes. Rory popped the cork and drank straight from the bottle, choking on the bubbles. She filled a glass and propped herself onto the bed with the computer on her lap.

"You'll never guess what happened to me tonight," she said when Silas appeared.

"*Tell me about it,*" he grumbled.

"This sounds bad."

"*You first,*" he said.

Rory described their trip in and finished with the hospital. Silas listened intently, only rarely interjecting for details. She appreciated this trait more than she might have guessed.

"*It might be a coincidence,*" Silas said after she was done. "*But I doubt it.*"

"He could have killed my mom. We need to stop

this."

"*I spoke to Waylen. He tried to contact you…but now it makes sense.*"

"Where is he?"

"*Staying on Fifth, near the church.*"

He was so close, only a few blocks away. Waylen's presence calmed her. She sipped her drink, and Silas laughed.

"*Bubbly? Really?*"

"It's from the hotel. They heard about my adventure tonight." She set it down. "What about your day?"

"*I had a beer with Cody Sanderson,*" he said.

"The guy Jack mentioned?"

"*The one and only.*"

"And?"

Silas frowned and leaned closer to his phone's camera. "*He has the third.*"

Rory flinched and downed the rest of the glass. "They're all in New York."

"*Yeah,*" Silas said. "*That worries me.*"

"The funeral might be dangerous."

"*I think so.*"

Rory had the urge to leave, or at least send her parents home. What if her father was right about selling in Woodstock? They had enough money; they could vanish to another state. "Where's Sanderson now?"

"*He said he had a hotel room in the East Village.*"

"All three are within walking distance of one another." Someone knocked on the door, and she lifted a finger. "Give me a minute."

"*Take your time.*"

They'd left the delivery in the hall, and Rory took the tray, removing the shiny silver cloche. Under the dome sat the juiciest burger she'd ever seen. When she dropped to the bed, Silas was there with a beer in hand. "*Figured you could use some company,*" he said on her screen. "*Cheers.*"

Her mother was in the hospital after being robbed. Rory had been struck for the second time in three days, but Silas put her at ease. Her stomach ached where the stranger had hit her, and her cheek was tender to the touch.

She took her first bite as the clock struck midnight.

9

"You sure you won't come into the office?" Silas' father asked.

Silas exited the car and watched his dad. "Next week."

"Take your time," Arthur said. "Barney's covering."

Silas grimaced but didn't comment. "See you at the house later."

Someone honked at Arthur for double parking on the narrow street. "Be careful, son."

"I will."

Arthur gave the delivery truck a wave and drove off. Barney was the kind of employee who lurked in the shadows for an opportunity. It didn't help that he'd graduated a couple years before Silas with, according to Barney, the honor of being his class salutatorian. Silas wasn't sure if he believed that, given the man's penchant for overselling his skills and under-delivering.

But if Silas was serious about quitting his job, it eased his mind that his father could fill the position with someone he trusted. Silas had been around the business long enough to understand that no one was irreplaceable, himself included.

He climbed the steps to his building, and the door flung wide. "Welcome," Carl, the new doorman, said.

"Roger still out?"

"Sick," Carl told him again.

Coming home was a bad idea, but he'd left without any of his stuff after deciding to crash with his parents until after the funeral. Silas hurried to his suite and began packing in earnest. He didn't know why, but he suspected he'd be leaving the city shortly. Maybe it had to do with the attack on Rory and her mom, or the fact he'd talked with Cody Sanderson and couldn't imagine not learning what the real purpose of the Delta was.

Silas paused before leaving his apartment. It was fancier than anything his parents had ever owned. He loved the black quartz countertops, the dark hardwood and clean modern lines. His sister told him it was "Art Mano," claiming no woman could handle living among such overwhelmingly depressing colors, and now that he saw it with a fresh perspective, she was right. Silas locked up and lugged his suitcase to the elevator.

Meet Rory and me in twenty minutes.

The text from Waylen included a pinged address. Silas responded, saying he was on the way, and his rideshare appeared when he reached the sidewalk. He avoided talking to Carl, not trusting Roger's replacement. He knew he was probably being paranoid, but that might keep him alive.

The driver wore oversized sunglasses, and Silas was glad he didn't start a conversation. He texted Cody from the SUV. *We should get together.*

Sure, where?

Silas gave him the address and told him to be there at one. That would give Waylen, Rory, and Silas a head start on their plan. He closed his eyes as they navigated heavy traffic. Moving through southern Manhattan to Midtown wasn't a simple task. He'd stayed up far too late chatting with Rory, and while he didn't regret it, his lack of sleep was deeply affecting him.

"We're here," the driver said, and he realized he must have dozed off.

"Thanks." He grabbed the luggage and hauled it to the street. The area was busy, and Silas' gaze drifted to the beautiful church down the block where Peter Gunn's service was scheduled in a little more than twenty-four hours. How his father had secured such a place on short notice was beyond Silas. Peter wished to have his service in Campbelltown, but given the issues they'd experienced in Loon Lake and Gull Creek, they'd chosen another option.

"I thought that was you." Waylen smiled from the corner, his tie flapping in the breeze. He offered a hand, and they shook like business acquaintances, rather than cohorts in a bizarre mystery surrounding a mission to the Moon.

"You look good," Silas told him. Waylen had shaved, and he only had a hint of dark bags under his eyes, contrasting Silas.

Waylen motioned to the hotel next to them. "It was the bed. Softest duvet I've ever slept with."

Silas peered into the lobby. "Rory here?"

"Her mom was being released, so they were having a late breakfast. Sounds like Kathy's doing better."

"Do you think it's related?" Silas asked.

Waylen shrugged and picked up Silas' luggage. "Who knows? This is New York, and it was dark. In my opinion, it had nothing to do with the Delta, and all to do with a crime of opportunity."

"Where did you hear that name? Delta?"

"Fred Trell's lawyer."

"Ah, Sanderson told me yesterday."

"Speaking of, will Mr. Sanderson be joining us?"

"At one. I hoped we could talk first," Silas said.

"Good call. Have you ever thought about joining the FBI?" Waylen asked with a grin.

"No, but I am considering quitting my job."

"Really?"

"The idea of returning to my desk after what I've been through seems futile."

"Want me to stow this in my room?" Waylen asked.

"Sure."

Waylen left, and Silas kept an eye out for Rory. He was nervous to see her again, even though they'd talked for a couple of hours last night. She was nowhere in sight when Waylen showed up and gestured at the restaurant. "Shall we get a table?"

Silas' stomach growled at the thought of food. He'd skipped breakfast, too anxious to eat, but now he was ravenous.

They were seated by a grumpy hostess. Waylen asked for a spot by the window so they could see Rory or Sanderson coming, and the woman reluctantly obliged. Silas read the laminated menu, and they both accepted coffees from a different server. Silas dumped a cream into his, and Waylen added nothing.

For a second, all he heard was the clinking of the spoon in his cup; then Rory was there, standing on the other side of the glass. Silas almost spilled his drink as he lunged for the window, knocking on it to get her attention.

Rory smiled when she recognized him, and entered the diner. She sighed the second she slid into the chair. "What a week."

"How's your mom?" Waylen asked.

"She's fine, but shaken up. We spent the morning talking to the banks and canceling cards. It's not quite the trip to the city we'd expected." Rory glanced at the cups, then the menus. "Did you guys order? I'm starving. We were on hold forever and didn't even make it to the hotel restaurant."

"We waited for you." They flagged the server down and ordered lunch. Silas finished his coffee. "Sanderson is coming in a half hour."

"The tokens will be together." Rory didn't have to elaborate. They understood what she was implying. Waylen's hand reflexively slid to his suit pocket, and Silas hoped no one was watching them. It would be obvious he was holding something important there.

"Do you think this will be the first time since...they returned to Earth?" Silas asked quietly.

"From the sounds of things, probably," she answered.

"I visited the Archives in DC yesterday, and there are almost exactly two hours on the surface missing. No images, sound bites, or data. It was wiped from the history books." Waylen pursed his lips when the server refilled their cups. When she was out of earshot, he spoke again. "How did they pull it off?"

"Which part?"

"Bringing the Delta from the Moon to Earth, then convincing NASA there wasn't anything else worth exploring."

Rory shook her head. "Grandpa Swanson always said they were looking for any excuse to cut the program. It would have taken a miracle to fund another trip."

"Like the Delta?" Silas asked.

"What I don't comprehend is why they hid it. How bad can it be?" Waylen's food arrived, with their meals following shortly after.

"Does it have to be bad? Couldn't it just be...odd? My grandfather and the others might have thought that society couldn't handle whatever it was. This was during Vietnam. People were protesting, the economy was on the fritz."

"Sounds familiar," Waylen muttered. "Every generation thinks they're special, but it's the same crap." He bit a fry in half.

"Was it their decision to make? They traveled to the Moon on government funding—" Rory cut herself off. "Sorry, that's something my ex would have complained about, and I am *not* him."

Silas noticed how methodically Rory ate her salad, then poked at the bowl. "Whatever they do, it'll be good to figure it out. Then we can pawn them off to the FBI or whoever Waylen thinks best. If the guy searching for them knows that we no longer have the Delta, they might stop harassing us."

Waylen didn't comment.

"We *are* going to relinquish them to someone, right?" Silas asked. After another moment of silence, he laughed. "What are you thinking, Waylen? A trip to the Moon?"

Waylen squirted ketchup on his plate. "Don't be silly. But before I give these up, I have to know who's after the Delta."

"How about we start with the charity event I attended last year? Jack was there," Silas said.

"Francis Jack Barker," Waylen corrected.

"Fine. Then we check the records, see who paid for Jack's seat at the event, and we have a lead."

"I wish I had a team on this one. Send me the details, and I'll ask my partner to dig into it," Waylen said.

"Why are you acting solo?" Rory asked.

"This isn't my wheelhouse. I stumbled on the case and ran with it. I'm lucky the Assistant Director hasn't pulled me entirely. Believe me, he wanted to. I made him touch the token."

They both stared at the FBI agent. "What did you do that for?" Rory set her fork down. "What if he's involved?"

"Then he would have snatched them off the boardroom table and bounced."

Silas checked the time and searched for Cody Sanderson. "He should be here soon."

They finished their meals, and Silas found himself twitching from the caffeine. He refused a third refill, while Waylen continued to drink it like there was a shortage on the horizon. Rory barely consumed any liquids, and he noticed the redness of her cheek. "Is that from…"

She nodded, absently raising her hand to her face.

"Does it hurt?"

"Not really. I took an acetaminophen."

"If I find out who did that, it'll take more than an over-the-counter pain pill to fix him," Waylen grumbled.

Silas glanced at the agent, wondering if he'd said the comment out of affection for Rory Swanson. In the end, he figured Waylen was just that kind of guy.

"Where is he?" Silas noted it was ten after. "I'm going to text him."

You're late. ETA?

Rory peered at the screen with him while they waited, her hand resting on his arm.

It beeped, and he read the incoming message. *I'm running behind. Do you have them?*

Silas peered outside and slid the phone to Waylen. "I don't think it's him," the agent said.

"Why not?"

"Call it intuition." Waylen pulled a fifty-dollar bill from his wallet and left it on the table. "We should go." Instead of heading out the front, he caught the server's attention. "You have a rear exit?"

"It's for deliveries," she said, and he slipped her a twenty.

"Pretend I work for the USPS."

She shoved it into her apron and let them pass.

They pushed outside, and Silas narrowly avoided tripping on a garbage bag. The grease trap reeked in the warm air, and he looked away, refusing to inhale. Waylen led them around the bend and held a hand up, gesturing to a white van across the street from the diner. It was unmarked, and a bearded man sat staring at the sidewalk.

"You were right," Rory said.

"Where was Cody staying?"

"A hotel in the East Village."

"You don't know which one?"

Silas shook his head. "We didn't get into details. I doubt he would have told me if I asked."

"He's probably dead," Waylen said.

Rory pressed her back to the brick building and took a deep breath. "I can't keep doing this. I just wanted to write a book."

Waylen turned east and hurried his steps. A block later, he hailed a taxi, and they piled in. "We have to find out where Sanderson was holed up."

Silas removed his cell from his jeans and scrolled through the images, stopping on one from yesterday. "It's his rental. Remember? I didn't want to get in without you having the plates."

"Good work." Waylen dialed a number on his phone.

10

*T*he 9th Precinct sent the deputy inspector, a skinny man around fifty-five years old with wire-framed glasses. Waylen waited near the impound gate, not wanting to ruffle any feathers. He had a feeling he'd need a few favors before the weekend was through.

"You didn't have to come, sir. I know you're busy." Waylen shook his hand. "Special Agent Waylen Brooks."

"Deputy Inspector Harry Truman."

"Like the president," Waylen said.

"Thanks for reminding me."

"I appreciate you taking the time."

"The FBI is a valuable institution, one I'm personally fond of. My sister works at J. Edgar."

"A DC woman. I was just there," Waylen said. Technically, he hadn't been at headquarters, but if it gave him any advantages with the leader of the East Village Police Department, he'd gladly take it.

"What's this about?" Harry lost his conversational tone.

"It's a long story. Can you tell me where you found it?"

"In an illegal parking zone by Tompkins Square Park at eleven last night. Officers had it towed."

"Did they look inside?"

"Not likely. We have better things to do than give

parking tickets," Harry said.

"What's at Tompkins?"

"It's a decent place. Dog park. Lots of drugs after dark. It's not the first time someone went for a hookup and passed out on the benches. We tow one or two a week."

The lot attendant buzzed them through, and Waylen slapped a pair of gloves on.

"Is this a crime scene?" the police commander asked.

"It might be." Waylen located the car near the entrance. He reached for the handle, and it opened. He scanned the interior, not finding much. There was a tourist book on the passenger seat and an empty fast-food bag on the floor; otherwise, it was unremarkable. He flipped the visor down, and the key fob fell.

Waylen stood up and walked to the rear of the sedan, hoping his instinct was wrong. He held the trunk release, and it beeped, then rose.

"Holy hell," the cop said, standing back.

Waylen stared at the body, the torn clothing, and…

It moved.

"Cody Sanderson?"

He gazed up, his lip split, the blood dried. "Thank God. I spent hours banging on that, but no one came." His hand was bruised purple.

Waylen examined the man. "Harry, would you mind calling an ambulance?"

Cody sat up, wincing as he held his arm. "Don't bother. I'll be fine. I slept it off."

"You were locked in the trunk. Don't these things have a safety?" Waylen searched for the trunk release.

"They busted it." The plastic triangle was in pieces near Cody's collarbone.

"Who did this?" Waylen asked, helping Cody from

the car. The man was thin, his hair stuck to his head. They'd done a number on him, but nothing looked life threatening.

"I didn't see their faces. I picked up dinner and noticed this car following me. I wasn't certain, so I looped around the area for a while, and there they were."

"White van?" Waylen asked.

"How'd you know?" Cody seemed surprised, and so did the deputy inspector.

"They were stalking me as well," Waylen said.

Cody hugged himself like he was cold, despite it being eighty-five out. "Do you have them?"

"The question is, did these guys get your token?"

"Not a chance. I wouldn't keep it on me," Cody said. "Wait, you're not walking around with…"

"Walking around with what?" Harry demanded.

Waylen ignored both questions. "Then where is it?"

"At the hotel."

"What did they steal?"

"Wallet. Phone."

"Room key?"

"Crap, yeah." Cody touched his lip. "Can I take the car?"

"Not before you tell me what's going on!" Harry shouted.

"Two men followed me. I pulled over near the park, hoping they'd pass, but they jumped out and dragged me from the rental. They checked the glove box, and every inch of me, before shoving me in the trunk. I was robbed," Cody said.

"And why were you the target?"

Waylen shook his head, trying to silence Cody Sanderson, and the guy seemed to clue in. "They must have seen an easy mark."

"I don't know what you two are hiding, but if you don't—"

"I'm working on a federal case, Harry," Waylen interrupted. "It involves the murder of at least three people, breaking and entering, and a few more attempted murders thrown in for good measure. I'm not at liberty to discuss, but I might need a favor or two in the next twenty-four hours."

Harry Truman chewed on the inside of his mouth and gave Waylen a nod. "What can I do?"

"For starters, we have a funeral for Peter Gunn tomorrow. Whoever attacked Cody will be present. They'll be looking for me. I'll require backup."

"That's not my precinct."

"But I assume since it's only a few blocks from your turf, you're on good terms?"

"Of course."

"Ten men will do, but twenty would be better. I'll brief them at eleven AM in the alley behind the church."

"Consider it done," Truman said.

Waylen was surprised by his quick agreement, and wondered for a moment whether Harry was on the take as well. "Why are you helping me?"

"As I said, I like the FBI. Plus, Peter Gunn was a hero of mine. I had posters of Helios 15 on my wall when I was a kid."

Waylen shook his hand again, grateful for the support. "You have my number if you need any more details."

"I'll be there in street clothes. I was already planning to attend." Harry motioned to the lot worker to let Cody leave with his car.

"You're using yourself as bait?" Cody asked.

"Don't feel bad for me. I'm using you too."

Cody stammered a response, but Waylen didn't listen. "I'll follow you to the hotel."

The place was on the lower end of the price spectrum, an old building with three stories and a sign in desperate need of updating. But the sidewalk was clean, and an older woman watered fresh potted flowers near the entrance.

Waylen appreciated the fact he could find street parking. It was far less crowded than the area surrounding Times Square, but he'd wanted to be in the middle of the action. It was easier to lose yourself in a crowd, yet more dangerous for the bystanders, should an altercation break out.

The lobby floor was spotless, the ceiling made with tin, like so many of these older Manhattan properties.

"Can I help you?" a man asked.

"Cody Sanderson. I have a room here, but I've lost my key."

"ID," the guy said.

"They took that too."

"I'm afraid…"

Waylen flipped his government-issued ID out, and the clerk mouthed the letters. *F.B.I.* "We need a replacement card, please. This is an investigation."

"Yes, sir." He quickly swapped it and smiled at Waylen. "You know, I wanted to work for the CIA."

Waylen tapped the card on the desk. "It's mostly filing paperwork."

Cody walked toward the elevator, but Waylen directed him to the stairwell. "It's only three stories."

He gestured at his torn clothing. "Fine, but it might take me a while."

Waylen touched his holstered gun when they arrived on the top floor and pressed through the doorway. It was quiet. "Stay behind me," he ordered, and Cody gave no sign he'd heard the comment.

The carpet was red and thick, worn in the center from years of use. It held the faint odor of cigarettes, and he noticed several suite doors were personalized with knick-knacks. Some of these old places had permanent residents with rent control. "What number?"

"309."

Waylen glanced at the closest one. 305. Something rattled ahead, and he unclasped his holster, clutching the handgun. He paused at the corner, guessing it was Cody's suite around the edge. Waylen took a deep breath and stepped out, aiming the weapon.

A man dropped an ice bucket and let out a whimper. He had on large white slippers, boxer shorts, and a tank top that said he loved the Big Apple. "I didn't do it!"

"Get out of here," Waylen ordered, and the man left the spilled ice, running in the other direction.

Cody's door was shut, and Waylen tapped the card to the electronic handle. It beeped green, and he depressed the lever, moving slowly. He listened before fully opening it, but there was no sound emerging from the suite. He entered, and Cody bumped into him. "They trashed it."

A suitcase was on the floor, every bit ripped apart. Clothing covered the bed, and the mattress was over-turned, the pillows sliced in half lengthwise.

"Did they get it?" Waylen asked.

Cody rushed to the closet and pointed at the hole where a safe should have been. Drywall dust lingered on the stained white cabinets, and it was clear they'd taken the entire thing with them. "It's gone."

Waylen had nearly brought all three pieces of the Delta together, but now it seemed impossible to finish the mission without everything coming to a head. He picked up the chair and sat on it, thinking of his next steps.

"What are we going to do?" Cody asked. "These guys will kill me."

"Why didn't they?"

"Huh?"

"Why are you alive?"

Cody shrugged, which seemed to pain him. "You tell me."

Waylen walked to the window and spread the dusty blinds. Had they set it up to trap him? Did they linger at the impound, then trail them back to the hotel, or were they stationed nearby, waiting for Cody to return with someone? Waylen was running on fumes, making poor decisions. For the tenth time, he wished Special Agent Sanchez was with him. "We can't stay here."

Cody crouched, gathering his belongings, and shoved them into the damaged suitcase. "Think they'll give me the deposit back?"

Where could they go that wouldn't be under surveillance?

Waylen remembered Silas mentioning the family event at his parents' house and figured it would be public knowledge. He suspected more than a few cousins or nephews might post about the gathering, trying to get likes based on their removed lineage from one of America's greats, Peter Gunn. But there were precious few other options.

Waylen hurried them outside after telling the desk clerk what had happened. The man didn't seem to care, but he scrawled the details onto a notepad.

There were no occupied vehicles parked down the block, or any white vans. "Leave the rental. They might think you're still in the room."

Cody climbed into Waylen's car and stared at the

driver's side. "Can I see them?"

"No."

Cody rolled his window down a few inches as Waylen headed from the East Village, taking the FDR north to Queensboro Bridge. He texted Silas at the lineup for the toll station, letting him know they were coming.

He was certain this organization would make their move at the funeral tomorrow, so Waylen needed to stay alive for another night if he was to have a chance at bringing them in. He'd never noticed how many white vans there were in the city until he was on the lookout for them.

"I want to know everything about the Delta," Waylen said, driving through Long Island.

"It isn't much."

"Start at the beginning."

"I met Fred Trell when I was twenty-nine…"

11

Rory checked her reflection, finding both cheeks red. She'd over-applied her blush, hoping to make her injury less obvious, but she just looked flushed. Silas' parents' house was lovely and modest. She appreciated how well they'd done financially, and yet, they lived in a home they'd owned for three decades.

She wondered what it felt like to be so grounded, connected to a place. Maybe it wasn't the house but the memories associated with it that kept them from moving. They'd watched Silas and his sister Clare grow up, and now they had grandchildren running through the same halls their children had used. It made Rory think about her parents, and how they'd owned a home for nearly the same amount of time.

The sentiment was alien to Rory, but perhaps there was a missing piece she hadn't understood until that moment. They were in love. Kathy and Oscar were infatuated, and from the brief interaction she'd had around Arthur and Alice, it was obvious their flames burned deep.

"You okay?" Silas asked through the door.

"Fine." She opened it and accepted a glass of wine.

"Waylen's coming," he said. "With Cody."

"Is he… Did they…?"

"Waylen's driving, and he wasn't any more forthcoming than that."

Rory stepped into the living room and glanced at the assortment of Silas' family members. Twenty of them crowded around the TV, a baseball game playing loudly. "You have a big family," she told him.

"And everyone stayed in the area." He lifted a glass when a man who looked to be his uncle nodded at him.

"Did any of them keep in touch with Peter?"

"Uncle Marty." Silas pointed to the right side of the couch. The man was old, a beer in his grip, his eyelids fluttering between awake and sleeping. "But I don't think they'd seen one another in ages. Marty's got a heart thing."

The Mets must have scored a run, because the group cheered. Marty almost spilled from the can as he sat up-right.

"You're Rory," a voice said, and she turned to find Clare approaching, with Arthur on her heels.

"Yes."

"Colin Swanson's granddaughter," Arthur said. "Is your father coming tomorrow?"

"Yes."

"Rory and her mom were jumped last night in the city, so they stayed at the hotel tonight instead of joining us for dinner," Silas said.

"What a travesty." Clare sipped from her wineglass. "That's why we moved to the suburbs."

Rory didn't know who *we* were, but figured Silas would fill her in later.

"That must have been horrible. Did they take any-thing?" Arthur asked.

"Our purses."

"Was it because of…" Arthur made a triangle with his fingers, and Rory shot Silas a glance.

"Turns out my dad saw it once," Silas said. "By the

way, Special Agent Waylen Brooks is coming for dinner too. With a mutual friend of ours."

"A friend? You seem to find all sorts of those these days, son." Arthur gazed at Rory. "I hope whatever's going on is dealt with soon. We don't want any trouble while we honor Peter. He may have been a tough old badger, but he was still our family."

"He also didn't deserve to be shot in the chest in his own home," Silas said.

"That's true." Arthur turned when the doorbell rang and left without excusing himself.

"Don't mind him. He hates funerals *and* his dad, so this is a double whammy," Clare said. "I like your outfit."

"Thanks," Rory said. "I like yours too." She peered at the door, finding Waylen entering. The man with him looked to be in rough shape, and Clare muttered something about letting vagrants into their private celebration before storming off.

"What happened to him?" Arthur demanded.

"Dad, just give us a day. We don't know where else to go," Silas said.

"Fine, but clean him up. You can offer him some of my clothes from the giveaway pile in the garage."

Waylen urged Cody inside, and only a couple of Silas' relatives broke their gaze on the TV. "You two holding up?"

"Better than Cody, by the looks of it," Silas answered. "Come on, Cody. Let's get you changed."

Waylen stayed with Rory at the end of the hall as the other pair wandered deeper into the home.

"Found him in the trunk of his car," Waylen said. "They stole the Delta piece."

"That's not good."

"No, it isn't. But on a positive note, the commander

of the 9th Precinct has promised me ten officers tomorrow for the funeral."

"You're actually doing it, aren't you?" she asked.

"Drawing them out? Yes."

"With all those people around?"

"You have a better idea?"

"I don't like it." Rory would have to convince her parents not to attend the service, and her dad might be an easy sell after the two incidents their family had gone through since Peter Gunn was killed.

"Wait until you hear everything. Then decide." Waylen loosened his tie and checked his phone.

"Expecting something?"

"Martina…my partner."

"What about her?"

"She hasn't responded today."

"Is that unusual?"

"Not really. She could be in the field. I don't really know what case she was thrown into." Waylen leaned on the wall, surveying the crowded living room. "I feel like an intruder."

"Same here. We'll try to stay out of the way," Rory said. "Wine?"

"Nah, I'd better not."

Silas returned, and Cody seemed slightly improved, though the pants were obviously too large at the waist for his slender frame. The fabric bunched up under the belt, and the shirt hung loose on his shoulders. "Rory, this is Cody."

"Nice to meet you."

"The famous author and granddaughter of Colin Swanson. I spoke to him once, did you know that?" Cody said.

Rory shook her head. "No."

"I wanted to see if they had any interest in bringing the Delta together, against Fred's wishes. He was polite, but firm, and had no desire to allow the sections in the same state, let alone the same house."

"What happened to those three men?" Rory asked. Cody looked ready to comment when someone clinked a glass with a utensil.

"Dinner's buffet style. Sit where you like, but please, give deference to your elders," Alice said crisply.

Silas joined his family at the main table, but Rory hung back with Cody and Waylen, opting to eat in the living room. The TV remained on, but the volume was muted. Two younger cousins stayed glued to the game.

"I'd like to propose a toast," Arthur said. "Peter Gunn was challenging, but I have fond memories of him too. He won America's heart as an astronaut, landing on the Moon when it should have been impossible, and showing the world what the United States represented. His flaws notwithstanding, Peter deserves to be respected for his accomplishments, and I am eternally grateful for his patriotism. To Peter."

"To Peter!" the family echoed, and Rory lifted her glass too, feigning the action.

Marty, awake after his nap, rose, using the table to brace himself. "My brother loved precious few things, but they included his country, Jack Martin, and above all, his wife, the beautiful Patty. May God rest her soul. But he loathed the Moon. I never understood this, considering he'd landed on it, and had the pleasure of experiencing something so few ever will. I've often wondered why. He left as a strong, loving father, then came back broken." Marty lowered his chin and held his beer with a shaky hand. "I love you, Petey. Both versions. May you find peace in the stars."

"Peace in the stars," Arthur repeated quietly.

"That was nice," Cody whispered. "You'd be different too if you traveled to another planet."

Waylen glared at the newcomer. "Keep it down."

Rory listened to the various stories as Silas' family shared their memories of Peter, ranging from childhood fist fights at the school grounds to the years after his retirement. Silas looked engaged, smiling at the stories. She offered to help clean up, and slowly the family departed until only Silas, his parents, and their group remained.

"Did you have a good time?" Rory asked.

"I haven't heard most of those anecdotes." Silas peeled the label on his beer bottle. "It's cool to think he was a normal kid before he flew into space. It's difficult seeing him as anything but that iconic image."

Rory knew the one, the famous photo of Grandpa Swanson and Commander Gunn as they stepped onto the Moon.

"Let's go to the basement," Waylen proposed. "We have to talk."

Silas went ahead, turning the lights on. The basement felt cozy, filled with crocheted blankets on retro furniture. A large flat-screen felt out of place in the time warp. The light fixtures had amber globes, casting a warm light, adding to the ambience. There was the faint odor of marijuana and incense. She glanced at Silas, wondering if he was the culprit or if Clare was to blame.

Waylen sat with Cody and Silas headed to a minifridge, pulling out a couple of beers. Rory didn't feel like drinking, but took one when the others accepted. "I think we're going to need this," Waylen said. "Cody, tell them your theory."

"No preamble? Introduction? Foreplay?" Cody smiled, but lost the grin when the room stayed silent.

"The Delta is an alien tool, and it can't be destroyed. Fred tried everything."

"Why destroy it if it's alien?" Rory asked.

"Because it could be the downfall of life as we know it," Cody whispered, then took a swallow from his beer. "Or not. I can't see the future."

Rory found Cody's answers evasive and a little condescending. "How is it dangerous?"

"Again, I'm not positive what it does. Fred wouldn't say precisely. He swore it was better for me not to be aware of its actual function. He also reminded me I'd never have the entire Delta, so it didn't matter."

"What have you deduced about the tokens?" Silas pressed. Judging by his expression, he was as annoyed as Rory.

"The Delta holds memories," Cody said. "Silas, you mentioned you saw the Moon. That's different than the one Fred had."

Rory's arm hair rose. "What did you see?"

"Another world. The sun was harsh, the ground gray and cracked, like a desert in a drought. There were rocky cliffs and red skies." Cody finished his beer, setting the bottle down. "The Shadow was present."

"Shadow?" Rory rested her elbows on her knees.

"The hole with black tendrils of mist. I think that's the portal."

"Does the Delta make them?" Silas inquired.

"I believe so, but I can't be certain. The Shadow might always be there, and the Delta merely acts as a link between them."

"How many times have you viewed the echo of this planet?"

"Probably a hundred?" Cody mused.

"A hundred!" Silas laughed nervously and sat on the

couch, kicking his feet up on the worn coffee table.

"Didn't it make you sick?" Rory shuddered, reminiscing on her view of the Moon.

"Sure, at first. That wears off. Your brain becomes used to it, I guess."

"Show us." Waylen removed one from his pocket. "This was Colin's."

Cody licked his lips, reaching for it, and Waylen snatched it away. "Could you look any creepier?"

"Sorry," he said. "I've wanted to see the other two for a decade."

Waylen extended his arm, and Cody gently accepted the section of the Delta. He slipped it from the bag and set it on the table without touching the surface. "It's quite simple. You merely—"

Cody placed his palm on it, and his chin shot up, his eyes rolling into his head as he gargled a bizarre noise.

Cody paled and convulsed. "Get it away from him!" Rory shouted, and Waylen pried his hand off. The bookmark-shaped token fell to the carpet, and Cody slid off the couch, landing beside it. They turned him over in case he threw up, but only a string of drool emerged.

Rory was ready to take someone's phone to call an ambulance, when he gasped and flopped onto his back. "What the actual—" Cody coughed, not finishing his sentence.

"What did you see?" Waylen heaved him onto the couch, and Cody clutched the armrest.

"Earth…from the Moon. The Shadow was on the surface, and… I sensed something behind me."

Rory peered at the stairs, perceiving they were being watched, but no one was there.

"I thought you said the brain acclimated to them," Waylen said.

"Mine did. I could go anytime with the token. It must not transfer between the different sections." Cody wiped his lips with a sleeve. "That was intense. I forgot how powerful they can be."

"How did anyone learn about its function, and who are they?" Rory asked.

"That's what I have to find out, and quickly," Waylen said. "I'm being pulled from the case after the weekend, and if I don't satisfy Assistant Director Ben, he's going to demand these pieces of the Delta."

"At least we'll be done with it," Rory said. "What do we care if these people take it?"

"They killed my grandfather and Leigh. You were kidnapped. Cody was thrown into a trunk. We're not letting them get away with this," Silas proclaimed.

Waylen checked his phone and smiled as he opened a message. "The field office found out who sent our friend Francis Jack Barker to the charity event. It was Governor McKenzie."

"Seriously?" Rory had read articles about the woman and thought she had a good head on her shoulders. She was a lawyer, pivoting into politics in her late fifties. Her mother adored the governor, and had a hardcover of her biography in the living room back home in Woodstock.

"My office contacted her people, and were advised that McKenzie was busy attending a prominent funeral, but could talk on Monday," Waylen said. "I think we might have found out who's in charge of this operation."

Cody stared at the relic on the carpet, unblinking.

"Cody, you said you wanted to gather the entire Delta. What were you going to do with it?" Rory asked.

He broke his gaze, got up, and grabbed another beer from the small fridge. "What anyone given the opportunity would do. Travel to an alien world."

12

Silas entered the church three hours before the service was scheduled to begin. From the outside, it was almost menacing, with Victorian Gothic spires and giant wooden doors that could likely fend off any attack. The stained glass depicted images of Jesus, seemingly from various cultures. Inside, it radiated a warmth that probably extended to the congregation during sermons. The ceiling was ornate, with domes and molding from another century. At the far end stood the largest organ Silas had ever seen.

He strode in, the carpet between the aisles of pews softening his footsteps. He touched the carving on the first bench, astounded by the level of intricate details.

"They don't build them like this anymore," a man said. He wore a black robe, with a blue bowtie beneath.

"You're not kidding."

"I'm Reverend Grant." He offered his hand, and Silas shook it.

"Are you leading the service today?"

"I am. You're family?"

Silas gazed to the front of the aisle, where a coffin sat closed. A team arrived, setting up easels with an assortment of photos. "Yeah, Peter was my grandfather."

The reverend studied him intently. "*To everything there is a season, for every purpose under heaven. A time to be born, and a time to die.* Your grandfather was stolen from us in a horrific manner, but you may take solace in the fact he's now being protected by the God who's called him home."

Silas wasn't religious, though he had no qualms with the faithful, but claiming God wanted Peter to be gunned down in a home invasion was pushing it. But the reverend was attempting to comfort him, so he didn't argue.

"It's going to be a packed house," Grant said.

"Yeah?"

"The press is already causing grief outside."

Silas had seen a couple of news vans pulling up before entering, but nothing they hadn't expected. He walked toward the coffin as the last photo was put into place. Seeing Peter Gunn in various stages of his life was strange. Funerals seemed odd to Silas. It was like you had to wait for someone to die to hear who they really were. Why hadn't he had a relationship with his grandfather? Silas could have picked up a phone or flown out to visit him.

He set a palm on the coffin, closing his eyes. He pictured sitting on the end of the lake house's pier with Peter, sipping a cup of coffee as the sun rose. Mist lifted from the calm water; inky black coils stretched and reached for Silas' pant cuff. The Shadow lingered on the lake, a hole without borders, a portal to another world. He squinted in the dream state, feeling a coldness emanating from the Shadow, and he saw the ends of his fingers turning blue. When he turned to check on Peter, his grandfather wasn't there.

"Son, are you all right?" Reverend Grant tapped his shoulder, and he broke contact with the smooth mahogany casket.

Silas peered at his hands, but they were fine, unaltered by his imagination. He patted his pocket, feeling the familiar rectangular shape.

"Son?"

"It's just hard to believe he's in there." The line worked, and Grant let it go, walking to the pulpit. He flipped a Bible open and adjusted the microphone.

"We have some finishing touches before the ceremony. Would you care for a room to gather your thoughts?"

"No, I'll manage." Silas almost ran from the church, careful not to look conspicuous. He stopped when he pushed outside, finding dozens of photographers snapping his picture.

"Mr. Gunn, did you see his body?" one called.

"Silas, what is your response to the news that they caught the killers?"

"Do you think they really flew to the Moon, or was he murdered because he threatened to expose the truth?"

The catcalls continued, and Silas shoved through the crowd, disgusted by their questions. He hopped into the chauffeured car his father had rented, and the paparazzi followed.

Rory had a new phone, and he sent it a text. *Want to meet up?*

With my parents. Give me a few?

Silas knew a breakfast place a few blocks east, and directed the driver to it while passing the location to Rory. It was pretty busy, with all the patio bistro tables filled with happy couples on a sunny Friday morning. Silas preferred the indoors anyway, in case someone recognized him.

He went to the counter, where three empty stools sat in a row. He tilted the one next to him and reached for a menu.

A woman dumped coffee into a filter. "Didn't I just see you on TV?"

"I don't think so," he said.

She gestured at the flat screen to the right. Footage of Silas appeared, with the subtitles scrolling on the bottom. *Peter Gunn's grandson, Silas, was spotted at Gull Creek before a mysterious fire killed a young woman at a grocery store. The station's heard that he was also present in Rye, New Hampshire, when the suspect was gunned down. Two others are reported to be in custody, awaiting their arraignment. The FBI has failed to respond to our request, but the local PD in Rye gave a detailed interview.*

It showed the new chief frowning as he stood outside the police station. *"The FBI botched our investigation, and I've filed an official complaint. It was actually the Rye Police Department that caught the killers."*

Silas rolled his eyes and accepted a coffee from the server without even asking.

"Big day for you," she said.

"It's just a funeral."

"Were you really there?"

"I'd rather not talk about it."

"Want something to eat?" she asked.

He read Rory's text when it arrived. *Dealing with my parents. I can't get away. See you at the service.*

Silas understood, but he didn't want to be alone, not while there were people hunting down the tokens from the Moon. Waylen's plan seemed too brazen, and the fact it would minimize Peter's funeral didn't sit well with Silas. But if it was over after today, he would accept the situation.

"Sure, I'll take the pancakes. Extra bacon."

"Coming right up."

Silas watched as the image of the church panned out, and the newscasters switched to another story. Tomorrow, it would be done, and they could all move on.

"We can't hide in our hotel room, Rory," Oscar said. He adjusted his black tie and scratched at his chin. He'd shaved, and it left a red patch on his skin.

"Your father is correct." Kathy wore a nice black dress with gold buttons and a matching paperclip-chain necklace.

"You're not listening to me!" Rory blurted. "They attacked us on the streets. Mom, they could have killed you."

"I'm fine. We're in New York, and we got mugged. It could happen to anyone," she said.

"Four days after Jack abducted me from our home?"

"They'll have security and cameras," Oscar added. "We'll be safer in the church than here."

Rory had tried everything, but in the end, it was their choice. The service was in an hour, and she still hadn't gotten dressed.

"Let me help you," Kathy said. Rory reluctantly permitted her mom in from the adjoining room. "This place is a mess."

There were two outfits lying on the desk, and a bag with supplies from the drugstore a block away. Hardly what Rory would call a mess, but she didn't take the bait. "Which one?"

Kathy eyed them and pointed at the dress. "You're young. Wear this."

Rory slipped into it and turned in the mirror, checking both sides.

"You look nice," her mom told her.

The rare and elusive compliment. "Thanks." Rory spent ten minutes applying makeup and trying to fix her hair while her parents talked quietly in the next room, the door propped open between them.

"I've asked the concierge to get us a car," Oscar said, and exited to the hall.

Kathy had a new purse, something from the department store on Fifth. Rory had opted for a cheap black clutch, since apparently the strap didn't prevent her from being robbed anyway.

It was bright out, the sun high overhead. She realized she rarely saw it in the city, unless it was being reflected off the insane number of glass panes on the enormous buildings lining the claustrophobic streets. The park looked busy in the distance, and Rory longed to skip the funeral and wander through Central Park instead. She could visit the zoo, row herself under the bridge, and storm Belvedere Castle. Rory might hear an acoustic version of "Imagine" in Strawberry Fields, or circle Jackie Onassis Reservoir while runners passed her on the right.

Instead, she went into the front seat while her parents occupied the back, and the driver flicked his blinker on, turning toward Madison Avenue.

"You know Commander Gunn?" the guy asked. He had a thick local accent, likely from a nearby borough, born and raised on New York pizza and a steady stream of baseball. He was the kind of character she loved introducing into her books, never to be seen again.

"Yes," Oscar answered. "He was my...godfather."

"No kidding. Imagine his life," the driver said. "Everyone considers the destination as the entire mission, but I think the journey must have been the best part. Speeding through space, hoping like hell the nerds at NASA programmed that old computer box properly. One false move, and..." He slapped his hands to the steering wheel, startling Rory. "Sorry 'bout that. I remember watching the launch when I was just five. I'm surprised he was still alive. I figured they'd all passed ages ago."

Rory wanted to ask him to stop talking, but since the drive was short, she held back. Traffic was lined up in both directions, and she knew they should have just walked. But given the recent incident, she understood why her parents had opted for the ride.

"Hold on, I have a secret way." The driver honked and cut into the left lane before darting in front of oncoming traffic into the world's narrowest alley. "Told you…" He swerved to avoid a delivery courier on a bike, his basket stuffed full of Chinese takeout bags.

After five minutes of slow yet extremely bumpy alley roads, he stopped and gestured at the back of the church. "See?"

"Great. You don't mind if I send you my chiropractor bill, do you?" Oscar asked while climbing out. He offered his hand to his wife, and Kathy emerged from his side.

Three squad cars sat a few yards ahead, the lights off. Down the way, Rory spotted more, and wondered if Waylen had briefed them on his plan yet. It was dangerous, and Rory couldn't help but feel slightly used by the agent. Waylen didn't come across as callous, but it was clear he wanted to figure this case out before he was pulled from it. Would he place innocent people in danger to accomplish that?

She opened her clutch as the car drove off and peered at the slender token within. He'd given her the piece of the Delta before they separated last night. Silas had the other.

"Oscar, slow down. Do you see the size of these potholes?" Kathy grumbled.

They entered the slender space between the church and the neighboring building, and Rory paused as they stepped onto Madison Avenue. The road was blockaded on both ends, closing the avenue from 73rd to 74th. A helicopter lingered in the air above, and she noticed the news channel number on the exterior. There were dozens of vans, and fifty reporters and camerapeople stationed around the entrance.

"Quite the spectacle," Kathy murmured.

Rory watched as a limousine arrived, parking at the barriers, and two police officers opened the doors. Out came Governor McKenzie, along with a man that looked vaguely familiar.

"That's her," Kathy said. "Do you think I could get her autograph?"

Rory hadn't mentioned the governor might be involved, given the woman's association with her kidnapper.

"And that's the administrator of NASA," Oscar said. "I read an article about him last month. Did you know the president chooses the incumbent?"

Rory had known that because of her extensive research on the subject three years ago for her book. "Let's find our seats."

Silas hung at the entrance with his parents. Clare met Rory's gaze, then rushed off to chase her kids as they played in the pews.

"This looks lovely," Kathy told them.

"Oscar, how nice to see you again!" Arthur shook his hand, then kissed Kathy on the cheek. "And, Kathy, it's been too long."

"Since Colin's funeral. We have to stop meeting like this," she said with the hint of a smile. Her mom, always good at small talk. Alice gave her a light hug.

"We're sorry for your loss," Oscar told the pair.

"The country lost a good statesman," Arthur said.

Silas waved Rory over and leaned in. "I haven't seen Waylen yet. He didn't respond to my texts."

Rory glanced at the front of the church, and there he was, standing with a police officer. She gave him a subtle wave, and he returned the gesture with a curt nod. "I don't like this," she told Silas.

"Me either. Come on, we saved you some seats with the family."

13

Waylen despised funerals, but he supposed most people did—except the businesses catering to the industry, perhaps. Death was a constant, and he suspected the margins were high when it came to shiny coffins and premium real estate in mausoleums.

Everyone had gathered, the church past the pews filled with visitors paying their respects in the standing room only section. The front doors were closed, with the reporters and photographers waiting for the pallbearers to carry Peter Gunn away.

"You seriously think the person responsible is going to show?" Deputy Inspector Harry Truman asked.

"Yes." He watched Governor McKenzie and tried to imagine a world where she was seeking alien artifacts and leaving a trail of bodies behind. It didn't add up. The NASA administrator, Clark Fallow, was there, seeming like a corpse himself. His pallid skin had a sheen of sweat, and from the looks of things, his hairpiece was askew. "I have to speak to both of them afterward."

"We've cordoned off the block, and we're keeping our eyes out for any white vans." Harry turned his radio down. "If these guys are coming, we'll be ready."

They'd ended up getting twenty-two officers to patrol down Madison and the adjoining avenues of Fifth and Park. Waylen was happy, but it would be overkill unless whoever paid Jack's salary had sent others to acquire the last two tokens of the Delta.

He'd wanted to leave Cody Sanderson at the hotel, but he'd demanded to be part of it. He claimed his close relationship with Fred Trell gave him the authority he needed to witness Commander Gunn's service. Waylen could monitor him better here, so he'd relented.

Instead of sitting, they stood off in the shadows as Reverend Grant took to the lectern. Waylen gazed at the photos. On the left, Peter was maybe six, with spiked hair, the sides shaved. He had a pair of black plastic sunglasses on and smiled widely, revealing a missing tooth. Beside it, a photo of him playing basketball in high school. It must have been in the early fifties, given his timeline. He'd gone to the Moon in 1972, at thirty-five. Next, his college graduation picture. He'd started to look like the man in all the magazines and newspapers from his glory years.

He scanned the rest. A wedding. Holding a baby that had to be Arthur. A shot of him in the Air Force, resting his hand on the hull of a fighter jet. He'd lived an incredible life summed up in ten still photos, ending with a picture of him on the Moon, and then a candid one of him on the pier with his tea, observing Loon Lake.

Waylen scanned the crowd, furious that someone possibly in this room had orchestrated his murder, all for a piece of metal. He noticed Peter's only daughter was in the pews, wearing a black hat with a feather in it.

Reverend Grant spoke, but Waylen didn't focus on his words. He watched the individuals instead. Rory sat with Silas, centered between each of their parents. Cody was a few pews behind, eyes darting around the church. After a while, some of Peter's relatives made their way to the stage, discussing their feelings for the departed.

He observed the governor, who didn't flinch at any of the eulogies. Waylen wondered if Silas or his father might speak, but neither got in front of the crowd. Eventually, it ended with a prayer, and Waylen glanced at Harry, who nodded as he pressed the radio speaker to his ear.

"Something?"

"We found a van. Unmarked, like you said, with cuffs and duct tape inside. A shotgun, too."

"Did you get them?" he asked.

"The vehicle was empty. We've left it and are scoping the area now. I have a team in civilian clothing. If they return, we'll get them."

That meant at least one armed assailant presently stalked nearby, searching for the Delta. It was a gamble splitting them up with Rory and Silas, but they were the only pair he trusted. Sanchez was MIA, not responding to his messages for two days, and the cop beside him might be on the take. Waylen didn't know how far the reach went.

When it finished, the organ player keyed a mournful tune, and the crowd dispersed. The casket remained closed, but people still filed up to pay their respects. Waylen bypassed the pews and caught up with the governor and the NASA executive. "Excuse me, I'm Special Agent Waylen Brooks, and I'd like a word with you."

"Me?" Clark Fallow asked.

"Both, please."

"My secretary told me someone from the FBI had called." McKenzie smiled when she turned toward the guests, but frowned when no one could see her.

"It won't take long." A security detail escorted them to a private office in the church, and he asked Governor McKenzie to join him.

"Am I supposed to just wait?" Clark snapped.

"Please give us a minute." Waylen closed the door.

"What can I do for you…?"

"Special Agent Brooks." He motioned to a chair and sat on the desk when she took it. "Does the name Francis Jack Barker mean anything to you?"

"Should it?"

"You paid for him to attend a children's hospital benefit last autumn."

"I did?"

"Your office sent him," Waylen said.

"What is this about?"

"Governor, the man you're linked to is awaiting trial for abduction and attempted murder. He's also connected to the person who killed Peter Gunn. Imagine the story if it broke. Not to mention you attended his funeral, on the same day they announced their discovery."

"I assure you, I have no relationship with anyone by that name."

Waylen assessed her answer, and nothing about her voice or body language showed she was lying. But she was well-practiced, being a politician. "Will you find out who authorized him, and if he was ever on your payroll?"

"Yes, I'll get right on it."

"Does the word Delta mean anything to you?" he asked, attempting to catch her off guard.

"It's an airline I avidly avoid booking with," she said jokingly.

Someone banged on the door, and Waylen found Harry Truman impatiently entering. "We got him."

"Mrs. McKenzie, please stay put. I'm not done yet." Waylen nodded at Clark, and gestured to the police officer remaining behind. "They don't leave."

"Yes, sir," the woman said.

Sirens sounded from the south, and that was the direction Harry led him in. "Scour the area, there could be more!" he called into his radio.

The sun reflected off the tall glass buildings, glaring into Waylen's eyes as they jogged through the crowded street, barricaded for the service. Reporters had shifted their focus to the scene unfolding three blocks from the church's stairs.

Waylen had a passing thought, wondering where Rory, Silas, and the tokens they held for him were, but it vanished when he saw the giant man fighting with three officers. The guy was at least six-foot-four and two-thirty, making it difficult for anyone to handcuff him. Even with six guns pointed at his chest, he refused to give in.

Waylen glanced through the area, finding bystanders recording the altercation with their cell phones from dangerously close positions. He counted twenty officers, meaning most of the support he'd requested was currently trying to subdue this suspect.

He peered toward the church and had a sinking feeling. "It's a distraction," he said.

"What?" Deputy Inspector Truman asked.

The giant from the van was pressed against it, fighting to wrestle free. He was making a lot of noise and kept looking north. "We have to go back." Waylen ran. Above, the news copter continued to circle, and most of the cameramen were recording the police takedown.

He spied Cody Sanderson backing up, an expression of abject fear plastered on his face. Waylen detached his holstered gun and crept to the edge of the building.

———————

*T*he cars waited at the edge of the alley, parked behind

the building. Silas' great uncle Marty and his wife were already entering the first, and Silas smiled as his niece and nephew piled in right before his parents. "You guys coming later?"

"I think so," Rory said. "You sure you want us there? You're already going to have a full house."

"Mom loves the company, plus it's been a tough day for everyone. My dad may seem like he doesn't care that his dad is dead, but it's really bothering him. He probably wishes they could have hashed things out before he passed," Silas told her.

"Guys…" Cody bumped into Silas.

"What's—"

"That's the guy that hit me. He took the piece of the Delta," Cody whispered.

Silas paused as the pair entered the alley. On the far side, two other men wearing black suits, probably to blend with the funeral crowd, cut off their escape path.

"Hand it over," the leader said. He lunged to the corner of the building, thrusting Clare forward. Her cheeks were covered in tears, her makeup running. His partner grabbed Silas' sister and clutched an arm around her neck, pointing a handgun at her temple. She sobbed, trying to claw her way free, but the guy tensed his muscles, choking her. "I said give them to me!"

Silas reached into his pocket and removed the token, carefully dangling it between two fingers. Rory muttered something unintelligible and did the same.

"They're right here. Let her go!" Silas shouted.

He peered past Clare and saw Waylen sneaking up behind the duo with the deputy inspector. Silas couldn't risk their enemies noticing Waylen's arrival. "You want this?" he shouted, drawing everyone's attention. "You can have them. We're sick of this."

He let it fall to the cobblestones. Rory did the same, and Cody knocked over a metal trash can, aiming to hide himself.

The moment it clanged on the concrete, the leader fell to the street. Clare shrieked as the man holding her dropped his gun, and multiple gunshots echoed in the alley. Police had the two suspects by the parked limousines surrounded, and they lowered their weapons.

Waylen crouched by the injured men as an ambulance broke through the barricades, screeching to a halt near the bodies. Cameramen had returned to the scene, filming the dead bodies, and Clare scrambling to her feet, rushing Silas. He hugged her, trying to calm his frantic sister. Her dress was sticky with the perp's blood.

Sirens rang loudly, and voices shouted while Silas ushered them to safety. Rory clutched the tokens, each wrapped protectively in their bags. Waylen made eye contact with Silas as he checked the dead man's pockets. He pulled an object out and held it up.

Two dead, two in custody, and three tokens.

The funeral had finished, and Silas thought his grandfather must be turning over in his coffin. Peter Gunn's worst nightmare had come true.

They'd reunited the Delta for the first time since its discovery on the Moon, fifty years earlier.

PART FOUR
ECHOES OF THE PAST

1

Rory gazed through the police station's third-story window, watching the low reflection of the setting sun. Deputy Inspector Truman allowed their group to use the facility while they gathered their thoughts, and Waylen had escorted them to the room two hours earlier. After more dead bodies, Rory was tired of witnessing such brutal violence.

She checked her phone, sending her parents another text. They were in the hotel room, staying out of sight as instructed, and were constantly asking for updates.

"This was not the funeral my grandfather would have wanted." Silas sat in a worn chair, bits of fabric missing along the metal frame. He idly picked at the edges.

"No one wants a funeral," Cody Sanderson said. His stare rarely left the table where the three tokens were placed. He reached for one, and Rory shot him a glare.

"Don't." Rory didn't have to keep the threat going.

"This is incredible. We have the Delta." Cody took the seat next to Silas and checked the clock. "We'll bring the tokens to San Diego and test it."

Rory let him have his fantasy, but she highly doubted Waylen would allow them out of his sight before delivering the tokens to someone up the chain. Possibly to the NASA administrator he was visiting down the hall, but more likely the military.

Silas absently rubbed his knuckles. "They could have killed my sister."

"But they didn't," Rory said.

"Why did they shoot? The deputy inspector might have missed."

"She's alive and safe."

Silas continued to peer at the floor. "I'm over this."

"Me too," Rory admitted.

"Guys," Cody interjected. "We have something that can change the world."

"Jack said the same thing, and look where he is. The state penitentiary." Rory walked to the exit. "Anyone want another coffee?"

They both grumbled acknowledgments, and she paused before leaving. "Don't touch the Delta."

"Is she always so demanding?" Cody asked Silas.

Silas finally smiled. "I don't mind."

Rory strolled through the hall, heading downstairs. The room had a bunch of desks, most filled with clutter and messy paperwork. Each had an old phone, along with computers that appeared to be from another decade. A couple of officers chatted by the main doors, and a few were on their cells, scrolling or talking to someone.

"Can I help you?" a woman asked. She wasn't in uniform, but her pantsuit indicated she was on staff.

"I'm trying to find some coffee," Rory said.

"You're with the FBI agent, right?"

Rory read the badge hanging around her neck and saw the woman's name was Ling. "Yeah, we shouldn't be here much longer."

"I'm Amy Ling, NYPD homicide. What were those people doing attacking the family at a funeral? It has me wondering—is the furniture company a front for something else? Money laundering?" Ling asked.

"I don't…"

"I looked up Special Agent Waylen Brooks, and he's with the Financial Crimes division, so that would make sense. These guys had priors and are well known around the city as hired help. It's possible Arthur Gunn employed them himself."

Rory stepped back. "Why are you telling me these ridiculous theories? The Gunns were targeted. I was taken hostage last week and almost died!"

Amy shrugged and gestured to the edge of the room. "Coffee's there. If you need me, I'm in the bullpen."

Rory stiffened and had to walk around Ling, who defiantly blocked her path.

She yearned to go home, but she wasn't certain where that was. Surely not her apartment in Boston with Kevin. Her parents' house, always so warm and safe, felt tainted after Jack's intrusion. If this was genuinely over, what would Rory do with her life? Was the offer to buy her a condo in Montpellier still on the table? She'd have to ask her father, but then she hated the idea of abandoning her parents so quickly after the trauma they'd all experienced.

Rory gathered the cups and balanced them, trying not to spill them or burn herself, and walked upstairs, only dripping a few times along the way. The door sat open a crack, and she pushed it with her shoe. "Coffee's here," she said, and dropped the three paper cups.

Cody was on the floor, leg twitching while Silas grabbed at something in his hand. His eyes were frantic. "I tried to stop him!"

Cody Sanderson ceased moving, and the token fell from his grip, clanging to the floor.

"Is he..." Rory knelt by him, reaching for his wrist when he sat upright to catch his breath.

"I was there. On the Moon."

"That's how it works," Silas muttered. "What the hell were you thinking?"

"I had to know these were real. You don't understand. I've been waiting ten years for this, and you weren't even going to let me test them," Cody said. Spit fell from his lips, and he didn't bother to wipe it. His eyes were red around the edges, his breathing ragged.

"What did you see?" Rory asked.

"It was different from Fred Trell's, far different. The Shadow lingered nearby. I must have been Commander Gunn. I saw another astronaut, and I believe it was Swanson." He gazed at Rory, then at Silas. "Your grandfathers."

Silas helped Cody to a chair, and Rory looked at the mess on the carpet where she'd spilled the coffees. "What else did you notice?"

"That's about it. It'll tell us a story, if we're patient. Remember, every time you use the token, the effects lessen."

Rory considered what it would be like to keep exploring the echoes. Would it explain anything? "Are you okay?"

Cody nodded and grabbed his bottle of water. "This happened after Fred gave me the token, and it eventually subsided. The FBI won't take it, will they?"

"Someone will," Silas said. "And I'll be relieved."

Rory agreed, but there was also something fascinating about the echoes emanating from the cold metal objects. A connection to the past that no longer existed in their reality.

She didn't want to admit it out loud, but Rory couldn't let them go. Not yet.

"Should I speak with a lawyer?" Clark Fallow asked.

"Clark, I'm not accusing NASA of doing anything deliberately. There were two hours missing on the Helios mission, while Commander Gunn and Colin Swanson were allegedly gathering rock and mineral samples. I'm just asking how to get hold of the blacked-out time period."

Clark's skin was white and papery. The fluorescent lights made him look ethereal, his cheeks hollow and his eyes bulbous. "I've been in charge for four years, and not once has anyone mentioned this."

"Will you investigate it?"

"If you let me leave this godforsaken room, I'll do anything," he said. "I came to the city to pay my respects to a great man, Peter Gunn, and now I'm being interrogated about something that happened when I was in college."

"It could be important."

"How?"

Waylen pushed his chair out to stretch his legs. "They found something on the Moon, and hid it from NASA." He figured if he told the truth, it might inspire the administrator into action.

Clark laughed and started to rise. "You've been watching too many late-night history shows, Special Agent Brooks. Aliens don't exist. The universe is a deadly and inhospitable environment. The communication was cut off because it was 1972, and they were on the longest moonwalk ever recorded. Things happen that aren't predictable. I suggest you let it go, and we—"

"Peter was murdered because of this secret," Waylen said. "Now there are two more deaths related to it, and you have the audacity to say it's not important. I want to know what happened during those two hours, and you're going to help me."

Clark sank into the chair. "Yes. We'll get to the bottom of it, Special Agent Brooks. I apologize for my insensitive comments. I'd be honored for you to visit us in DC, and I'll put a team on it Monday morning."

Waylen labored to his feet and shook Clark's hand. "Thank you, sir. I appreciate it."

One down, one to go. He had a feeling the next wouldn't be as forthcoming.

"Am I free to leave?" Clark's bony fingers paused on the lever.

"Yes. Have a good night. I'll contact the office after the weekend."

Clark left without another word, and Waylen sighed while heading to the second door. He entered without knocking, finding Governor McKenzie on her cell phone, playing a game. Little bell sounds emanated from the speaker, and she hurriedly turned it off.

"It's about time," she muttered.

"Governor McKenzie, I'm sorry for any inconvenience."

"Please call me Vickie." The remark didn't seem to hold malice.

"I'm Waylen, then."

"Waylen, what is it you want from me?"

"Your office sent a man named Francis Jack Barker to a charity…"

"Yes, you've already said that. I've spoken to my assistant, who wasn't there at the time, but she did notice something. It appears that Planetae Inc. requested we send someone from their organization as a bit of a cross-pollination."

"Planetae?"

"It's a big tech company out of New York, though their primary operation is in DC. They're aiming to build a facility north of the city, and are trying to jump through regulatory hoops to garner all the tax benefits befitting a company of that size. We're talking a five-hundred-thousand-square-foot facility within an hour of Manhattan. Five thousand jobs, with growth opportunity. I had to listen, and he's got a pile of lobbyists working with Congress on his behalf."

Waylen strained to piece it together. "And just what does this tech company do?"

Vickie clicked something on her phone and slid it across the table. "A bit of everything. But mostly, military development."

The website appeared to be there as a domain placeholder. It showed a picture of a facility, with chain-link around it. *Planetae protects the world.*

"That's quite the claim," Waylen said. He thought about the comments he'd heard from Bobby in the hospital that his boss was in DC, and that he was a powerful man. Could the same guy oversee this defense company? "They do contract work for the US military, then?"

She stared at him. "I'm not privy to the details, but I suspect they're working for clients outside our borders as well."

Waylen recalled Assistant Director Ben's warning that he'd been asked to ensure the case was closed. When he'd inquired by whom, Ben had said Waylen wouldn't believe him. Then he'd admitted it was Jacob B. Plemmons, the current Secretary of Defense.

"Are you satisfied with my answers?" Vickie asked.

"Who's the CEO?"

"Leo Monroe."

The name was vaguely familiar, but Waylen wasn't into business or investing. He threw his pittance of an offering to his 401K every year, and let some hedge fund team deal with it.

He marked it into his phone. "Have you met him?"

"Leo? Sure, at a few fundraisers."

"So he supported your campaign?"

Vickie tapped the table with a red fingernail. "Many people did. This state was ready for someone who saw things from a new perspective. I prefer to look to the future, rather than the past like the rest of our dusty old politicians. I want progressive change, and that begins with tech investments in our great state of New York."

Waylen listened and understood why she'd garnered so much support. Job creation in a city with millions was obviously important, especially in the volatile and often shifting economy. "And facilitate that by allowing a weapons manufacturer to operate less than an hour from Manhattan?"

Vickie's brow didn't budge, given the Botox, but her anger was obvious. "Would you rather we not support them and have Planetae select another country to work with?"

Waylen didn't take the bait. "What's your assessment of Leo?"

"Do I have to answer that?"

"It would be advisable."

"Leo's built differently. He's analytical, and not overly personable, but that's what you need. His team is friendly, and he's…"

"An asshole?"

A laugh escaped Vickie, and she nodded once. "He's driven. Does it rub people the wrong way? Sure."

"Thanks for your time." Waylen extended his hand, and it took a solid second for her to react. They shook, and Governor McKenzie was at the exit.

"Leo Monroe has a lot of friends, Waylen. At the top. Don't go in unless you have undeniable evidence, because you'll find yourself unemployed." Vickie gazed at her shoes. "If you're lucky."

Waylen stayed for a minute, replaying the conversation in his head. It was obvious the governor thought Leo was a dangerous man, or that his connections were. A company such as Planetae Inc. would be privately owned, not traded, which kept them under the radar of public scrutiny. He'd thought they might be in the clear, after today's altercation, but if this corporation was involved, they'd only scratched the surface.

Waylen couldn't give the Delta up, no matter what his superiors commanded of him. He got on his phone and searched for a short-term rental in Brooklyn. After creating a new profile, he paid with an app not linked to his name.

The three remained in the same room he'd left them, looking somber. "I know you all want to go home, but it's not   over   yet."

2

"You aren't staying?" Arthur asked Silas.

"We rented a place, but I can't tell you where it is," Silas told his father.

"That doesn't sound safe."

"No kidding, but we have to talk it through. Dad, I'm sorry the funeral was all messed up."

Arthur squeezed his shoulder. "None of this is your fault. I'm the one who should be apologizing. I let you stay at Peter's house on the lake and forgot about his little secret."

He peered into the living room, where Rory's parents sat drinking wine with his mom. It was strange to see the Swansons in their family home, but everyone seemed comfortable enough. "Thanks for letting them crash for the night," he said.

"Our pleasure. It'll be nice to catch up."

"How's Clare?" Silas asked.

"Sleeping it off. The kids are with her in her old room."

"Good."

Silas saw the three squad cars parked around their corner lot. "You'll be the talk of the town."

Arthur smiled. "I've been meaning to create some neighborhood gossip. It was this, or I refuse to decorate for Christmas."

Rory kissed her mom's cheek and embraced her dad before coming to the exit. "We'll see you soon, Mr. Gunn."

"Please, call me Arthur."

Rory passed by Silas, heading to Waylen's car.

"Rory's nice," his dad said.

"Yeah, she is."

"Pleasant on the eyes too, isn't she, son?"

"Dad…"

"All I'm saying is your mother and I want you to—"

"Not now," Silas said. "I have enough to think about, and my parents meddling with my love life isn't one of them."

"Love is often found in the face of adversity," Arthur told him.

"Is that a quote?"

"I think I read it in a fortune cookie."

Silas waved at Rory's parents, then said goodbye to his mother in the kitchen as she opened another bottle of wine. Her cheeks were damp, and she dabbed them with a dish towel. "Be careful, Silas."

"I will."

He strode to the car and took the backseat beside Rory, while Cody stayed in the front. Waylen rolled up to the nearest police sentry and talked momentarily before driving off. Silas watched the house shrink through the rear window, and saw his dad's silhouette in the living room.

"Is this necessary?" he asked Waylen. "We have the police protecting my parents' house. Shouldn't we stay?"

"He knows the Delta is together, and in the city somewhere," Waylen said.

"Then give it up. Call your boss or ship it overnight to another address." Silas thought his options were sound.

"Not until we know what it does. Why is a weapons manufacturer killing for this damned thing?" Waylen signaled, heading to the Grand Central Parkway leading to Brooklyn.

"I already told you. It's a portal," Cody said.

"To where?" Rory's voice was quiet.

"To the Moon, for one," Silas answered.

"And the third token?" Rory asked. "Where did it bring you, Cody?"

"You'll have to see for yourself." Cody craned his neck, grinning at them. He'd mentioned it earlier, but his description was vague at best.

Rory was on her phone, the glow brightening her face. Outside, the sky was dark, the streetlights barely illuminating the cloud-covered night. Trees rattled and shook with a gusty breeze while Silas watched the road.

"Find anything?" Waylen asked her.

"There's next to nothing about Planetae Inc. online."

"They're probably paying good money for that," Waylen said.

"Don't most companies want exposure?"

"Not in that industry. It's all top-secret stuff," Cody answered, as though he understood the business.

"What is Planetae anyway?" Silas asked.

"Latin for *planet*," Rory said. "*Planetae protects the world.*"

"What do you think that means?" Waylen slowed and pulled over on the cramped Brooklyn street.

"Maybe they literally mean just that?" Cody asked.

"From what?" Silas countered.

"Someone outside of Earth."

"Aliens? Leo Monroe is running an anti-alien defense corporation?"

"It's possible." Cody rolled his window down, letting

in fresh air. "Where is the place?"

"221," Waylen told them. "Anyone see it?"

"There, three down." Silas pointed between the two front seats to the right. In the darkness, it was difficult to read the house numbers. The streetlights were dim, the kind of yellowy-orange that showed next to no color in its glow. Most of the homes didn't have driveways, or if they did, they were located in a rear alley. Waylen pulled up half a block and backed in, parallel parking with ease.

The four of them exited the car, bringing whatever luggage they had with them. They must have looked suspicious, but from what Silas could tell, no one was watching. Silas glanced as a doorbell camera blinked on, recording their passage.

Waylen grabbed his phone and used the lockbox on the handle. This home didn't have security, at least none that was obviously visible. Silas lingered, checking over his shoulder, then entered, noticing the faint odor of patchouli lingering in the air.

"It asks that we remove our shoes," Waylen said.

Cody's were already off, and he stalked into the small living space with his socks. Silas did the same, and Rory neatly set hers on an empty rack.

"Can you tell me why we're staying here?" Silas asked.

"Because ..." Waylen's hand rested on his holstered side piece, and he crossed into the kitchen, checking the back door to find it locked.

"They won't know where you are," Rory said.

"That's the idea."

Silas thought about the doorbell camera and wondered how inventive this leader of Planetae was. Rory flicked the lamp on, and Cody was already seated, activating the gas fireplace with the press of a switch. The pilot ignited, and the flames lifted behind the glass casing.

"Give me a minute," Waylen said, trucking his bag to the second story. He turned and called down, "May as well claim your bed for the night."

Silas grinned at Rory and realized they'd all be separating tomorrow. Cody would head to San Diego, which wasn't an enormous loss, considering they barely knew him. Rory would go to Woodstock with her parents. And Silas… he wasn't sure what to do, but working in the furniture business felt like a waste of his energy now that he'd discovered the Delta. How could he return to mundane spreadsheets when there were actual worlds to explore? He wasn't positive these artifacts did anything but offer an echo from the past.

Rory went ahead of him, and Silas followed along, noticing Cody on the couch. "You coming?"

"Nah, I'll stay here." He patted the cushion. "I prefer to be close to the exit."

The stairs creaked under Silas' weight, and he spotted chips in the paint and dents in the plaster. It was rare to see an old Brooklyn house in pristine shape, given the age, particularly when they were rented out by the night. For a moment, Silas pondered if he'd own a home someday; maybe not in New York, though. He watched Rory checking the bedrooms and questioned if she was happy living in Vermont with her parents.

His family still had the house in Loon Lake, but could he settle in the place where Grandpa Gunn had been shot?

"I'll take this one." Rory tossed her bag to the bed. That left a room for Silas, with a double bed and a nightstand with a colorful lamp.

When they went downstairs, Cody was up, putting his shoes back on.

"Where do you think you're going?" Waylen asked.

"I saw a corner store a couple of blocks away. I can't live here until the morning without snacks."

Waylen reached for his footwear. "You're not going alone."

"You stay," Silas said. "With the Delta. Better to keep it behind a lock."

"Any requests?" Cody asked.

Silas made a mental note of Rory and Waylen's orders. They'd skipped dinner, none of them willing to eat after the stress of the day, but after the adrenaline faded, Silas found himself ravenous. "Where was it?"

Cody started north. "Not far."

Silas only saw a few cars as they went, taking long strides. Cody walked with purpose, and Silas appreciated the pace. "You could be a New Yorker, you know that?"

Cody laughed and kept moving. "Nah, I prefer the beach."

"We have beaches," Silas said.

"Sure." Cody gestured at the end of the block, where, as promised, there stood a twenty-four-hour store. They entered, a digital chime ringing to announce their arrival. Silas saw the TV and went up to the counter.

"*...gunned down on Madison. It's the sixth officer-related shooting this month, and the citizens of New York deserve answers...*" The man being interviewed was agitated, and a crowd gathered behind him with protest signs in Times Square.

"You hear about this?" the old guy behind the counter asked. "Right in the middle of the day. What's happened to our city?"

Silas shrugged, not willing to discuss the incident. Cody had his arms full of chips and pretzels and balanced a six-pack of soda on top. Silas grabbed some beers and found a few microwavable dinners that didn't look freezer burned.

He doubled up on bags, making sure they didn't lose their supplies on the short trip. The TV continued to reference Peter Gunn's funeral, implying the city was on edge.

"You flying home tomorrow?" he asked Cody, to make conversation.

"What choice do I have? I was thrown into a trunk and left for dead. Plus, Waylen confiscated my piece of the Delta. This wasn't what I anticipated when I came to New York," Cody said.

"You expected to take them to California?"

"No, but… I want to use it."

"To go to the Moon." Silas failed to keep the sarcasm from his voice.

"And elsewhere," Cody added.

"And how are you planning on making that happen? How will you breathe?"

"I have a solution," Cody said.

"Really?" Silas paused, noticing a shadowed figure behind the steering wheel of a sedan a short distance away. They were facing the opposite direction. He grabbed Cody, dragging him behind a tree for cover.

"What…"

Silas set the bags to the grass and put a finger to his lips. The individual observed the houses on the block and peered around, as if searching for something.

The house they were staying in was five down, light casting by the drawn drapes. He snatched the snacks, then cut into the alley between two homes. Cody trailed behind him, moving much more loudly.

"They could be waiting for someone," Cody whispered. "Maybe it's an Uber."

"I didn't see the sticker."

"It's dark, and we were on the opposite side of the car."

Silas crept on, coming through the passageway. The small yard was fenced, and he flipped the latch, swinging the gate inwards. He must have tripped a motion sensor, because a bright beam flashed over the yard. Silas hurried up the steps to the compact wooden deck and hoped it held their combined weight. An old barbecue leaned on the railing, and he could smell grease.

Silas knocked gently, then louder, after no one let them in. Finally, Waylen gazed between the curtains with his gun drawn.

Waylen held the door open. "What are you two doing crawling in the back?"

"I think we're being watched," Silas said.

"What?" Waylen looked up, and the light flicked off.

Silas went to the living room, unplugged the lamp, and motioned to the street. "Sedan, five down."

Waylen squinted as he peeked past the drapes. "I see someone." His cell buzzed, and he frowned when he read the message.

"What is it?" Rory asked.

"My partner just texted me." He flipped it around, showing them.

Hey, Brooks, I'm in New York for the case. You up?

Silas glanced outside, where the figure in the sedan held a phone. "What's your partner doing here?"

3

*W*aylen had to read the text twice. "It might be unrelated. Everyone's on their phones." His fingers hovered above the keyboard. This wasn't possible. Martina Sanchez was his rock, his foundation with the Bureau. Without her, he'd have sunken into paperwork purgatory during his tenure as an agent. She'd kept him moving, pushing him to be better. She'd been recruited under his guidance, and there wasn't an ounce of Waylen that believed she'd betray him.

He pictured her at the airport, the touch of her hands, the kiss that could have meant 'goodbye' or maybe 'I'm sorry.' Waylen took a deep inhale and confirmed. *Where have you been? I couldn't reach you.*

Waylen surveyed the parked car and recognized the moment the message arrived. Either it was her, or someone had her phone. He used his own camera, filming the person surveilling them, and zoomed. It was grainy, but he'd recognize her dark, wavy hair anywhere. "Damn it."

"She's been bought off," Cody said, opening a bag of chips.

"Would you put those away?" Waylen snapped. "Think…"

Martina was in town and watching him from outside. He hefted his cell, sure now that she'd tracked him by its GPS. Clearly, it didn't pinpoint his precise location, but she'd gotten very close. It wouldn't take her long to figure out which house he was in if she flashed her credentials and started knocking on doors. The first resident would confirm which place on the block was an online rental property.

Waylen glanced at the corner of the window, seeing the TRUSTED HOME sticker from the company he'd used. If she saw it...

"I have to draw her out," he said. "Then talk sense into her."

"She knows you're on this street." Rory wrung her hands nervously. "Why can't this be done with?"

Silas perked up. "There's a place for sale nearby. The sign's in the front yard. It looked empty to me. Dark, with a realtor box on the handle. It could be rented too. Like the owners were subsidizing it while waiting for it to be sold."

Waylen nodded. "What's the house number?"

Cody crunched on a potato chip. "That would be 213."

Been busy. Where are you staying?

Waylen prickled at the comment. He prepped the message, using 213, and removed the Delta from his pocket, handing it to Silas. "There's another gun in my room. Go take it."

Silas didn't look confident.

"This is important. I have to find a way to make this Leo stop sending people to kill you, but right now, you need to trust me." Waylen nodded at Silas. "Go upstairs, lock the door, and keep my gun ready. Got it?"

He felt terrible, given the fact Rory had already killed a man, and Silas was recovering from his flesh wound, but there wasn't much of a choice. Assistant Director Ben's orders for him to leave the civilians out of it parroted in his mind, but he lacked the time to come up with a better plan.

"Be careful," Rory said before jogging up the steps.

Waylen waited until he heard the door shut, and went through the kitchen, down the rear porch, and past the fence. He stopped at the home for sale, and hit send on his text.

Her reply was instantaneous. *I'm in the area. See you soon.*

Waylen jumped the fence, hiding in 215's yard. The residents were watching a late-night talk show, which was all about the incident from Gunn's funeral. How quickly someone's tragedy became a punchline in Hollywood.

The sedan's door opened, and Special Agent Martina Sanchez emerged. Did she have backup? More likely, she planned on surprising him and taking the Delta for herself. He couldn't believe someone had gotten to her.

She eyed the realtor's sign and paused, double-checking her cell. Martina didn't go straight for the front door. She circled to the side yard and tested the gate. Waylen was only a few feet from her, secured in the neighboring lot. He tried the gate latch, which was thankfully unlocked. Martina had continued on, and he rounded the corner, finding her peering through a window.

Waylen's faith in humanity had already been challenged countless times over his years on the force, then with the Bureau, but to see Martina skulking in the dark sealed it.

He held the gun, aiming it at her. "Why would you do this?"

Martina jumped, nearly hitting her head on the window's shutter. "Brooks…"

"Don't." She reached into her jacket, and he waved the barrel slightly. "I'm not messing around, Martina."

She pulled out a piece of paper. "I have a message for you."

Waylen frowned and took a single step closer. He could smell her perfume on the breeze, and almost lowered his weapon. "Did you expect I'd give it up? Or were you sent to kill me?"

"Neither," she said. "I swear, Waylen, I would never—"

"Save it. Be honest. When did he contact you?"

Her posture slumped, as if someone had cut her puppet strings. "When I started the other case."

"How?"

"He called the landline in the field office. They patched it through, and he told me how dangerous the artifact was in the wild."

"He's killed people, Martina."

"You understand nothing," she said.

"Then explain it to me."

She peered around. "Can we go inside?"

"No."

"Waylen, I want to help."

"By lying?"

Waylen heard a car door close somewhere down the block, and imagined more armed contractors stalking around the nearby homes.

"He won't stop until he has them, but I'm here to make you an offer," she said.

Waylen kept his gun raised. "I'm listening." He was really just biding his time, wondering when he'd find himself surrounded.

"We can all escape this in one piece," Martina said, her voice steadier.

Waylen doubted that, but was he willing to risk his life, or those of the people waiting for him a few houses over? "I said I was listening."

"He swears Jack acted on his own will. The other guys too. No one was supposed to be hurt. These were simple grab and goes."

"What about the attackers at today's funeral?"

Martina genuinely looked upset, but it wouldn't work on Waylen. Her betrayal stung beyond anything he could have expected. "He hired outside contractors, but we both know they'll take it as far as is required."

"So Leo Monroe is a saint?" Waylen asked.

"Don't even say his name," she warned him.

"Why?"

"He's an important man, working for individuals in prominent positions. The highest."

"Are you trying to tell me Leo has the President's blessing?"

Martina gave him a tight-lipped nod. "Maybe not directly, but I wouldn't be surprised if they spoke on occasion. Leo's exposed the threat, and he's been asked to deal with it."

"You're saying Leo told the President of the United States of America about the Delta?" Her silence was confirmation. "What's the deal?" he asked.

"Give them to me, leave, and go on with your job."

"And you?"

"Are you going to tell the Assistant Director?"

"How much?" Waylen inquired.

"What?"

"How much did he pay you?"

"Waylen, you know my parents could use the money. My dad's company was sold, and they're living on scraps while he's struggling to find a legitimate job."

"So you betray your country and your partner for a little cash."

She gazed at him. "It's not a little."

"I thought we had something," he said. "We made a hell of a team."

"We still can."

"There's no world where I work a case with you now."

"What'll it be, Waylen?"

"You take the Delta, then what happens to us?"

"Nothing. You and your band of misfits walk free. Isn't that what they want?"

Waylen figured it was, at least for Rory and Silas. Cody Sanderson would have other ideas, but in Waylen's estimation, his vote wasn't as important. He'd chosen to be involved, unlike the astronauts' grandkids. "I guess we'll have to ask them."

"Yeah?" Martina gestured at his gun, and Waylen lowered it cautiously, but he didn't holster the weapon.

"It's this way." Waylen led her to the actual rental. He stopped when he noticed the front door was ajar, the frame splintered where someone had pried it open. "Call them off!"

———————

Rory stared at the chair leaning against the handle, knowing it would never hold should they actually break in. The knob was locked too, but Kevin had often reminded her that locks only kept honest people out. Even now, she was hearing his whiny voice, and she hated him for it.

"Did you catch that?" Silas asked.

Cody picked up his bag of chips, the noise filling the small room. Rory slapped it from his hands, spilling them everywhere.

"Would you cut it out?" she hissed, and Cody hopped to the bed, landing on the end.

"You guys don't know how to chill."

Rory watched the guy, wondering how he was possibly so calm. He'd been beaten up and tossed into a trunk, then witnessed a shooting only a few hours earlier, and here Cody was, having a great time.

She turned her ear. "Footsteps."

"Maybe it's Waylen?" Silas didn't look confident with the gun he held. Rory almost asked him for it, considering she'd proven her ability to use it when push came to shove.

Rory heard muffled whispers, and someone opened the first bedroom door, then the second. They were close. "Dammit."

She moved behind Silas when the handle rattled, gently, then with more aggression. "Open up!" a deep voice shouted.

"What do we do?" Silas asked.

Cody fiddled with something in his hoodie pocket and walked to the closet where Silas' jacket sat draped on a hamper. Rory flicked her attention from whatever Cody was doing to the attempted invasion happening in real time.

She'd been through so much in the last week, and it felt like her life was nearing its end. All for what? Some pieces of metal that showed echoes of a Shadow, or whatever Cody had named it.

Silas took a single step farther from her, the gun aimed at chest level. He breathed in long inhales and exhales, probably trying to steady himself.

Outside in the hall, more voices sounded: a woman's, then a counter from the deep-toned man. They banged on the door, making Rory jump.

"It's okay!" Waylen shouted. "Let them in."

Rory swallowed and glanced at Cody, then at Silas. "What if he's being coerced?"

"Then we give them up and hope they don't shoot anyone," Silas said.

"Okay."

Silas shoved the chair out of the way. "We just want to go home."

"You will," a woman said.

Silas gave Rory a nod and flicked the knob's lock, stepping back.

Waylen was the first one there, and he kept his hands raised. "Guys, I think we're out of time."

Rory stayed where she was, while Waylen entered with the woman.

"We've been offered a trade. Our lives for the Delta. I know it's not what we'd hope for, but I couldn't decide without you."

"Not a chance," Cody said, and the guy wearing black aimed a gun at him.

"Enough of that!" the woman ordered. "Give it over."

"On second thought, I have another proposition for your boss," Waylen said.

"What?"

"Get him on the phone for me," Waylen demanded.

"He won't—"

"Try."

They seemed to have a familiarity between them, and Rory suspected this was indeed his partner at the FBI, Martina Sanchez. Waylen must have felt so let down in that moment.

Sanchez dialed on her phone, mumbled something,

and held the cell out for Waylen to take.

"Mr. Monroe." He paused while the man on the line spoke. Rory wished she could eavesdrop on both sides of the conversation. "Yes. I have the Delta, and you'll get it, but only if we personally meet." Another delay. "I want to deliver it so you can show me what it does. Then I'll leave. And you will never bother Cody Sanderson, Silas Gunn, or Rory Swanson again, understood? Sure, Wednesday in DC. I'm there."

Rory paused with her breath held, hoping against all odds that this was actually over with.

Waylen gave the phone to Sanchez, and she listened without speaking, then hung up. "Waylen, this is dangerous. You don't actually think he'll wait until Wednesday, do you?"

"Why not, if he's as innocent as you claim?" Waylen said. "Get the hell out of here."

She glanced into the room, making eye contact with Rory. "We should talk."

"No. You won't see me again," he told her. "Ever."

"Come on," she sighed. "We're going."

The two men eyed the FBI agent, then shrugged and let themselves out. Sanchez lingered in the hall long enough to get her last word in. "I'm sorry."

"I don't care." Waylen kept hold of his gun while they left the house. Rory trailed after the agent, and he shoved the exit shut, managing to bolt the lock despite the damage the perps had done. He leaned on it and sighed heavily.

"Are we safe?" Rory asked.

He smiled, nodding slowly. "Probably not, but Monroe assured me he'd called them off. He could have forced us to relinquish it tonight."

Rory lunged at Waylen, hugging him. She wasn't able

to hold the tears at bay, and they poured out, her relief overwhelming.

"You did great, Waylen." Silas shook the agent's hand while Rory wiped her cheeks. "Are you sure you want to do this?" He reached for his pocket, but must have realized he'd left the Delta upstairs in his jacket. "Give me a second."

Cody lingered in the kitchen, munching on his chips again. "Why do you look so smug?" Rory asked him.

"Me? I don't."

Silas returned, carrying the three separate tokens. Two were in the whiskey bags, one in the brown wrapping Cody had brought. He thrust them at Waylen, probably glad to surrender them again. "So we're good? It's almost done?"

"Unless Leo Monroe lied to me." Waylen peered through the blinds. "He asked me to come to DC for a meeting next Wednesday."

Rory was surprised. "He's giving you that long?"

"I guess he's overseas. This shows trust, right?" Waylen would leave Manhattan tomorrow. "You guys don't have to stick around."

Rory glanced at Silas, the pair making a silent agreement. "We already have our things upstairs, and it's paid for…"

"And who knows when we'll see each other again," Silas added. "What about you, Sanderson?"

Cody washed his hands, watching them while he soaped up. "I should be going."

Rory didn't blame him one bit. "It was nice to meet you. Sorry it didn't work out like you'd hoped."

Cody gathered the few belongings that hadn't been destroyed in his hotel disaster and said his goodbyes. A taxi showed up, which meant he must have called one while upstairs, and he exited, not looking back.

"Strange guy," Waylen said.

Cody climbed into the car and waved once before it took off, probably heading for Manhattan and his car rental.

Rory fell to the couch and stared at the gas fireplace. "What do we do now?"

Silas smiled and grabbed the beers from the fridge, cracking one before handing it to her. "We celebrate our freedom." He lifted the can. "To Peter and Leigh."

"Peter and Leigh," Waylen and Rory repeated.

4

Silas walked up to his parents' house, lighter in his step than he'd been in ages. The police cars were gone after Waylen had called Deputy Inspector Truman a couple of hours earlier. Saturday morning in Queens was spectacular. He paused on the front steps, gazing at the neighborhood as the calmness washed over him. Sprinklers ran, a dog barked a few houses away, and he watched a boy and girl speed by on bicycles.

It was difficult to imagine he'd almost been killed just last night.

"Silas?" Arthur stood behind him, the door wide. "You didn't knock."

"I'm... existing."

Arthur plunked on the steps beside him, holding a cup of coffee. "I'm glad this is done. I don't care what they want with the artifacts your grandfather found, if it doesn't involve my family any longer."

"Same here, Dad."

"Since we've dealt with the funeral, let's discuss your absence from work."

"About that..."

"What?"

"I quit," Silas said.

Arthur sipped from his cup. "I thought you might."

"You did?"

"I never believed it was your passion. You're too ambitious to manage our finance department, which, let's be fair, comprises a payable and receivable clerk. It was a shoehorn position because I wanted the family to be part of *my* dream. What I've learned since Peter's death is we should all live our own lives to the fullest."

"You were going to fire me," Silas said with a smile.

"Nothing so drastic."

"Any chance at a golden parachute?"

"You'll be okay. Speaking of, Grandpa's lawyer finally got his act together. He's leaving it all to you and Clare."

Silas stared at his dad, trying to follow. "Me?"

"And Clare."

"Why?"

"You were his only grandkids. Clearly my sister and I weren't in his good graces, not that we need an inheritance at this age. I'm glad he thought about you two."

"And the house?"

"That's between you and Clare."

Silas pictured the A-frame, the peacefulness of the lake. "Where is she?"

"In there with the kids."

"And she knows?"

"She's already deciding what car to buy." Arthur sighed and finished his drink. "Come on in for some breakfast. You can talk."

Clare was at the table, scrolling on her tablet, when Silas entered. She wasted no time jumping to her feet and hugging him. "Can you believe it? Grandpa Gunn coming through from beyond the grave."

Clare had a great position in the company, and her ex-husband was paying her a hefty child support sum, but Silas was glad she wouldn't have to worry anymore.

"How much are we talking?" he asked.

"Someone needs to go to Campbelltown. Peter's being buried there too."

"I'll do it," Silas said without thinking.

"You've gone through something extremely traumatic," his mom said, joining the conversation. She set a plate of food in front of Silas, sliding it forward as if urging him to eat. "You should be with family."

"Since Dad fired me, I have the time." Silas spooned a mouthful of scrambled eggs.

"You did what?" Alice blurted.

"It... he wanted... sure, I canned my own kid."

"I'll go to Loon Lake, meet with the lawyer, and see to Grandpa's burial. I assume that's good with everyone?"

"It's a shame we couldn't honor him properly, but considering what happened at his funeral, it's best to leave it private," Arthur said.

"Mommy, what's a will?" Eva asked.

Clare patted her on the head. "Never mind, honey. Keep coloring."

"Clare, I'd like to hold on to the house," Silas said in between bites of bacon.

"Really? It's in the middle of nowhere."

"He loved it."

"What's it worth?"

"Take it out of my inheritance. I don't care."

Clare watched him as if he was one of her scheming children, seeking an advantage. "Is that so..."

Alice smiled, putting her hand on Silas' shoulder from behind him. "I think your parents would be thrilled Silas wants to keep it."

"The sad thing is, I have no idea," Arthur said.

"What will you do there?" Clare asked. "You're coming back soon, aren't you?"

Silas was flying by the seat of his pants, with no

thought behind it. "I just learned we were getting the estate two minutes ago, so let me process the information for a while."

He stayed and talked with his family for a while, then opted to return to the city. He got to his condo at one in the afternoon and rolled his suitcase to the doors, happy to find the regular doorman on site.

"Mr. Gunn, nice to see you. Sorry to hear about your grandfather," Roger said. He coughed into his hand.

"Thanks, Rog. You feeling better?"

"It was a doozy, but nothing can keep me out of the game for too long. Have a splendid afternoon, Mr. Gunn."

Silas felt better knowing his temporary replacement hadn't been a plant, and that Roger actually had been sick. Not that he wished any ill on his doorman.

Silas entered his suite and hefted the luggage in before falling to the couch. He stared at the TV screen, reflecting the view from his window, and lay down, kicking his shoes off. He watched the ceiling, listened to the subtle sounds of the surrounding city, and pictured the pier at Loon Lake.

It was time for a change.

Silas hoped Rory had made it home. Waylen had a few days before meeting with Leo Monroe, and he claimed he'd be safe, considering his hired help could have shot them all and taken the Delta at the rental. What would he find behind the physical walls of Planetae Inc.? He worried about Waylen, because everyone working for Monroe carried a gun and was eager to use it.

"You're out," Silas told himself. It was better to forget all of it and move on.

He closed his eyes, his breathing growing deeper.

As he fell asleep, hints of the inky black Shadow crept

into his mind.

———————

"You sure it's okay that I'm here on a Sunday?" Rory asked Justine.

She wore a taupe blouse, and her hair had been curled. "Rory, I wasn't expecting any patients today, but as I told you on the phone, I'm happy to lend an ear."

"You weren't going on a date or anything, were you?"

"A date… oh, the clothing. I was at church," Justine said.

Rory noticed the golden cross hanging at the end of her necklace. "Do you find it helps?"

"Church? I suppose."

"Have you always gone?" Rory asked, following Justine to her office.

"Since I was a young girl. My parents were devout. We'd dress up, grab good seats, and sing all the hymns. I loved it." Justine clasped her hands near her chest, smiling. "I started going again when I moved to Woodstock. It's lonely in a new place. Where better to make quick friends than in a congregation?"

"I wouldn't have thought of that," Rory admitted.

"You should check it out sometime. No pressure, but it's not as stuffy as you'd think."

"My parents belong to the local club, so I'm plenty used to stuffy," Rory joked.

"Would you like some coffee?" Justine was already moving to the kitchen, and Rory had no choice but to follow her.

"Is this normal?"

"Which part?"

"Talking to me about your religion?"

"You asked, and I just answered."

"That's cool. I've never done"—Rory wagged a finger between them—"this before. I always pictured a therapist like one of those British armed guards with the enormous hats."

"Some are more standoffish, but I have nothing to hide. Pretending we're not human is more unsettling. It's easier for my patients to talk if they see that." Justine went through the motions of making two single-serve cups. She didn't have a regular drip machine, and Rory clutched the cup, careful not to spill it as they went to the office.

"Now what has you calling me on a Sunday for an emergency session?" Justine picked up her notebook, flipping to a pink sticky note.

"I told you about the abduction."

"You did."

"It almost happened again, but I only had guns pointed at me in a general sense… twice."

Justine's pen stopped moving. "Care to explain?"

"Not really. I can deal with that on my own, but I need some advice."

"Are you presently in danger?" Justine's gaze drifted to her open window, where the breeze blew at a white see-through linen curtain.

"Not anymore."

"That's good. Rory, I don't know how you're taking this so well."

"I'm very practiced from years of forcing my emotions into a bottle and keeping it sealed," she answered, giving Justine a smile.

"Then it's a good thing you're coming to see me, because I have a corkscrew for such occasions."

Rory liked the woman, but one didn't become friends with their mental health care professional. It was a classic Kathyism, and she realized her mother was right about most things.

"I want to write," Rory said, changing the subject.

"Why don't you?"

Rory pointed to her temple. "This has been a little preoccupied."

Justine waited, not prompting her, which in itself was a form of a prompt.

"I'm also having visions," Rory whispered.

"Can you elaborate?"

Rory adjusted in the seat and glanced at her fingers. A dark fog twirled around her index, and she held it up for Justine. "Do you see that?"

Justine squinted and shook her head. "What am I looking for?"

"Besides a terrible need for a manicure?" Rory asked. "Never mind. I'm just tired." When she checked again, the mist had subsided, vanishing into her periphery. The Shadow was always there, barely out of reach. All because she'd touched that stupid token from the Moon.

She imagined her grandfather, Colin Swanson, from when she was a child, about ten years old. He was vibrant and youthful for his age of sixty-four. Colin was a role model, but also a fun excuse to go on adventures. Together they'd explore the forest south of town, with her grandpa pausing to explain different species of trees; then they'd walk the path by the winding river leading back to Woodstock, where their day would end with a big bowl of ice cream.

"I miss him," she said.

"Who?"

"My Grandpa Swanson. He died of Alzheimer's disease ten years ago. I was in college, and it became so difficult to see him like that, so I stayed away, almost refusing to come home unless it was for Christmas. Even then, I couldn't watch the man's mind degenerate in front of my eyes. He was such a presence, and…" Rory suddenly wished they hadn't given up the Delta, if only for that connection to him. "He inspired *View from the Heavens*. Without Grandpa, it wouldn't have come to fruition."

"But it's not his story."

"No."

Justine sipped her coffee. "It's Maddy's life. Don't forget that."

"How could I? She's so much stronger than I've ever been." Rory scanned the degrees on the wall, then looked out the window, where the beautiful Sunday afternoon loitered teasingly. What was she doing? "I don't know where to go. Can you tell me?"

Justine shook her head. "I'm only here to help guide you to that answer."

They spoke for a while longer, with Rory's attention slipping from the conversation. She'd needed to talk about her experiences, but the more that she did, the less she wanted to reveal. She skipped the details of the Delta, and after they discussed her current situation with her writing and her future paths, Rory took the cue and headed out.

She didn't get two blocks before her phone chimed. Rory checked the message.

It came from Greg, the determined doctor. *Coffee?*

Rory noticed another text from Silas. *Leaving for Loon Lake.*

She smiled and sent a reply.

5

*W*aylen eyed the clock on the wall, the second hand slowly rotating around the circumference. He loosened his tie and sighed.

"This is all we have, Special Agent Brooks." The young woman, Hannah, dropped the last of the files onto his desk.

"Can you bring up the one before the feed is cut again?" Waylen asked.

Hannah, who'd been overexcited the entire time, looked to be wearing out after six hours of repetition in a cramped office. He'd arrived at the NASA headquarters early, right when they opened, and it was well into the afternoon. He had two days before his meeting, and was determined to figure out everything he could about the landing.

"Here you go." Hannah clicked her mouse, and the projector showed the dip and rise of the voices.

"Pelican, this is Helios, requesting updates." The voice belonged to Fred Trell.

"Helios, coming in loud and clear. We're loading the cart, and…"

There was a muffled sound before Swanson's voice cut out. "Can you clear that?"

She highlighted the last four seconds, clipped it, and

began working on the controls. "This is the best we can do."

"Play." Waylen leaned forward, closing his eyes.

"…holy…spac…don…ouch"

"Sorry it's not better," she apologized. "What do you think happened, Special Agent Brooks?"

"Call me Waylen." He gazed at the woman, probably in her early twenties, working for such a fine establishment as NASA. He admired that someone her age would seek employment in the field. "The comms were on the fritz, as reported by the engineers."

He listened to a few of Fred Trell's worried communications to the surface, and when he didn't receive responses, Fred contacted Houston, relaying the issue.

"And the first one after the comms returned?" Waylen asked.

"…back. Come in, Helios," Commander Gunn said.

"Thank God. You two okay down there?"

"Musta run into some interference. Looks to be in the clear. How's the window?"

They discussed the orbital rendezvous, and it all became technical, with Houston interjecting. Waylen wasn't getting anywhere, but something had transpired during the missing two hours. He suspected they wouldn't learn the truth, but it didn't matter. Gunn and Swanson had returned to Earth with three tokens from the Delta, all separated, and vowed never to allow them to connect.

Had they traveled to another world? That sure as hell would have messed with their communications. The garbled words replayed in his mind. *Holy.* Maybe they'd said 'hole,' then 'don't touch.'

"Anything else, Special… Waylen?" Hannah began to clean up the mess.

"No, thank you for everything today. It's appreciated." Waylen glanced at the time, realizing he'd be late.

Waylen hurried from NASA headquarters, pressing into a cloudy Monday afternoon. It was only a seven-minute drive, but he could walk it in around the same by cutting through the streets. He started north, and the moment he crossed the road, his phone rang. Waylen didn't recognize the number, but he knew the area code. Boston.

"Special Agent Brooks," he answered.

"Hello, I'm returning your call. Darren Jones."

Waylen hadn't wanted to resort to a self-proclaimed UFO specialist, but he'd been given the man's contact information by Assistant Director Ben. "Darren, thanks for getting in touch. I have somewhat of a sensitive matter to discuss, but I'd be more comfortable dealing with it in person."

"Where are you?" Darren asked.

"DC."

"That'll pose a problem, because I'm all the way up in Providence," he said.

"The number's Boston."

"Work phone," he responded.

"Would you come to Washington tomorrow? My office will book the flight," Waylen said.

"The FBI does that?"

"Sure. It's important."

"Can it wait until the weekend? I have a seminar at Harvard to prepare for."

Waylen was surprised to hear a UFO fanatic was speaking at the Ivy League school, but didn't say so. "No, I'm afraid it can't wait." *Because I might be dead by the weekend.* The thought popped into his mind, and he had to have a contingency plan. He'd arranged all of his time-sensitive meetings, and was on his way to an important one now.

"*Okay, but I don't like the window seat. Aisle, please. And if you can put me near the back, it's statistically...*"

Waylen sighed and looked both ways before jogging through a Don't Walk signal. The FBI headquarters were ahead, and he stared at the building. "We'll be in touch with the details. I'll pick you up at the airport in the morning." He ended the call and started for the J. Edgar Hoover Building. It was a bland, beige structure with five rows of evenly square windows for each office within.

He entered, giving the security his credentials, and saw Assistant Director Ben across the lobby, with a tall man Waylen had never met.

"There he is," Ben said. "Waylen Brooks, this is Gary Charles."

They shook hands. "You were working the case in DC, right?" Waylen asked.

Gary nodded. "We should talk."

They headed to the elevator, taking it to the top floor where Ben was stationed. Waylen nodded at Ben's administrative assistant and closed the doors behind him.

"Did you find something?" Waylen asked.

"While you were running around the country shooting people, Charles was getting somewhere. He tracked the van rental from the Smithsonian heist to a shell corp, but after some burrowing..."

"You found a connection to Planetae," Waylen finished, and Ben seemed impressed.

"How did you..." Gary reached for a tablet. "Once I started investigating—"

"Against my wishes, since I shut him down," Ben added.

Gary smiled, and Waylen appreciated that he'd continued despite Ben's orders. That's what he would have done. "I noted a lot of red flags popping up. There appear to be numerous connections between Leo Monroe and our government, which is why I visited the White House to ask around. I was ignored, almost commanded to leave, and finally, someone in the administration spoke with me. That's when the Secretary of Defense called and told me to drop it."

"He phoned my office too," Ben said.

"What are they trying to hide?" Gary asked.

Waylen nodded and removed the bags from his jacket pocket. He deliberately separated them and placed them on the desk. "These are the reason."

Gary furrowed his brow and reached for them.

"I wouldn't do that if I were you," Ben warned.

"Why?"

"It's okay, they're covered," Waylen said.

"I don't understand," Gary said.

Waylen was going to walk into the snake pit on Wednesday afternoon, and he couldn't do it without support. "I'm putting my trust in the pair of you."

"We'll do what we can, but…" Ben stopped. "Go on."

"Here's what I know." Waylen's shoulders were tense, and they loosened as he spoke. "Helios 15 was the last trip to the Moon in December 1972. It was a monumental occasion, but the fact that they'd lost contact with the orbital ship for two hours went unrecognized. I believe that Colin Swanson and Peter Gunn encountered these while gathering samples. They found a portal to another world and possibly stepped through it. Whatever they discovered was enough to scare the living crap out of them. They separated the Delta—what we're calling the triangle they form when assembled—and split it between the three crewmates, promising to never tell a soul."

Ben and Charles listened with rapt attention, neither appearing to take a breath as he talked.

"Colin did an interview before his illness really took hold, almost breaking the story wide open, but he must have thought better and clammed up. Peter's remained hidden in a safe below his hardwood floors, and they killed him for it. The same men broke into Fred Trell's storage unit, stealing a fake. Swanson's was secured at his home in Rye, where you know we had an incident last week."

"And these are the three genuine pieces of this Delta? From the Moon?" Gary asked.

"Yes."

"They go together, and make a… what did you call it? A portal?"

"Leo Monroe's hired a lot of professionals to secure the tokens, and…" Waylen had the opportunity to call out Sanchez, but he couldn't bring himself to do it. He pictured her expression, the story about needing money for her parents in Florida, and he let it go. "Monroe won't stop hunting until he has them in his possession. I've set up a meeting, and basically traded the lives of the astronauts' families in exchange for the Delta."

"He's untouchable," Ben said. "Planetae is sealed tight, under direct orders from our government."

"What about the Attorney General? We can talk to her…" Gary started, but Ben shook his head.

"Then call in the Director; he'll knock on the right doors," Waylen said.

"And tell him what? That one of our military's top manufacturers wants to travel to another planet?"

"I'm walking in there on Wednesday," Waylen said, "and I intend on walking out."

"We'll see to it," Ben assured him.

"This will be dangerous, Ben." Waylen stared at the artifacts. "These men saw something that scared the wits out of them, and we're going to hand the tokens to a man willing to kill innocent citizens to possess it."

"It'll prove difficult to connect Monroe with the crimes. I guarantee he'll have a thousand ways to discredit your evidence," Ben said. "Not to mention support from the White House itself."

"Do what you can. Please, Ben. It's a matter of national security. Isn't that what we're here for?"

"I'll touch base with my pals at the CIA. They'd be interested in this."

They both answered to the Director of National Intelligence, but that was where the similarities ended. "I don't care who you call. I'm afraid of what Monroe will do with these. I've already seen what he'd do *for* them."

"What about the third?" Gary asked. "You mentioned the pair from Gunn and Swanson and a fake from Trell. Where did you get the last one?"

"A man named Cody Sanderson. He's a space paraphernalia collector out of San Diego, and he befriended Fred Trell. He was never told exactly what the Delta did, but he had his suspicions, which align with my own. Cody met up with us for the funeral and was nearly killed in the process."

Ben's gaze held on the tokens. "You should leave these with me."

Waylen almost ran, taking the offer, but gathered them instead. "I told Monroe I'd deliver them, and I'll see it through."

"Very well. Brooks, watch out. This man is clearly willing to do anything for those, and you're walking around DC with them, which puts a large target on your back. I'll contact our director and set up a meeting with

Intelligence. If we're talking about alien worlds, we can't let them into the hands of a citizen, particularly a private arms manufacturer. I wouldn't believe a word of it if I hadn't touched that damned thing back in Atlanta. I can still see the Moon when I go to bed."

"Out the window?" Gary joked.

"No, not quite." Ben grew quiet, then rose, buttoning his jacket. "Keep me posted. Gary, offer Waylen support if he requires it."

"Yes, sir."

Waylen walked out of the building and emailed the office, providing Darren's information, and got the confirmation ten minutes later that the alien expert was booked for a six AM flight out of Boston.

He felt the urge to dial Martina, but pushed the thought away.

"Should we grab dinner? Will you show me what all the fuss is about?" Gary gestured at his chest, where the tokens were secured.

"Believe me, you don't want to do that. Sure. I could eat." Waylen kept his phone out. "But I have a call to make first."

6

*T*he area was far different upon returning. Silas drove through Gull Creek, avoiding the main street where the grocery store had been burned to the ground with Leigh in it. He pictured her easygoing smile and the sound of her voice. Another casualty of the Delta.

"It's over," he told himself, and continued on the highway into Campbelltown. They were burying Peter Gunn on Wednesday morning, and it was strange that he'd be the only familial witness. Silas had already been to the house, ensuring no break-in attempts had happened during his absence.

Campbelltown was a decent size, and it had everything any big city would offer, but he quickly realized he might be too late. A hardware store was already closing shop, a couple of teenagers breaking down sidewalk displays out front, while an older woman swept the entrance.

He pulled up to an electronics store, finding they were open for another ten minutes, and grabbed two wireless cameras, one for each end of the lake house. Silas paid with cash, not wanting to leave a digital footprint while he was here. He'd taken a few thousand dollars from his account back home, preferring to go cardless until Waylen's meeting with Monroe.

Next, he gathered groceries, filling the vehicle with essentials. There was nothing in the kitchen, so he bought pasta, rice, and soups for the pantry, as well as produce for a few recipes. Since he was currently jobless, he may as well learn to cook. Silas unloaded the bag filled with beer, coffee creamer, and soda, and closed the hatch.

"Damn it," he said, checking the time. Silas dialed the lawyer's office, letting them know he'd be ten minutes late.

The office was nice, and the exterior suggested the practice was as old as the town. Silas noticed how well-manicured the lawn was, and admired the bright flowers lining the cobblestone path leading from the street to the entrance. The sign said they were closed, but a man came to the door and unlocked it when he saw Silas.

"Come in," he said.

"Sorry for the delay."

"My wife prefers me at the office," he assured Silas. "I'm Quinn Martin."

"Silas Gunn."

"Your grandfather spoke kindly of you." Quinn brought Silas into a large corner office with L-shaped windows, giving him a wonderful view of the grounds. Perhaps there was something to living away from a crowded city after all.

"He did? We didn't really know each other."

"He followed your schooling, kept in touch with the administration," Quinn said.

Silas was shocked. "Seriously?"

"And after that, he spoke to your father's assistant. Were you aware of that fact?"

"No."

"Beverly worked for him in the Nineties, when he was running his consulting firm. They stayed in contact."

Silas remembered how often Beverly would ask about his life in the break room. Sometimes she'd go out of her way to have lunch with him. He'd liked her, and now he understood she'd been a mole for Peter. He smiled, thinking about the woman's discussions of her own grandkids, and how proud she seemed to be of them.

"You're here for the will," Quinn said. "Clare wasn't able to make it?"

"No, she has the kids, and work…"

"That's all right. I take it you'll fill her in on the pertinent details?"

"Yes, sir."

"Please, call me Quinn. I work for you, Silas."

Silas sat across the oversized desk and searched for a computer, but didn't spot one. Quinn was probably in his seventies, and hadn't gone digital.

"Okay." Quinn licked a finger and flipped a page in a folder. "You and Clare are the beneficiaries of everything in his estate. The money, the retirement funds, and the house. Then there's the cars, and of course, his royalties."

"Cars? Royalties?"

"Commander Gunn had his likeness used for various licensing deals over the years. Don't you remember the 50th anniversary edition of those building block sets, or the cereal boxes? It was a good contract. It wasn't a lot of money, but he was proud of them. His wife acted as his manager for a couple of decades, and they scored a few lucrative endorsements. Car dealerships, that kind of thing." Quinn gazed out the window. "It's a shame what happened to him."

"It sure is."

"And the vehicles are in storage, right here in town. The keys are in this package." Quinn shook a sealed envelope. "He was into those Sixties muscle cars. Patty hated him wasting money on them, but I think for someone who's flown to the Moon, a boring sedan just doesn't cut it. You get me?"

Silas laughed and nodded. "How many cars are we talking?"

"Five. It's all in the packet. Some of this will take a while to clear, but when we're done, you'll have around four million dollars," Quinn said.

"That's incredible. I'm so grateful Clare and I can split this."

"Sorry, you misunderstood. The accounts alone sit at over eight million in total. Plus the house and other assets."

Silas couldn't even talk. He'd gone from nearly dying to being rich in the span of a week. "Thank you, Mr. Martin."

"Peter was glad he could offer his family something. Oh, before I forget, there's one more thing." Quinn stood up slowly, his knees creaking. He pulled a key from his pocket and undid a barrel lock on a desk drawer. "Peter made me swear never to read this, and I've avoided it for the last two years. He didn't want it in the house, and said to keep it somewhere safe. I suggested a bank, but he refused."

Silas' heart leapt when he saw the journal. The leatherbound volume had cracks on the spine, and the edge of the pages looked dark from smudges. "Is …"

"It's his journal, Silas. I hope you find a connection." He offered the book to Silas, who rose and accepted it without opening the cover. "We need a few signatures, and then we'll be done."

Quinn slid the paperwork toward Silas, but all he saw was the book in his hands.

"Y̶ou're making a mistake," Oscar said.

"Dad, for the hundredth time, I'll just be in Loon Lake for a few days," Rory told him.

"I don't understand why you have to go." Kathy lingered at the exit, like she was defending her daughter from the outside world.

Rory glowered at her father. "Silas is alone, and they're burying *your* godfather."

"Given the circumstances, you should stay here."

Rory smoothed her hair behind her ears and grabbed the suitcase. "I love you two, but I'm still leaving. I'll be home soon."

"When?"

"Soon!" Rory didn't want to be late for her red-eye flight. Silas would be so surprised to see her. She considered keeping it a surprise, but with recent events, it might be better not to show up unannounced, banging on the windows.

Hope you don't mind, but I'm coming to Loon Lake.

Seriously? Silas texted. *When? How? Why?*

Rory laughed as she drove the hatchback toward the airport, using her voice-to-text feature to respond. *Landing at five. On an airplane. Because I choose to.*

I'll be there waiting. Jackson? Silas meant where she'd be landing.

That's the one.

The next few hours were a blur of short lines, security clearance, and boarding, followed by the world's most boring flight. The cabin stayed dark, since it was the middle of the night, but Rory left her light on, thumbing through a mystery novel she'd picked up at the airport. The plot was predictable, but that was a comfort. It seemed like the author wanted the reader to be connected so they could solve the mystery. In this one, Rory guessed the killer was the protagonist's boyfriend from back in high school, and as she skipped ahead, she found exactly that. Rory flipped it closed and turned the light off, waiting for the tires to screech on the tarmac.

She must have fallen asleep, because she woke to the jerking of the plane as it landed. Fog clouded her brain momentarily, but it cleared as she remembered where she was. Rory lifted the window cover, finding a hint of dawn in the distance. She yawned and stood, with her entire row to herself. It wasn't long before she had her carry-on rolling to the airport's exit, and she texted Silas that she'd arrived.

The place was dead at this off hour, and there he was, leaning on an old blue car with his arms crossed. He had a jean jacket on and looked to be transported from another era. Silas hugged her, then took the bag, tossing it into the backseat.

"Whose ride?" she asked.

"Mine, I guess." He opened her door. "I'll explain on the way."

It smelled old inside, kind of stuffy, but in a comforting manner. Silas shifted it into gear, speeding from the arrivals. "Good flight?"

"Nothing happened."

"In my experience, that's a great flight, then." Silas signaled and exited the grounds. "Why did you really come?"

"I couldn't stay there for another day in my old bedroom, trying to write a book. Not until Waylen gets back to us after his meeting on Wednesday. Plus, I didn't want you to be alone."

"I'd be fine," he said. "I've spent the last decade on my own."

"You know what I mean. In that house."

"Thanks. I'm glad you're here."

Rory rolled her window down a crack as they hit the highway, heading west, and breathed in the fresh country air.

"I met the lawyer."

"Yeah? I figured. Unless you were randomly in the market for a classic car," she said.

"I guess I'm rich now."

"That's awesome." Rory beamed. "How wealthy? Like buy a chateau in the south of France rich, or only have to work part time at the coffee shop rich? On second thought, it's none of my business."

He laughed at the comment. "That depends how big of a chateau."

"Impressive. I visited at the right time, before the ladies of Loon Lake knocked down your door bearing casseroles." She said it and regretted the joke. "I wasn't suggesting that's why I was here. I just got out of a…"

"Don't worry, Rory. We're friends." The way he looked at her made her think otherwise. He did have a nice smile.

The drive was quick in the early hour, with next to no traffic aimed for Loon Lake. Silas slowed and turned as they passed the lake on her left. She stared at the large body of water, gazing as the slightest sliver of orange appeared on the horizon. "We made it," she whispered.

"That we did."

"I hate that we gave up the tokens, but I also never want to hear about them again. You know what I'm saying?"

"One hundred percent." Silas brought them to a gravel road, the engine rumbling as they took it slowly. "This is my place. Sounds weird when I say it."

She glanced at the house number, displayed on a rectangular sign. "Beachcomber Way. How charming."

"Isn't it? Wait until you see the sunrise."

Silas took her bag and unlocked the home. Rory noticed the camera above the door, the light glowing green. It was a lovely property, and she recognized why Silas chose to visit. It was the polar opposite of living in the city, even from her parents' place in Woodstock. This was serenity at its finest. Birds called out in the lake, and she found herself drawn to the pier. "Do you mind?" she asked.

"Go ahead. I'll be right there."

Rory removed her shoes on the porch and crossed the grass in bare feet. The wooden dock swayed slightly as she walked to the end. She set a hand on the back of the chair. "I'm sorry, Peter," she breathed. "We let someone learn your secret."

Silas arrived after a few minutes, carrying two cups of coffee. They sat, staring at the water as the sun rose higher. The area had felt foggy, almost oppressive in the darkness, but with the light, it changed before her eyes, becoming energized and beautiful.

She reached out, taking Silas' free hand, neither of them speaking.

Rory was where she was meant to be, for the first time in her adult life.

7

Waylen was used to airports, particularly Reagan National, but he still hated them. They were too busy. People were rarely in good moods, leaving or arriving home. The lines were endless, even at the pickup station. He impatiently drummed his fingers on the steering wheel, searching for Darren Jones. He'd looked the man up online, and guessed he'd be able to pick him out of a crowd.

There was one day before his meeting with the CEO and founder of Planetae, and Waylen both dreaded and eagerly awaited the encounter. He could be rid of the Delta and move on with his life. But why had these astronauts been so determined to keep them hidden? What had they seen on the Moon that would drive them to basically break contact with each other, and never share the fact they'd actually confronted something... alien?

That the Department of Defense had an interest in the objects didn't sit right with Waylen. Just what were they up to? Clearly, Jacob B. Plemmons knew what they might be capable of, but how? And where did Leo Monroe ever learn of the Delta?

Fred Trell was likely the culprit. From the sounds of it, he'd told his lawyer, Daniel Klein, and Cody Sanderson, the collector. He thought about his own father for a moment, and one of the infamously common sayings he'd used throughout Waylen's childhood. *Loose lips sink ships.*

Peter Gunn seemed the most serious about keeping their secret. Colin Swanson had done that interview, sparking some speculation, but even that was short-lived. Colin hadn't lived much longer, then Fred passed shortly after. Waylen wondered how it was for Peter to know they were both dead for an entire eight years while he kept his token secured. He might not have worried about the other two, since they required all three to form the Delta.

Can we talk? The message appeared from Martina, and Waylen's pulse instantly quickened. He muted the conversation and tossed the phone aside. Waylen could forgive a lot, and had over the years. His parents, his former boss… himself. But this was beyond anything he'd justly exonerate.

Waylen squinted as a man walked from the airport, a leather duffel slung on his shoulder. He didn't look like the type of person with a vested interest in aliens. Waylen pictured him swapping his tweed jacket out for a leather vest and a motorcycle helmet.

Waylen threw his hazards on, staying double parked with a taxi next to him. "Darren!" he called.

They met gazes, and Darren strode closer. "Special Agent Brooks?" he asked, his voice gravelly.

"Call me Waylen."

Darren omitted a handshake and tossed his bag into the back seat, climbing in. Waylen started it, shoulder checked, and pulled out.

"What does the FBI want with me? Have you finally found them?"

"Them?" Waylen asked.

Darren leveled a hand near his chest. "Little green

men."

"Nothing so thrilling, I'm afraid." Waylen waited behind another ten vehicles at the red light. He peered in the mirror, finding a black SUV, the windows tinted dark.

"Then what is it you couldn't tell me on the phone? I'm a busy man." Darren seemed agitated.

"Don't enjoy flying?"

"Not particularly."

"I'm the same… let me guess. You were stuck between a chair leaner and a screaming baby," he said.

Darren laughed and flipped the visor to block the sunlight. "Are you clairvoyant, Waylen? What division of the FBI did you say you worked in? Does it start with an X?"

"I'm in Financial Crimes."

"If this has anything to do with that real estate investment fund, they reimbursed my cash, and I'm out of the lawsuit," Darren said.

"No, it's not about that. I can't really tell you, but I can show you." The SUV broke off, and Waylen continued south toward Alexandria.

"Where are we going?"

"To Alexandria."

"You live in DC?"

"Nope. Atlanta."

Waylen hated asking a favor from Charlotte, but he hadn't known what else to do. His hotel room was probably bugged by now, or at least under surveillance. He'd contacted her office with a staff member's phone at headquarters, and dialed her through the main line to make the trace more difficult.

To his surprise, she sounded pleased to hear from him. It had been a while since they'd spoken, but from the quick conversation, she was doing well in her career at the White House. When he'd asked to use her home for a meeting, Charlotte had paused. He'd pictured her brows scrunching up as she considered his odd request. After a few questions, she'd reluctantly agreed.

"Why do I have the feeling I'm getting involved in something I shouldn't be?" Darren asked.

"You'll want to see this." Waylen turned off Duke Street, heading over the creek. "Have you heard of Planetae?"

Darren's reaction showed his cards. "Yes."

"What do you know about them?"

"Leo Monroe runs the place. They do government contract work, mostly suborbital satellite defense, and according to rumors, invisible missiles."

"Invisible missiles?"

"Not truly, but they're undetectable to any established radar."

"That might come in handy," Waylen said.

"Until the schematics are conveniently leaked, and the Russians or North Korea end up with the same technology. That's how people like Leo operate."

"Interesting."

"Planetae also protects the UFO division."

"UFO division?"

"There's a reason people believe we're harboring alien technology."

"Actually, I don't know anything about it. I've been working a lot…"

"The government began its operation a couple of administrations earlier," Darren said. "I'm uncertain how much even the President knows about the program, it's that tight. Your boss might have an inkling, or at least his boss."

"Where is it?"

"I have a few theories."

"Area 51?" Waylen asked.

"Nah, that's a joke. That was the Fifties. We were getting out of the war mentality. People were buying up houses, driving big cars, distracting themselves with music and ice cream sundaes while the economists were doing everything to grow and protect the country. We're talking about the Korean War, then the Cold War, leading into the space race. I believe aliens hadn't landed yet, but the government was letting people discuss it. Anything to keep funding rolling their way, right?"

Waylen listened, not wanting to write Darren off. So far, he'd made sense.

"I bet the FBI could use some extra funding, couldn't they?"

Waylen shrugged and turned into Charlotte's neighborhood.

"The real facilities didn't get built up until 2014."

"And Planetae assisted with them?"

Darren nodded. "Yeah, from my research, it's the obvious answer. It wasn't easy, but I dug into shipping manifests, shell corp documents, and any public information I could find on the Department of Defense. Not to mention job postings for the crews that would be necessary. I called the heads of a few construction companies, but it was obvious they'd signed NDAs."

"Have you gone public with any of this information?"

"Not yet. There are enough speculating UFO nuts out there to keep the masses satisfied. I prefer to have concrete evidence first," Darren said.

Waylen pulled onto her street and slowed. There were no homes across from her, just overgrown trees and bushes. It looked wild, and he remembered going for a few walks with Charlotte on his visits years ago. At the time, he was so rarely in Atlanta, and this almost felt like home.

"This the place?" Darren asked.

"Up there."

"What are you waiting for?"

"Making sure we weren't followed."

"Followed? What's going on, Waylen?"

He watched a woman drive on, frowning at her kids in the back seat. "You'll see."

Waylen parked on the street so he didn't block in Charlotte's nondescript sedan. She'd always been practical, and he appreciated that about her. Her house was petite, with red brick and black shutters framing the living room window. He got out and inhaled the scent of her thriving daylilies.

Darren exited, staring at the door. "Whose home is this?"

"A friend's."

Charlotte appeared at the entrance. She looked the same, but her hair was slightly shorter, and dyed a lighter blonde. She wore her work clothes, a smart suit with short heels. "Waylen."

He smiled. "Charlotte."

"Oh, that kind of friend," Darren mumbled.

"This is Darren. Thanks for letting me come. I figured it would give us some privacy."

Darren walked up the steps, visibly admiring the setup. "Nice porch."

"It's a *veranda*," Charlotte said, a little forcefully.

Waylen glanced at Darren, silently urging him to let it go. He kissed her cheek, and she held the door while Darren entered. Charlotte held Waylen back. "Are you in trouble?"

"A bit."

"You aren't dragging anything into my life, are you? I can't afford to—"

"No. I'll be gone in an hour. Then you won't have to see me again," he said.

She softened and set a hand on his arm. "That's not what I'm saying. To be honest, I was relieved to hear your voice last night. I almost thought you were kidding about using my house for a meeting, and that you'd smartened up."

"You dumped me, if I recall," he reminded her.

"Not like I had a choice. I never saw you."

Waylen sighed, letting the past go. "You look great." He hoped it would diffuse the obvious tension in her shoulders.

"Same with you." She walked around Waylen. "Lock up when you're done. Place the key under the pot."

"You're leaving?"

"I can't be involved with whatever this is." She paused at the bottom of the steps and met his gaze. "If you ever want to talk or have dinner, let me know."

"Friday," he blurted.

"Friday?"

Waylen had his meeting with Monroe tomorrow, but for some reason, he was trying to make plans for a date. Seeing her and the home brought a bout of nostalgia and comfort to his hectic life. It also gave him motivation to survive the upcoming day.

"How about that place near your office with the dark wood and moody jazz band?" he said.

"Seven?"

"Seven." He watched her go, and she waved before backing from the driveway.

Darren stood inside, laughing to himself. "A special agent with game. Who knew?"

Waylen locked the door and glanced at the living room. It was mostly familiar, with a few new pieces of art on the walls. He removed the tokens from his pocket and showed them to Darren, not intending to waste any more time. "These came from the Moon, and I believe they can be used to travel to other worlds. Have you heard of them?"

Darren reached for one, but Waylen snatched it away. "It's true. The Delta exists."

8

Silas wasn't used to such a normal day. Being around Rory was effortless. She didn't mince words, and openly told him her opinion about everything. They opted to stick around, rather than head into town. They were going to Campbelltown in the morning to bury his grandfather, but today, they'd relax. He had a stocked kitchen, a killer ride, and energy to burn. They walked on the gravel road, and a truck stopped, rolling the window down.

"Silas, right?" the man asked.

"Mr. Greenthumb," Silas said.

"You remembered." Gabriel had driven him into town when he'd shown up, dropping him at Leigh's grocery store. It felt like months ago, not a handful of days. "Back in town?"

"Yep. For a while."

"Still on foot, I see," Gabriel said.

"City folk. We prefer to walk. Hey, have you seen Carol and Bitsy?"

"She's moved out of state to her daughter's. They didn't want her out here alone, especially after that home invasion, and what happened to your grandpa."

"That's understandable."

"You need anything, you have my card." He drove off, not waiting to be introduced to Rory.

"Already friends with the neighbors?" Rory joked.

"Apparently."

The skies started off clear, but a darkness had blown in over the water. They were a mile from the house, and he worried the storm would hit them. Rory didn't seem to mind, and she strolled with grace, almost floating without a care in the world.

"I'm lost," she said after a moment of silence.

"Well, the lake is right there." Silas pointed through the tree cover. "My place is back ten minutes, and Gull Creek is about thirty in that direction."

"That's not what I meant," Rory said.

"I quit my job and moved to Loon Lake. I prefer to think of it as the 'finding myself' phase."

Rory kicked a rock into the ditch. "I wish I'd never touched that stupid token."

"Same here." Silas had experienced no visions since Rory's arrival, and he counted his blessings.

"But we did meet."

"We'd met before," he said.

"Not really, though. Sometimes it takes a reason to connect with another human." Rory looked up as a few raindrops fell.

Silas inhaled the scent of ozone while the downpour began. He hung at the side of the road, facing Rory, and first noticed something was wrong when he spotted the Shadow in her eye's reflection. He spun around, but it wasn't there. "Rory…" he croaked.

She grabbed hold of his shoulders. "It's in yours too."

"What does it mean?" he asked.

"That damned Delta marked us," she said.

"How do we … unmark ourselves?"

Thunder cracked overhead, and the dark sky grew blacker as the storm cultivated. Lightning snapped through the afternoon sky, tendrils of it sparking above the lake.

"Let's go to the house!" Rory jogged the way they'd come from.

When they reached the porch awning, he panted for breath. His feet were soaked, along with every other inch of his body. Each step made a squelching noise, making Rory laugh. It started off light, but he could tell it wasn't a healthy sound after a moment. "I can't do this," she said, wiping her face with a sleeve. Her makeup was smudged, but the reflection of the hole from the Moon was no longer in her pupil.

"We'll be okay," Silas promised her. "We're in it together. Once Waylen hands them off, it'll stop. Or it's a time stamp. The token's effects might only last for a while."

"No," she said. "Now I understand why all of them were so messed up. Grandpa Swanson, Commander Gunn, and Trell. Everyone said Peter was a changed man. It's because he had visions for the rest of his life."

"What about Colin? He seemed pretty normal."

"He just put on a friendly face," she said. "But it probably ate at him."

The idea of having dreams of the Moon forever was more than unsettling.

They hurried in, and he locked up while thunder shook the large panes of glass. Even with the blinds open, the room was dark. They stood together, watching the storm ravage the lake. Trees bent and twisted in the gale-force gusts, and he noticed the top of a pine snap near Carol's property. Water pooled under them, gathering on the hardwood, but neither moved.

At some point, he put an arm around Rory's waist. She shifted closer, and he became fully aware of their proximity to one another.

Before either of them could speak, they were taking their drenched clothing off, tossing them in heaps by the windows. They fell to the bed, a tangle of limbs and wet hair.

For a time, Silas forgot about the Delta and the visions from the Moon.

———————

"*W*hat do you know about the Delta?" Waylen snapped. "Better yet, how do you know?"

"I have my ear to the ground," Darren said. "There were a few reasons to suspect something strange from Helios 15, but it's more than the interview Swanson gave that triggered most of the discussion. I wanted to investigate, but Trell died shortly after. Peter Gunn wouldn't return anyone's calls. He was a brick wall. The word *Delta* circulated for a while, but I have no idea who coined the term."

"You ever heard of Cody Sanderson?"

"No. Should I have?"

"Probably not. He's a collector who befriended Trell, and was the one who brought this." Waylen lifted the token wrapped in brown paper.

"There's always been rumors of devices that can form a portal between two worlds." Darren sat on Charlotte's living room chair. Waylen took the couch and set the Delta on her rustic coffee table. "I've subscribed to the theory of UFOs and UAPs because it seems more likely, but I understand that line of thinking might be wrong. Many people in the scientific community will attest that we default to imagining things similar to our own world. Because *we* fly around in ships doesn't mean an alien would, you get my drift?"

"Hence the portals," Waylen said.

"Exactly. The issue with that is, there must be a mechanism to control it."

Waylen peered at the tokens, each covered so the echoes wouldn't be stirred. "What do you mean?"

"Judging by the name, Delta, and the fact there are three of them, I can only assume those form a triangle shape."

"Yes."

"But you haven't tested it?" Darren asked.

Waylen shook his head. "Not a chance."

Darren pursed his lips. "I'd be willing…"

"That isn't a good idea, especially here." Waylen imagined activating the Delta in Charlotte's house and somehow transporting her entire place to the Moon, leaving a crater in the neighborhood. "What were you saying about a mechanism?"

"Let's hypothesize it's a triangle, with the power to activate portals to other worlds, or the Moon, or wherever you imagine. How can you make it work without a tool to choose destinations, et cetera?"

"We have to think outside the box." Waylen tapped his head. "What if it's done cognitively?"

"That's a possibility, but I bet there's a physical device," Darren said. "I've heard of a few artifacts being found overseas, barely mentioned in the forums, but enough that it piqued my interest. Mysterious pieces that can't be melted, broken, or cut. Sound familiar?"

"Very," Waylen admitted.

"What are you doing with them?"

"I'm going to Planetae to give Leo Monroe the Delta tomorrow."

Darren lifted his eyebrows and scratched the stubble

on his chin. "You're kidding me."

"I wish I was."

"Why?"

"Because he's sent an army against the grandkids of the astronauts, all with the objective of securing these three tokens, and it was the only way I could get him to call off the dogs," Waylen said.

"Incredible. It sounds as though Gunn and the others understood how dangerous these were."

"That's an understatement."

"And you're resigning them to a man who builds invisible missiles."

Waylen didn't respond.

"I may be an alien enthusiast, but I question the likelihood that they're among us. But… if it's really a portal between worlds… the situation might change."

"In your expert opinion, is it possible that three pieces of metal could indeed link to a different planet?"

Darren shrugged. "There's no proof, but it's plausible."

"I've touched one of them." Waylen described the experience, and Darren listened intently.

His gaze lingered on the tokens, but he didn't ask to see them up close, or to undergo the strange sensation that accompanied making contact. "The Moon… as it was seen through Peter Gunn's eyes. Incredible."

"What could the purpose of the tokens be?"

Darren sat back, crossing his right leg over his left. "At this point, all I know for certain is that they hold an echo, as you called it. The hole, or Shadow, is the intriguing element. It must be part of the portal. These being placed on the Moon in the same location of the final NASA destination is surprising. Is that a coincidence?"

"Are you suggesting that aliens were watching our

NASA reports and placed the Delta on the surface of their landing zone?"

"More presumably, the Delta was on the Moon for ages. Since they don't tarnish and can't be destroyed, again, in theory, they might have been dormant for thousands of years. Millions, even."

"I need a coffee. You?"

"Sure."

Waylen knew his way around the house, and Darren called to him from the other room. "There is a fair bit of conjecture in my circles." He walked to the kitchen, taking a seat at Charlotte's small island. His knees bumped the cabinets, and he adjusted the stool.

"What's the theory?" Waylen dropped a coffee pod in and turned it on. The machine vibrated as the water heated.

"The idea is this," Darren said, lifting his hands like a professor in front of a classroom. "Aliens have visited our solar system and many others, leaving behind artifacts that only a spacefaring race might encounter. They wouldn't come to Earth and abandon the device, because anyone could stumble across it, and that doesn't meet their criteria."

"The Delta might be a test," Waylen said.

"Yes."

"And if they used it on the Moon, fifty years ago?"

"It's possible that triggered an alert."

"To whom?"

Darren shrugged and accepted the coffee when Waylen slid it to him. He made another and contemplated their conundrum.

"If you saw the Shadow, the Delta is functioning. Perhaps the astronauts didn't 'activate' the Delta. If it was running when they arrived, then the trigger may not have happened."

"Until Leo Monroe snaps it together tomorrow when I offer it to him," Waylen finished.

Darren blew in his cup and sipped it. "That's only one hypothesis, of course, but it's solid. Aliens can't be wasting their time traveling to and from every solar system. This would be a logical way to connect with possible intelligent races."

"Or give them the excuse they need to blow us to smithereens," Waylen countered.

"I don't subscribe to the theory that all aliens are hostile."

"Sure, they'll just enslave us and steal our resources, right?"

Darren laughed, but Waylen's comment struck a nerve. "Think of it this way. If there are extraterrestrial beings, they probably don't need anything from Earth. They're mining moons and asteroids. One asteroid the size of Rhode Island would build a fleet of starships and give them enough water to meet the requirements of a continent like Africa for a decade. If they have the power to fly between galaxies, they can mine and process things better than I could imagine."

"I've never paid much attention to aliens," Waylen admitted.

"What *does* catch your interest?" Darren asked.

"Nothing, really. All I do is work. Financial Crimes division for the Bureau."

"Is it how you found out about Planetae Inc.? Followed the paper trail?"

Waylen set his cup aside. "Not this time. I got to them the old-fashioned way, by interrogating a governor."

Darren laughed again. "Wait, you're not kidding?"

"Nope."

"Let's talk it through," Darren said. "Leo Monroe is willing to kill for those tokens. Why didn't the government become involved? If the military is working with Monroe, they could have sent a team of Marines in helicopters over Loon Lake. No one would have died."

"That's a good question. He probably wouldn't want to be associated, should something go wrong."

Darren rapped his knuckles on the island's countertop. "You'd know better than me, since you're employed by the government, but would they authorize such a careless mission? And the moment word leaked about Gunn being killed, Plemmons would have retreated, especially after the token wasn't found. If it was my case, I'd assume that Monroe is acting independently."

"You're a smart guy," Waylen told Darren. "I've drawn the same conclusion. I'm waiting for my assistant director to talk with the Department of Defense before my meeting, but I'm not holding my breath."

"What happens tomorrow? You walk into Planetae and give the Delta to an arms manufacturer?"

"At this time, yes."

"Monroe wishes to use it for his own selfish motives," Darren said. "Imagine if you had the ability to travel through this Shadow to the Moon anytime you chose? He'd have an entire stranglehold operation on mining the Moon. It would be a multi-trillion-dollar endeavor. Monroe could build a facility up there and hold a monopoly, maybe hold Earth hostage."

"Sounds a little comic-book evil villain to me."

"Probably, but I wouldn't put it past him. Money does strange things to people."

"And the trigger? If you're right, Leo Monroe might notify an alien race that we've used the ancient artifact and are ready to meet," Waylen said.

"I didn't think I'd live to see aliens."

"Or nightmares. I've read *The War of the Worlds*, and this isn't a story I want to experience." Waylen finished his coffee and set to cleaning up. He wouldn't leave a mess in Charlotte's kitchen after she was gracious enough to offer her home.

"Do you mind if I stick around DC for another day?" Darren asked. "You have me intrigued, and I'd love to learn how tomorrow goes."

"Sure, but I thought you had a lecture at Harvard to prepare for."

"Some things are more important. This might alter the course of history, and I plan to be in attendance."

The weight of his words washed over Waylen.

9

"It was a mistake," Rory told Silas. "I didn't come here for that. We were scared and vulnerable, and it'll never happen again."

Silas stared at the flickering fireplace, feeling quite the opposite. They shared an undeniable connection: both being grandkids of famous astronauts, having to grow up with their looming presences overshadowing their families.

"Silas, would you say something?" Rory sat on the chair closest to the hearth, her legs crossed beneath her.

"Something."

She rolled her eyes, looking exasperated with him. "That's not funny."

"What do you want me to do? I like you, Rory."

"I like you too, but that doesn't negate the fact it was an error in judgment."

"Why does it require a label? Is there really anything wrong with what we did this afternoon? We're two consenting adults capable of making decisions."

Rory averted her gaze. "You don't want to be involved with me."

"Why not?"

"First off, I'm a loner, and I'm spoiled rotten."

"So am I."

"Not like me. My dad is going to buy me a condo,

and I didn't pay for my schooling. When Kevin blew my advance, who do you think bailed me out? I fought so hard to take care of myself in those years after college, but I've never known what it's like to fear where my next meal was coming from, or had to worry about my future, which makes me an utter and complete failure who can't write another book. I just don't have it in me. I'm clearly attracted to psychos, present company excluded."

Silas smiled and took a drink of his lemon tea. That was one thing his grandpa had in ample supply. "But you said you like me. That's a nice start."

Rory's frown finally vanished, and she clasped her tea close to her chest. "It was fun. I don't know the last time I stopped thinking. Do you ever feel that?"

"Probably."

"I'm in my head so much that I can't turn it off. I'm constantly annoyed with myself. Can't I shut up for a minute and hear the world around me?"

"I don't have that problem. I've never been much of a thinker."

"Sure, the finance major doesn't use his brain."

"I understand what you're saying," he said. "Our brains are difficult to ignore."

"I sit and watch people, having dinner with friends, laughing, sharing stories, and existing… It's missing in my life."

"It's called being happy, Rory."

"Is that what it is?" She smiled at him. "Are you happy?"

"I'd say I'm quite content, but given the recent situation? It's tough to remember what normal is." Silas motioned to the room they sat in. "Grandpa Gunn was literally killed two weeks ago, and we've been through more than we deserved. But great things are around the corner.

I can sense it."

"I'm glad one of us has your optimism." Rory sighed and drank her tea. "I need a splash of honey or something. You good?"

He offered his cup. "I'll take a refill."

Rory left and banged around the cupboards in the kitchen. She returned a few minutes later with two steaming cups and an open bottle of tequila—the same one Leigh had brought to the house. Silas paled, and it all flooded back.

"You okay?"

"I was thinking about..."

Rory glanced at the bottle and seemed to understand. "Oh, you two were..."

"No, we weren't, but it was one of those... what might have been." Silas made eye contact with Rory. "She died because of me."

Rory sat on the couch next to him. "It's not your fault."

"We bury my grandfather tomorrow. Then what?" Silas took the tequila and splashed some into his lemon tea. Rory did the same, and they clinked glasses.

"Then we live," she said.

"To living." Silas frowned at the taste, but kept hold of the mug.

His phone buzzed, and Silas checked it, finding a message from Waylen. "It's our friend at the FBI."

"That's a sentence I never expected to hear. What's it say?"

"*Don't worry, I won't let you down. Consider this over on your end.*" Silas read it twice, and started a response.

"There's no reason for Monroe to continue to come after us, since Waylen's delivering the tokens. I feel so free. We can do anything."

"Or nothing. I *am* retired for the moment, remember?"

Rory laughed, and the air in the room seemed to get lighter. "Not everyone's independently wealthy."

"Oh, poor Rory." Silas poked her in the arm. "I refuse to be sad for you."

Rain started up again, drawing his attention to the window. It was pitch-black outside, the world drowned by dark clouds. It made the indoors of his new lake house all the more enticing. Drops splattered onto the massive windowpanes, one after another, in a continuous random pattern.

Be careful, and remember, it's someone else's responsibility soon. Silas hit send and waited for the response.

"It's true. We can start fresh." Rory set her cup aside and leaned on Silas, giving him the idea that her earlier statements didn't coincide with her genuine feelings.

"How about that game of Monopoly?"

"Fine, but I *will* throw the board if I lose," Rory said.

"Of course you will. I'll be the bank."

---

*T*he storm lingered, refusing to pass through the area. The heavy black clouds were anchored from Loon Lake and persisted all the way to Campbelltown. Silas' mood matched the weather as he pulled into the cemetery. This was a somber affair, not a ceremony so much as just bearing witness to Peter Gunn's burial.

Silas didn't know the man, and even staying at his home had done little to change that. He kept the journal with him, but couldn't bring himself to read it. He wanted the tokens to be gone from their lives forever. If he opened the journal, they'd continue to hold power over him.

Rory had a black outfit, and Silas wore a dark suit. They'd stopped at the store in town, grabbing two matching umbrellas, but there were only white and red polka dots left. He parked his Chevelle under a large oak, then climbed out and popped the colorful canopy.

"At least we won't be soaked," Rory said, taking the rare role of optimist from him.

Silas checked the clock, knowing that Waylen had three hours before his own meeting in DC. The seconds seemed to tick slower with the pending arrangement, and Silas had woken up with a headache because of it. Rory, on the other hand, was almost perky.

They greeted the woman in the brick office building, and she smiled warmly as they dripped on her entrance mat.

"I'm so sorry for your loss, Mr. Gunn. We loved Patricia. She and I were in a knitting club together, and she always gave me the best slow cooker recipes. I miss her every day." She rubbed her palms, then blinked. "Whoops. I suppose I should have told you my name. I'm Dolores Newton, and I manage the place."

"Nice to meet you, Dolores. I'm Rory."

"You look familiar," she said.

"I get that a lot."

"No, you said Rory?" Dolores beamed. "She gave me a copy of your book!"

"Who did?" Rory asked.

"Patricia Gunn. It was a beautiful tale of a courageous woman breaking through glass ceilings and venturing to the Moon. I loved it."

"My grandma read your novel," Silas quietly told Rory, then focused on Dolores. "Could you tell me some stories about them after?"

"It would be my absolute pleasure, dear." Dolores looked to be around his own parents' age, but she sounded like his other grandmother, a kind soul who'd passed when he was around fifteen.

Twenty minutes later, they stood at the edge of a dug grave, the coffin from the funeral sitting on the lowering device. The freshly-dug dirt trickled in the heavy rainfall. Dolores had asked if they'd prefer to wait it out, but since the radar didn't show it dissipating, he'd opted to proceed as scheduled. Silence filled the air, and Rory held his hand as Peter's body descended into the ground.

Beside his gravestone sat the plot of Patricia Rose Gunn. Silas had visited it before during her whirlwind funeral, but couldn't recall what the stone said. His gaze flickered to Peter's, and he read the inscription on the bottom. *Your footprint on our lives will never be forgotten.*

Silas tugged his umbrella closer as emotion welled in his chest. Peter should have lived longer, and Silas should have tried to know him. He supposed most regrets were irreversible; otherwise, they'd be called something else.

When it was over, he was numb.

"Let's go talk with Dolores," Rory said.

They spent an hour in the office, with the cemetery director excusing herself twice to deal with random issues. Silas learned about Patty, as she affectionately called his grandmother, though Dolores had little first-hand experiences with Peter. Eventually, she had to go, and Silas thanked her for spending so much of her morning with them.

He closed the umbrella near the car, tossing his into the backseat. "Lunch?" he asked Rory.

As they pulled away, he noticed a black van following them, the wipers on full.

———————

*W*aylen paced the office, continually checking his watch. The meeting was in an hour, and Assistant Director Ben hadn't shown up yet.

"Can you call him again?" Waylen asked Ben's assistant.

"As I've told you five times, he's in a meeting with the White House," she said haughtily.

Darren Jones had talked his ear off yesterday at the hotel bar, until almost midnight, and he'd found the distraction helpful. The moment he'd gone up to his own room, Waylen couldn't sleep. He lay in bed, staring at the ceiling as the window-mounted AC unit clicked on and off. Twice, he'd removed the tokens from their hiding spot, spread them out on the desk, and considered assembling it. He had to know if they were really a portal to alien worlds.

He'd kept in touch with Silas and Rory, and ignored another two texts from Martina. Then, when he'd given up hope of ever relaxing, his eyes closed, and Waylen recognized the brush of the Shadow on his mind. Tendrils clung to his appendages, dragging him into oblivion. He'd woken at seven AM on the dot, his head clear of distractions.

Waylen sat, tapping his toes until Ben appeared in the hallway. He jumped to his feet when his superior waved him to follow. "What's the word?"

"You'll see."

He entered a meeting room with Ben, and spied Plemmons at the table, along with another man he'd never met.

"Special Agent Brooks, take a seat." The Secretary of Defense gestured across from him.

Waylen glanced at Jacob B. Plemmons, then at the man with him. He was younger, around Waylen's age, with a fresh haircut and shiny cufflinks that didn't look cheap. Plemmons had a blue tie on, with a small golden American flag pin on his lapel.

"Gentlemen," Waylen said.

"It's come to my attention that you're going to Plane-tae Inc. today," Plemmons said.

"In an hour, sir."

"Leo Monroe is on our untouchable list," he told Waylen.

"I'm not going to arrest him."

"Monroe had several important contracts with our government, but it's also clear he's not above selling technology to the opposition. We've warned him before, and I believed he would stop. He hasn't. I've watched his business closely, and while we're still in a partnership with him, that may come to an end."

Waylen listened intently to each word. "His men tried to murder me, sir."

"So Ben has said."

"He killed Peter Gunn, a national hero," Waylen said. "He may not have pulled the trigger, but the blood's on his hands."

"I know."

"Are we doing anything about it?"

Plemmons leaned on the table, pointing to Waylen's chest. "Show me."

Waylen shot Ben a nervous glance, but the Assistant Director only nodded his confirmation.

Waylen removed the packages and slid one token on-to the table. The younger man with Plemmons almost drooled at the sight.

"Who is this?" Waylen asked.

"He's with me," was all the answer Plemmons offered. He reached for the token. "May I?"

"Don't." Ben grabbed his arm. "You have that heart condition."

Plemmons loosened his tie and sat back. "Proceed to the meeting at Planetae. Give him the Delta and make a quick exit. We'll do the rest."

"You're taking him down?" Waylen asked.

"Yes."

Waylen filled with relief. As dangerous as the Delta was, he somehow felt better with the concept of it being in the government's hands, over those of a private company's deranged CEO.

"Bring them. We'll deal with Monroe."

"Why not just go arrest him?"

Plemmons frowned deeply. "He's feeling the heat. He might skip town and hide at one of his foreign plants. But he won't leave with the Delta in the city."

Waylen stood, knowing his timeline was tight.

"And Special Agent…"

"Yes?" He stopped at the door, with the tokens securely tucked into his pocket.

"Does anyone else know about these?" Plemmons asked.

"No one we need to worry about."

The man with him whispered in his ear, and the Secretary of Defense pursed his lips. "Don't tip Monroe to what's happening. He's dangerous, and we can't allow him the opportunity to evade us."

"No pressure," Waylen muttered to himself as he left.

Special Agent Charles met him in the lobby. "Everything good?"

"It will be. Thanks for your work on this, Gary."

"Any time."

Waylen found his car in the parking garage and began his drive north.

He first realized something was wrong when he smelled the burning. A hiss of smoke rose from the hood as he hit the freeway, and he heard a snap. He pressed the brakes, but they no longer worked.

Waylen guided his car to the shoulder and yanked on the emergency brake. It pulled up with no resistance, and he slid into the guardrail, scraping the side of his doors. He did everything in his power to avoid striking another vehicle. The car was slowing since his foot had retreated from the pedal, but the steering wheel locked up. Waylen could only watch as he aimed directly for an overpass and hoped he'd make contact with the orange impact barrels. The car hit the barricades at twenty-five miles an hour, and Waylen smashed into the airbag the second it deployed.

Pain erupted in his face, and his neck tingled when the airbag deflated with a hiss. He tried to grab his phone, but it must have fallen to the floor. Waylen undid his seatbelt and reached for the handle, hearing a strange noise. He glanced up, finding a black helicopter landing in the middle of the exit.

A man stepped out.

Leo Monroe had brought the meeting to Waylen.

10

"We should have heard from him by now," Rory said. The restaurant was pleasant, probably the finest dining experience Campbelltown had to offer. She'd opted for the seafood, and Silas had ordered the Cajun chicken, neither of them finishing their meals.

"He was going there at one. It's two thirty." Silas stabbed a steak-cut fry and bit it in half before setting the remainder on the plate. "They might still be talking."

"Talking," Rory said. "About what? It's not like Monroe will want to be besties with a special agent after trying to kill him. He bribed a federal agent, and from what I gather, Waylen took that one personally, if you catch my drift."

"You think so?" Silas seemed surprised.

"It was obvious, at least to a woman." Rory waved the server down and asked for the check.

"It's on me."

"My entitlement continues," she said.

The place was quiet on a Wednesday after the lunch rush, but a couple of people lingered near the windows. They'd opted for a quiet booth, tucked in the back of the dimly-lit establishment. Rory felt like hiding from the world on this gloomy day.

"Let's give him another ten minutes."

Rory wanted to dial Waylen's number, but wouldn't

allow herself to follow through. The last thing an FBI agent in the middle of his duty needed was to be pestered by a civilian.

"Are you staying?" Silas asked, after paying cash for their lunch.

"That depends on you."

"Me?"

"You probably want the place to yourself. I could book a hotel in town," she said.

"No way. You're welcome to the lake house for as long as you'd like. You planning on starting the book again?"

"I am."

"Good."

"When Waylen calls us and confirms it's done, I can move on," she said.

Silas dangled his car keys. "Rain's let up. Ready to head back?"

"Sounds good to me." She stopped Silas at the exit. "He'll be all right."

"Waylen can take care of himself."

The clouds had finally parted, offering a peek of sunlight through the darkness. Silas cursed under his breath. "There's that van again."

It was parked a block down, facing the other direction. "This is a small town. Probably has nothing to do with us."

"I hope so." Silas manually unlocked her door and opened it for her.

Rory wasn't used to this kind of treatment. "How chivalrous."

The moment Silas started the car, the van ahead took off.

"See, we have to stop being so paranoid."

Silas put the car into gear and moved from the curb, driving past the main drag. Soon they were through town, and he was on the highway that led to Gull Creek and eventually to Loon Lake. Rory held her phone in her lap, willing Waylen to contact them with good news.

"Shit," Silas said. "He's following us."

Rory's pulse quickened, and she felt on the precipice of a major panic attack. "This shouldn't be happening."

Silas reached under his seat, brandishing a gun. "I'll take care of it."

"What are you doing?" she shouted. "You can't whip that out whenever you want."

"Things are different in Wyoming, Rory." He slowed, and she watched through the mirror as the van did the same. Rory exited, wishing he'd just leave it alone, but obviously Silas was done being pushed around. He backtracked on the road and stepped further onto the shoulder as a massive semi-trailer whooshed by. The van had tinted windows, and Silas jogged to it, gun raised. "Get out of the van! Why are you following us?"

Rory was certain this was it, that a team of Monroe's killers would tumble from the vehicle and end their lives. She tensed as the door opened, and all she could hear was Silas' laboring breath as he kept the handgun aimed for the van's driver's side.

Someone emerged, landing on the asphalt. "Don't shoot!"

Cody Sanderson spilled out, hands raised.

---

*W*aylen rubbed his neck and peered from the moving helicopter as they departed DC. "Where are we going?"

Leo Monroe sat one row ahead of him, a sneer on his stubble-covered face. He was tall, his shoulders narrow beneath an expensive blue suit. Waylen glanced at the man beside him, and then at the barrel pointed at his chest.

"You know this is all kinds of illegal," Waylen said.

"Mr. Brooks, it's my understanding that your superiors were about to infiltrate my operation, and I couldn't allow that to happen. Not before I got my hands on those." Leo's voice was cultured.

Waylen checked his pocket, where the tokens remained. "You could have killed me."

Leo's expression held zero remorse. "You look fine."

Waylen realized they could easily throw him from the helicopter once they secured the tokens. And there was only so much resistance he could muster with a bullet wound.

Leo reached closer. "Give them to me."

Waylen looked at the hired help, then at Leo, and grabbed the three bags.

Leo smiled, baring his teeth. "Perhaps you'll be persuaded to cut ties with this agency and work for me? There are much better perks in the private sector."

"Isn't bribing one FBI agent enough?" he asked.

"One? You have to be kidding, Brooks. I have members of every organization in my pocket, the President included."

"Are you forgetting about the incoming raid you just evaded?"

"They'll change their tunes after I send the video we're about to film," Leo said.

Waylen watched as Leo held the tokens almost reverently to his chest. He didn't remove their coverings, and that was for the best while in a traveling helicopter.

Leo Monroe went quiet, and no one spoke for a good chunk of time while they flew north, heading close to the Atlantic coast. The copter flew quickly, and the pilot talked quietly, probably giving someone on land his authorization.

"I'll ask again. Where are you taking me?"

"I assume you spoke to Governor McKenzie?"

Of course he knew the details. "Yeah, what about it?"

"I've built a facility outside of the city, where I'll change the trajectory of Earth's economic future," Leo said. "Imagine what will happen when I prove there are other planets within our grasp. Everyone's been thinking about starships, and how to build an engine capable of leaving our solar system. The entire time, we've had the Delta on the Moon, with the ability to lead us to these alien worlds."

"You're a murderer, not a hero," Waylen said.

"On the contrary, Special Agent Brooks. Those men killed Peter Gunn of their own volition. Jack, Shane, and Bobby had a personal vendetta against the man. I was never involved." Leo looked forward as he spoke, and the pilot shifted angles when the Manhattan skyline appeared in the distance. They headed to New Jersey, and he continued north, hugging the edge of the Hudson.

"Have you stopped to think this through? What if you encounter hostile life across the Shadow?"

Leo's face twisted into a grin, and Waylen had to fight to keep from lunging at him. "Then I'll still be a hero, Brooks. After all, *Planetae protects the world.*" He said the company slogan slowly.

"You're delusional. If you use the Delta, you could trigger a cataclysmic series of events." Waylen shifted in the seat to watch the Jersey shoreline as they sped by.

He'd given the Delta to this megalomaniac, and no

one could help him. Waylen had been hoping to survive the day, but his odds were dramatically declining with every passing minute.

———————

Silas turned down his driveway and made sure Cody was trailing him before continuing to the house. He cut the engine and waited while Cody parked his van, backing it closer to the front porch. "What's he doing?"

"I have no idea." Rory exited.

Cody emerged, smiling at them like he had a secret and couldn't wait to share it.

"How did you find us?" Silas asked.

"I knew you'd go to Loon Lake," he said. "I wasn't expecting Rory. Are you two…"

"No!" Rory quickly replied.

Cody shoved his keys into his jeans pocket.

"You came all the way from San Diego?" Rory couldn't believe he was there.

"Yep. Drove through the night, caught a couple of hours of sleep at a rest stop. Almost hit a deer at dusk yesterday, but somebody up there likes me."

"You want a cup of coffee?" Silas asked.

"Do I ever. I haven't stopped for three hours. Also, I could use a refresh."

Silas unlocked the door and held it for Cody. He jogged in and vanished down the hall.

"What's he doing here?" Rory whispered.

"Maybe he didn't want to be alone either. This has been a seriously messed up time, and we've all been through the same thing." Silas glanced at the van again, wondering what Cody had stowed in it. If he wasn't carrying gear, what was the point of driving the clunky old vehicle? It probably had terrible gas mileage, and he doubted it could even reach the speed limit on the interstate.

Cody came into the living room, cracking his knuckles. "Whew. How about that coffee?"

Silas made a pot and shucked his tie off.

"You guys look nice. You make quite the couple," Cody said, sitting at the wooden kitchen table.

"We're not... why did you come?" Silas asked.

"Well, I have a confession." Cody drummed his fingers on the table.

Silas fought to keep his jaw from clenching. "Are you going to tell us what it is?"

"I'm still deciding." Cody rose and poured himself a coffee.

11

*T*he facility was huge, with a giant chain-link fence running a mile in both directions around the complex. It was impressive, and Waylen wondered how much of the funding came from the US government. There appeared to be three rows of offices near the top of the main building, but the glass was a dark blue, the light reflecting off the panes.

The helicopter landed within the fence on a designated pad, and the rotors slowed when it touched down. Leo disembarked, and Waylen took the hint when the gun shoved closer to him.

"Can you ask your man to relax?" Waylen shouted over the noise.

Leo gestured at the guy, who reluctantly holstered the weapon. More armed guards were present, standing near the entrance, and they didn't react when Leo tapped a keycard to the screen by the doors. "Welcome to the future, Brooks. The offer's still on the table," he said.

Waylen stepped into another world. The floors glimmered with gold specs; the walls were molded poly, and it resembled a television science fiction starship. There were computer screens, with the name *Planetae* lingering on them in a white font.

The front desk was empty, and Waylen didn't see any other staff members. Leo waved him on, the tokens gripped in his left hand.

Their footsteps echoed in the halls, and Waylen took in the sights. "It must have taken you ages to build this."

"Three years."

"McKenzie said you were seeking permits to operate in New York," he said.

"In my experience, it's better to ask for forgiveness than permission. I've shaved years off every project that way. And in the end, my contacts always push it through, just as they will on the Delta development."

He stopped when they encountered a barricaded wall. Cameras were angled at them, and Waylen noticed the blinking green lights.

Leo leaned over a screen, and it scanned his face, giving him access. "Waylen, this will be a shock to you. You'll understand why no raid can stop what I've begun."

Waylen kept quiet, but nodded once.

With the touch of an icon on the display, the doors hissed and spun aside, giving him a view of the massive warehouse space beyond. The lights clicked on sequentially, until the area was covered in a soft white glow. There were countless desks, each equipped with monitors and black computer towers. In the center of the room, a hexagonal platform was raised a foot off the ground, and it was surrounded with a clear casing.

"This is Operation Delta." Leo walked in long strides toward the case. "With it, I'll harness the Shadow linked to these tokens, and we'll be able to travel to other worlds."

Waylen glanced at the sections of the Delta. "You're going to test it?"

"Of course I am. I've waited years for this," he said.

"How did you know their purpose?"

"I visited Colin Swanson once, after the interview. He

told me things you'd never believe," Leo said. "I couldn't act until I had this prepared. Planetae wasn't nearly as powerful as we are now, but I was patient. Then Peter Gunn refused to die of natural causes like the others, so I had to…" He watched Waylen, and stopped from giving a confession. "Now I have the Delta."

He gestured at an industrial storage closet, and scanned his face again before opening the metal slabs. Five spacesuits hung inside, with helmets above in cubbies. The Planetae logo—a basic spherical world with a slash around it, implying it was spinning—was on each suit's upper left breast.

A team appeared from the far end of the laboratory, wearing gray lab coats and carrying tablets. Leo removed his jacket and passed it to Waylen, who took the garment before setting it onto a desk.

"You plan to use the Delta," Waylen said.

"Yes."

Leo undressed and slipped into a jumpsuit, then began clipping the suit on. The team of three ran through processes, consulting with Leo as they completed the steps. He reached for the helmet and stared at Waylen. "You're about to witness history in the making."

He put it on, and a blue light illuminated the clear mask. "I will now prepare the Delta." His voice came out of a speaker, sounding deeper.

Waylen noticed numerous cameras pointed at the cordoned-off platform. Leo stepped to it, entering the safety of the protective casing. Waylen guessed it was twenty feet wide, and when he peered up, it went on for twice that in height. His fingertips tingled in anticipation of the monumental event. Waylen took a few steps back, almost without thinking, as the Planetae team talked amongst one another.

Leo sealed the containment area and relocated to the center of the platform. He stopped at a white pedestal with a flat top and set the covered tokens on it. He cautiously removed them from their bags, until all three lay in a row. He lifted one and scrutinized it, then did the same to the other two. Because he wore a spacesuit, no part of him could contact the token, saving him from experiencing the power of their built-in echoes.

Leo turned to a specific camera and stood tall. "I am Leo Monroe, with Planetae, and I'm about to connect the tokens. Swanson and Gunn discovered these on the Moon during their Helios 15 venture, and returned to Earth with the Delta. They separated the pieces and vowed to keep them disconnected. This was never their decision to make. Today, we discover how incredible the tool can be. I will personally test it."

Waylen wondered if it would be possible to chance an escape. Even if he made it outside, would the guards shoot him on sight? What was he going to do, hurtle a twelve-foot fence?

He braced himself as Leo lifted a token, then attempted to bond a second to it. The token fell to the platform.

Leo's head snapped up, and he glared at Waylen. "You... where are the real tokens?"

Waylen swallowed and shook his head. "Those *are* the real ones."

Leo tried again, any which way, to create a triangle, but nothing worked.

An alarm sounded, and Leo stared at a screen off the platform. Dozens of vehicles stormed the grounds, and Waylen grinned when he recognized them as FBI SWAT. Two helicopters arrived, hovering over the facility.

"Time to give it up, Monroe. They have you surrounded," Waylen said.

———————

Rory was growing tired of Cody's evasive comments. "If you don't tell us this instant, you can turn around and go back to San Diego."

"Fine." Cody set his cup down and reached into his windbreaker's pocket. He removed three envelopes.

"If it's a wedding invitation, I'm busy that weekend," Silas said.

Cody took the first and dumped a token onto the table.

Rory's heart pounded, and she sat again. "What…"

"You didn't think I'd let someone else take them, did you?" Cody laughed and dropped the other two out.

"Waylen." Rory checked her phone, but there was no response from their messages to the FBI agent. "You might have given him a death sentence."

Cody fidgeted with his coffee cup. "I didn't mean to… I just couldn't allow Leo Monroe to use the Delta."

"When did this happen?" Silas demanded.

"When they broke into the rental, everybody was distracted with the betrayal by Waylen's friend, and I swapped them. Fred had a few copies made, like the one from the storage unit, and they sure came in handy."

"What are you planning on doing with those? Are we going to hide them again?" Rory asked.

Cody shook his head. "That's why I came."

Rory couldn't stop her hands from shaking. Silas flicked the fireplace on and returned with a frown. "Put those away."

"No."

"I won't let you do anything stupid, not in my house."

"You don't want to learn what happens beyond the Shadow?" Cody's eyes gleamed in the firelight. It was getting later in the afternoon, and the clouds had grown darker again. It seemed to fit the mood of their conversation.

"No, I really don't," Silas admitted. "Take them and go. The moment Leo realizes they're not real, he'll come here."

Rory stared at them and pictured her grandfather on the Moon with Commander Gunn, stumbling across the Shadow and Delta on the surface. They'd done miraculous things in their lives, and because of this, their futures were forever altered.

Something extraordinary was within reach. All they had to do was take hold.

"Rory, what's that look?" Silas asked.

She didn't answer as she rushed to the exit. A few raindrops fell, splatting on the sidewalk near Cody's van. The other two followed her, and she tugged on the rear handle, finding it locked. "Open it."

Cody fumbled with the keys and swung it wide. There was a big trunk, and he used another key before opening the lid.

Rory gawked at the retro spacesuit inside.

Cody smiled from ear to ear and pointed at the sky. "Who wants to go to the Moon?"

12

*T*he next few minutes were a whirlwind, with Waylen nervously waiting for the SWAT team to infiltrate the building. When it was abundantly clear Leo wasn't planning to defend himself in a last-ditch effort, Waylen headed for the exit, opening the barrier to the laboratory. He raised his arms, declaring himself as an FBI agent, and his counterparts moved past him, securing Leo Monroe, who sat on the edge of his platform's entrance, stuck in his brand-new spacesuit.

"Do you have any idea who I am?" Leo shouted. "Unhand me."

Waylen watched as they apprehended the Planetae CEO, dragging him out of the lab. His employees stood helpless as the place was scoured.

"Thought I'd find you here," a voice said from the hallway.

Martina Sanchez strolled up, stowing her handgun into her shoulder holster.

"You did this?"

"I heard through the grapevine that Planetae was being raided in DC, and when they found your car, I had a suspicion this was where he'd brought you," she said. "That Jack guy also confirmed my theory when I grilled him."

"But you're working for Leo."

"No. He paid me to intermediate for the tokens; that's all. I thought I was doing you a favor, and at the same time, protecting those friends of yours. Without the Delta, you were no longer a target."

Waylen observed her, and while he couldn't forgive her for taking a bribe from a dangerous man, he figured her heart might have been in the right place.

"I was in New York and called the field office for the SWAT. They were happy to oblige once Ben gave them the green light. Our friends from DC are on the way now." Martina shouted at someone, and they gathered the staff members in lab coats, moving them from the enormous space.

"I have to check something," Waylen said.

Martina walked with him, whistling when she spotted the contained platform. She lingered by the closet, grabbing a helmet. "He really thought they'd take him to space? I guess he was wrong."

Waylen wasn't so sure. He went to the clear door and stepped onto the raised section. The tokens were there, two on the podium, one on the floor.

"You should leave them for Ben to handle."

Waylen didn't listen, and crouched, picking the fallen token up. It didn't send him into a trance or reveal a vision of the Moon—or anywhere else, for that matter. It was a dud. He rose and tried the next piece of metal, getting the same result. The last was no different. "I don't understand what happened."

He closed his eyes, struggling to determine if they'd ever done anything. He'd collapsed when he'd visited Silas and Leigh in Loon Lake, and they'd seen it too. Assistant Director Ben would attest to the power behind the version he'd made contact with. So what was he missing?

"I should have known," he said.

"What is it?" Martina asked.

Waylen had a strong suspicion he knew where the tokens were, but without his cell, he didn't have their numbers. "Can I borrow your phone?"

"*I* asked who wants to go to the Moon!" Cody repeated.

Rory and Silas gazed at one another.

"No way, not going to happen," Silas said.

But Rory touched the fabric and couldn't help but smile. "I'll do it."

"Rory, you're kidding me. There's no way you can wear... *that* and walk on the Moon."

"Why not?" Cody asked. "This is a real pressure suit from the mission. Well, not exactly, but it was a backup. It was used for a couple of years in training, and I have the certification. The oxygen is good, updated last month, and I've had it tested many times. It's a working spacesuit, for all intents and purposes."

Rory felt like she was watching herself through a lens, no longer in control of her voice or actions. "Let's get me into it."

"Hold on, we don't even know if the Delta works. Cody, have you connected it?"

"Nah, I didn't want to until we were all together and in agreement."

"We're not agreeing to anything," Silas said.

"This is a democracy, then." Cody pointed at himself, then at Rory. "I'm sorry, Silas. It's two to one."

"Can I speak to you?" Silas peered at Cody over her shoulder. "In private."

Rory went under the awning with him as the rain fell

with more intensity. She let him argue, knowing that nothing he said could dissuade her from this experience.

"You can't put on a suit from the Seventies and expect to wander the Moon. It's impossible."

Rory smiled, a calm uplifting her senses. "It's okay."

"No, it's…"

"I'll be fine. I have to see, don't you get it? We've been given something special, a chance to view life from another perspective, to explore places beyond our reach."

"Then why did our grandparents waste their whole lives hiding it?" Silas asked.

"I intend to find that out, and if I return with the same idea, then we'll get rid of the Delta," she said. "I promise."

Silas paced the front porch, hands clenched into fists at his sides. "I hate this."

"I know."

"Someone wanna give me a hand with this? It weighs a ton." Cody had the trunk halfway out of the van.

Silas helped him carry it in, and Rory listened carefully as Cody explained the suit. Apparently, it wasn't uncommon for him to wear it on a Friday night and play video games. It had a strange odor, a musty scent that wouldn't shake no matter what. They activated the air and tested it, Rory inhaling with the helmet on. It was odd wearing something on her head, and she felt exposed in the suit, even though it was meant to do the opposite. Her steps were heavy, the suit weighing far more than she expected.

Rory slowly and carefully walked to the bathroom, and stared at herself in the mirror, seeing her main character from *View* instead of herself. Maddy had followed in her grandpa's footsteps, and now Rory would as well.

It was bulky, with a NASA insignia on it. She touched the embroidery with a glove and lumbered to the living room. "Let's do this."

"The suit is an A7-LB, a newer version. It has the proper insulation and reflective materials necessary to survive the elements. If this works, and brings you to the same landing destination as Helios 15's Pelican module, known as LM-12, you shouldn't have any issues staying alive. If you can return through the Shadow, do so quickly, just in case."

Rory nodded her understanding.

"Here's the camera. It's a lot smaller than the ones your grandfathers had," Cody said. "I'll turn it on before you leave, so we can witness the entire trip."

"If the Delta's real," Silas added.

"Yeah, if the tokens do what they're supposed to," Cody agreed.

Silas could barely meet her gaze, and it was obvious he didn't think they should use the tokens at all, let alone consider leaving Earth through the Shadow they would create. Rory didn't let that discourage her.

"Bring the Delta," she said. Her voice sounded strange within the helmet, and she cleared her throat, finding her lungs tickling with the canister air.

Cody licked his lips and put on a pair of yellow nitrile cleaning gloves. They'd already cleared the coffee table and a chair, making room for the staging area. He lifted one token and touched the end to another. They magnetically snapped together and buzzed. The lights dimmed and flickered when he connected the third piece to them, and it became a perfect triangle, the excess seeming to fold over the exterior's 120-degree angles.

The outer edges glowed blue, and a misty darkness filled the space between.

"It works," Cody whispered in awe.

Silas' mouth was closed, and he looked ready to tear

the tokens apart.

Rory remained motionless while the black fog spat out of the Delta, forming a floating hole in the air. The Shadow shimmered and darkened before their eyes, and finally stopped moving at all. "You guys see that too, right?"

"Oh, yeah." Cody pressed a button on the camera and thrust it at her. "It's your turn."

Rory peered at Silas, and he gave her a supportive nod. She heard Silas' phone ringing as she started forward, and she hesitated. Then she stepped into the Shadow, vanishing from the face of the Earth.

EPILOGUE
THE VIEW FROM HEAVEN

*D*arkness.

A pitch-black eternity from which there is no return.
Weightlessness.

The sensation of floating upside down and sideways, all at once.

The Shadow lifts, breaking away, until Rory sees the surface. Her feet touch it, and a tear falls.

She stands, still holding the camera, and confirms it's recording. She can't tell the temperature, but believes she'd die within seconds without the suit.

To her right sits the descent stage of the Helios lunar module, Pelican.

They were here.

Rory blinks and takes a deep breath, feeling light-headed from a wave of vertigo. In the distance, she sees Earth and struggles not to fall apart. It's brighter than she expected, and the lower half is covered in a shadow, like it's being enveloped by space.

"Is this real?" she asks, but of course, there is no answer. Rory's always felt alone, yet now, it's the utter and inexplicable truth.

She rights the camera, not wanting to forget her mission. The Shadow remains intact, offering hope of returning home to Loon Lake. Rory sees the piece of the lander and touches it. It's really here. She is too.

It's like a dream as she scopes the ground out and sees foot-

prints, actual impressions in the regolith. Commander Gunn's boots were larger than her grandfather's, and Rory steps closer to the smaller set, her movements light and calculated. She has the intuition that if she kicks off, she might float away into oblivion, so she makes intentional steps.

Rory thinks about her character Madeline's big moment, and can't believe she's on the Moon. It was impossible, but here she is, in the same place Grandpa Swanson visited long before she was born.

She investigates the area, and guesses at the location where they'd discovered the Delta. Rory realizes it's back on Earth, and that she's here without it. What would happen if it shut down? Would she be stranded? Her breathing speeds up with the thought, and she fights to relax.

Rory's been on the Moon for somewhere around ten minutes, a good first visit, and she returns to the Shadow, eager to leave. Something is imprinted a short distance from her position, and Rory moves closer, filming the surface.

Her grandfather's words from the interview play in her mind as she sees the indentation.

'They're out there. Waiting for us.'

Rory records the finding with a shaky hand, and understands why they never told a soul about the Delta, or what they'd discovered on the Moon.

The imprint is clearly not human.

They're not alone.

THE END
Of
Echoes From the Moon (The Token Book One)
Find out what happens in
Shadows of the Earth (The Token Book Two)

ABOUT THE AUTHOR

Keep up to date with his new releases by signing up for his newsletter at www.nathanhystad.com

Sign up at www.shelfspacescifi.com as well for amazing deals and new releases from today's best indie science fiction authors.

Printed in Great Britain
by Amazon